Last Seen in Bangkok

A Novel
by
Dominic Lavin

ISBN-13: 978-1-84753-964-9

All characters in this book are ficticious and any resemblance to actual persons, living or dead is purely coincidental.

Gone but not forgotten
RIP

Max Deveraux
Frank Truman
Hannah Fish

When'er to Drink you are inclin'd,
Or Cutty Sarks rin in your mind,
Think ye may buy the joys o'er dear,
Remember Tam o'Shanter's Mare

Robert Burns 1790

Every day Deacon Mau

Tussanee October 2003

don't know

Vinny had been dreading that day since he'd got there. It was his fourth trip. On the last three, departure had been torture. To add to his torment he'd met Jeed. They were cornered up in Bulldog and he had his elbows on the bar. To strangle time he picked at the foil on a bottle of Carlsberg. His farewell night had been heavy and he was a fourteen-hour flight away from Bolton and an empty flat.

Jeed, seductive as ever, was leaning back in her chair, right leg crossed over left and wearing his Wanderers top.

"Honey, talk to me, no talk to bottle." She exhaled a chest full of smoke and leaned towards him. " I think you all the time and send for you email every day."

Vinny looked up and smiled. Jeed leaned over and kissed his neck. He smiled again and kissed her on the lips.

Hopefully, after the scheming he'd done with Pete Jensen, this was going to be the last time he'd be returning to England. Pete had been on at him for a week and had closed his pitch two days previously with, "I know it's risky but nothing ventured, nothing gained. The greater the risk, the higher the reward."

Pete had even made it sound legitimate and Vinny had agreed so long as he didn't tell Jeed. He'd shaken his hand, scribbled his name and address on a scrap of paper and downed a shot of whiskey to celebrate the Rubicon he'd just agreed to cross.

Outside Soi Yamoto was bustling as normal. The midday Pattaya sun beat down on its host of misfit residents and bleached the signage of the bars, shops and guesthouses.

The usual assortment of farangs, long and short term, sat around the bars in various states either recovering from yesterday's abuse or embarking on another attempt at the drinking grand slam. They were all throwing their unspent baht about and girls in their twenties hung around hoping to catch a spare thousand or so.

"Honey, you make me feel like young man again. I miss you at home." Vinny had been speaking a hybrid of English and Thai for a fortnight and was going to have to adjust to English again. He kicked the sports bag at his feet and gestured with his head towards the street. "We get taxi airport now, honey?"

Jeed started to lift off his football shirt.

"No, no, keep. When Bolton play TV you wear and think of me."

It was three sizes too big for her and added to her waifish charm.

Tom popped his head up from behind the *Pattaya Mail* he was reading from the cooler recess of the bar. "You off then?" His Cockney lilt added a lighter tone to every occasion. He could make handing out the death sentence sound like a quip between mates. Not that Tom was ever likely to be in a position to hand out the death sentence, not in an official court of law at least.

"Yeah. Off home for me chips and gravy, mate." Vinny bounced between Th/English with Jeed and proper Bolton with the English farangs.

"No doubt see you in four or five months then, Vin."

"Ayc. Probably be Christmas, kidder."

He'd been boozing in Bulldog of an afternoon since his first trip two and half years ago. At 39, ICF Tom was one of Pattaya's elder statesmen. He knew everyone you wanted to and quite a few people you didn't. Corpulent and shaven headed, Tom was a textbook hooligan. Vinny marked him down as 'all right'. He'd been one of West Ham's more notorious supporters and was reputedly wanted for murder, which prevented him from returning to England. Whether the rumour was true or not, Tom did little to quell it.

Vinny hoisted his bag over his shoulder and waved as he padded out of the bar into the searing heat. Jeed grabbed his hand and led him out onto the concrete plinth that acted as a pavement. She jumped off the ledge onto the red-brown dust-covered tarmac so she could flag down a cab. One of Pattaya's 80 million predatory taxis stopped without pulling over. Oblivious to the traffic backing up behind him, the driver pressed the window button and leaned over to the passenger side.

Jeed started jabbering in Thai to him and he responded with what sounded like, "Two thousand baht."

Jeed recoiled. "*Pahng mahk!*"

She made a downward movement with her right hand and delivered a look of disgust with her pretty Isaan face.

As she turned towards the pavement the driver issued a frantic "OK! OK! OK!"

Jeed turned round and re-entered the negotiations, punctuated on either side with frowns and alternate nods and shakes of the head. Eventually she turned round and winked at Vinny, thumb aloft. "I get for nine hundled baht."

He nodded 'OK' and picked his bag off the floor where he'd rested it during the Orients' version of the Maastricht talks.

By the time he'd hopped off the pavement and into the road the middle-aged taxi driver, in his blue shirt undone to the waist and jeans riding at slightly above the ankle, was by his side and hauling the bag off Vinny's shoulder and into the boot.

"We go say goodbye." Vinny nodded towards The Rising Sun.

They dodged motorbikes and flea-bitten mongrels on the way over.

All the guys were there: Fatty Jarvo, larcenous old Pete Jensen, Ken the Boss and Underworld; they called him that because he used to be a tunnelling engineer.

Vinny hopped up onto the pavement and stood at the entrance to the open bar front that acted as reception and dining area for the guesthouse he'd stayed in.

"I'm off now, lads." He hid his hands in the back of his shorts.

They all pretended not to notice.

"Fuckin' cunts."

Underworld stifled a laugh and buried his head in his *Bangkok Post*.

Jarvo looked over to Jensen, smirking. "You hear summink, Pete?"

"Oh, it's that Vinny fella." Pete looked at Vin with a feigned air of distance. "Or should I say Mr Bradley?"

Vinny felt a tug on the pocket of his shorts and looked down. A girl no older than 10 was looking up at him with an angelic brown face, offering him the pieces of chewing gum in her hands. He shook his head and looked back at the guys but could still feel her big brown eyes staring up at him.

"Fuck yers, you lucky cunts, I'm off." He waved and sloped back to the taxi.

He heard some faint mocking from behind him. "Oh, don't go, Vinny," and a chorus of laughter.

The guys were a sardonic bunch, good to be around, different backgrounds and outlooks but with a common bond in the appreciation of female company and alcohol.

Vinny got in the back seat having successfully avoided a collision with an unbaffled motorbike bearing down on him at six miles an hour. It was always a relief to actually get into a taxi alive anywhere in Thailand. Jeed hopped in after him, pulled the door shut and slid across the vinyl seat to sit next to him.

The driver started the engine and trundled into the flow of traffic.

Jeed frowned. "Honey, why Pete call you Mr Bladley?"

"It joke!" He smiled and gave her an evasive shrug.

Jeed kissed him lightly on the neck. She leaned her head on his shoulder and rested her slender olive-skinned hand on his thigh. The taxi edged onto the Beach Road, then turned into Soi Post Office and onto 2nd Road heading out of town. Once through the hustle and bustle of north Pattaya's streets, which were constantly filled with taxis, motorbikes and baht buses, they hit the Trat Highway, the hundred-mile stretch of concrete that ended in downtown Bangkok.

Vinny caught the driver's eye in the mirror. "OK for cigalette?"

The driver nodded and wound down the rear window so he could add his ash to the veneer of dust that covered most roads in Thailand. He fumbled in his shirt pocket and dragged out a crumpled soft pack of Marlboro Lights. There was always one pack with a few left in it after a night out. It took a bit of fucking about to drag two flattened, bent fags out of the corner and he popped one in Jeed's mouth, the second into his own.

The driver looked at him expectantly so Vinny passed him the pack, hoping it would be empty.

Jeed reached in Vinny's pocket for a light and lit his first, then hers. Like a lot of the Thai girls, Jeed's had this magical gift of making a cigarette in her mouth appear the size of a Cuban cigar. It was shit hot watching them.

Once half his ash was on the road and the other half on the taxi carpet, he dispatched the butt out of the window and started taking in the view. The taxi was the same as most in Thailand, meter with turbo switch for guys new to the country, vinyl seats that defied age, driver with jet-black swept-back hair and tough leathery skin like an old brown cricket ball. There was a picture of the driver that looked like it had been taken fifteen years ago selotaped to the windscreen so that you knew he wasn't a murderer; well, at least not one who couldn't afford the hundred baht to fake his licence. Vinny hadn't been in a car in Thailand that didn't have a selection of mini Buddha's, pictures of the king and famous monks stuck on the dashboard. This one was no different. They were there because they had Buddha's charm, and without them you couldn't go the wrong way down one way systems or pass through red lights in rush hour without getting killed.

After examining the inside of the cab, Vinny weighed up what was going on outside. Pattaya was five miles behind them and the hotels and bars had thinned out. There was a 95-mile thoroughfare ahead. Palm trees, abandoned trucks, industrial equipment and the odd bit of a hill were all he could see. The sort of stuff that cropped up on that road still amazed him. You could drive for miles without seeing a sign of life and then, in the middle of nowhere, they'd have a shop stood on its own selling bog seats or staircases.

Jeed wasn't up for conversation. Last night had obviously taken its toll and, other than the odd rub of Vinny's crotch or squeeze of his leg, she was motionless. So he started daydreaming about football. Bolton had started the season well. They'd just been promoted to the Premiership and Vinny fantasised about sitting in Bulldog with Jeed in eight months time watching them beat Man U in the Cup Final. Then he got this picture of himself thirteen months later sat in Bulldog as the gaff's new owner, with his beautiful wife Jeed tending the bar. He'd already renamed it The Burnden Park, and was watching Wanderers beat Real Madrid in the Cup Winners Cup. Just as David Beckham, the new captain of Bolton, lifted the trophy he was interrupted.

"Internatonal or Dometic?"

"What? Err, International, Terminal 2."

“You cam from Engrand?” The driver smiled in the mirror waiting for a nod.

Vinny shook his head and ignored him.

A lot of the roads over there were made of concrete sections, so when you were travelling the tyres made a ‘thrub, thrub, thrub’ noise. It sounded like you had a puncture. With that, the warmth of Jeed pressing against him and a 26-bottle hangover, Vinny soon nodded off.

Six thousand miles away Keith was lying on his couch wearing his leopard-skin Gucci briefs and black socks. There was a half-empty bottle of Tesco’s vodka on the table and a square of paper cut from a magazine that had, until ten minutes previously, contained cocaine. A plastic Fiat 127 with an Italian flag stuck in the roof stood proudly on top of his telly, and the screen a naked black girl on her hands and knees was staring out at him, the gentleman kneeling behind her with a stern look of concentration on his face – the sort of expression you’d expect to see Kasparov sporting in the middle of a world championship.

Keith licked the empty wrap, tossed it in the bin and took a slug from the bottle. He walked over to the window and pulled back the curtain. Outside it was starting to get light and the drizzle gave the cobbles in the back alley a glaze. He let the curtain fall back, shook his head and headed for the bedroom.

When Vinny woke, his crotch felt warm and his shorts were round his ankles, Jeed was doing what she’d done every midday after they’d woken for the ten days since they’d met, and for that matter after afternoon tea when they’d been for a nap, and at three or four in the morning when they’d returned home from Marine Disco. Vinny lay back and smiled as Jeed’s lips lapped gently against the part of him that British girls had refused to acknowledge.

He closed his eyes for a moment then jumped up. “Fuck me.”

He’d forgotten they were in the back of a cab.

Jeed looked up from the job in hand. “It OK, Winny. Man go from some dlink.”

She pushed with her left hand against his stomach and he leaned back into the corner of the seat, glimpsing out the window. They’d pulled up at the side of a roadside Seven Eleven.

Thai service stations were a bit surreal. Models of Millennial consumerism decked out in sparkling chrome and steel and stocked with gleaming cans of Diet Coke, Haribo Sweets, Sloppy Joe hot dogs and Western Cigarettes, set against the semi-primitive second-world landscape of intra-urban Siam.

Vinny looked back down at Jeed working like the expert she was but now with her hand instead of her mouth. Their eyes met and, for the first time since they’d got together, Vinny could distinguish between the dark brown of her irises and the black of her pupils. Most of the time they’d been awake together had been after sundown, making it hard to tell. His groin twitched. His lower back tightened then his prime Lancastrian genetic information spat onto Jeed's cheek. She pulled away, sat upright and wiped the edge of her cheek and lips like she was wiping biscuit crumbs from her mouth at a vicar's tea party. He lay there flustered for a bit then buttoned up his flies. Jeed finished wiping up then kissed him on the lips and turned to her make-up mirror.

"Honey, you get cigalette for me?"

Vinny stumbled out of the taxi. The heat hit him as he approached the service shop. The air conditioning above the glass door made the hair on his forearms stand on end and he tilted his head back to soak up the cool. At the counter the driver was leaning on one elbow with two bottles of Sprite in his hand. The King of the Chromium Empire was in his early twenties. Smartly dressed and preened in Seven Eleven uniform, and standing upright with arms wide on the counter. He looked at the driver unimpressed but listened to his diatribe. King Chrome glanced up as the door opened, and clocked Vinny cooling himself. The driver noticed him and raised his hand, nodding and smiling. He turned from the counter uttering an ignored goodbye to the assistant and tottered back to the car.

"Marboro Ligh, *ka loon na*." Vinny's fourth visit to the Land of Smiles hadn't been completely wasted. He'd learned that *ka loon na*, or something similar, meant 'please'. There wasn't even a raised eyebrow during the transaction, which pissed Vinny off enormously considering his defiant act of private indecency moments earlier.

He scooted back to the car enduring the heat plus residual air con and threw the fags on Jeed's lap, then joined her and kissed her on the neck like a soft cunt. If Keith had seen him he'd have ripped the shit for Vinny being a smitten bastard.

The car pulled back onto the highway and Vinny stared at the road ahead. He had one of the crappy moments of realisation he'd been having once or twice a day since he'd got there. Most of the guys holidaying in Thailand had them once or twice a day. They usually lasted three minutes max. First, they'd think, "I've got to go back to all that shite in England/Germany/Holland/Australia/The States." Then they'd convince themselves that life back in the real world would be better. Even though this doting creature provided them with everything they'd missed out on back home, she was, after all, being paid to. "I'll be here soon on a permanent basis," is usually the last thought, before the cuddle in hand breaks the depression.

When he glanced up at the driver's mirror, Vinny caught him weighing him up but he glanced back at the road to avoid eye contact, then buried his manners and stared at him full on in the mirror.

"Girfliend you go." He nodded expectantly.

"Whatever." Vinny had been using the dismissive about ten times a day, either on attentive female entertainment staff whose hips were just that millimetre too small or legs just that inch to short. It came in handy for taxi drivers talking shite and, when accompanied with a forward-waving hand gesture, it'd send street vendors offering decorative rice paper umbrellas scattering.

The cosy little career girl and customer carrier started to approach the edge of Bangkok. It was 3pm and the humidity and traffic fumes that Bangers was famous for (among other things) shrouded the skyline. For an ordinary guy like Vinny it was an impressive place, but a lucky twat who was being paid a Western salary to pretend to be an engineer and cheat on his Mrs in South East Asia had told him that, "Architecturally, it's not a patch on Hong Kong or Singapore."

There were more shiny highrises than he'd seen anywhere in the world, although to be fair his world had been limited to the UK and the Med until he'd come to Thailand. The Highway rose up from ground level and they stopped at the pay point for the toll road that allowed wealthy foreigners the privilege of passing unhindered above the interlocking mass of taxis, tuktuk's, buses, trucks, motorbikes, private cars and handcarts that clogged up Bangkok's highway system like cholesterol. The driver passed on 40 baht to the attendant and glided on up the ramp. Thai taxis were surprisingly smooth runners considering they all looked well over ten years old. Before he knew it the lights and aerials of the airport were more than just distant blobs to Vinny's right. The departure lounge was imminent.

The taxi veered off to the left and then doubled back under a flyover so that the terminal buildings were on the left-hand side. After passing the Domestic Departures they pulled into Terminal 1. The car stopped in the taxi bay and the driver turned and smiled. Vinny couldn't be arsed reminding him that the KLM flight for Amsterdam departed from number 2. He pulled his wallet out from his safari shorts and passed the driver two 500-baht notes.

The driver rummaged in his pockets and made a charade of trying to find the hundred-baht change. Vinny gestured for him to keep it. With the baht in his shirt pocket the driver was rooted to the seat, leaving Vinny to haul his bag out alone and stagger sweltering in the Bangkok humidity to the baggage trolley. Jeed was waiting for him. As he trundling the trolley towards the automatic doors Vinny stopped. Jeed's arm was linked loosely in his.

"Honey, we have cigarette before go check-in?" he said.

Jeed nodded in agreement and they veered off towards the row of plastic seats on the pavement. Vinny sat down first and could see thunderclouds gathering on Jeed's face.

He lit a fag and passed it to her. She rummaged in her handbag and produced the piece of paper he'd written his email address on.

"Honey. Your name Winny Clotton?"

She held out the slip with *Vinny_Croston@yahoo.co.uk* written on it.

"Yes."

"Why Pete call you Mr Bladley?"

"He joking." Vinny stared into space.

"You bullsit me, I kill you." She put the paper back in her bag.

They sat and smoked, avoiding each other's gaze, both fearful of any upsetting eye contact.

Once Vinny had finished his cigarette he broke the silence. "You come to check-in with me then go for some drink?"

"OK." She pecked him on the cheek, threw her cigarette to the floor and stubbed it out. At BKK International, or Don Muang to use its proper name, you were miles away from beer-bar country, and respectable Thais looked down on bar girls.

Vinny pushed himself up from the seat, grabbed the trolley with one hand and trailed the other behind for Jeed to grab. She took hold and clopped along behind him through the brown-glass door.

They entered the departure hall of Terminal 1, all decked out in marble. It should have been majestic, a room the size of two football fields clad in white and brown polished stone but Don Muang Airport had the feel of a building that had been grand twenty years ago. These days it could do with a refurb.

Because of the numbarse driver they had to walk to Terminal 2, but it was a good chance to people watch. The place was always packed.

The security guards stood around in groups of three and four with walkie-talkies hanging from the waistbands of their dark brown uniforms. Boots polished and clothes neatly pressed, they looked menacing but the clothes appeared to have been pressed every day since 1975. As Vinny and Jeed passed one would always be distracted and give Jeed the once over. Face, feet, then up the legs to pause for a carnal moment on her arse, then back to the conversation with his mates. Perhaps a collective glare from the whole group would follow as he pointed a six or seven out of ten to his buddies. Young porters scurried around with their shirts hanging out of the back of dark blue trousers, stopping occasionally to confer with a mate over the contents of the chit in their hand.

Pairs of fat grey-haired, middle-aged farangs wheeled trolleys around stacked high with expensive luggage and golf bags. They squared off the details of their stories for their partners. Yes, it had been a good trip even though it had been a bit hot. The buyer had agreed or the vendor had given a good price. They'd played golf on the two free days, eaten in the hotel every night bar one and retired early after a long hard day of negotiations on the days of the meetings (nudge, nudge, wink, wink). Oh, and they'd probably have to go back in seven weeks to keep the customer sweet or the vendor on his toes.

The odd Western family would pass through, husband looking at couples like Vinny and Jeed through the corner of his eye so as not to alert the Mrs, but planning a business trip for the future; kids oblivious to the fact that these guys were with working girls that they'd probably regard as abominations in years to come; wives would use the hundred-yard stare and refuse to look the 'perverts' in the eye, even though their husbands were planning a week of the same soon in the name of business. Some of the wives would look in disgust at the affluent Westerner walking along with his downtrodden Eastern woman then play hell with her husband that night just for being male.

Occasionally a female airport worker would glance fancifully at Vinny, then respectfully at Jeed. She might get dirty looks off respectable Thais but she was earning five times more in the bar than some receptionist at the airport, and being spoiled rotten by a generous, if slightly portly, Westerner. That reassured Vinny. If Jeed was only there for the dollars (which she had, in fact, refused from Vinny) at least other Thai women found him attractive. It probably gave Jeed a bit of pride as well. Not everyone disapproved of her line of work.

They passed through the corridor into Terminal 2 and waited by the lift for the departure hall. A Japanese family with trolleys squeezed into the lift with them, then reversed out next to the escalators. Heading towards the check-in desk, Jeed slowed a little. Vinny was pissed off by the sadness on her face.

"Honey, why not *sabai*." Not happy. "I want remember you smiling, not sad."

Jeed moved her head from side to side, trying to shake it off. They got to the queue for the luggage check-in and joined the line of departees. Vinny kneeled down next to his bag and unzipped it so he could dig out a sweater for when he got home. The bag was brimming with smelly undies, shoes, wash kit and that pair of boxing gloves he'd bought in Bangkok on the first night. He'd meant to try and get to the Muay Thai gym but had been too hungover every day. He finally found his target, a thick grey Nike sweatshirt that would insulate him against the October chill at Schicpol, and hopefully in Manchester as well. He tied it round his waist and hoisted the bag onto the conveyor to be scanned for drugs, firearms, ammunition or livestock. It passed under the rubber flaps of the x-ray machine and he walked to the other end to await the outcome. There was a brief second of paranoia while it was bombarded with electrons. What if the taxi driver had been part of a Triad cartel who'd planted a kilo of heroin on him? What if Tom had slipped a handgun in while he'd nipped to the bog in Bulldog? What if…? His bag emerged looking amazingly like the one he'd put in the front end a moment before. It stopped at the end of the conveyor as two young guys in blue uniforms held it in a machine to be encapsulated in blue 'BKK Airport Security Checked' tape. This was the fourth time he'd left Bangkok and he still hadn't sussed how the machine worked. Vinny picked his bag up and went over to the check-in queue. Security checks completed, he could have safely put a couple of kilos of heroin in the side pocket, or that endangered snake he'd bought off a guy in Happy A Go Go.

The queue at the desk wasn't moving. A group of four Nigerian guys in flowery gowns were busy causing chaos. They had suitcases big enough for a double bass each. One of them was open and they were frantically emptying 400 or so brand-new T-Shirts, still in cellophane, into a bag. Their mate was helping them. He'd be taking them back to his apartment for the next time someone was leaving the country. It was obvious that they knew their allowance but had chanced it anyway.

Everyone waited patiently. At the check-in desk a girl appeared in a KLM blazer and skirt.

"Pleese queue a thit desk, pleese." She tried to make herself heard but Thai ladies' vocal chords weren't really made for shouting.

No one needed telling though, and people were already shuffling over before she had issued her order. Vinny was at the desk in no time and lifted his bag onto the conveyer. He plonked his folder of travel documents on the desk and rummaged through all the papers and shite, the outbound ticket, old boarding cards, travel-cheque stubs and insurance documents until he found the return ticket and passport, and pushed them across the counter to the girl. She smiled, took them in her hand and opened them up in front of her screen. Vinny looked at the badge on her lapel. 'Royal KLM Airlines, Rungnapa Thomadee, Check-in Assistant'.

"Pleese, sir, you no reconfirm fly."

On all his trips to Thailand he'd avoided reconfirming the flight from Bangers in the hope that it would be overbooked.

"I forget." He smiled helplessly.

She tapped in a few figures on her keyboard.

"OK. Depar flom gay forty two. You must be a gay fipty minit beefor fly depar." She passed back his papers. "Enjoy your fly."

"*Khop khun krup*." He'd learned how to say thank you on his first trip.

Faced with the reality of departure, Vinny felt like a kid taking his dog to be put down and his bottom lip creeped up over his upper one. He was left with two hours to kill before saying goodbye to Jeed. He headed back to where he'd left her by the x-ray machine, but couldn't see her among the faces at first glance. He eventually caught sight of her and she looked sad, but as their eyes met she brightened up. When he got nearer her she bounced towards him and clasped his arm with both hands and smiled. She didn't seem to care that it was unseemly to show affection in public away from the bar. Vinny felt his groin tighten and cursed the lack of short-time rooms near the airport.

"We go for some drink and food, then I go in two hours."

There was no answer, just a pull towards the escalator that led towards the Bill Bentley pub on the upper floor.

They got on the escalator, Jeed a step behind Vinny. She was still nervous about escalators. She'd lived in Pattaya and worked the bar for two years but they didn't have escalators upcountry in the village near Ubon where she was from. Getting onto the moving staircase was still a trauma for her and she hesitated the way 5-year-old kids did in the UK on their first trip to a shopping centre. Halfway up, with his right hand clasped in both of hers, she turned round and surveyed the mass of internationals twenty feet below. Up until her 21st birthday three years ago, she'd never set foot outside her village and had only had one Thai boyfriend who'd helped her family on the farm. She'd eaten in wooden huts and had a new item of clothing every twelve months. Now she was being treated to drinks by a foreigner and passing through an international airport. Jeed often had moments like farangs do, who pity themselves for having to return to the West, except hers were more of amazement at how different her life had become since working in the bar.

They walked into the Bill Bentley pub, with Burger King and KFC concessions through the opposite door. Vinny hovered over the thought of Burger King for a moment, contemplating getting his stomach used to Western stodge again, but thought better of it.

The Bill Bentley was just like a typical boozer back home. It was carpeted and contained dark wooden chairs and tables adorned with glossy menus, beer mats and dark green ashtrays with a yellow livery.

Jeed clambered onto the stool next to a high table. Vinny untied the sweatshirt from his waist and draped it over the adjacent chair. With his hands on his hips he gazed around for a moment. There were framed photos hanging on the walls depicting Western sportsmen or front pages from the *New York Times* chronicling disastrous days on the stock market or assassinated dignitaries.

"This same pub in England," said Vinny. For all his enchantment with Siam there was still a little bit of reluctant Westerner in him.

The 300 square yards or so occupied by KFC, Burger King and the Bill Bentley served as a bit of a of a decompression chamber for those making the cultural jump from East to West. Around them there were couples in similar situations, or groups of lads sat around ploughing through their last fistful of baht and reminiscing about the night one had been caught out by a lady boy in Pat Pong, leafing through the photos they'd picked up on the way. An older mixed couple sat at the table close by. The bloke farang, grey haired and overweight, stared into his beer the way Vinny had on Soi Yamoto while the lady Thai, obviously of a similar age but looking much finer than a Western lady of her years, smiled as she saw Vinny and Jeed. Her face gave that look of 'that was me and him fifteen years ago when the airport and fatso over here still looked dashing'. She looked back at her other half. Her face straightened and she went back to her book.

Vinny got his wallet from his back pocket then eyed the menu and weighed up how much cash he had.

"Honey, *mai satang*." No money, "I go cash cheque, you order drink."

He gestured towards the Bureau de Change.

On his return he was greeted by two bottles of Carlsberg, one in Jeed's hand and the other waiting to jump down his throat, and he stuffed the hundred pounds' worth of baht in his wallet. Jeed looked down at her beer. It was like the eye contact would upset her too much. She had a tissue in her beer-free hand. During the quick dash to the money vendor Vinny had decided once and for all that he was going to amass an enormous amount of cash in an amazingly short period of time back home and return to sweep Jeed off her feet. She looked up when he touched her arm. There was a small tear making its way out of the corner of her eye. He picked up a tissue and wiped it from her cheek.

"Winny, I cry because I'm lub you too much." She looked down again and he kissed her forehead. Jeed looked away. After a quick swig of beer she turned back and seemed to have composed herself. She touched his leg and sniffed, then a smile broke through. A quick rub of his leg followed to reassure him she was OK.

"Honey, tell me what you do when home England."

"OK. When I get home it 10pm. I get taxi to my house then go to pub for drink with friend."

"What friend name?"

"I don't know, it depends who's out." She looked at him confused. He'd started speaking English and quickly. The decompression chamber had brought that on.

"Him name Bill Bentley."

Jeed laughed. "You joke. What you do when go to working?"

That depressed him. "You know I working sell computer."

Smiling now the conversation was flowing, Jeed followed on with the playful interrogation. "What people like in working? Many lady?" She had him on the run.

"I don't know. I start new job on Monday." A whole fucking Sunday to sort his head out and get rid of the jetlag.

"You big liar, you have many lady at working and in pub."

She knew it wasn't true. What would he be doing holidaying in Thailand on his own if he was Bolton's answer to Tom Jones?

"Honey, I start new job selling big computer and making many money so can come back Thailand see you." He touched the top of her two clasped hands and waited for her to catch his gaze again.

"Winny, you know I'm lub you too much." Jeed's emotions started to slide again.

"Honey." he lightened his tone to cheer her up. "What you do when I back in England?"

"I get bus Pattaya and go back work bar Soi Eight where meet you." She sighed.

"Tommy Bar?"

"Yes, Tommy Bar."

"You always work Tommy Bar?"

Some of this was old ground but it filled the time and stopped the tears.

"No before when come to Pattaya, I work go-go bar Soi 2, name Classloom." He'd stalled the tears but she wasn't getting any happier.

"Why you move to Tommy Bar?"

"Dancing all time in go-go make tired and feet hurting. Then meet friend from Ubon. She tell me she work Tommy Bar and make money same go-go but no hurting or make tired so I'm go to work with her."

A friend had cropped up in the conversation. It lifted her spirits.

"What friend name?" The tears were at bay. He was back on safe ground.

"Her name Na, she nice lady. Always joking very *sooway*." *Sooway* was one of the first words farangs learned in Thailand. 'Beautiful', essential for sweet talking the girls.

"Have I met Na?"

Not surprisingly enough he remembered more than one pretty girl from his nights on the town with Jeed but the name didn't ring a bell.

"No, no. She go back Ubon six months. Mama sick, she help with farm and childlen."

Jeed clasped the cigarettes on the table. Flustered and embarrassed at having shown a tear, she reached into the packet and popped a fag in his mouth. She kissed his cheek and lit him up before repeating the process for herself. Playing the doting girlfriend seemed to cheer her up as she mopped his brow. She was back in the driving seat.

"Winny, when you go home I want you take care because England colt. You get sick, have flu. I not want you working too hard because that make sick also."

Thai girls could really turn on the compassion when they wanted to. "No, no. When I go home I stop smoking. Then I not have flu. Also I start to go to boxing again so I stop being fat."

This was met with a look of disapproval. He'd dabbled in Thai boxing after his first visit; he'd gone along to the local gym in the hope of meeting some Thai birds but there were none. It had got him out of the flat at night but eventually it had got in the way of his drinking. Obviously he'd been no great shakes because of his lifestyle. He'd not even competed, but had trained for a while just to keep fit.

"I not want you boxing. Lady have man who boxing alway have bad life." Jeed was putting her foot down. The Thais were proud of their national sport but in some quarters it was regarded as a peasants' game.

"Why lady have bad life from boxing man?" The comment made him a bit indignant.

"Because she worry too much. Also fix him face when broken."

She pressed hard on his leg, forcing the point home.

"Honey, I not do boxing for fight, I just do for keep fit. It stop me from be fat."

"If you not have fat I not recognise you." She lightened the pressure on his leg and smiled. She was willing to call it a draw but not without making her point. Jeed gently stroked his stomach then went back to her nearly empty bottle.

Vinny noticed a matter of urgency. Thais were concerned about losing face in social matters and he was keen to ingratiate himself with their customs. He was mindful as well of the last remaining crime to carry the death penalty in Bolton – being seen in a bar with an empty bottle.

The waiter answered his beckon and was soon at the table.

"Two Carlsberg." He turned to Jeed. "Honey, after this beer I go." He got a nod as a bit of a sullen reply.

The beers arrived and were placed on fresh beer mats. The waiter cleared the empties and was turning to go.

"No no … *Check bin*!" Vinny shouted at him as he turned away.

The waiter turned back and totted up the total for the table. "Seven hundred and twenty baht, please."

Vinny and Jeed looked at each other in shock.

"*Pehng mahk!*" Too expensive, Jeed stabbed at the waiter.

"Let me look," said Vinny. He grabbed the bar tabs and compared them against the price on the menu.

"Hundred and eighty fucking baht a bottle."

It was triple the Pattaya price for the same round. He shook his head again in disgust and dumped the money on the tray without a tip. The waiter scurried off. He obviously hated charging those prices as much as the customers hated paying them. The fucking beer was warm as well and, as Vinny took his first gulp, he used his free hand to grab Jeed by the wrist. Another gulp and the bottle was half empty. Vinny looked in his wallet. He needed 500 baht departure tax, and a thousand or so for cigs in the duty free.

"I'll give up after I've smoked my allowance." He always lied to himself about smoking; every pack was his last one. He pulled the remaining currency from his wallet and pressed it into Jeed's hand. There was well over 3,000 baht. It was about a week's wages in the bar and probably six months' wages in the rice fields, but nothing like what he should have paid if he'd bar-fined her every night and paid her fee on top. That's what it was with Jeed, she didn't take his money like bar girls normally did. She was with him because she liked him. Obviously he bought her food and booze and that and gave her a couple of grand to send to her mum. But to him it was a proper relationship.

"Come on, we go." He swung away from the seat. In the act of ordering another beer he'd saved himself from death by verbal abuse in a Bolton bar-room court but in leaving he'd still committed a less sinister but no less forgiven crime. Not finishing his drink.

Jeed trailed behind him. She wanted to slow him down and spend more time with him, but he hated goodbyes. There were still 45 minutes before the pre-determined time to be at the gate. He wanted the emotional safety of the transit through Passport Control and an amble round the duty free. The sooner the farewell was over the better. He could try and close off the compartment in his heart that Jeed occupied, leaving it to be opened when he checked his email in the mornings, and when he reminisced over the photos in the evenings or when he was in the pub listening to Keith slating his latest bird.

They stood on the escalator with their arms round each other, befire heading to Passport Control. The pair stopped a yard away from the vending machine where passengers paid their departure tax. There was a group of English guys in their mid-twenties trying to club together the 500 baht each they needed to leave the country.

"Jeed, I send you pictures as soon as I get them." He kissed her on the forehead. She looked up and kissed him on the lips. The kiss lingered until he pulled away but he had to lean back and kiss her lips one more time. The tears were welling up now and about to break onto both cheeks. Fuck it! He hugged her and pulled her head to his chest. She looked up with tears still halfway down her face. He took the tissue from her hand and wiped her cheeks dry. It was the second time he'd done that in an hour and he was getting used to being the Casanova.

"Not cry, honey. It make me sad."

Jeed pushed him toward the ticket machine. She blew her nose and shook her head.

The 500-baht note slid into the slot and he got his exit ticket. He turned and saw Jeed with a tissue over her nose, pointing at the hole in the partition with 'Passport Control' printed above it. Once he was through the gap he was in the machine that woud stamp his passport as having exited, rush him past some tax-free goods and despatch him onto the plane. It would fly him over the Bay of Bengal and off towards the West to boredom, discontent, his hopefully lucrative job and his beloved Bolton Wanderers.

Jeed watched and waved. He waved back and now it was his turn. All he could feel was his nose blocking up. He tried to smile but his mouth puckered up with the corners pointing down.

Once he'd forced himself through the porthole he was sanitised again. The orderly queue of Thai nationals next to that of the non-Thai nationals were routinely having their exit cards examined and their passports stamped. He reached the desk. Farewell over, he was the single guy again. Free and on his way home, safe from heartbreak and the guilt of showing emotion.

The official took his passport and looked it over. "Boarding card, please." He didn't look up but stretched out his hand and Vinny handed over the document. He was sure it was the same guy who'd stamped his papers every time he'd left.

Everything seemed to be in order and the uniform stamped in the exit date, squiggled on the page and pulled out the tourist visa that had been stapled into his passport for two weeks.

Vinny trundled through into the departure terminal, separated from the runway and walkways to the plane by a huge sheet of smoked glass. The shops and stalls marked 'King Power Duty Free Shopping' were much the same as anywhere else in the world, stacked high with cigarettes, liquor, perfumes, sportswear and a selection of local and global bestsellers.

He made a beeline for the fags: 480 baht for 200; there was about 60 baht to the pound so it worked out at about 80 pence a packet. He pulled down two cartons and went to the till. The girl struggling with her ogre of a machine looked up from the piece of card she was keying in digits from and smiled. "One secont, pleese."

She put the card to one side and motioned to the stacks of cigarettes on the shelf. "Speshar offer, sir. Buy thlee carton, get one flee."

"Marvellous!" He could just make out the outline of her breasts beneath her semi-translucent 'King Power' blouse. Vinny smiled, hopped over to the shelf and grasped at two more cartons. With the extras he was 600 over his limit and he plonked them in the basket by the till. The till girl smiled. "One Thousarn nine hunlet twenti baht, pleese, sir."

Vinny couldn't help having licentious thoughts as he fumbled in his pocket for the cash.

"Bollocks!" He only had a 1,000-baht note and a couple of loose 10s in his wallet. He was going to have to use his Visa card but he wasn't sure if there was any credit left on it. He plucked it out and placed it on the desk. While she swiped his card a young guy packed the three cartons plus 'extla flee' in a 'King Power Duty Free Shopping' carrier. None of your cheap shite mind, these bags were heavy-duty plastic, soft yet durable. They were the sort of carriers you could keep for taking folders into the office when you wanted to look flash in front of the secretaries. They said, 'I'm quality. I've seen the world'.

There was an anxious moment as the card was validated. He stood there hoping he had enough credit. Had he paid his last bill? Chugga, chugga, chugga, chugg. The till spat out a slip for him to sign and he heaved a sigh of relief. While he scrawled his name on the line he tried to catch her outline beneath the blouse again.

"Sank you, sir." She handed his card back and placed the receipt in the bag, lifting it handles first out of the basket.

With enough Melvyn Braggs to last him five weeks, he headed into the 300-yard mall that led to gate 42. There were still 40 minutes to kill before boarding time so he ambled slowly in and out of the gift and souvenir shops. He eyed up glass paper weights with pictures of the Grand Palace etched into them, wallets full of postcards depicting Thailand in the past, carved wooden Buddha's, miniature replicas of the Royal Barges and other bits of tat that tourists paid through the nose for. He'd already bought a cast brass image of some Thai god or other for his old dear, so gifts were covered but it passed the time. Generally speaking he avoided books. A lot of his time at work was spent reading technical specs for new computers or bid documents for customers, so reading was low on his list of pastimes, but out of boredom he wandered into a book store. Nothing caught his eye. There was the usual section of war and crime fiction; the shelves under the heading 'Regional' contained hardbacks aimed at the tourist. *Thailand, Land of Smiles* with a picture of a hill-tribe girl on the front concealing 200 dramatic landscapes from the north, canal shots from Bangers and pictures of fishermen in the south hauling in their catch at sunset. *Cooking* – he gave that one a miss. The 'Language' section caught his eye. On this trip he'd started to notice the advantage farangs who had a bit of the lingo held over linguistic mutes like himself when it came to bargaining and asking directions, so he sauntered over. There was the stand of 'Berlois' dictionaries: Thai/English, Thai/German, Thai/French. They didn't appeal so he glanced across the shelf and noticed a heading 'Audio' and saw some boxed cassettes. One had a picture of a pretty young girl on the front, head tilted back and smiling playfully. *Hello Thailand.* The lettering below the picture claimed that the buyer would 'Learn 300 useful phrases without book or college course'. A round white sticker covering the bottom corner of the smiling girl proclaimed in pink lettering, 'Special price 500 baht plus free booklet'. The word 'free' was in bold and double the point size of the rest of the wording.

Bargain. He picked it up and weighed it in his hand. Not too heavy, not too light. It felt good. There was a pamphlet behind the box, encased in the cellophane so he flipped it over. The back of the pamphlet read,

> This helpful 90-minute cassette with booklet is designed to help the English-speaking traveller or businessman with 300 useful phrases such as:
>
> Can you take me to the airport please?
> Where is the nearest post office?
> Excuse me, where can I get a massage?…

No further info required, he walked towards the counter, box in hand. There was no one at the till. Walking off without paying was considered but he corrected himself a moment later. A longer stay would have been nice but twelve hours in an interrogation cell in the airport explaining why he'd half-inched a tape worth less than a tenner wasn't worth it. He rested both hands on the counter with his wallet clasped in his right. The squeak of rubber-soled shoes on the tiled floor signalled the approach of an assistant. She wasn't as pretty as the cigarette girl but her smile was more cheerful. Once safely behind the till she tilted her head slightly to the right and smiled again, running the bar code under the scanner.

"Fipe hunlet baht, pleese, sir." She packed the box away in a smaller but none-the-less impressive quality carrier. Vinny had forgotten the thousand or so cash he held, and was expecting to use his card, but he saw the fringe of the brown note popping out of his wallet. It was quickly transferred into the girl's hand and into the till. She counted out five red hundreds and plucked the receipt from the printer. The bag fitted neatly into the side pocket of his shorts. He grasped his bag of 800 fags and was off down the corridor towards gate 42.

There was a 'smokers' cabin' 50 yards ahead. It was a brown-glass object that looked like an indoor greenhouse with plastic seats and ashtrays full of sand at hand level. When he pushed the swing door open the nicotine hit him full in the face. Those places always stiffened his resolve to quit. Well, not immediately, but maybe soon. He sat himself down, distant enough from the other occupants so as not to encroach on their personal space, but not too far from the ashtray, then tapped in his pockets for his fags. Left? No. Right? No. Left side pocket? No. Right side? Jeed must have 'em, he thought. Check the shirt pocket. Fuck it. Open a carton. It was handy. Delving with both hands into the carrier between his knees meant avoiding eye contact with the others in Marlboro heaven who were looking but not looking at each other. Bingo! Twenty deck obtained, he sat upright and unwrapped the pack. It was fucking awkward picking out that first cig from a soft pack without fucking up the tip. The pocket routine started again for the lighter but, before he was halfway through the search, a large Western lady who was sat opposite in a big yellow dress smiled and offered hers. He nodded thanks, smiled, gave the lighter a quick flick of the thumb and passed it back. The first lung full provided relief from the smoke-free zone he'd endured for twenty minutes. The second was nauseating and the third started to constrict his throat. It made his stomach and chest churn. He didn't want to launch into a full coughing attack, especially in front of strangers, so he held the smoke in his mouth and breathed in through his nose. No use. A cough was on its way. His mouth gaped the smoke bellowed out and the cough 'BLWEHH' followed . It sounded like a child puking. Vinny's head lowered to chest level. Deep breathe in and back upright. He shook his head quickly and was back to normal. The Thai guy sat opposite looked back at the floor, avoiding his gaze, and the sweet-faced Western woman smiled in empathy.

The young European to his right hadn't even looked up from his book to take in Vinny's party piece. He took a short drag but didn't inhale and let the smoke seep out slowly. Same again, then he put it out. The last two drags were to show how manly he was. Never let a coughing fit stop you. He dipped the remaining third of his tax-free 'Marboro Ligh' out strategically to avoid ruining the Bangkok Airways logo in the sand. He collected himself, smiled at the lady in the canary outfit and walked out.

A quick time check fixed him at twenty minutes till final boarding, so he popped into another 'cancer cabin' en route for another fix before his twelve-hour nicotine depravation. This tab was uneventful. No need for the starting game of 'hide and cig'. All he had to do was grab the lighter off the armrest next to him and chuff away contentedly.

Ten yards from the boarding gate there was a final security check. Everyone's hand luggage and pocket contents went through the machine while folk walked through the metal detector. Vinny was pretty much certain he wasn't smuggling a surface-to-air missile in his body cavities so walked through the magnetic archway with a swagger. An airline pilot and the cabin crew crowded past him politely as a girl in airport uniform stopped him. The buzzer hadn't gone off but they still checked everyone with a hand-held scanner. She ran the device up and down the length of his body and crouched to scan his lower legs. It brought a cheeky smile to his face as he remembered one of the girls in Bangkok called Noi – or was it Lek? – who'd crouched towards the lower half of his body once before. Only she hadn't been holding a scanner in her hand. Check done, the uniformed girl stood upright and smiled.

"Thank you, sir. Plees ploceed to gay with boardin car leady," and she motioned with her outstretched hand down the corridor.

Vinny found an empty chair by the gate and plonked himself down on it. There were couples and families milling about. The tannoy had been calling out last calls for flights and urgent last calls for individuals, but there was no mention of KLM flight 4122 to Amsterdam. His mind was on the tannoy. 7355 to Dubai, nope, 6613 to Hanoi, nope. Not Mr Sparding for Frankfurt again, must still be in Bill Bentley's.

"Finar call for all passanger on fly 4122 to Amsterdaa. Plees ploceed too gay forty-two. The fly is now depar."

It might have been in her book, but there was no one at the desk and there was definitely no one onboard.

A group of stewardesses carrying radios nearly as big as their torsos appeared at the desk with clipboards and heavy make-up. A keen bunch of business travellers would always pounce on the desk before the staff were ready and today was no exception. The first guy to the desk was a greying fellow with awkward questions about what colour his seat was and if his car would be waiting for him when he finally stopped after two transfers. In fact, he'd put his documents on the desk before anyone was in the chair. The youngest of the three girls took her jacket off and mounted the chair. Old 'grey hair' was pecking at her before the computer was switched on.

"Plees show boardin car there." She pointed to her left without looking up from the screen. Mr Eager had to trace his steps back to the two girls the queue was forming next to, and show his card the same as everyone else, which made him frown. The queue started to move and the first few passengers headed down the ramp. Vinny was among them.

They entered a larger hall with a roped walkway to a door at runway level. There was a small strip of tarmac between them and the runway bus. Out of the air-conditioned sanctuary of the building the late afternoon heat and humidity tickled him gently under the chin. It sort of served as a depressing reminder that he was leaving and asked, "When you coming back,

Vinny?" Inside the bus he held onto the handrail as they rocked across to the plane. Once he'd crossed the tarmac and trudged up the stairs to the door of the plane he was virtually back in the West. Western hostesses greeted him at the door, inspected his card and motioned him towards his seat, 38 F, his nominated arse-sized home for the night. The sweatshirt he'd been wearing round his waist got plonked on the seat and he stuffed his bumper bag of fags into the holder above. He nodded at the two Arab-looking guys occupying the seats by the window, who'd probably been soaking up the Siamese culture the way he had. He slipped his sweatshirt on and started to look through the magazines in the pouch in front of him. It was the usual shite, duty-free this and that, special fortnight breaks in Montreal. Vinny rummaged in his pocket and found the little packet containing two pills. Before leaving Pattaya he'd popped into the chemist and been told by the pharmacist, "Thees pir no ploblem at airport. Take one, you sleep for fife hour." And at a hundred baht each it was better than twiddling your thumbs for an eternity.

A stunning blonde-haired stewardess passed his seat. It'd been two weeks since he'd noticed a Western woman. She was superbly well kept and healthy, nice tan and perfectly made up. Two and a half years ago she would've given him wood but now the thought didn't cross his mind. It was amazing how your tastes could change.

"Scuse me, love, can I have a glass of water?" She didn't acknowledge him but two minutes later she returned. He gulped down one of the pills and slipped the other one back in his pocket.

All the passengers seemed to be on board. The doors closed and the plane started to taxi. The captain ran through the pleasantries on the tannoy and the elegant Dutch ladies did their lifejacket workout at the end of their aisles. Vinny watched keenly as their breasts heaved and sighed through the lifebelt dance. They weren't brown and available at 49 pence a pair but he could still appreciate them.

The plane seemed to turn, and stopped. He plucked his contact lenses out of his eyes and flicked them on the floor. The engines fired up and the plane began to move, slowly at first but gradually gaining pace. The bumps of the runway started to feel like they were further away. Vinny felt woozy as the nose of the plane lifted.

oh, I've just

Keith pulled up ten yards past the Archways 24 Diner and sat looking at the old brick viaduct wondering how painful the proposition was going to be. He contemplated delving into the bag of coke in the glove box but for once thought better of it and watched the raindrops splatter on the windscreen for five minutes before braving the elements.

Archways 24 Diner is an interesting place. It's made of two portacabins welded together, knocked through and painted blue. Keynes would have been proud of the clientele and the microcosm they've formed. The workers from the nearby industrial estate who buy bacon on toast and cups of hot milky coffee for breakfast don't bat an eyelid at the thin lipped hookers, Asian taxi drivers and hard faced drug dealers who populate it day and night.

What operates there is a fine example of economic interdependence. The hookers do tricks and buy drugs. The drug dealers peddle and when they dry up get a taxi to Moss Side to restock. When a cabby's had a good fare he treats himself to a woman. Bypass Ronnie (who's called that because of his heart condition not his roadside bistro) sells them cups of tea and coffee and most of them are happy most of the time, unless someone overdoses in the bogs or gets short changed.

Keith pushed the door open and a couple of the more desperate whores looked up. His contacts weren't hard to spot through the smoke. The woman's clothes and jewellery were four or five rungs up the retail ladder than the Pound Empire garb of the low rent demireps around her and the bloke might as well have had 'Hong Kong Triad' tattooed on his forehead.

"Are you Vicky and Eddie?" Keith asked once he'd shuffled up to their table.

"We are," the woman said.

"I'm Keith."

"Sit down," the lady looked around and seemed uncomfortable in her chair.

She was sitting so that as little of her body as possible could risk picking up bacteria from the surroundings.

"You alright?" Keith flicked his eyes between the two of them.

Vicky smiled back and even held his gaze for a moment but Eddie seemed more interested in the stained menu on the wall and the female occupants of the next table.

Keith was anxious to get this underway as soon as possible, "So what is it you want to talk about?"

"Your debt."

"I know that. But what are the specifics?"

Keith looked round to see if anyone resembling a detective was listening. There was no one, but Bypass Ronnie glared at him for not buying a drink, Keith took no notice.

"How much do you owe him Keith?" Vicky fixed him with her eyes.

"It's about eight grand."

Eddie spoke for the first time, "You help us, we pay for you."

"Let me elaborate Keith," Vicky leaned forward and widened her eyes, "Your debt still stands, but if you help us complete errm a little project, it'll be wiped clean."

Vinny felt a judder. His eyes opened and he smelt food. He saw the beige fabric on the back of the chair in front and the KLM Royal Dutch Airlines logo on the back of the foldaway table.

It took him a moment to realise he was on his way home. The plane juddered again. He glanced to his left. The two Arab's were curled under their half tog blankets. He stretched his arms up and within seconds was wide awake. A quick glance at his watch told him it was 11.35pm Thai time. "Fuck me, five hours on the dot," he muttered.

Down the aisle he could see the rear end of one of the life-jacket strippers pulling a trolley full of efficiently packed airline meals towards him. Talk about timing. She pulled up next to him as the two Arabs to his left stirred.

"Would you like fish or chicken, sir?"

"Chicken."

She unclipped the foldaway table and placed a tray with a large foil-covered dish on it and three other smaller dishes covered in cellophane. To add to the delight of this none-juvenile pile of Christmas goodies were a plastic knife-and-fork set and some sachets of whitener, salt, pepper and sugar. Helga or whatever the blonde was called leaned past Vinny and repeated the same six-million dollar question to the Arabs. Her left breast was three inches from his face. Perhaps he could get used to Western girls again. He was forgetting they'd long since got used to healthier specimens than him. Helga turned back to the trolley and Vinny glanced over to the Arabs. He gave them that cheeky grin lads gave their mates when they'd been dragged on stage at a strip show to be covered in cream. The Arabs nodded at him, tongues wagging. Yep, they'd been up to the same as him and millions of others in the Land of Smiles.

Vinny peeled the foil back and tucked in. The meat was a bit too hot so he moved onto the spuds, dipping them sparingly in the sauce. Back onto the meat and then the spinach. Next he devoured the creamy desert thing. Not bad, quite sweet. Then the *piece de resistance*, mild cheddar cheese between two crackers, exquisite. He skipped the fruit course and nipped to the bog.

Good time to head for the loo on aeroplanes, mealtime. Everyone was busy. He squeezed in and sat on the seat. He looked in the mirror to his right. After two weeks of drinking solidly he wasn't a pretty sight. Not that he ever had been. No wonder he had to pay for sex. A red sign above the door to his left read, NO SMOKING. PASSENGERS FOUND SMOKING ON THIS PLANE WILL BE FINED 6,000 GUILDER. He dipped in his pocket for his fags and slotted one in his mouth. The tight space made Vinny dance awkwardly. Front pockets. Back pockets. Side pockets. Shirt. Fuck, no lighter. He slammed the white-tipped Marley down the pan and flushed.

"Might as well have a piss while I'm here." He smiled at himself in the mirror and waved with his right hand at his reflection, holding his best friend in his left. Airline bogs always bought the imp out in him. After a quick shake of the battle-weary soldier he buttoned up his flies. The lock slid, he pulled the door back to a queue of mothers who'd finished eating and were marshalling their offspring towards the mile-high bog.

Oops, he hadn't shaken properly. Light brown shorts as well. Not to worry. He pulled his sweatshirt down. None of the mothers noticed his garment irrigation because they were eye to eye with him. Vinny liked smiling at kids and one of the youngsters who stood at just below waist level turned and stared up at his mother in disgust.

He squeezed past and headed towards his seat. Just within earshot he heard one of the mums in hushed tones whispering, "Well,just make sure *you* don't do it."

Back in the safety of his seat he started to tidy the debris of his meal. This time a steward was pulling a trolley that was gradually being filled with used trays. There was no communication, he just whisked the mess away. As he leaned towards the Arabs, Vinny pushed himself into his seat to avoid unnecessary proximity with a nudger.

Close on his tail was another of the Helgas.

"Would you like a drink, sir?"

"Jack Daniels and Coke, please." He smiled.

He squirmed carefully in his seat so as not to dislodge the drink and produced the second of The Sandman's sweets. It went straight down his neck with Jack close behind. He looked round. In front there was a Tom Cruise film being shown on the wall of the next set of toilets. The plane buffeted and the film became hazy.

Surrounded by Helgas, having eaten Western food, and half-watching an English-language film without Thai subtitles, he could tell he was definitely back in the West…

"Sir. Sir."

Vinny twitched. His eyes opened and Venus herself in a KLM uniform with her hair pulled back from her face was smiling at him from six inches away. He shook his head and moved upright in his seat.

"Could you fasten your seatbelt, sir? We will be landing soon," she glanced at his waist. The patch of high nitrate wetland that had appeared in the lower agricultural region earlier had become arid and Vinny had obviously been dreaming about someone special.

Helga stood upright and walked on to the next row to check more seatbelts. Once in the galley she joked with her colleagues about the dark-haired English guy in 38F with a boner.

The plane's nose began to rise slightly in preparation for landing. It was almost in sync with Vinny's drooping. He felt the jets reverse to slow the plane down, and then they were gliding. Aisle seats don't generally offer much of a view of the outside world but what he saw didn't impress him. It was pitch black and the rain was pelting the window at 45 degrees. A glance at his wristwatch told him it was 3.55am in Thailand, about 9pm in Holland. The plane bounced on landing and rattled as it slowed on the runway.

Ping! "Would passengers please remain in their seats until the plane halts. Seatbelts must remain fastened until the 'fasten seatbelt' sign is off. May I remind you that Schcipol is a no-smoking airport"

Sighs of relief were heard and chattering resumed amongst the passengers. Most had remained silent during the landing. Anxiety always shut people up and with the landing officially over they could concern their imaginations and vocal chords with day-to-day chat instead of worrying whether their wills had divided their estates fairly.

Seven hundred red crosses appeared in unison across the FASTEN SEATBELT signs. Six hundred heads tilted back and three hundred and eighty aluminium spring-loaded buckles unfastened within a second of one another. This was followed by three hundred and twenty torsos appearing above the seats.

The lockers opened and people started pulling out bags and cases, and heading off down the aisle. This was the part that Vinny hated. Every four rows there was a passenger halting the exodus by struggling with something too big to get out of the locker. One of the offenders was the guy who'd been first in the queue at Bangers. Waiting to get on or in something wasn't too bad. Waiting to get off though…

Once the exit trauma was over he was in the concrete labyrinth of Schcipol. Finding your flight and gate without contact lenses was fun and three or four dead ends later he was at the gate. He deposited his cigs at the end of a row of seats, walked over to the smoked glass and stared vacantly at the runway. With his hands behind him tucked into the waistband of his shorts he tried not to become woeful at the sight of the liquid stair rods hitting the panes.

In the bat of an eye he was strapped into his seat on the transfer to Manchester with a complimentary *Evening News* folded on his lap. Smaller planes were always more fun in bad weather and this was no exception. Just like on a roller coaster, Vinny's hands gripped the armrest and his eyes focused on the gap between his feet. Once splashdown was over Vinny headed for Passport Control. He was still in a semi-slumbered state from the pharmaceutical. He headed for a desk with only two people queuing to have their passports checked. The spinach was starting to say hello, not in the solid form quite yet but, seeing as he was among strangers, there was no point holding on. Through his blocked nasal passages he noticed a bit of a smell. The people in front of him obviously didn't have as badly a blocked nose as him and looked round in disgust. The immigration guy looked up and also reeled in disgust. A couple of people approached to join Vinny's queue but once within ten feet they backed off and joined a larger queue adjacent to him. The official waved him through quickly.

After ten minutes by the luggage conveyer with his hand on his hip he was leading his trolley into the 'Arrivals' lounge. Fuck messing about, straight through the sliding doors for a taxi.

"Jesus Christ!" He didn't whisper. The North West weather knew how to say 'Hello'. A thousand follicles on his legs stood upright and goose bumps appeared a split second later. His cheeks felt the pellets of hailstone like the German machine-gun fire that had mowed down his granddad. As he turned towards the incline leading to the taxi rank the wind changed direction and pushed him back down the slope. Bending forward he soldiered on like Edmund Hilary on the final leg of his ascent of Everest. The first black cab in the queue had its light on and Vinny tapped the window. Without looking up from his paper the taxi driver hit the window switch and the glass lowered.

"Can you tek us to Bolton, mate?"

The driver nodded and Vinny heard the central locking click open. Vinny pulled the door and yanked his bag onto the floor. The trolley started to reverse down the slope and Vinny grabbed it. His mountain of nicotine sticks was still in the basket above the handle. Fags retrieved, he clambered into the back of the cab and pulled the door to. Vinny was privileged. That night Bernard Manning's younger brother was chauffeuring him. He looked out of the back window and saw his trolley on a wind-assisted kamikaze mission towards a newspaper stand. Among the other passengers he saw Jack Reilly, the saviour of Wanderers, do the same dash as he'd done a moment earlier. Dressed in slacks and cotton shirt, he pushed a trolley with two Samsonites and a Dubai Duty Free bag on it. Vinny smiled. At least the credit-worthy cunt couldn't buy the weather he wanted. Two years ago he'd sold his share in a supermarket chain he'd built and sunk it into the Wanderers. His funding had helped them get from the third to the first division.

Bernard Jnr folded his copy of *The Star* and started the engine.

On the flight from Amsterdam Vinny had contemplated getting a Visa for Jeed to come and live with him in Bolton, but after the SAS Harsh Weather Training course he'd just negotiated he was worried. What if Amnesty International found out?

"Whereabouts in Bolton is it?"

"D'you know Bolton?"

"No."

"Twenty-seven Greenbank, just off Millhouse Lane." Vinny was still in banter mode after the fortnight spent in bars. Bernard wasn't impressed. He glared at Vinny in the mirror. "Just head for the centre, mate."

Having made his stance on joviality Vinny decided not to share his joy at being home with Bernard but rested his feet on his bag and read the signs for the motorway. The good-humour gene obviously didn't run in the family.

In no time they were on the slip road for the M56. A silver Merc splashed passed Vinny's cab. Blonde piece driving while Reilly mopped himself down with a hand cloth.

He drifted back to Pattaya and was soon in Bulldog again. Banter about football. Chips and gravy quips being parried by references to jellied eels. Five-year-old girls selling flowers being directed towards the least genteel of the punters and Jeed on his arm mopping his brow and keeping his cancer chances high with a supply of lit fags.

"Are we heading the right way?" Bernard smiled at him in the mirror.

"Yeah, keep going." They'd turned off the motorway and were headed towards town.

"Do a right at the lights near Tesco." The ring road would take them up to Millhouse Lane, cutting out the centre of town. Vinny glanced at the meter.

"Forty-two pound seventy!" Jesus, no wonder Bernard had smiled when he checked his directions.

"We'll have to use the cash point at Tesco, mate." The journey from Fun City by the Sea that same day was over a hundred miles and had cost him less than fifteen nicker. Ain't it great to be home.

After a quick dash across the deserted Tesco car park Vinny returned to the cab with a fistful of tenners. The journey was almost over. They turned left off Millhouse Lane and onto Greenbank, a row of Edwardian townhouses converted into flats.

"Looks like you've missed last orders, mate." Bernard had a sense of humour after all. A black one on a sombre occasion's better than not having one at all.

The taxi stopped on Vinny's queue with the meter reading £47.83. Vinny pressed the five tens through the gap in the glass partition and waited for his change. Bernard took his time leafing through the notes, no doubt hoping his fare would waive the change, but Vinny was having none of it. A day ago a five per cent tip would have been nothing, but back then the fare would have been the equivalent of around £2.17.

Out in the dark tree-lined street Vinny wobbled a touch under the weight of his bag. He squeezed through the parked cars and scaled the steps to the front door. He'd already retrieved his key from the side pocket of his kit bag and was in the hall in no time. There was pile of costly looking letters waiting on the doormat next to his ground-floor flat, which he brushed aside with his foot as he opened the door to his home. A flick of the light switch revealed that he hadn't been burgled. Pity, the insurance claim would've funded a return trip. His kit bag propped the door open and he nipped back into the hall to pick up the bills. A quick shove with his foot moved the bag and the door slung shut.

Home and alone again, Vinny's abode of four years now had a temporary feel to it. Vinny and Kerry had moved in to 27a Greenbank after two and a half years together. The move had announced to the world that they were a proper couple. Her presence still lingered like the smell of a week old takeaway carton. After six months of domestic bliss Vinny had proposed using the 24-carat gold ring with a diamond cluster. "It didn't cost that much, sweetheart," was his line, but it had made her weak at the knees. How could she resist? Twelve months on she'd dropped it to him over tea that she had a new job in Newcastle, and didn't want him to move up with her. The engagement was off, even though a wedding had only just been talked about. That was that. Four years down the pan. Within a week the furniture they'd bought together was in the back of a van and heading up the A1. The flat was empty. She'd been considerate and not thrown the seven grand worth of metal and stone back in his face. Obviously wanted a memento.

Vinny had scrounged some bits of furniture and started to drink.

They'd had a flight booked to Thailand and were going to go up north, shag elephants, visit the hill tribes, that sort of thing. Vinny thought, fuck it, and went on his own. That's how he'd caught the bug. He wasn't sure if Kerry had been crafty and planned it so Vinny could shag his brains out abroad and lose any carnal desires he'd previously held for her. If that had been her plan, it had worked. The circle of couples they'd had dinner parties with started to shun Vinny, the single leper. Apart from Jason, Janet's other half who had a season ticket for the Wanderers with him.

The light on the answer machine was flashing and he strolled over with the bills still in his hand. He pressed play and the tape rewound. He flicked through the bills – nowt exciting looking – and stowed them on the mantlepiece.

Pweeep! "Hi, Vincent, it's Charles," the educated southern-English tones of his new boss rang out of the machine. "Hope you enjoyed your holiday and look forward to seeing you Monday." Bosses are meant to be like that though.

Pweeep! "Vinny, you tosser, it's Keith. I thought you were back today. I'm in town. Bell us on the mobile." Keith and Vinny had become mates not long after he'd split with Kerry. He didn't really work but had his finger in a lot of pies. They'd been out on the town chasing women. Keith's Italian heritage and lack of taste meant he was quite successful. Vinny got left behind. He was a touch overweight, a little too old and a far too cynical for the early twenties flirts found in the pubs and clubs of Bolton. Vinny pressed 14713.

The phone rang twice.

"Vinny!"

"Keith, ye tosser. What you up to?"

"I'm in town. When d'you get back?" The pub noises in the background gave his grid ref away.

"Just landed, mate, 'bout ten minutes ago."

"I'll call round. See you in five." The line went dead.

A trip to the bathroom was due. Travel tends to make you smell. The longer the journey, the worse the whiff and Vinny's hose control added to the aroma. He turned on the shower and dropped his clothes on the floor. Nice and warm. Budget guesthouses in Pattaya weren't always fitted with the best plumbing and the Fallen Angel on Yamoto had been no exception. The cold shower and the odd dose of the shits were about the only hardships he'd endured. There were some blessings to be found at home after all.

Bzzzz! Keith had arrived. Cleaned and with a towel round his waist, Vinny patted into the front room and pressed 'Enter' on the intercom. He unlocked the door to his flat and heard Keith's Saturday shoes clopping down the hallway.

Vinny stuck his head round the door. "You greasy Diego Wop."

He pulled the door back. Keith stared him in the face wearing a three-quarter length leather coat, black silk shirt, pressed grey trousers and Patrick Cox shoes. He ran his fingers through his slicked back hair.

"You fat sex pest. Good to have you back." His hand reached out and Vinny clutched it, holding the towel carefully with his other hand.

"You didn't tell me it was a toga party." He grinned and Vinny stepped aside to let him in.

"Sit down, I'll just be minute." Vinny slipped into the kitchen. The bedroom was off the side of the kitchen. "Fancy a beer?"

He didn't wait for the answer and got a can from the fridge. His last move before setting off was to get eight Stellas. He knew he'd miss last orders from the flight times and, despite his casual attitude to life, certain things had to be taken seriously.

He padded back into the living room and placed the can on the table.

"Fallen off yet, has it?" Keith glanced at Vinny's crotch.

"Na. Gone a bit green though and burns when I piss." He mimicked an itch in his groin.

Keith laughed and shook his head as Vinny disappeared into the kitchen.

He emerged a minute later, can in hand, dressed in sweatshirt and jog bottoms.

"What you doin', you gimp? We're off in town." Keith was disappointed. He'd had two weekend sorties into fanny territory without his accomplice and wanted to make up for lost time.

"How've Wanderers done today? They were away to Bradford." Vinny was sidestepping. The last thing he wanted was a club in Bolton. Two reasons, one, no bar girls, two, he was starting his new job with Personable Computers on Monday and wanted to be fresh.

"Fuck Wanderers, you're coming to The Mill." The Mill was Bolton's latest attempt at sophistication. It consisted of two floors of tacky house music and flirts in lame.

"I'm skint."

"It's on me."

Vinny shook his head. "I'll get changed if you tell me how they got on."

Keith submitted but did his best not to sound enthusiastic. Keith didn't share Vinny's passion for the Wanderers but sometimes went along to the big games for a scuffle.

"Two-nil at Bradford."

"Who scored?"

"Fuck knows."

Vinny emerged from the kitchen door a minute or two later in black trousers and a blue woollen-knit shirt.

Keith's head lifted from the table with a rolled-up note still in his hand.

"Line, Vinny?"

"Na. Staying off Pablo's Talc. Want be fresh on Monday for t'job." Vinny eyed the line Keith had done for him and sucked his lips in to ward off temptation.

"I can see you've kept away from any sort of Slim Fast," Keith popped with an impish grin as he looked up at Vinny, stomach bulging over his belt.

"A little extra weight's seen as a sign of affluence in Thailand," was Vin's indignant retort.

"You must be the richest cunt in the country then." Round one of the buddies' sparring session had started and Keith was a point ahead.

"Fuck it. I'll blame the jetlag." He knelt down by the table and held his hand out for the note. Vinny devoured the line. He passed the note back to Keith and set himself down in the armchair. He looked him in the eye and Keith's face was screwed up.

"What's that aftershave you're wearing?" Keith wasn't impressed.

"My better stuff's still in my bag." As if he'd need aftershave in Thailand.

"What the fuck's it called?"

"Image. It was a present off my mum."

"Fucking sewage more like." Keith threw a fag at Vinny. "So how was it?"

"Usual. Trip round the temples, crocodile farms, all that shite." Vinny smirked. "Come on, we off?"

They left the house and Keith pressed the button on his key fob to open his car. He drove a three series BMW. It was seven years old and the shape a touch out of date but it fitted his image. He sold sportswear on local markets and had a minor hand in satisfying the town's demand for cocaine. As a teenager he'd helped in the family bakery and was still weighed down by 'the Italian Sandwich Man' tag.

Sat in the car and heading into town, Keith prodded, "So what d'you do then?"

"Couple of nights in Bangers then off down Pattaya." Vinny was dying to tell him about Jeed but was wary of sounding besotted.

"Do many birds?" Keith was driving carefully. He was over the limit and didn't want attract attention from the local Five O.

"Did four in Bangers then met one in Pattaya who I stuck with."

"Stayed with the same one? Variety's the spice of life, you told me."

" Well, she seemed a decent sort and acted like she liked me," Vinny began to open up.

"She's a hooker, mate. That's her job." Keith was stating the obvious but wanted to know more.

"Well, I met her on the first night and did the job. Let's just say she's in the right line of work. She told me she'd wait for me the next night in the bar and I brushed it off. Next night I pulled this stunner from a go-go bar. Took her home and she just lay there starfish, so I fucked her off and went looking for Jeed." Vinny was in full flow and wanted to share his newfound love with his mate.

"That her name then?" Keith's mind was on his driving and the tender young flesh in The Mill.

"Yeah, she's superb. So anyway, I went back to the bar and there she was waiting for me. So we did a bit of Yoga again that night. In the morning she told me the usual shite. 'Honey, I like you too much. I wait for you again.' I started to get a bit suss so that night I sent a couple of guys I'd met to scope her out for me."

They pulled into the car park of The Mill and Keith reversed into a free space. He was beginning to get worried. His partner in crime was head over heels for some go-go slut in Thailand.

"Swift shnaffle before we go in?" The Ricky Martin look a like looked to his left.

Vinny didn't reply but dove in the glove box and got the owner's manual for Keith to rack up on. He plonked it on his lap and looked out at the stars. He was dying to tell him how Jeed had turned down astronomical offers from Chris and Geoff from Leeds to leave the bar. How she'd rung the bar saying she was sick for the following eight days so that Vinny didn't have to pay the bar fine. How she'd refused the money he offered her and even paid for her own meals for the first four days.

Keith stuck his nose plus note onto the logbook then looked up and passed it to Vinny, who held it in is left hand and looked down at his nemesis while his right hand waited for the note. He clasped his fingers round the rolled-up tenner and in an instant the whitener was gone. The lovelorn bachelor wiped the book clean then placed it back in the glove box as Keith folded up the wrap and put it in his wallet. The self-styled Ray Liota was in *Goodfellas* mode now. Tough, nasty, loaded with coke and on the hunt for molls. He pulled the front off the car stereo and leaned past Vinny to slip it in the glove box. The returning mercenary lifted his left butt cheek and let out a quiet rasp. There was a fortnight's worth of spicy Tom Yam soup and green chicken curry fermenting in his gullet and the particles in the gaseous phase had been pushing against his sphincter. Keith paused for a moment to get a hint of the South East Asian arse gas. His face screwed up. It reminded him of the time that the fridge they kept the meat for the pies in at the bakery had packed up on the Thursday evening before the Easter weekend. Come Tuesday the stench had been unthinkable.

"Fuck me, you could bottle that and drop it on the Kurds." Keith was out of the car the way Rubens Baracello jumps out of his Williams F1 after a crash. He looked back and Vinny was sniggering. He got out the car at his own pace.

"I couldn't really do it in the queue, could I?"

The pair strolled across the car park. Fortified with cocaine and a couple of beers, they were swaggering towards the door rather than the back of the queue. Keith knew the bouncers and always blagged in without paying. It would have only cost a fiver anyway but made him look important. Just inside the glass doors a youngish guy was trying to convince the doorman that, yes, he was eighteen and, no, he wasn't drunk. The black guy who was blocking his way snapped.

"Fuck off!" He sent the kid hurtling out the doors.

"All right, Jonah?" Keith smirked. " Customer-care course paid off then?"

"Silly little cunt."

"How's the Mrs?" Keith feigned an interest in her welfare. Guys always love talking about their partner's maternity.

"Fine, yeah. I'm off up to Farnworth on Monday with her for a scan." Farnworth was a district five miles away, still within the boundary of Bolton Metropolitan Borough and home to the square complex of brick buildings where the townsfolk went to give birth and, later in life, to die.

Jonah was a nice guy. One of the few West Indians in Bolton, 19 stone, some of it muscle and some of it not, he'd worked the doors for years. Keith and him had a reciprocal relationship. Keith gave him gear cheap so he could make a cut when punters approached the bouncers for drugs, and Jonah let him in clubs for nothing.

"We all right for a freebie tonight?" It was polite to ask rather than bustling straight in, even though he knew the answer.

Jonah motioned towards the door with his head. "Tight as a fish's arse, you are. Never paid for a club in your life."

"Never found one worth paying for."

They walked past the booth where ordinary people paid, and got a dirty look from two pale-skinned girls. Probably called Gayle and Michelle or something, aged about nineteen, twenty or so and wearing skirts that were wider than they were long.

Vinny and Keith pushed through the doors and entered the lower floor of Bolton's latest beer-selling venture. The first port of call was the bar. En route they passed the usual groups of lads and girls eyeing each other up. Not drunk enough to make the approaches but greasy enough to exchange winks and flirtatious smiles. Keith was in his element. Three or four years older than the competition with a flash car by Bolton standards and a gangster image, he couldn't go wrong. Not in his mind anyway. Once in place at the neon-lit bar Vinny ordered.

"Two pints of Carlsberg, luv."

The barmaid in her brewery polo shirt smiled and started pouring the pints. She was quite small and the pumps seemed to dwarf her. It felt like ages since Vinny had drunk a pint. Drinkers in Thailand trusted bottles from the fridge more than the Siamese draught systems.

"Five pound ninety, please." Her smile was straight out of the brewery training manual. He almost choked. Twenty-four hours ago £5.90 would have allowed him to take a miniature Patsy Kensit with jet-black hair and slanted eyes out of a bar for the day. Now it was two drinks. He delved in his pocket and pulled out a crumpled fiver. He placed the note on the counter and delved back in his pocket again. Embarrassment loomed. His fingers homed in on a pound coin in the corner of his pocket and he bounced it irreverently on the counter.

Keith had his mind on other matters. With his back to the bar he was engaged in furtive negotiations with a couple of guys in their late teens. The glare in the prospective buyer's eye suggested that he didn't really need any more drugs but hedonism has always been fashionable in Bolton. He was obviously living the champagne lifestyle. Three hundred quid a week for fixing boilers, he'd hit the big time and was spending every penny bar his keep for his mum and his car loan on narcotics.

"All right, forties then." Keith shook his head, hurt at having to drop his price, and motioned to shake the guy's hand, with a wrap of coke secreted in his palm. He turned to the bar and the guy pushed his hand discretely into the pocket of Keith's leather coat. Keith turned his head and checked the bundle of notes in his pocket. It felt like forty quid and people rarely took him for a ride.

"Cheers, mate." Keith glanced over his shoulder and saw the two guys scurrying towards the bogs. The gas fitter raised his hand in thanks.

Big-time Keith turned to his pint. The barmaid gave him a knowing smile and leaned with her hands behind her back against the fridge. Vinny was halfway through his beer. Keith's was untouched. Two weeks of drinking all day did wonders for your speed and stamina, and Vinny gulped while Keith sipped.

"What's this bird like then?" Keith was a bit more talkative now he was in profit.

"Shit hot. She's not the fittest I've done over there but top Donald Duck and a proper laugh."

"How old is she?" Keith could see the glint in Vinny's eye.

"'Bout twenty-five. It's hard to tell with Thai birds, they age better than this lot over here." Vinny's glass was nearly empty. He opened his mouth, raised his jar and emptied it. "Your shout." Standing up was thirsty work.

Keith shook his head. "You pissant." He glanced at the barmaid. "Carlsberg and a tube of VD cream for Michael Palin here."

She tried not to snigger as she filled a fresh glass for Vinny. Keith's last comment had made Vinny paranoid. He felt an itch in his groin and rubbed it, trying not to make it obvious. Keith shook his head.

"Case of Bangkok Bell End, is it?

"Na, just a bit itchy round the pubes."

Vinny was giving information to the barmaid that would ensure his chastity in Bolton for the next six months.

With a fresh pint in his hand Vinny turned his back to the bar and joined Keith in watching the carousel of dresses passing in front of them. Not a lot different from Bangkok, Vinny reckoned, just you had to charm them a bit more. He was still under the illusion that he was 'velly velly haandsom', that he spoke with 'sweet mouth' and that 'lady like man fat little bit'.

One or two caught Vinny's eye but his glances weren't reciprocated. He thought a blonde piece had smiled back but she walked past with an Asian guy five minutes later.

"Fag, mate?' Vinny had one of the forty packs he'd bought at the airport in his hand and offered one to Keith.

"Cheers." Keith lit his and waved his light towards Vinny, who leaned forward to get the flame.

"Bit strong, they are, mate." Keith's face screwed up as he picked the packet off the bar. He eyed the health warning written in Thai.

"They make me look debonair and exotic, they do." Vinny was defending himself and hadn't noticed that they were stronger than the Western strain. "'Ere, you couldn't lend us a tenner, could you? Taxi screwed us for fifty." Vinny didn't like borrowing but had spent a fortune on the trip to treat his tryst.

"You should have said, I'd have picked you up." He squeezed a crumpled brown note into his hand.

"Just nipping the bog, mate." Vinny followed the trail the two junior drug statistics had led to the tiled and tidy restroom earlier.

This trough was packed with guys, heads down and backs to the world. One or two swayed but they remained silent. Vinny stood a safe distance from the other guy who was waiting to take a leak. The gents was the last place you wanted to invade someone's territory. One of the guys paying homage to the porcelain started to do the shake. He straightened as he zipped and headed for the door. The invisible chicane he drove through gave away the fact that he'd had more than one pint. Vinny motioned to the gap with his head at the guy stood waiting.

"I'm waiting for the cubicle, mate." Obviously one of Keith's customers.

Vinny nipped into the gap and emptied his bladder. He shook then turned and zipped in the same movement.

"Fuck." Fearful of being caught wanking in the company of blokes, he'd not shaken properly and felt the same warmth and dampness he'd felt on the plane. He consoled himself that it wouldn't show through dark trousers. The coke was wearing off and he felt drowsy. Jet lag had started to creep up on him.

Back at the bar Keith was talking to two girls. They looked around 20 and weren't the cream of the crop but would have done. One with blonde hair, short skirt and a white boob tube was directly in front of Keith launching a full-on charm attack. Her mate stood to his side trying not to look impatient.

Vin pushed his way between Keith's admirers and was back in safe hands. Or at least his pint was.

"Sarah, you know Vinny, don't you?" Keith guided the girls eyes towards Vinny and added, "He's just got back from Thailand."

The girl smiled at him and relaunched her assault on Keith.

"What's your name?" Vinny asked her friend, more out of politeness than interest.

"Joanne." She looked sullen and turned towards Sarah, leaving Vinny to stare at the side of her head. He couldn't help sniggering. He was definitely home. Her response had been a far cry from the kiss on the neck and the stroke of the crotch he'd have got 7,000 miles away.

Joanne had managed to catch Sarah's eye and motioned to her mate that she wanted to be on a different planet from this 30-year-old tosser who smelled faintly of piss.

Vinny shook his head and remembered why he liked Thailand. Exotic climate, gorgeous food and birds willing to fuck you regardless of your appearance for the price of a cup of tea. Well twenty quid but there was no need to split hairs.

"I'll see you later." Sarah raised herself on her toes and kissed Keith's lips. In a flash they were gone, leaving the two amigos to themselves.

"Looks like my round." Keith was gulping down the last of his pint and Vinny was leaning over the bar to catch the ale maiden's eye.

"Two Carlsberg, luv." He turned back to Keith. "Who the fuck's that then?"

"Sarah." Keith looked disappointed that Vinny hadn't done a better job on her mate.

"I know that much. Who is she though?" Vinny didn't recognise her.

Keith turned and saw two freshly poured pints glowing on the bar and an expectant barmaid waiting for Vinny to make an offering to the till god.

He reached in his pocket and pulled out the crumpled tenner Keith had given him earlier. It was damp like his pocket from the cursory shake of the chopper earlier. Vinny flicked the note across the bar and turned back to Keith.

"Where'm I meant to know her from?" He looked over at the barmaid. In the mirror he could see that her face was screwed up in disgust. She was pinching the piss-soaked tenner between finger and thumb, and holding it as far away from her body as possible while she rung the numbers into the till. The change got passed across the counter without a glance and she dashed straight to the sink to clean her hands and forearms.

"Three Arrows."

"I've never seen her in there."

"You 'ave." Keith enjoyed teasing Vinny.

Vinny shook his head, clueless, then it dawned on him. "Oh, you stupid cunt, landlord's daughter."

He'd seen Sarah countless times but in leggings and a T-shirt, with her hair tied back and no make-up on while she collected glasses for her dad in their local.

"What's yer problem?"

Vinny shook his head and told him straight. "She's trouble. There'll be no end of grief once Sheila's onto you."

Sheila was Sarah's mum and, although it was her husband Graham's name above the door of the Three Arrows, Sheila was the boss.

"She's barely fucking legal."

"Seventeen's all right." Keith didn't rise to the bait. A shag's a shag and he'd expected a pat on the back.

Vinny had made his point and didn't want to labour it. "Anyway, I'm going to have to shoot. The jet lag's catching up."

"Take more coka," Keith proffered.

"Na. New job and all that." Vin was bored and tired.

The pair's eyes moved back to the carousel as the conversation ground to a halt.

"Although I could be tempted." Vinny saw what, in the dark of the club, looked like perfection. Mid to late twenties, shiny brown hair, big green eyes and an hourglass figure. It was apparent from a slight wobble that Gossard's designs hadn't interested her. She didn't need them.

"It's fuckin' Liz Hurley with big tits," Vinny whispered, pleasantly stunned. A smart looking guy was in tow but her confident stride told the world he wasn't that important.

The smile that came their way nearly knocked Vinny flat. He thought it was his but Keith knew better.

"Liz Hurley doesn't shop at Next." Keith referred to the red sequinned backless number she filled so gracefully.

Vinny looked at his feet and took a gulp of his pint. Keith was unflustered.

"Took it up the Council Gritter last week while you were shagging ladyboys."

"Yeah?"

Keith shook his head and laughed. "Did I fuck. I'm working on it though. She's called Vicky, I think."

Sarah appeared again. She was alone this time. Joanne had attached herself to a guy five years younger than Vinny who could control his bladder. The landlords progeny was starry eyed and gazed smitten into Keith's eyes.

"I'm giving my good friend Vincent a lift home in a minute. Do you want to tag along?" He was happy enough to eat baked beans while the salmon was being smoked.

"Yeah, I'll just tell Joanne." She tottered off with a smile on her face. A flash Italian guy with a BMW was a good catch for her and she didn't take long to return.

"You right then?" Keith turned to Vinny. Keith was ready for the off but was wary about the extra baggage that had appeared. He gulped the last of his pint down and picked up his fags. Vinny didn't need to answer.

They got to the car after a handshake and a 'Thanks' with Jonah. Keith occupied the front seat while Sarah sat in the back. It made her aware of her standing in the hierarchy.

"It's lovely, this car. Is it a Golf?" Sarah showed her age. Wiser women don't ask questions about cars unless they know they're on the right track. Vinny tossed a smirk at Keith as they pulled out of the car park. Keith scowled. Her ignorance was giving Vinny plenty of ammo for their next verbal tussle.

The car pulled up outside Vinny's flat.

"You two lovebirds having a brew?"

"Might as well."

He parked up and pulled the face of his Sony. Keith and Sarah took up residence on the sofa.

"Beer do you, mate? I can't be arsed brewing up."

"Anything." Keith wasn't that arsed and was more bothered about taking Sarah up the stairs at the back of the bakery. He'd agreed to come in to satisfy Sarah's curiosity to see where this character lived. It was handy. Stopped him looking like he was rushing.

“Beers fine,” Sarah chirped up. A classier bird would have asked if he had any wine and then taken a beer as a second choice.

Vinny returned from the kitchen with three Stellas cradled in his arms like newborn triplets. He plonked them on the table and popped back into the kitchen. He rummaged in his bag and returned holding a fake Ralph Lauren T-shirt. He’d bought it for three quid on a stall in Bangkok.

“Present off my holidays, mate.” He’d only worn it once. He chucked it at Keith. “Have a guess how much?” Keith had an eye for a bargain. Vinny knew that the price might wet his appetite for the Land of Smiles.

Keith picked it off the floor. He knew a bit about garments, having sold sportswear on the stall.

“Is it a fake?” He eyed it like a jeweller inspecting a diamond through his eyepiece.

“What do you think?”

“If it is, it’s a good one.” Keith frowned.

“Come on give us a price,” Vinny probed.

“Bout a tenner?”

“Two hundred baht. Three pound thirty.” Vinny nodded with satisfaction. “That’s a one-off, not bulk.”

Keith picked it up again and started fingering the logo. Vinny could see the neural activity going on behind his friend’s eyes.

“Fuck me. Halve it for bulk, that’s one seventy-five. Buy a hundred and flog ’em on the stalls for fifteens.”

“It’d pay for your holiday.” Vinny liked the idea of showing a first timer the sights. He could just see the look on his face as he walked into Nana Plaza. The capital’s biggest red-light area, Nana Entertainment Plaza to use its proper name, was a sort of amphitheatre. The floor area was filled with beer bars and the three floors of the complex surrounding it were crammed with go go bars. It was Vinny’s idea of paradise with something like 5,000 sweethearts willing to be your bird for the night. He was saving that part until Sarah’s tender ears were out of range.

“What’s Taiwan like?” Sarah pulled another corker out the bag.

Keith shook his head. Vinny tried not to laugh.

“Thailand.” He ignored her blushes. “Shit hot.”

“Is it true they have those lady men things?” It was an innocent question but it was Keith’s turn to smirk. Vinny had admitted to Keith when he was pissed up after his first trip that he’d been caught out. He’d taken the fucker home and kissed it and only noticed the lump when he’d clambered on top and was about to take her dress off. Keith had kept it to himself but liked seeing Vinny squirm.

“Oh aye, yeah. They do shows and that.”

“What are they like?” Sarah obviously had an interest in the offbeat.

“They look just like women. Some of ’em are a bit manly so you can tell but otherwise you’d never guess.” Vinny was in his element.

Keith put the T-shirt back on the table and gulped at his can. The sap had started to rise and he didn't want to appear rude by leaving his beer untouched. He plonked the half-empty can on the table and let out a burp.

"We off then?" he asked his limpet.

"If you want." She did her best not to sound like she was gagging for it.

Keith grabbed his fags off the table and picked up his new leisurewear. He gave it a sniff.

"You didn't have to wipe your arse on it." He winked as Sarah trailed behind him.

Vinny lifted his feet onto the table. He could dispense with the graces now his guests were leaving.

"I'll see you round, like a doughnut," was Vinny's parting gift.

"I'll bell you through the week." Keith headed home for a night of naughtiness and the door slammed closed behind him.

Vinny was alone and knackered. He finished his can and headed for his pit.

Vinny woke in bed at midday. He had a headache from the powdered arrogance and was foggy from the seven or eight beers. Considering the states he'd got used to waking in for the last two weeks it was a modest hangover. He let out a silent fart that nearly made him wretch. The results of the special thoughts he'd had the night before about Jeed were wrapped in tissue by the side of his futon. Kerry had taken the bed with her when she headed for her new life in Tyneside and a mate had lent Vin the futon. Since he'd started pissing most of his wages up the wall he'd not got round to replacing the bed. He convinced himself it was good for his back, regardless of the harm it did his credibility. Spurred by the urgent need to take a crap he jumped out of bed. En route to the smallest room in the flat he picked up the protein-enriched parcel and threw it down the pottery porthole on arrival. Shorts round his ankles and arms folded on his knees, he sent the last of his roadside food-stall nourishment heading towards the Mersey. If you could invent a chilli that was hot on entry but not on exit you'd make a fortune, he thought. He'd have to make a note of that one in case he ever met anyone involved in genetic modification. The wipe was a painful experience with his exit wound still smarting from the spicy delights of the East. He didn't do too thorough a job with the tissue, opting to rinse his ring in the shower.

Douched and dressed it was time to head for the shop. A hundred yards down Millhouse lane there was a convenience store, and he needed a paper and a bottle of milk.

He rummaged in his unpacked luggage to find his glasses. Contact lenses were his preferred method of bringing the world into focus but he liked to wear specs once or twice a week to let his eyes breathe. They were proving to be evasive and the pile of clothes was turning into a can of worms that he decided not to agitate.

"Use the force, Luke," Vinny muttered to himself and set off down the street specless.

Outside the flat he felt the October chill on his face. Armed with a Marlboro Light and with his collars turned up, nothing could harm him. At least it wasn't raining and the cold did freshen him up a bit. Bolton didn't seem that bad after all. It had been his home for as long as he could remember. Despite the lack of go-go bars and the price of the beer, it had a lot going for it. It was the home of the Wanderers. The bloke who invented the Spinning Jenny had lived there. Ghandi had paid it a visit once.

"Bollocks!" It was a town where people let their dogs foul the pavement.

He stopped and leaned against the nearest lamppost. He raised his lower leg at a sideways angle and inspected the damage to his Reeboks. He'd bought them specially for his trip and was distraught when he saw the shite smeared up the side of the soles. The bigger chunks came off easily by scraping against the kerb and he soldiered on to the shops. Worse things have happened at sea, he thought. He reached a patch of grass and started rubbing his soiled foot in the damp blades. It cleaned most of the lightly perfumed putty off but there was still enough to carry the aroma wedged into the tread. He flicked his fag into the road. It narrowly missed a jogger who'd crept up behind him. She had a blonde ponytail bouncing above her head and a finely shaped behind covered by Lycra shorts. She glanced over her shoulder. Her cheeks were flushed by the cold and exertion. She didn't need to call him an arsehole, her face said it for her.

Not bad, thought Vinny.

There was a cash machine built into the wall of the Co-op and he needed a few quid to get him into Manchester in the morning. A company car came with the job, a Golf he'd been told, but he wouldn't pick it up until he started. In the past he'd been used to driving BMW's as company cars but was grateful just to get an offer off Personable.

The backside turned into the Co-op ahead of him and, forgetting his canine cologne, he decided to save the cervix till 'til later. You never know, she might fall at his feet and give him her number, he mused. Jeed would never have found out if he'd been unfaithful. He entered the shop but Mary Decker was nowhere to be seen. He grabbed a copy of the *Sunday Sport* from the pile of papers and headed over to the fridge for a pint of milk. Semi-skimmed. You've got to take care of yourself. He heard the sound of trainers on the tiled shop floor and knew she was still there. He was in with a chance. The walk to the till from the fridge was carefully timed to enable maximum contact with Blondie but on arrival she wasn't there. He plonked his paper and milk on the counter. The assistant, a 50-year-old woman in a Co-op pinafore picked up the paper and ran it under the scanner, then noticed the whiff. She looked away and covered her mouth, coughing. She turned back and Vinny heard the trainers creep up behind him. He paid for the goods with the remnants of Keith's tenner, took the milk and turned. Blondie was a safe distance behind him as he looked her in the eye. She was staring at his feet and her nose was turned up in disgust at the stench. He tried to start walking, looking cool, but his copy of the *Sport* slipped out of his hand and landed face up on the floor. His free adult toys catalogue had slipped out of its safe haven within the folds of 'Britain's Raunchiest Read', and the bimbo on the front page in a g-string with stars on her nipples, who was announcing her romp with a cabinet minister, stared Vinny straight in the face. He picked up his paper and headed out. As the door pulled shut behind him he heard the 'Pschhh' of air freshener being sprayed.

Milk and paper in hand, he keyed his number in the cash point and selected 'Cash Withdrawal'. He hit the ten-pound button.

'Insufficient funds available.'

"Cunt!" He kicked the wall. The Co-op door slammed shut. Blondie, bag of fruit in hand, had heard his outburst. Health hazard, skint, smelly pervert. Obviously husband material. She seemed to be running much faster than before. Must have been the breather she'd had in the shop.

He trudged home with the paper under his arm and his milk in his coat pocket, wondering what the fuck he was doing in the UK. Less than 48 hours ago he'd been in paradise, soaking up the scorching sun, sat in a ramshackle bar surrounded by gorgeous dark-skinned girls, with one special one doting on him. Now it was four degrees C, the clouds were dark and the only satisfaction he could hope for was a hand solo over some bird in the *Sunday Sport*.

He got home, pulled his scented shoe off in the hallway, limped along single shoed through his flat and dumped his trainer in the back yard. Better get that fucker clean before its turns into concrete, was his logic as he ran the hot tap into the bowl he used to wash plates and added a dash of soap. He carried the bowl into the yard. The cold bit at his hands and the chill off the concrete flags gnawed at his one socked foot. He shuddered. He didn't want to stay around long enough to get used to the weather. He placed the bowl on the floor and looked up. His second-best mate was sat on the wall separating next door's yard.

"All right, Casper? That faggot feeding you properly, is he?" He padded over to stroke next door's cat. When he got near the wall and raised his hand Casper's back arched and his jet-black fur stood on end. He hissed and disappeared into safe territory. The local cats liked him as much as the local women. Vinny smiled. He took it as reassurance that he should be living somewhere else.

He placed his left hand inside his shoe and started working away with the brush at the muck smeared up the side. It lifted off easily and he turned his attention to the sole. Getting the waste out of the tread proved more taxing and required more elbow grease.

The phone rang. He walked into the house and through the kitchen, still scrubbing away at his shoe, spraying the lino and the carpet with a mix of dog shit and Fairy Liquid. The answer machine kicked in and he heard Keith's voice.

"Vin, you tosser, get out of bed and ring us back, you cun—"

He managed to reach the phone and, with a rare display of co-ordination, clasped the brush in his left hand along with his shoe and threw the handset between his right shoulder and chin. He started talking and, ever the paragon of efficiency, put the brush back in his right hand and carried on scrubbing.

"Keith, you paedophile." Vin was proud of the brush–shoe phone-juggling act he'd just performed. If it had been an Olympic sport he'd be getting 9.8 for style and pride glowed in his voice. "What you up to?"

"I'm round the corner. I've just dropped Sarah back at the Arrers. What you doin'?" Keith sounded quite young on the phone and his chirpiness after last night's result accentuated it.

"Cleaning shit off me shoe."

Keith sniggered briefly. "Sounds lovely, mate. I was just gonna pop in for a brew."

"Whatever. Yeah. See yer in a sec." Vin dropped the phone back down towards the receiver but the handset missed its port – 5.6 for effort. He nudged it back into its cradle with the brush and headed out again to the yard, scrubbing as he went.

By the time Keith rung on the intercom he'd done as good a job on his shoe as he could and had left it on the windowsill to dry.

Keith swaggered into the flat with a grin on his face. Obviously had a tale to tell but was trying to keep a lid on it.

"Brew?"

"Aye, fuck it, you only live once."

Vinny sneezed as he headed to the kitchen. His nostrils had been spared the assault of freebie lines off Keith for a fortnight, and last night's couple were playing on his sinuses.

"So how was she?" Vinny raised his voice to be heard in the living room.

Keith waited for him to get back before he replied.

He shook his head. "Did she seem pissed when we left here?"

"Not really."

"Oh I tell you! Gets her home, right. Fucking walking up the steps she had to hold on the handrail and starts swaying, don't she!" Keith had a fire escape staircase leading up to the flat at the back of the bakery. "Gets inside and has a job keeping her eyes open. Only one thing for it." He sat up, proud of his scoundrelish act.

Vin shook his head, feigning disgust. "Not content with shagging the landlord's daughter but you get her addicted to class-A drugs."

Keith was put out that his narrative had been interrupted. " So anyway, I racks up dun I, and she's like, 'What's this? Is it speed?'" Keith mimicked Sarah's whine. "Once it's down her she's straight out her chair and in the bog hooping up. All I could hear was her wretchin'. Put me right off, I tell you."

Keith paused for breath and gazed out of the front window waiting for his prompt. He loved playing to the crowd.

"Go on then."

"Well, after a good puke she comes out wiping her gob on the back of her hand." Keith gave a demonstration of her clean-up act. "And then drags me into the bedroom."

Vin tried took look impressed but knew that young birds in Bolton weren't a patch on the world champions he'd been tussling with in Thailand. "Any good?"

"She nearly yanked my fucking cock off." Keith made an up-and-down gesture with his hand.

"More enthusiasm than experience?"

"Aye, summat like that. Then jumps on and she's at it all fucking night like a bird possessed."

The kettle clicked and Vinny turned, interrupting his mate's dialogue.

"Fuck the brew, our kid, are we down the Arrers for a pint?" Keith liked a beer on Sunday lunch.

"Skint."

"It's on me!"

"Are you serious!" Vin was a bit put out. Not by the offer of money but at how stupid the Itai cunt could be sometimes. "You've just shagged the landlord's daughter and you want to go and have a pint in his pub?"

"All right then, Crown?"

Vinny slumped into his armchair. "Fucked!"

He flicked the TV on with the remote. He'd spent the afternoon tight lipped, playing pool in the Crown with Keith and sipping at four or five pints. He was half kicking himself. The cunt looked better than he had in the fake Ralph Lauren. That wasn't the main reason he was quiet though, he was distraught at having to start work again tomorrow. Back to the daily in and out, trying to convince clients he could get the Unix machines cheaper and quicker. The one plus point was they were a new outfit, sounded full of bright ideas. He turned his gaze to the TV. The sound was off and he could see a church choir with hymn books in full flow.

"Sunday fucking Worship." The jet lag, cocaine washout and four or five pints were trying to hold him in the chair and push his head to one side but there were still three cans of Stella left in the fridge. It took every ounce of muscle he had to haul his carcass out of the armchair. He mooched over to the kitchen and flicked the light on. Instead of heading straight for the fridge he wandered to the sink. It faced out onto the yard. He rested his elbows on the worktop and gazed out to try and get a perspective on things. He saw a shadow scamper away and noticed his shoe, a pool of light in the yard. He tutted. Another fucking effort to get his shoe from the yard. He opened the back door and stood in suspended animation for a second. His body told him it was 2am. It should have been twenty degrees C and the air should have been still. Jeed's slender arm should have been linked into his. The clock on the kitchen wall said 7pm, and it was two degrees C. A gust of wind hit him. A small droplet welled up in his left eye. If anyone had been there it could have been mistaken as being caused by the breeze, but it wasn't. He soldiered out into the yard and remembered that he'd left the shoe on the ledge. His nostrils flared. "Casper, you little fuckin' cunt." His best mate after Keith had been using his new trainer to sharpen his claws on. Maybe it was an act of revenge for calling his owner a faggot. Or he could have been under the command of the go-go god, passing on a message: "Don't stay in England, Vincent, everything's shit. Your presence is required elsewhere!"

He picked the shoe up and sneezed. It felt more like he had a cold than the aftermath of the South American Sinus Slayer. He eyed the damage to the Reebok and only once he was back inside could he see that half the white sheen had been scuffed off the upper. Cunt could have scratched the sole.

He rubbed his hands as he opened the fridge door. There was no blood getting through to his fingertips and when he grasped a can of beer it was painful. Two days ago a cold bottle had been a pleasure to behold. They were great for rolling across the brow to cool you down if you'd just walked fifteen yards to the next beer bar. Now it was like having arthritis.

from nine to five I

Vinny woke curled on his side and rolled up inside his quilt. He was wearing jog bottoms, a T-shirt and socks. His head then his bladder told him it was time to get up. He turned to his right and as he did the cocoon he'd made himself cracked open and let in cold air. Not enough to make him shiver or gasp, but enough to make him grasp the quilt to close the gap. His head turned an extra 40 degrees and he saw the glowing red digits of his alarm clock. 5:27. On Thai time it would be about the time he normally got up, apart from on the last day when he'd had to be up at a shockingly early 11.30 to check out before midday. He shut his eyes and tried to doze off again but his bladder was saying, "Empty me". He stumbled into the bathroom and rummaged in the front of his jog bottoms. The cold weather wasn't doing him any favours. Jack Frost had stolen half his penis but left him with his original foreskin, there was barely enough to fit over the waistband. He stood in front of the WC motionless, staring at the wall. Why did it always happen like this? Seconds ago he was bursting but now there seemed to be a seal that needed breaking. He looked down and the flow started. Nice and easy for 12–15 seconds or so then a respite. There was still waste that needed disposing of and the flow started again then trickled to a halt. He shook and put his best friend back in his trousers.

The first couple of strides into the living room were done with a sense of pride. No dribbles this time round … oops, spoke to soon.

He sat in the armchair and lit a fag. The craving for tobacco had been another factor forcing him out of bed. The telly lit up as he hit the switch on the remote. Channel 5 was showing Canadian Baseball and Vin's eyes glued themselves to the screen but there were no neural messages going down the optical nerve. He made mental calculations. Start at 9, 8.05 train gets in 8.35, plenty of time to get into the office. Bus about 7.45 should drop me off in time. That means dressing at 7.10. He looked at his watch – 5.45. That left him with the best part of an hour and a half to kill. He drew a final drag on his cigarette and stumped it in the Greenhall's ashtray he'd nicked from the Arrows.

"Might as well have another fag," he said to himself and drew his knees up to his chest to get a bit more body heat.

Second fag finished, he padded back to bed and cocooned himself in his quilt again. There was no sign of sleep so a wank seemed like a good idea. He put his right hand down the front of his keks and started to rub. No signs of life. He put his left down there to try and raise a bit of support as he shut his eyes and thought of Jeed writhing around naked on top of him. What felt like an erection started to appear. It felt warm but only half the size it had been in the heat of Chonburi province. He started to work single handed but the life drained away from the old chap. His cold, slightly rough hands weren't the tonic that Jeed's red-hot inner sanctum had been.

"Bollocks." He let go and felt his best friend slump to one side. He turned round and looked at the clock, still an hour and ten minutes to kill. Thoughts of how to perform well at work started to enter his head. He'd lasted six months at his last place selling (or not selling) high-end computer systems. He'd done all right selling all different types of heavy-duty computing equipment for five years or so but after Kerry's departure and his first trip to Thailand there'd been a downturn in his productivity and he'd walked out after the pressure from above got too heavy. At his next place he'd done OK for six months but then started to knock around with Keith. After going on the missing list for two days he was dismissed over the phone.

Personable Computers was realistically his last chance. A lucky lifeline; most people in his sector knew he was a waste of time. He had been about to be sacked from his second job since leaving the place that had taught him his trade under the watchful eye of Kerry, when he saw Personable's advert in the paper and applied. He'd made up some cock and bull about them having poor supply lines and failing to deliver on sales he'd made.

"Right, no fucking about, get my head down and put the effort in, do everything to earn the cash so I can go see Jeed at Christmas. No pissing it up in the week, no drugs, give it one hundred per cent." He did a good job of convincing himself he was going to pull it off.

The pale-skinned Siamese exile rolled around and rubbed his cock to keep warm till the digits on his clock read 6:50. He'd been wide awake for well over an hour and headed for the shower. Nice and refreshing. Once clean and with a towel wrapped round him he padded over to the sink and eyed himself up in the mirror. He still had a tiny bit of a tan from catching the sun for ten minutes a day walking from The Fallen Angel to Tommy Bar on Soi 7 via

Bulldog. There were horrendous bags under his eyes though. All that boozing on top of the jetlag had taken its toll.

Wear glasses today, they'll cover 'em up, he thought as he shaved.

Scrape complete, he headed for the living room in his towelling toga. He squatted over his bag and rummaged through the smelly undies and shirts for his glasses case and that bottle of aftershave he'd bought at the airport. The warm water from the shower started to evaporate and suck the heat from his body. The join at the front of the towel left his tackle half exposed and he gave himself a rub to get the warmth back.

Once he'd found the Dolce & Gabbana glasses case and Jill Sander aftershave he retreated and dressed in the bedroom. He'd had his best suit dry cleaned for the new job, ironed a week's worth of shirts (he only had six that were still wearable) and polished his Church's shoes. He still looked the successful salesman, even if the hem on the cuffs of his two-year-old Hugo Boss suit did fall down occasionally, and if he wore it without the jacket you could see where his wallet had worn a hole in the cloth near the back pocket.

With his sensible blue woollen overcoat on, the hi-tech hawker headed for the bus stop. Keith had lent him another tenner, which saved him having to go on the scrounge to his mam and dad. That could wait till that night. There was a smile on his face as he stood at the bus stop drawing on a fag. He was looking forward to his day and, despite a new job having become a regular occurrence recently, he was excited. They'd told him they were going to recruit a team to generate leads for him so he could concentrate on closing the deals. It sounded like they meant business.

The bus dropped him off and he felt superior walking into Bolton Railway Station. The bus had been full of college kids, school kids and middle-aged women in cheap work outfits. Not a patch on him.

He headed down to the platform as a train pulled away towards Manchester. It wasn't that big a problem, he was early for the train he'd planned to get. A nice greasy bacon barm from the café on the platform stopped the growls that had started in his stomach.

When the train arrived it was full so Vin and the 80 or so other commuters crammed themselves into the aisles and walkways. The train rolled and clattered its way to Manchester, stopping at Salford Crescent, Salford Central, Deansgate and Oxford Road.

Vin got off at Oxford Road and walked down the ramp out of the station. The ticket inspector hadn't managed to reach him so he'd got a free ride. He joined the countless workers milling the streets heading for their offices. He was faceless and anonymous. Did any of them know he was a sleaze bag who paid impoverished women to sleep with him? A proud smile crossed his face. These cunts didn't know what they were missing out on. They were happy to sit and pay a mortgage and sleep with a fat twat, work all their lives to pay for ungrateful kids then die in the cold. He shook his head. I'm not long for these parts, he told himself.

Quite what he was going to do when he fucked off was still an unknown factor in the equation but there was little doubt over the destination. Trundling down Whitworth Street he felt the chill. His hands were in his pockets and his shoulders were hunched up. The mist from his breath hit his face as he walked into it. It felt like ages since he'd seen his breath. Turning left turn onto Princess Street signalled the imminence of his arrival at his new place of work. Like a prisoner about to be executed he lit his last fag until lunch and wondered what the training he'd been told about would be like. A sense of trepidation hit him as he hovered outside Number 4 Princess Street, the converted warehouse that was identical to half the office blocks and hotels in Manchester. Its sandstone face gave it an austere appearance. He took three deep drags of his fag before flicking it in a graceful arch into the traffic. He walked up the steps to the entrance. The ascent would have been quicker without the jitters. At the lift at the far end of the granite-floored entrance area he hit the up arrow and waited. The doors opened and he saw himself in the mirrored back wall. On the journey up to the fourth floor he patted his hair down, making sure he didn't look unkempt on his first day. When he'd been interviewed for the job the office had been undergoing refurbishment and he was curious as to how the place had taken shape over the last six weeks. There was stillness as the lift reached its destination and then the doors opened. Vin put on his best smile and the nerves helped it grow broader than usual. Like a kid on his first day at a new school he approached the pine-veneered double doors at the end of the corridor. An intercom had been fitted since his interview. With a purposeful push he hit the sign saying RECEPTION. Two women appeared behind him. They'd been stripped of their overcoats and smelt heavily of perfume. New Boy looked over his shoulder and saw one slightly older than him in a dark checked suit and heavy make-up who had a Mediterranean look about her. Dark hair and olive skin, she could've been Jeed if she was four sizes smaller with slanted eyes. The other was about a foot shorter than the Latina, paler skinned and a good foot wider to go with it. Their chatter stopped. They were a little out of breath, having used the stairs not the lift.

"Who've you come to see?" probed the taller of the two as they both put on their best 'I'm so fucking happy it stinks' smile, the one reserved for male clients, male superiors and newbies they wanted to look content in front of.

"I'm starting work here today." Best grin like a daft cunt myself, he thought, if that's the order of the day, and he gave them his best glow.

"Oh well, you'll be in the induction course with Charles this week. That's in the boardroom. I'll take you down there in a moment." She was holding a pack of menthol cigarettes and a disposable lighter in her hand. She waved her fags at a small panel next to the intercom. The swipe card she had hidden somewhere in the same hand caused a buzzing noise. Latina pushed the door and probed again. "What's your name?"

"Vincent Croston." He used his full name rather than the abbreviation he kept for friends.

"Oh, I've heard about you," gushed Latina. " I'm Sue Robbins, Regional Sales Manager. You're doing the high-level stuff, aren't you. This is Toni, she's running the consumables section."

Sue pushed the door open to reveal the newly decked-out office. It was the size of four tennis courts. The carpet was deep blue and the floor space was carved up by fabric-coated partitions. There were pine-veneered desks matching the door sitting flush against the partitions, with a brand-new PC on each and a brand-new swivel chair pushed up against each desk. Half the desks (about 60 or so in total) were occupied, mainly by females, busy chatting either on the phone or to colleagues. Most of them seemed quite healthy as well at first glance. Toni scurried off and started chatting to a blonde that he could only see from behind. The smell of new carpet and wallpaper paste finally made it's way through Vin's blocked nostrils. The place had the feel of one of those operational centres the bad guy had in a Bond movie – clinically clean and full of 'Y' chromosomes. Two large windows with slatted blinds occupied the far wall, each with a door matching the corporate pine veneer next to it.

Sue turned to Vinny wearing a helpful look on her face, rather than the gushing smile. "Just wait here and I'll show you where to put your coat and take you downstairs." She pottered off towards one of the goldfish bowls at the far end.

She was stopped with, "Hi Sue," from almost every member of staff she passed within ten feet of. Some of the ones with browner noses stopped her to compliment her on her suit or her perfume or her blusher or the new way she'd set her hair. Vinny felt a sneeze coming on. Maybe it was all the new carpet, maybe the cocaine, maybe he was getting a cold like he'd had every time he'd come back from Thailand.

"Attchew!" It wasn't too loud. His hand had managed to muffle it. His favourite wanking hand had also managed to prevent a good measure of crystal-clear snot from spraying his new colleagues.

"Fuck." A nice pawful of mucus and any moment now he was gonna get his hand shook. He wiped his palm on the inside of his overcoat pocket, smiling politely at a young girl in blouse and skirt heading, Silk Cut in hand, for the doors behind him. She flashed her teeth at him, more of a polite gesture than a friendly one.

Sue reappeared out of her goldfish bowl at the end of the office and tottered back towards Vinny. Her beam was a different this time. "I am very important and everyone kisses my oversized dark brown tights-clad arse," was the message this particular smile semaphored to him.

"Right then." The smile was even broader now. "You can put your coat in here." She headed towards a door on the wall that housed the main entrance and pushed it open. By now his nostrils were clear and it took no time for the smell to hit him. It was like a tart's boudoir. About 25 women's overcoats were hanging on pegs next to a shelving unit housing stacks of paper, pens, Post-it notes, mugs with the blue 'Personable' logo printed on them. The collective mass of excess perfume packed a punch.

"I'll keep my coat with me for today, thanks, Sue." Vinny smiled to mask his horror. If his coat started to smell like that he'd have queers trying to mount him on the train home.

"And the kitchen's next door." She smiled. Our hero followed her back into the office. Down at the other end he spotted his first male member of staff, a black guy in his thirties. Obviously as scared of salads as Vinny, sporting a brand-new grey suit made of heavy cloth. He was pacing up and down, gesticulating aggressively to the person on the other end of the phone. His words were inaudible above the office, but from his mannerisms they obviously weren't kind ones.

Sue headed for the main door and out into the corridor. Opting for the staircase rather than the lift, she started descending ahead of Vinny, side-on to project her words at him.

"So how did you hear about Personable?" The interrogation was underway.

"I saw the ad in the *Evening News*." Non-plussed.

"Oh, I see. So Charles didn't approach you himself?"

"No." Should he have done?

"So do you know anyone who works here?" Her face straightened.

"Nope." And he sounded like he didn't give a fuck either.

Sue's tone became a sterner now as if not knowing anyone was a bit of an issue. "You see, a lot of us used to work for Charles at Meg Computing before he left to set up the UK operation for Personable. Have you heard of them?"

Who hadn't? Big mail order operation. Half their clients were domestic users buying toners and blank disks over the phone. Real grotty stuff. They advertised in things like local free papers and delivered a week later. The stuff was usually damaged in the post or the wrong order. Vinny hadn't even realised they sold to companies, let alone got involved in the sort of machines he sold worth upwards of two or three hundred grand.

"Oh yes, of course. Hasn't everyone?" He smiled. At least they were well known and he was trying to play on that to placate her a little.

The conversation hushed as they reached the ground floor. Sue did an about turn at the bottom of the stairway and waved her swipe card at the panel next to a pine-veneered door tucked away behind the staircase. An identical buzz to the one upstairs sounded and Sue pushed the door open with her arm.

"This section's still being decorated," she said over her shoulder as she walked down a narrow corridor to another pine door. There was no carpet down yet, just bare concrete. This door didn't have access control on it and she pushed the steel handle into what appeared to be the boardroom. It was about an eighth of the size of the office upstairs. Most of the space was taken up by a large pine-veneer table matching the corporate look, with a royal-blue carpet, white walls and around twenty easy-ish chairs round the table, upholstered in the corporate shade of blue. Half the chairs were occupied, again mainly by young ladies in their best attempt at business clothes. Sue was leagues above this lot. The chorus of, "Hi Sue," was a little less resounding than earlier. A lot of these were obviously new to the company. Vinny felt like a PhD student at a degree ceremony for ordinary graduates when he eyed everyone quickly and guessed the average age to be 21.

Plenty of vacant places were available but Vinny wanted to pick carefully. He saw a fat guy with light brown hair and a slightly gaudy pin-striped suit on with a space next to him. He'd be safe in male company. There was a spare seat next to him and he shuffled past the backs of a few sweet-smelling young girls.

"All right, mate? This seat taken, is it?" Might as well be polite.

"Feel free." The fat guy looked up, appearing disinterested. He weighed Vinny up as he removed his overcoat and put it over the back of the chair.

Vinny pulled out the chair, conscious of his movements. The women were pretending not to notice a male entering the room.

In Situ Vinny relaxed and smiled. Seat equalled safety and he could afford to show his human side.

"I'm Geoff." The fat guy offered his hand and Vinny accepted. Geoff wore a gold bracelet with a panel that obviously displayed his name, although he couldn't see the engraving, and he'd also acquired quite a large gold-coloured ring with the name 'Geoff' making up the face of it.

"I'm Vin, Vinny Croston. How's tricks?" He was used to working with classier people but decided to try and put snap judgements aside.

"Not bad, mate. I'm told Charles'll be here in fifteen minutes. You coming for a fag?" Obviously the friendly type.

"Aye, why not?" Vinny pushed his chair back and clutched his coat. They two scurried out of the building with another guy close on their tail. Vinny fumbled around in his pockets momentarily as Geoff offered him a Benson & Hedges.

"Bit strong for me them, mate." Vinny produced his Siamese ciggies. He became aware of the curiosity they aroused as he pulled a white-tipped cigarette out of the packet. Geoff thrust a light in his face.

"Been on holiday, mate?" Geoff had that friendly tone that most fat people tended to possess, and a jowl that hung over his collar. Judging by his accent he was from Lancashire rather than Manchester.

"Yeah, just got back from Thailand the other day." Vin looked away. He was trying not to make a big deal of it and knew that if he got talking he'd give away too much info.

Geoff must have sensed Vin's reluctance to let him explore that opportunity, or maybe he was just more interested in work. "What section you working on?"

“I’m setting up the high-end section. You?” Vin followed etiquette and stuck to work topics.

“I’m in charge of peripherals in the commercial sector. You know, printers for offices and schools, that sort of thing. Have you worked for Charles before?” Geoff was inadvertently backing up Sue’s tack of ‘are you an ex-employee of Meg’s?’.

“Nah, just saw the ad in the paper.”

The other guy that had followed them out of the boardroom was stood by himself and was talking into his mobile while he enjoyed a cigarette. He was a little more demure and not overweight. His clothes looked more like a school uniform without the badge on the blazer. You’d have been forgiven for thinking he was on work experience. He certainly didn’t look old enough to smoke. Conversation over he hit a button on his mobile and strode towards the two new friends.

“All right, Geoff?” The youngster had a spark in his voice.

“Yeah, Geoff, not so bad,” fatty replied.

“Fuck me, two Geoffs in one office. Must make life interesting. Know each other from Meg?”

Little Geoff piped up, “I was there for three years till I heard about this place and Charles running it.”

Geoff and Geoff carried on with tittle tattle about Meg and who was and wasn’t coming on board while the three of them finished their fags.

A black cab pulled up as Vin dropped his glowing ember on the pavement and erased the light with his foot. The two Geoffs looked alert and almost in unison thrust their hands behind their backs and turned to face the cab as if it were the trooping of the colours. Might as well stop around to see what the fuss is all about, thought Vin. A large beige object appeared to be moving inside the cab. It was Charles in a camel overcoat. Vin remembered him from the interview, huge guy, must have been at least 22 stone and ruddy faced. Fat Geoff was obviously imitating his jowl but had only just got it over the top of his collar. Charles was leagues ahead. Vinny had forgotten how bovine his new boss was. Having spent two weeks in a land where the average weight of blokes is 9 stone seemed to amplify him in Vinny’s eyes.

“Morning, Charles,” was the unified call from the Geoffs. “Good flight, Charles?” piped up fat Geoff.

“Fine, thank you, Geoffrey,” he mooed over his shoulder as he paid the driver. He even sounded like an Oxford educated ox.

Vinny had started to head back, but thought better of it and decided that a bit of brown nosing of his own might not do him any harm. As the head honcho headed his way he turned and smiled.

“Ah, Victor, how are you?” the fat fucker spat rather than spoke. The effort of getting out of the cab with a briefcase left him breathless.

“Fine. I must say I’m looking forward to the training.”

“I was hoping to catch you before we started actually.” Charles took in a deep breath to get his heart rate back down. “With your background you may find it a little, erm … a little basic. I’d appreciate it if you could play along really.”

“Fine.” Vin was happy to oblige. “Where did you fly from?” He could see fat Geoff scowling. Only been there five minutes and stealing his thunder.

“Heathrow. I live in Twickenham so it’s only ten minutes by cab.” Vinny politely thrust his hands behind his back and plodded along around a foot behind him on his left-hand side. “How are you finding the high-end market at the moment?”

“Fine. Reasonably buoyant.” He tried to look unconcerned. Before he’d gone away a lot of ex-colleagues had been commenting on a downturn. “It’s just the other office’s we’ve opened have found that sector a little harder to get off the ground than the others. We may need to keep a close eye on things,” he huffed and walked ahead.

That was music to fat Geoff’s ears and, as Vin looked over his shoulder, he could see an enormous smirk on the his face.

Back in the boardroom Charles was ahead of them, briefcase open and overcoat hung on the coathanger in the corner. Sue had miraculously appeared by his side. She looked in raptures to be privileged enough to be within a foot of his 64-inch waist.

I’m so happy it stinks again, and she said it without moving her lips.

Two stooges and an outsider fumbled themselves back into their seats as Charles started.

“I need to get copies of the training material for everyone,” he boomed and muttered to Sue by his side, “Twenty copies of that, please.”

“Yes, Charles. Do you want them binding?” His lady in waiting was avoiding eye contact with the inductees and apparently looking at the chief’s crotch.

“If you can.” He readdressed the crowd. “While we’re waiting for the course material we can do the introductions and ice-breakers. For those of you that don’t know me, I’m Charles Grantwell, Managing Director. Previously I was Managing Director of Meg Computing for ten years, and prior to that I ran my own company selling spare parts for home computers…” He droned on about how he was aiming to make Personable the leading supplier to domestic and commercial users of all sorts of bits and pieces for computers, and how he’d set aside £10 million of his investors’ money for advertising, and how they had a superb distribution network established through five giant warehouses running an automated delivery system across the UK.

After Charles’s introduction the inductees had to introduce themselves to the assembled.

The first three were girls in their twenties who’d given up jobs in record shops or call centres to get into selling computer spares. Next was a girl who’d worked for Charles at ‘you know where’ for eighteen months and whom in January had won the coveted 'Customer Service Award' in the Manchester office. A couple more of Charlie's stalwarts harped on about generating £15,000 worth of sales in this month or the other, and how they were expecting to make the same amount in the next month. Then it was Vinny's turn, now singularly unimpressed by his new colleagues to introduce himself.

"Hi, I'm, er, Vinny Croston. I'm Team Leader of the High-End Solutions division." He was doing his best to smile and sound keen but laid back. "I've been selling the larger commercial solutions for around seven years now, mainly Sun and HP, and I'm hoping my team can generate around £2 million in year one." He smirked and sat down. That should put Charles's two-bit arse lickers in their place.

Intros over, it was time for the ice-breakers. Everyone present had to stand up and talk for a minute (non stop) on a subject of Charlie Boy's choosing. There were some fumbles and a few gaffs but it seemed to work quiet well and ease the tension. Quite why Vin had to talk about cider would be one of those mysteries that remained unsolved.

Once the swooning Sue had delivered the training material it was on to the serious matter of working through the training literature. The content was basic. It started with how to answer the phone to customers responding to adverts and shitty stuff on how to get a customer to buy a pack of 24 floppy disks instead of 12. Vinny switched off. Everyone had to do role plays with Charles. Vin did badly. Maybe it was the jet lag, maybe the cocaine, perhaps it was because he wasn't listening, possibly it was because he couldn't be arsed or, dare he think it, the fat ponce was trying to trip him. Whatever the reason (probably a combination of them all), he fucked it up, knew it and wasn't bothered. He wasn't the only one to be less than a hundred per cent. One of the girls without experience was trying her best and would've got her name wrong if she'd been asked what it was in public. Strangely Charles seemed to throw tougher questions at the guys, while the young ladies, especially the prettier ones, got an easier ride. Vinny put that observation down to cynicism on his part.

The course dragged on and Vin tried not to look at his watch even when the Fat Controller looked at his own.

"Now seems like an appropriate time to break for lunch." He smiled. "Let's say back here in fifty minutes from now."

Most of the throng didn't want to look over keen on leaving the room, and stayed to chat with their neighbours for a while. Vinny had other thoughts. He knew that Jeed would have emailed him at least once in the two days since his departure and it was gnawing away at him that he hadn't checked. A second but no less important factor that dragged him out of the chair was nicotine. Fags cost eighty pence a pack in Pattaya and with nothing to do all day but sit and play Connect 4 or Jackpot with your loved one, smokers tend to increase their habit.

Like a greyhound when the trap goes up he was out the door with a lit fag and chasing the email rabbit to a cyber café three hundred yards away.

CyBar was a cross between a coffee shop/bar and a cyber café. Young guys in skate gear sat at tables trying to look cool in front of their mates while sipping an unusual coffee or a new brand of imported beer. Geeks who looked like PhD students sat in front of the bank of PCs that sat at the side and back walls, tapping away and pausing while a page was sent or downloaded.

Vin approached the bar and the warm air made his cheeks flush after the cold and damp of outdoor Manchester. The bartender pointed him towards a free terminal in the corner. The lonely man was soon in position logging into his Yahoo account.

"Fuck, this PC's slow," he mumbled to himself as the machine churned its way into his inbox. The black girl sat next to him with her sister or cousin leaning over her shoulder gave him a sour glance because of his blue language. There were a couple of messages from some porn site that had managed to get his email address and kept sending him updates. A quick look down the list showed two from Jeed Pornsutto so he clicked on the first with his hand trembling.

"Vinny Tilac

I miss you so much. I hope you are in England OK. How are you? Please
tell me. I want to know how about your job. This time don't work too hard. It's make you tired. There are so cold, please take care yourself when boxing and not make hurt yourself.

I worry about you. I'm fine. don't worry me. If I reply mail to you late, don't angry about me. Because I don't have time for check mail. But I still want your mail to me alway. Please keep touch. If I get your mail, it's make me feel good. I'm glad someone who I love, he is mail me.

Love you so much.
Chok Dee for new job.

Jeed"

Vinny had to touch the corner of his eye and sniffle a little. There was a soft smile on his face. He could sense the black girls smiling even though he couldn't see them. His foul words were forgiven.

The back button was slow and once in the inbox he clicked on the next mail to see what the second mail she'd sent on the day he'd departed said.

There was no script in this one, only a couple of attachments. He clicked to open them and waited. His hand grasped the top of the screen as a picture started to make its presence felt. It appeared from the top downwards agonisingly slowly, eventually showing a picture of his Tilac stood in front of a waterfall in some shopping mall or other wearing a baseball cap, dark sleeveless top that finished above her naval, shorts and training shoes. He paused for a moment and took in the view. She looked so cute he stroked the screen. His heart started to bump. He scrolled down to the next one that still hadn't loaded, then scrolled back up to the full photo and gave the next one a moment to download. The smile he wore was a proud one now. The second photo once complete showed the love of his life in the bar with three friends; one he knew as Ohn but the other two crowding into the frame and laughing were anonymous. Jeed took up the centre spot and was wearing the baseball cap back to front. That one didn't capture his attention as much and, mindful of the cost, he hit reply and started to type.

"Jeed Honey

It so nice to hear from you. I'm back in England and it very cold. The picture you send it very beautiful. Who are other girls in bar? I only start new job today it OK I think. I want come and see you soon but have problem with money. Maybe Christmas I'll come Pattaya again. I send you mail again soon and also photo.

Take care
See you soon

Vin
XXXXXXX"

The send button took time to acknowledge being pressed. Message sent Vin signed out and headed back to the bar.

"Two pounds fucking fifty," he cursed as he walked back into the cold. After the bacon barm, that left him with a fiver out of the tenner he'd scrounged off Keith. The sandwich he grabbed in a newsagent's was unimpressive and he headed back to the office for the afternoon's training. With three pounds to his name he was more bothered about making ends meet till payday than absorbing any shite off Charles about smiling on the phone and welcoming the customer.

A couple of the new starters were stood outside the office nattering and enjoying their cigarettes. They were all female apart from fat Geoff, who was trying his best to sound important in front of the better looking and slightly older of the four young women. As Vin drew near he dipped into his pocket and dragged out a fag. "Got a light, Geoff?" He had one himself but wanted to make conversation.

"How you finding it?" Geoff quizzed as he waved a light towards Vin.

"Fine. Bit basic, like, but you've gotta cover all the bases, haven't you?" Vin lied. Fucking shite, he felt like saying.

"If you actually follow what he's saying, it does work. I use those standard lines every day." Charles's self-appointed second lieutenant turned back to the brown-haired girl he'd been trying to impress and hardly showed anything of a scowl.

Vinny finished his fag alone and stared at the traffic in Princess Street. He had more than a slight feeling that there was trouble ahead. Fuck it, he thought, I've made my bed…

Jeed entered his mind and popped her head round the post at the corner of the bar smiling. "Oooh, sexy maan, sexy maan," and she blew him a kiss before scurrying off to natter with a friend.

Blink blink… Na, still in Manchester. The fag end landed gracefully in the grid in the gutter. Vin half shivered, half shrugged his shoulders and turned once more unto the seats, to spend the afternoon learning how to ask if it was OK to send the customer a catalogue.

At 6:30pm Vinny was sat in his armchair in jeans and a thick jumper with the training book on his lap, waiting for the central heating to kick in. The afternoon had dragged. Charles had only humiliated him once before closing the session and telling everyone to learn the day's sales pitches off by heart for tomorrow. The Personable training bible literature was drivel and reading it made Vin nauseous so he put it on top of the neatly folded *Sunday Sport* next to the armchair. His stomach was growling as well. An inspection of the fridge showed that, unless he could make a meal with half a tub of margarine and a month-old stick of lemongrass, he was going to have to go on a harsh diet. Feeding himself took priority over learning the patter for Charles. The options available were painful. Ringing the parents would mean relying on his family and he was 30 years old, for fuck's sake. He felt a twat scrounging off Keith. There were three other options: shoplifting, becoming a rent boy or using his credit card. After a moments deliberation he pulled his card from his wallet and rang the customer services number on the back. Vin's telephone was well past it's best and punching in his personal ID number and security codes took three attempts before he actually got his balance.

There was three hundred quid of available credit. That would sort him out for food till payday.

With his winter jacket, baseball cap and freshly scuffed trainers on he headed out the door and down the road to the 24-hour Tesco. Shopping was always boring and this occasion was no exception.

It took him 45 minutes in total to walk there shop and walk home.

Back in the newly heated home he placed the eight cans of Fosters for the price of six in the fridge, well, six of them anyway. The other two went in the cooler compartment to chill quicker. He peeled the packaging off the red Thai curry, pricked the lid and slammed it in the microwave. Next on his list of fattening exercises was to pour himself a glass of Coke.

While he waited for the microwave to ping he leafed through the *Sunday Sport* he'd bought the day before. The nipple count was a stunning, 63 this week, although only about 4 of them seemed to be sat on top of non-surgically enhanced breasts. Not his cup of tea. He'd once had the pleasure of playing with a pair in a massage parlour in Manchester and his best summation of them was that it was like playing with a two-pound bag of sugar in a one-pound bag. The fuckers were rock solid and didn't move. As usual, there was nothing newsworthy so he skipped to the list of classifieds at the back. A quick survey revealed that no new massage parlours had opened in Bolton while he'd been away. Luxury Lounge on the edge of town was still Bolton's only offering to the town's ugly and heavy sacked desperados. The microwave pinged and he could smell the garlic from the curry wafting through the seals on the microwave doors.

Brrrrrinnng! Brrrrrinnng! Brrrrrrinnng! "Fucking cunt." The phone never rang in the middle of Sunday Worship or when Jehovah's witnesses were button-holing you on the doorstep.

He picked the phone up. "Hello." He wasn't pleased by the intrusion and it told in his voice.

"Hello, Vincent, this is your mother." He'd known who it was, of course, as soon as she'd said hello.

"Oh, hiya." He did his best to sound pleased to hear from her. She must have had the poshest phone voice in Bolton. She was a teacher and always spoke with an air of suspicion. "Look, Mum, I'll call you back in ten minutes." He tried to sound polite but was thinking of his curry going cold.

"What's up, don't you want to speak to your mother?" She sounded dejected but the suspicious tone took a higher rating in her vocal characteristics. She was a worrier and always suspected him of some hideous crime or misdemeanour if he didn't give her his undivided attention.

"Look, Mum, my tea's ready. I'll call you back in ten minutes." He wanted to slam the phone down but knew how much stick he'd get for it. Like most worriers, she never listened.

"How was Thailand?"

"Lovely. Look. My tea's getting cold. I'll call you back." He put the phone down gently so it didn't sound like he'd slammed it, and glared at the handset. He could just see her laying into his dad at home.

"He didn't want to speak to me. I think something's wrong."

Parental contact wasn't Vinny's favourite pastime and it took the edge off his curry. To stop the pot it came in burning his lap he used the training book as a tray. At least it had some uses. The microwave meal went down a treat. Not quite as hot as the real stuff and there were no damsels in denim mopping his brow with tissues or stroking his leg while he wolfed it down but it brought the memories back. It was probably the first time he'd had a genuine smile on his face since his return.

The cans of Fosters in the icebox were nice and cool and the first one seemed to jump into his hand. He lit a fag and sat back in his armchair like a successful industrialist in his Park Road gentleman's club, sipping a brandy and puffing on a cigar.

Brrrrinng! Brrrrrrinng!

"Hi, Mum." He was chirpier now with the taste of Thailand fresh in his mouth and a cold beer and a fag in his hand.

"Oh." She sounded flustered. "How did you know it was me?" Suspicious tone again.

"I just guessed. How are you?" Barraging her with questions would throw her and prevent an interrogation.

"Fine."

No chance for her to catch her breath. "And how's Dad?"

"Oh, you know, he's fine as well. He's just taken the dog for a walk."

Vinny smiled. Since his dad's heart attack, his mum had insisted that he give up smoking. For a guy who'd been smoking 30 a day a for 40 years (Woodbines as well), he'd done exceptionally well to last 6 months but for the last 5 years he'd mysteriously been taking the dog for 20 walks a day that lasted no longer than 7 or 8 minutes.

"So what's been happening then?" Vin had become an expert in staving off questioning. Get her talking, stops her mind working overtime and asking questions.

"Well, I've been rehearsing a lot and it was parent's evening at school on Friday." She was glowing down the phone. How sweet.

Vin grinned. Fuck me, the fast lane lifestyle of a 55-year-old high-school teacher.

"What are you rehearsing for?"

"I'm in the chorus for Oklahoma. Do you want tickets?" He could see her beaming down the phone at him. She couldn't sing to save her life but had insisted on getting involved in Bolton's amateur operatic club.

"When is it?" He tried to sound enthusiastic.

"Oh, let me check." Vin heard the phone get put down and the sound of scurrying and paper being rustled. "It's running from the twelfth to the fifteenth of November at the Town Hall."

Vin sucked his lips. "Work have said something about a conference in Brighton that week. I'll have to give it a miss." He'd need to think of another excuse as well. There was a conference every time she was in a play.

"Oh well. Never mind."

Vinny had to smile; she was in sweet old-lady mode, "How was Thailand?"

"Fine."

"Only fine?" Her natural interrogational instincts were starting to shine through but he'd sweetened her up by sounding interested in her wellbeing, and her tone wasn't as suspicious. "What did you do?"

"Oh, same as usual, err couple of days in Bangkok then err flew down to Ko Samui." Ko Samui doesn't quite have the reputation enjoyed by Pattaya for being the world capital of sleaze and alcoholism so in his mothers mind that was where he went.

"Where is Ko Samui?" Her memory was starting to go. He'd told her on his previous three trips that it was an island in the southern part of the country.

"It's an island in the south, Mum. Look, there's someone at the door. I'll call up to see you in a couple of days." Amazing how the door always rang when his mum phoned.

"OK. See you soon. Pwst." She blew him a kiss. It always made him cringe.

He put the phone down and took a good long slug from his can of Fosters. Speaking to his parents tended to put him on edge. With both of them being in the teaching profession they always made him feel like a naughty schoolboy, but in the last two years with mounting debts and his dubious lifestyle he was always guilt ridden after contact with them. He knew how mortified they'd be if they knew he'd built up masses of debt engaging in sins of the flesh and sinuses.

Distractions over, Vin returned to his armchair and started reading over the day's training course.

Vin felt dazed. His bladder was forcing him out of bed again. The alarm clock on his bedside table read 6:45. Jet lag was starting to have less of an influence on his sleep patterns. Clouds had miraculously formed in his head and the first slash of the day relieved pain more than pressure in his bladder. Along with the jet lag wearing off his intolerance to the cold was subsiding. Once the toilet seat had been splashed he headed into the kitchen for an early-morning caffeine fix. He switched the kettle on and spooned some brown granules into a mug.

"Silly cunt." Once he looked into the fridge he understood why he'd slept so soundly. Eight full cans of Fosters had been demolished. It probably explained why the cold wasn't biting as much. Dressing proved to be a muddled affair. Lager made him lethargic and could make him clumsy. It took three attempts to fasten his tie and a good five minutes to fasten the button on his collar. Venturing into the open for his stroll to the bus stop, he lit his first fag of the day. It tasted awful and added another layer to the film of mucus lining his throat. Today the bus was full and he had to stand and hold onto the ceiling rail to prevent him careering into old women as the bus went round bends.

Vinny was having a slash in the platform lavatories when the 8.05 to Manchester left. There was another due at 8.17 but it didn't arrive until 8.25. Its lateness was forgiven though; there was a seat on this one and a conductor. Reluctantly Vin passed over his credit card and signed the bill in return for a seven-day pass. Ever conscientious, he started to pore over the training book. He remembered heading for bed confident that he knew it all – beer did that to you. Looking through the literature again in the morning only made him aware of how little he actually knew.

He arrived in the boardroom at 9.05. He was flushed from walking briskly from the station. Charles pretended not look annoyed at the latecomers but was making mental notes of who they were. The seat next to fat Geoff was free again so he shuffled past the occupied chairs into his home for the day.

Tuesday's performance in training was awful. Vin cursed himself throughout the day as Charles picked on him at every opportunity, much to the delight of fat Geoff.

That night at home, in an unusual display of discipline, Vin sat and devoured the training. Pride was at stake. By the end of Thursday Vin was starting to shine and look like the smartarse teacher's pet he'd been when he'd worked at Intra Tech, his first computer company.

The training course was complete and Vin was proud of himself, even though none of what he'd learned had been relevant to his speciality.

At 5pm on Thursday Charles drew the course to a close in a self-satisfied and superior tone.

"We've covered all the work we need to go through now. Tomorrow we'll start with a short quiz and then we're going to have a little competition as part of a team-building exercise. I'm going to put you in teams of three and you're going to have to perform a couple of tasks, but before that I'd like to invite everyone for a drink in Del Sol and something to eat in China Town." The throng of trainees swooned. Vin perked up as well. A bevy on the gaffer was something he'd never turned down.

The evening passed without event. About 80 per cent of the staff arrived at Del Sol and politely tried to smarm around their seniors and not drink too much. Vin got himself acquainted with the black guy who'd been irritated on the phone on Monday. Sounded similar to himself, Nigel his name was and he'd moved up from Nottingham to be with his girlfriend. Personable was proving to be problematic as far as he was concerned and the two drowned their sorrows at the bar in the company of Mick the Logistics manager. Mick was in his thirties and had no sales responsibilities. He had to make sure the orders went to the warehouse properly. His was an easy life and he had the sense of humour you'd expect of someone who'd moved up from the warehouse and didn't have any pressure.

On Friday the inductees had to make a structure that would hold a can of Coke, out of A4 paper. Vin couldn't be arsed, he just let the two girls he'd teamed up with bodge it and they came last.

Get me away from

Vinny got home bored and tired on Friday night. It had been a hard week, taking in all of Charles's nonsense, adjusting time zones and trying to stay interested. Keith had left a message on the answer machine to see if Vinny was playing out, he'd had to decline due to fiscal difficulties. He stayed in and moped while he pined for Jeed and ploughed his way through a stash of beers. Saturday was much the same, although he managed to pluck up the courage to open his mail. He was maxed out at the bank, on his credit card (almost) and had a pile of bills to pay. Things weren't looking good.

On Sunday Keith rang mid-afternoon to see how he was.

"Call round, our kid." Vinny was happy to make contact with a human being. The only person he'd been close to since Friday tea time had been the owner of his own right hand.

Keith arrived ten minutes later grinning like a Cheshire cat.

"How was your weekend, scumbag?" He was glowing and obviously had another tale to tell.

"Marvellous, mate. Sat and pulled my pud and watched telly. How was yours?" Vinny was trying his best not to sound sarcastic.

"Productive!" He smirked. Productive was their byword for having achieved some sort of leeway with a female.

"Not Sarah again?" Vin shook his head.

"Aye, well, I did that last night, like," but there was more to the tale.

"Spill the beans."

"Remember 'Liz Hurley' from The Mill last week?" Keith was gushing now, oblivious to the touch of jealousy he was stirring up in Vincent.

"Aye. Go on." Vin raised his eyebrows.

"Well, I'm stood on the stall yesterday, rough as fuck from Friday night, and she totters up, don't she." Keith always gave a good narrative. "Well, I've got a load of these lycra gym vests, haven't I. Proper tackle, like. Low cut and all that. So she starts looking at 'em, picking 'em up and holding 'em against her to see how they look, and then she asks, 'What colour do you think'd suit me, Keith?' I nearly choked. She knows me fucking name!" Keith was sat back in the chair trying to look unflustered. "So I put my best charm on and says, 'Well, I think the blue'll go with your eyes. You can try one on in the back.' So she totters off behind the canvass at the back of the stall. I tell you what, fucking gave me a semi." Keith paused to light a cigarette. "She's fumbling about for a bit then I hear her say, 'Can I try a red one?' So I went round and passed her one. She's only stood there behind the tarpaulin, like, with her top off and her arm over her tits, left nipple poking out, and she's smiling at me like there's nowt wrong." Keith was doing his best to hide his excitement. "Well, she comes out a minute later with her clothes back on and says, 'I'll take them both,' passes me a tenner and walks off. I were stunned." Bolton's answer to Georgio Armani took a drag on his cigarette and exhaled.

"Cheapest thrill I've had this weekend's been Cat Deeley on kids TV," said Vin with a smirk.

"That's not all…" Keith could talk. "I looks at the tenner, like. The tops were marked up at five ninety-nine, but I weren't complaining. She's given me a piece of paper as well. It just says 'Vicky' and her mobile number."

Vin shook his head. He was proud of his mate despite his envy. "You're a lucky cunt, you. If you fell in a barrel of shite you'd come up with a penny in your mouth. So what about Sarah?"

Keith turned his nose up. "Bollocks to her." He sniggered.

Vinny started his first proper week at work and was sat next to Nigel in the office. The first thing he did was check his Yahoo account. There was one from Jeed.

Hello Honey,

I'm miss you too much.

Today Jeed go to temple and make gift and praying for Buddha so Vinny come back Pattaya stay with me. I want you stay with me forever same husband because my heart I love you too much.

Yesterday customer asking me go him room. But Jeed saying cannot. Have boyfriend.

Please coming back soon for make happy again.

Jeed

It was difficult to keep his mind on work after that.

He started to find his way round the computer system and gleaned a few bits of information from his new buddy. Nigel had been brought in to sell commercial databases, the sort of software banks use to keep a list of their clients. He'd been promised a team the same as Vinny, who'd generate leads for him. In the month he'd been there nothing had materialised. The advertising department kept 'forgetting' to place his ads in the trade press and his promised company car still hadn't arrived. These snippets did nothing to motivate Vinny but he soldiered on. Over the next few lunchtimes Vinny used his desktop email to tell Jeed how much he was missing her and how he'd come to see her again soon. Jeed's replies were in the same vein as Vinny's, although miss-spelt and in the wrong syntax. It didn't matter, it added to the charm. He also surfed round the less graphic websites catering for travellers to Thailand. The first proper week went as gradually as it had come. Vinny was still skint. He was waiting for payday and the new Volkswagen Golf Personable had promised him. When the weekend came round he was glad of the break. The database system at work eventually became less of a mystery and he managed to speak to a few old clients who didn't need to upgrade their Unix machines, so the chance of immediate sales looked bleak.

Vinny had to decline an offer to play out over the weekend again with Keith, so Keith came round on Sunday to update Vincent on the state of his love life.

"How's tricks?" Vin was still happy to see Keith but didn't smile too much. He was bored and was starting to feel depressed. Thailand seemed like a lifetime ago. There was no sight of earning a ton of money in the near future and there was no trip to the Land of Smiles on the horizon.

"Not bad, mate." Keith looked tired.

"What've you been up to?" Vinny was expecting the usual onslaught of lascivious tales from Keith, especially considering his lucky encounter with Vicky last week.

"Took that Vicky out on Tuesday and again last night." It wasn't often that Keith was so economical with his tales. Vinny was starting to get intrigued. Had something gone wrong? Had she wound him up or done some despicable deed that had left Keith lost for words?

"So how did it go? She worn you out, lad?" Vinny enjoyed seeing his mate shellshocked.

"Well, I arranged to meet her Tuesday and go for a bit of nose bag, so I took her down Lucciano's." Lucciano's was an Italian restaurant in the centre of Bolton. Keith's family knew the owners so he always got special treatment. "Anyway, I'm trying to get some info on her like what she does and where she lives and that and she just clams up, says fuck all, or avoids the question or asks me summat about myself. So I'm thinking, this is a bit suss, like. Is she Drugs Squad or summat?" He was starting to get his wordiness back but still looked pale and worn out. "Comes to the end of the meal. So I said what do you wanna do now?" He paused for effect. "She just comes out with it, don't she. 'Let's go back to yours and have sex,' she said. I couldn't fucking believe it." He was talking slowly but not for effect this time. Vinny could tell that his mate was still in a genuine state of shock.

“Must have give you the ride of your life, you cunt, if she’s left you in that state.”

Keith chirped up a bit and grinned. “She fuckin’ did that all right. I tell you.”

He was suddenly back in full flow. “I gets her home, right, and it’s just, ‘Right then, where’s the bedroom?’ I points at the door and she drags me in and undresses me.”

Vinny lit a fag and nodded in approval.

“Starts sucking me cock, like, and fuck me, it’s superb. She’s a real master, that one, I tell you. Then she fucks off into the bathroom and comes back naked and mounts me.” Keith threw his head back with his eyes half closed and paused for a minute as the smile grew on his face. “I tell you what, I shot in no time. She’s tight like a virgin and I’m sure them tits are false. So she gets me hard again with her mouth and makes me do her from behind and then fucks off once I’m done.” He shrugged his shoulders, looking bemused.

Vin had been all week without a beer, what with his ever-worsening financial state, so he tried his luck. “Fancy buying us a pint in the Arrers then?”

“Fuck that.” Keith coughed and gave Vin a dirty look. There was more to tell. “Took her out last night in town and runs in to Sarah in The Boulevard.” The Boulevard was one of the bigger town centre pubs that the local twenty-somethings hit before moving onto a club.

“Ouch,” Vinny winced. “What happened?”

“Well, I said, ‘all right?’ like, but she just blanked me. When we gets outside she’s in tears with that Joanne bird trying to comfort her. So looks like the Arrers is off limits.”

“Crown then?” Vin could taste the lager.

“Aye, fuck it, why not,” and Keith was himself again.

Sunday afternoons in the local were always nondescript. This one was no different. Keith whooped Vinny 6-1 at pool although Vinny told himself it was best to lose deliberately because Keith was buying the beer. Vinny managed to extract a bit more information about Vicky: she wasn’t local originally but lived somewhere in Bolton. Whereabouts was still a mystery. She’d spent her early years living in Spain. Her age was still undetermined as was her occupation.

The week at work was dull. Vinny had been used to getting leads to sell decent-sized computers from a team of telesales staff who made cold calls and took responses from advertisements in the trade press. He started to query Sue about when the ads would start to run, when his car would arrive and how soon the telesales people would start focusing on his requirements. She was vague. She had important stuff to deal with. One of the new starters had managed to sell three printers to a company in Rochdale and was being fussed over like she’d managed to get in a million pounds’ worth of business. Vinny was starting to get worried. How was he supposed to make a sale? Nobody seemed bothered that they'd set him up in a division. They were just trying to flog printers and scanners.

On Friday Vinny was glad the week was over again. There was only a week until payday so staying in that weekend wasn't a big problem. Anyway Bolton were at home. They'd been away the last two weeks and, even though it was early days being almost the end of October, second in the league was a good spot.

Vinny settled into his armchair after he'd fed himself. He looked forward to an evening of his only pleasure of the moment; carnal thoughts about Jeed and the 25th of his 40 packets of Thai Marlboro Lights.

Bbbbrrrriinnng! Bbbbrrrriinnng! Bollocks. Vin contemplated not answering the phone. His mum hadn't rung for a couple of weeks and he was due an update call. He eventually reasoned that he was sober enough to pick up the call. There was nothing he could say wrong in his current state.

"Vinny." Keith still sounded young on the phone.

"Keith." He was glad to hear from his mate. "How's things?"

"Not bad, kidder, I thought I'd pop round." Keith sounded purposeful.

"Look, you can't talk me into coming into town. I'm skint and can't pay you back." Vinny was hoping Keith would pay for a free night out.

"Nah, just thought I'd say hello." Vinny could hear that Keith was in his car.

"Yeah, whatever." He cheered up a touch and mentally prepared a few pops he could have at Keith about the mysterious Spanish señorita.

"Be about ten minutes, our kid. That all right?" Keith sounded like he was in a good mood.

"Aye, see yers in ten." Vinny put the phone down and picked up the dirty plates that had gathered over the last three days in the living room, and dumped them in the kitchen.

The buzzer rang and he pressed the entry button. He heard the front door open and he could hear two sets of feet coming down the corridor. One of them was in stilettos. Vinny smiled a sort of perverted smile to himself. Keith was bringing Vicky for him to ogle.

"Hope she's wearing summat low cut," he muttered to himself before opening his door.

True enough Keith had brought the mysterious one with him. Keith was in his usual weekend leather jacket and looked and smelt like he was trying to impress. His left hand trailed behind him as it clasped onto a sunbed-tanned paw. Vin could see a long black fur-collared overcoat behind Keith in the corridor, with a shock of silky auburn hair trailing over the collar.

"Come in." he smiled and was more reserved than he usually would have been in welcoming his mate due to the presence of the lady.

Keith was smiling as he led Vicky into the front room, proud of his conquest and a little nervous. She was overpowering and men weakened in her presence.

"This is my mate Vinny, the one I was telling you about." Keith had loosened his grip on her hand and she made her way to the settee.

"Hiya." Vinny was blushing a bit. It wasn't often he got within touching distance of an eight or above out of ten.

By now she was half reclined in the corner of the sofa. "*Sawasdee ka.*"

Vinny stopped in his tracks on his way to the armchair. She'd said hello to him in Thai and he was flummoxed.

"*Sawasdee krap*," he returned as he sat in his chair. "*Sabai dee mai?*"

The two men in the room were both looking perplexed. Keith didn't have a clue what was being said and Vinny was taken aback that Keith's latest shag could speak Thai.

"*Sabai dee ka.*" She threw a flirtatious smile at Vinny.

"Would you two mind speaking in a language I can understand?" Keith looked bemused.

"It's all right, Keith," she purred. Vicky didn't have a squeaky voice the way most of the girls that he'd picked up had. She obviously wasn't in her late teens, "I just said hello to Vincent, he said hello back and asked me how I was, and I said I was fine." She looked pleased with herself and gleamed at Vinny.

"How come you speak Thai?" Vinny felt superior to Keith now. He may not have known much Thai but being able to open a conversation in an unfamiliar language put him a step up the intellectual ladder from his mate.

"An ex of mine was posted there for work so I lived with him for a while." She put her hand inside Keith's arm to stop him feeling isolated from the conversation and looked down at her feet momentarily.

"It's all right for some. Where did you live?" Vin was keen to talk about Thailand at every opportunity.

"We lived in Bangkok. You know Soi 18?"

"On Sukumvit. Yeah, I think I know it." Vin mimicked a frown, as if he 'sort of' knew where Soi 21 was. He had more than a vague idea. It was the road that led to the city's second most popular red-light area after Nana Plaza, Soi Cowboy. He'd been there plenty of times.

Vicky was obviously trying to be diplomatic, but the knowing smile still showed on her face.

"Keith said you'd been a few times. When are you going again?" she asked.

"Probably Christmas if I can sort the cash out. Head down to Samui or somewhere, you know." Vinny told virtually everyone he went to Samui. The stigma of paying for sex was one that could cost you a lot of professional and social credibility, and Vin was keen to keep a lid on the fact that he'd spent most of his time whilst in Thailand in Pattaya.

"Certainly sounds like you've got the bug, Vincent." She smiled and pulled at Keith's arm. "Are we off then?"

The visit had been short but sweet. Vinny was making the most of her presence and trying to get a glimpse up the short dress she was wearing. The section of thigh just above knee was showing as her overcoat was open. It looked tanned and well toned. I bet she can thrust a bit, he thought as he stared.

"Can I just use your loo, Vincent?"

He looked her in the face; she'd caught him peeking.

"Yeah, just through there second door." He pointed over his shoulder into the kitchen and she tottered towards the toilet. Vinny cringed as she left. Being a bachelor he never spent a great deal of time cleaning the bathroom and held his head in his hands hoping he'd flushed the toilet within the last couple of days.

"Fucking hell, Vin." Keith looked indignant. "You've had more info out of her than I have and I've shagged her six times."

"I'd rather have the shags than the info. She still as vigorous?" Vinny was using hushed tones in case she could hear them from the lavatory.

"Fucking too right. Doesn't stop the night though. Always fucks off when the job's done and I like a dawn strike these days." There were no secrets between these two.

The sound of the toilet flushing hit them and they heard the bathroom door open.

"So we should beat Swansea tomorrow and then it's Wimbledon at home in the cup next week." Vinny was an expert at changing subjects.

"I might come with you to the cup game." Keith smirked as Vicky appeared in the door. It wasn't like him to be under the thumb. Most of his birds were usually a lot younger, but with a good result like Vick he was putting on his best act. He was out of the settee in a flash and holding the flat door open for his first decent siren in nearly two years.

Vinny looked up as they left and could see Vicky's well-defined calf muscles above her stilettos. He shook his head as she left. Fuck me, there's some revs in that one, he thought, Keith's got himself a proper sporty version there.

Ordinarily he'd have got seriously jealous of Keith getting himself a bird like that but he knew that Jeed was waiting for him. He closed his eyes…

Bolton's Oriental Relations officer lay on a big wide bed in a posh hotel room in Pattaya. He'd taken his shoes off but was still in his cargo shorts and Bolton Wanderers top. Steam was slowly coming out of the slats in the bathroom door and he could hear the tone of the water hitting the floor of the shower changing as Jeed moved around washing herself. The shower stopped and he heard a few drips of water. There was a moment of silence and then he heard the door open. Vinny sat up and looked over. Jeed was walking towards him. She stopped and smiled as he caught her gaze. She had a big white towel wrapped around her. Jeed had a slight auburn colour in her hair – it was from a bottle; it was naturally jet black. It was damp and pushed back from her forehead, and her beautiful face with wide, high cheekbones glowed from the hot water of the *douche*. The towel was wrapped and knotted loosely above her petite but firm breasts, and covered her knees. Her slender figure was superbly outlined and Vinny got off the bed and walked over to her. He put his arms round her and held her tight. She nestled her wet face on his chest and felt warm. At five-foot two she was seven inches shorter than Vinny. Vinny pulled back and looked down at her. He ran his finger down her nose gently. Compared to a Westerner she didn't have a nose, not with a bridge anyway. He'd laughed once when she'd tried on his sunglasses and they had kept falling down because there was no bridge for them to rest on. Vinny clasped at the top of the towel and tried to undo it. She slapped his hand.

"Go have shower," she said and reached onto her tiptoes, kissed him and pushed him towards the bathroom.

Vinny always played that game with Jeed. On his trips he must have slept with over 30 Thai women and they'd all made him shower first, and Jeed was no exception. He remerged a couple of minutes later, himself wrapped in a towel, to see Jeed tucked up in bed waiting for him. Her size made the bed look even bigger than it was. The towel Jeed had worn was crumpled on the floor and Vinny let his slip to the floor and climbed into bed. Jeed's body was warm and she held him close.

Vinny opened his eyes. He was still in Bolton, he was still skint and he still had no beer. He flicked the TV on. Chris Tarrant was quizzing some bloke. The contestant was trying his best to win a million quid. Vinny settled back in his chair and thought about Keith wining and dining Vicky. He thought about Jeed charming punters in the bar, and then reflected about his own situation. He had to escape.

When Vinny arrived at work on Monday morning he was in a good mood; probably the best mood he'd been in since he'd joined Personable. His beloved Bolton had beaten Swansea convincingly in the League in front of a home crowd 4-0, a proper result. Jason, his match buddy, had driven him to and from the new stadium in Horwich, a cold uninviting windswept town on the outskirts of Bolton but within the boundary of the borough. Tranmere, who had been a point clear at the top, had lost, leaving Bolton in pole position. He'd had his usual Sunday drink with Keith and was keen to get into work. Bolton's performance had inspired him to perform well on the sales front.

He strolled into the office. It was payday on Friday as well so this week didn't seem like a chore. Nigel looked up from his desk as he approached. He was smiling as well. Vin liked him; he was intelligent and good conversation. It was the first time he'd seen Nigel smile and that added to his confidence. He clicked on his mouse and scurried over to the printer before Vinny was in his chair. It was 8.50 and work wasn't due to start until 9. Despite his enthusiasm there was no need to go overboard. He leaned over and picked up the *Daily Mirror* that was folded on Nigel's desk and started to read. The football section was the first port of call and he went straight to the League table. Bolton were top of the first division, two points clear with a game in hand. Promotion to the Premiership seemed imminent and Vinny looked up as Nigel returned from the printer with a single sheet of A4 in his hand, looking confident and content.

"All right, chief?" Vinny smiled as he greeted his colleague.

"Marvellous, Vincent." Nigel spoke with a plumb in his mouth and always used people's full name.

"Look pleased with yourself, kidder. Mrs open the back doors for you at the weekend?" He loved using sewer-level vernacular around prissy young women.

Nigel's smile broadened. "Better than that, my fine friend. On Saturday I got a written offer from a company who know what they're doing, so as soon as that sycophantic cow Susan turns up I'm resigning." He leaned over his chair and waved his official notice he'd printed off a moment earlier with a boyish kind of satisfaction.

"Tosser. Leaving me to fend for myself." He covered his jealousy with a smile. No company worth its salt would offer Vinny a job with his work record. "Who's it with?"

"Not at liberty to say, my friend, not at liberty to say." Nigel smirked and threw his head back, looking down his nose at the office as his head turned to survey the gaggle of young girls trying their best to flog printers over the phone.

Sue emerged in her overcoat from the main doors carrying a brief case and a large bag from Marks and Spencer. Her face was flushed from the cold outside. The chorus of 'Hi Sue's rang out as usual and she headed towards her fish bowl.

Nigel winked at Vinny as she approached and smiled his warmest smile. "Oh, Hi Sue." He put his poshest voice on and Vinny smirked and looked down at the paper. She all but ignored him. He followed her to her office and stood behind her, holding the door open as she plonked down her heavy load in her glass haven.

Vinny heard the door shut and looked up. Nigel was stood in front of Sue with the letter secreted behind his back. He was dying to see the look on Sue's face when Nigel gave her the news but his view was obscured. He shook his head and looked back at the paper.

Vinny was on the phone when Nigel emerged from the office. He was trying to get hold of Keith to sort out tickets for the cup game on Saturday. Without a word Nigel grabbed his jacket and disappeared. Didn't even bother logging off.

A few of the more attentive ones in the office had seen what was happening and could spot scandal a mile off. Vinny put the phone down. Keith was on voicemail. As soon as the phone was down it rang again. Vinny was a little surprised. He picked it up. “Vincent Croston,” he said in his best ‘how can I help?’ tone.

“Vincent, it’s Toni.” He was taken aback. She had a sexy voice on the phone considering how fat and ugly she was. “You sound shocked.”

“It’s the first time me phone’s rung. I’ll put a note in my sales diary for that. Incoming call received.”

“What you like?” Toni was tickled by his sarcasm. “What’s gone on there?”

“Where? What do you mean?” he said innocently.

“You know what I’m on about. Nigel!” She was hungry for gossip.

“Couldn’t tell you, love. Ask Sue.” He liked being one up on the rest of the office. “Got to go anyhow. Expecting a call from Bill Gates.”

He put the phone down and went back to his paper. The match report on Bolton was sensational, hailing them as the giants of the first division. It was so good he read it twice. Once he’d completed the sports section he worked his way backwards through the news. About halfway through the paper was a holiday section. It was aimed at the family reader and gave reviews on a couple of bland resorts across Europe. There was also a glossy pamphlet inserted from a credit-card company. ‘Apply now. Credit Limit up to £10 000. Instant Decisions.’ Vin flicked past it, but the picture of a beach in the holiday section had set his mind to work. He turned back to the pamphlet and started to read it.

Within 30 seconds he was dialling the freephone number.

“Merchant Card, how can we help?” The voice was female, British and without a recognisable regional accent. She sounded professional.

“Hi, I’ve seen your advertisement for a credit card, and I’d like to apply.” Vinny’s heart was racing. If he was successful he could be spending Christmas with Jeed.

“Certainly, sir. I’ll just connect you to the New Accounts department.” The hold music was soothing but not enough to slow his pulse.

The lady who took his call sounded stressed. She had obviously been taking a lot of calls and Vinny could hear a lot of voices chattering in the background.

“Good afternoon. I believe you’d like to apply for the Merchant Card.” He could hear her tapping away on a computer keyboard. He smiled and held back a snigger.

“It’s morning, love.” He was relaxed at finding her more stressed than him.

“Oh, did I say afternoon? I’ve just been sooo busy.”

Vin could tell that anyway.

She ran through the list of basic questions: name, address, occupation, salary, bank details and what credit limit he'd like.

Feeling brave Vinny went for the £10 000 limit.

"OK, let me process that request, sir." She sighed as she tapped her keys frantically. "Oh, I'm sorry sir." There'd been a short wait while his details had been processed. "Your application has been declined."

Vinny's heart sunk. For a moment he'd been sat on one of the deck chairs on Pattaya beach with his gut hanging over his shorts, sipping a Carlsberg with Jeed mopping sweat off his brow.

"Do you know why that is?" He did his best not to sound dejected.

"Let me just try and find out for you, sir."

He went back onto the hold music.

"It seems, sir, that your current earnings at the rate you quoted will not support a credit limit of £10 000." She at least sounded polite.

"What credit limit would they support?" He sounded a little cross. He'd spent time on the phone just to be knocked back.

"I can find out for you." He could hear keys tapping again. "It appears on your current earnings the maximum credit available to you would be £5000, sir."

Vin gulped. "I'll have that then."

He could sense Victory. He could taste the free peanuts that were left out for customers in Tommy Bar.

"OK, sir, I just need to process that. Can you wait one second?" *Tap, tap, tap.* Fuck, that keyboard was getting a hammering. "Sir, your application has been confirmed. Your card will be despatched to your home address within forty-eight hours." They both heaved a sigh of relief. She prattled on about security, interest rates and signing the confirmation slip to be returned but he wasn't listening. He could taste the aeroplane food.

He slammed the phone down and didn't do a very good job of suppressing his urge to punch the air.

"What's up, Vincent, got a sale in?" Toni was marching towards Sue's office to get the lowdown on Nigel.

"Nah, just got the all-clear from the VD clinic." He smirked.

"Ooh, you're so sophisticated." She smiled and soldiered on, trying her best to look seductive as she pushed her hair back from her face. The floor shook in time with every step she took.

Vinny winced. "Nah. Never," he mumbled to himself, trying to banish the despicable thought from his mind. There was a mental image of him sliding about on top of sixteen stone of blubber. "No," he told himself firmly.

Nigel's departure had dented his will to be productive, but now with available credit he was completely thrown. He sat back in his chair and started to daydream. Should I go straight to Pattaya from the airport or have a night or two in Bangers? He could visualise himself at the airport taxi rank in the humid embrace of Bangkok. Dropping his bag in the boot of a cab.

The phone on his desk rang. "Vincent Croston."

"Sound like you've won the pools, mate." It was Keith. Vinny could hear the sounds of activity on Bolton Market.

"Nah, you've just taken me into previously unprecedented phone-activity figures." Vin was as happy as a pig in shite and his voice was sparkling for a change.

"Eh?" Keith didn't understand office talk.

"Two calls received in one day. And it's not even ten o'clock."

"Is that good?" Keith didn't recognise the banter. He'd obviously become a little drained (in more than one way) after the weekend with Vicky. "Anyway, I just got yer message. What did you want?"

"Yeah, I was just seeing if you could get tickets for Saturday. I can't get to the ground 'cos I'm in Manchester." Vin had left it a too late to get cup tickets because of his financial situation but Keith could be relied on in emergencies.

"Aye, yeah. I'll bell you later. Listen, gotta go. Laters." The phone went dead.

With nothing to do now his commercial ardour had quelled he decided on a cigarette. It had been a good start to the week. A bit of gossip, Thailand round the corner and tickets for the third round of the cup on the horizon.

Vinny stood in the cold at the front of the office and weighed up how long he could make his duty-free fags last and whether it would be possible to be in Thailand before they ran out.

The clip-clop of a pair of high heels descending the sandstone steps at the front of the office disturbed his train of thought and he looked over his shoulder. Toni was trying to look ladylike on her way towards him with her cigarettes in her hand.

"Oi, Vincent Croston. I want a word with you." She was smiling like it was her birthday. Sue had obviously furnished her with the news of Nigel's resignation. "What's all this acting innocent like you don't know a thing?" It was a friendly attack.

"Well, I couldn't really say anything, could I?" No point pretending now.

"Apparently he gave her a right mouthful about not getting his car and building a team." Toni pretended to be shocked at Nigel's directness. Stoicism was obviously something the staff at Meg had learned over the years.

"You can see his point of view really though." Vinny decided not to play along with the character assassination that was on the way.

"You could use that to your advantage you know." Toni was standing quite close to him now. It was almost uncomfortable, but a bit warming as well. She lit a cigarette.

"How do you mean?" Vinny was a bit taken aback by on old Meg hand siding with one of the only outsiders.

"Well, if you have a moan about not getting your car and stuff today…" She didn't end the sentence, enough had been said.

Vinny's brain started to churn. Could be a good day to ask about booking time off at Christmas. He finished his cigarette and trotted back upstairs.

Back in his chair he checked his email. There was one from Jeed. The day was getting better by the minute.

Subject: Miss you my honey.

Sender: Jeed Pornsutto

Hello Handsome Vinny,

I'm hope you are OK and everything with your working. How is England. Before you saying it cold a lot. You must take care for your self. Wear thick jacket and if get sick with flu must eat medicine to make good.

Please not angry me for not send email but working many long hour and not have time for send.

I want you stay with me forever OK.

I'm now have mobile phone number me 863 4577.

Hope you can ring and talk with me honey.

Waiting for you call

Jeed.

Vinny smiled. He looked at his watch. Eleven o'clock. That made it around 6pm in Patters. He hit 9 for an outside line and started to dial. His hand was trembling as he started to punch in the numbers. Shit. In his eagerness he'd started to dial without the code for Thailand. He picked up the receiver briefly and let it fall back into the cradle to cut the call. He wracked his brain for the dialling code and started again nervously, dialling 9 again for an outside line, then 0066. He looked back at the screen and then around the office. For a moment he imagined speaking Thai/English in a loud voice in front of the whole office. Before continuing he paused. He pictured himself in Sue's office, hands behind his back like a naughty schoolboy trying to explain why he'd phoned Thailand at the company's expense in the company's time. He cut the call. Better not chance it. He hit 'reply' on his email.

Jeed Honey,

It so nice to get your message. I miss you too much. Work is 'Mai Dee' and England cold mak mak. I come to Thailand at Christmas to see you maybe stay forver. On Saturday Bolton will play on TV. I hope you can watch.

See you soon Tilac.

Vinny

XXXXXXX

Hitting 'send' made him smile. He sat back and spent the morning pondering how he was going to make Nigel's departure work to his advantage.

Vinny returned from lunch and looked in Sue's office through the window. She'd obviously popped out so he sat at his desk and played with a pencil. It was amazing how holding one end of a pencil, tapping it and letting it run through your fingers to the other end could amuse even the most educated of minds. After ten minutes he decided to see what Nigel had left behind. Trying his best not to look like a scavenger he leaned over and opened his desk drawer. He flicked through the tray. A cursory search produced one pound coin, two twenty-pence pieces, a five and two ones. The real trophy was a complimentary book of matches from Manto's, one of the gayest bars in the 'Gay Village'. Superb! The scandal that could be raised was monumental. Nigel had claimed that he lived with his bird. It could have been a smokescreen. Maybe he was straight, maybe gay. No point letting the truth get in the way of a good story.

Vin was bored now. Toni made her presence felt. He gazed over at her desk. She was definitely not the best looker in the world. Well overweight and her face didn't make up for it but she had a sort of spark in her personality.

"Nah, can't do that. Mustn't. I'd be hung drawn and quartered." He looked up and saw Sue walking towards her office. Her face was grey. She'd obviously taken Nigel's notice personally, seen it as a failing. The old Meg lot were just so happy to be working there and didn't make demands. Nigel, like Vinny, had been used to working for a decent-calibre outfit. News of Nigel's departure had obviously spread through the office and people could read her face. Hardly anyone said "Hi Sue" as usual. It was heads down. Vinny waited a minute for her to settle in. Before heading for her door he straightened his tie and brushed his hair with his hand. He could see his reflection in the computer screen on his desk. With a deep breath he plucked up some courage and walked to her office. He tapped gently on the door with the knuckle of one finger. It wasn't very loud. The office went quiet. People saw him and were thinking the worst. "Is he handing his notice in?"

Sue hadn't heard his knock and got out of her chair, heading for the filing cabinet in the corner, then saw Vinny through the narrow pane of glass in the door. She scurried over and pulled the door open. Vinny got a faint hint of gin on her breath as the door opened. She'd taken Nigel's news worse than he'd expected.

"Hi, Sue. Can I have a word?" He gave her his best 'softly softly' smile. She smiled back. Best to keep up appearances. "I was just wondering what I have to do to book a holiday, Sue?" His smile had gone but he was giving her his 'I'm a nice schoolboy' look, trying his best not to give away the fact that he wanted to take time off to gorge himself on sins of the flesh on the other side of the world.

"Not a problem." She was visibly relieved. Two resignations in one day would have been more than she could take. "Just get a form from Admin and I'll sign it for you. When are you going?"

"I've not booked yet. I was just checking before I do." He'd got what he wanted.

"Oh well, let me know. Is there anything else?" She was relieved he'd not played hell about a lack of a team or his company car not turning up.

"Well..." He paused for effect once he knew he'd got her on the run. "I was wondering when my car was going to be delivered."

Her face dropped. She looked uncomfortable.

"I've been trying to find out about that. The cars were due last week." She stressed the 'were'. "But there's been some sort of hold-up." There was a bit of a frown on her face. Vinny could tell she sensed mutiny. "Can I get back to you on that?"

He tried to cover his pleasure. She'd be panicking now and putting a rocket up the fleet supplier to get his car delivered. The car problem didn't really bother him though, in all honesty.

Work was now definitely low on his list of priorities. Booking a flight went to the top of his activities list and he was straight down the phone to reserve a seat. The young lady in the telesales department of Travelbag remembered him from his last booking and gladly gave him a list of options. KLM seemed like the best one for him. The outbound flight left on Saturday the fourteenth of December from Manchester at 2pm. They could get him back to Manchester at teatime on the third of January if he left on the second.

"Can you book that for me? I'll get my credit card details for you by the end of the week." He put the phone firmly back in its cradle. Who said Mondays were depressing?

He spent the afternoon on the phone trying to generate some sales. The phone call he'd made to Travelbag was going to cost him the best part of two and a half grand including spending money. No luck.

Back at home he sat in the armchair, exhausted. A lot of nervous energy had been expended that afternoon. When Keith rang his tiredness made him sound grumpy.

"Vin."

"Yeah."

"It's Keith." He'd obviously had a decent day on the stall.

"Oh, right."

"What's up? You sound pissed off."

"Knackered, mate." Vinny yawned.

"Done a days work, have yer, lad?" Keith could use anything as an excuse to have a pop.

"Booked a flight at Christmas, so pulling out the stops to get some business in." Vinny would have put the phone down if it was anyone else but he hung on as it was his best mate.

"When?" Keith sounded interested.

"Fly on the fourteenth, back on the third."

"Might come with you, our kid. Who did you book with?" Keith sounded like he meant it and it lifted Vinny's spirits.

"Yeah. Fuck me. I can just see you in Nana Disco now with a *katoey*." Vinny was grinning from ear to ear.

"What's Nana Disco?"

"You'll find out when we get there." Vin could picture the pair of them propping up the bar in his favourite after-hours drinking den. "I'll just get Travelbag's number for you."

"It's all right, Vin. I'll pop round tomorrow. Listen, I've got tickets for Saturday. *Bolton Evening News* Stand, front row's all they had."

Vinny had forgotten about the match with all his excitement. "They'll do. Cheers, mate. What do I owe you?"

"Just twenty. Mate, I've got to go, Vicky's coming round. I'll call over tomorrow." Keith put the phone down.

For the second time in 24 hours Vinny threw an uppercut into the air. "Wicked!"

Getting Keith to come to Thailand with him had been on his list for the last eighteen months. The tickets were of secondary importance. Front row in the *Bolton Evening News* stand was a bit of a short straw. If it rained you didn't get the cover from the roof and the view of the pitch was limited but it was late in the day and better than watching it on telly.

Tired but pleased, Vinny sat back in his chair and made mental plans. Where could he take Keith that would shock him? How could he wind him up without going too far?

He slept well that night. He'd done a lot and, as he curled up, there was a satisfied smile on his face. Trying to picture Keith's expression as they wondered into Nana Plaza kept him happy all night and for a good part of the week.

Keith came round on Tuesday night and dropped off Vinny's ticket for the third round of the FA Cup. They were right behind the goal. In return Vinny gave him the details of the flight and the number for Travelbag. He smiled as Keith scampered off to Vicky waiting in the car.

"See yer Saturday, mate." The door shut behind him as he ran off to get rid of his ballast.

Friday was payday and by lunchtime Vinny was weary. The phone hadn't left the side of his head all week as he tried to drum up some interest in his selection of Unix machines for sale. Vinny finished his cigarette at the end of the lunch break before returning to the office. Toni had joined him on his fag breaks since Monday and made small talk.

"So are you coming for a drink after work?" She looked away while she waited for his reply. There was money in his bank account now, albeit a hundred quid after his overdraft.

"Aye, might as well." He'd worked up a thirst and never said no to a drink when he could cover the costs.

Back at his desk he started to frown. Fuck, she was getting familiar. He hoped there'd be more people coming along. Imagine that, he thought, a nice cosy date with Chubby Checker.

Five o'clock took an age to arrive. Vin was starting to lose interest in making sales calls and he spent his time surfing the web for news on Bolton Wanderers and places to stay in Thailand. People started to pack up and head home for the weekend. Bang on five, the thirst was starting to grow. He sauntered over to Toni's desk, trying not to look impatient.

"Where's everyone goin'?" He had his hands thrust in the pockets of his overcoat and was toying with his cigarettes.

"Del Sol, I think." She looked over her shoulder. "Janet, where we off to?"

Janet was the office blonde, not bad looking, and Toni seemed to be her bosom buddy.

Janet tutted. "I just don't know. Amir, are you coming for a drink?"

Amir was a smartly dressed young Asian guy. His shirt and tie were always perfectly creased and his shoes were always brightly polished.

Vinny shook his head, his impatience starting to show. "Well, I've gotta nip to the cash point. I'll see yers in Del Sol."

He headed for the door. Janet smirked and he could hear the beginning of a girly bit of piss-take aimed at Toni as he dipped in his pocket for a cigarette.

Outside he was cursing. "Fucking British birds. Can't do summat as simple as go for a pint without delay and arsing about." He lit his fag. Jeed had spoiled him, always at his heel like an obedient dog.

He headed for China Town; there was a cash machine that would take his card there. There was already a queue of thirsty office workers at the machine. Obviously payday in other companies as well. Vinny waited semi-patiently for his turn to get his money. A woman in her early forties was at the front of the queue and was fannying about. She'd waited till her turn to get her purse from her bag, then rummaged for her card, then she had the cheek to get a statement before ordering cash. The queue began to sigh collectively. Eventually the machine spat some cash at her but she waited till it was safely in her purse, then until the purse was tightly zipped in the right section of her handbag before she left the cash hatch free for use. The young guy in front of Vin stopped the stopwatch on his digital watch and showed it to his mate. "Six minutes, twenty-four seconds."

Vinny sniggered and the two guys turned round. "Passes the time, dunnit?" the watch owner quipped to Vinny. He'd made a new friend. Vinny hadn't noticed the time that much; he been trying to get a glimpse of Oriental females near the Chinese Bakery.

He was anxious when he got to the machine just in case his wages hadn't gone in. But the machine obligingly spat out five crisp, brown ten-pound notes and he strode off purposefully to Del Sol, folding four of them into his wallet and keeping one in his pocket.

At the bar he was a proud man again. This was the first drink he'd bought with his own money in around a month. The pint of lager arrived in a trendy tall, straight glass and was placed neatly on the bar on a paper beer mat. By the time his change arrived he'd gulped a third of his pint. He turned his back to the bar and weighed up the scene. Del Sol was part of a chain of pubs decked out in a modern Mediterranean style. The floors were thin strips of polished wood. It was spacious and the spiral staircases had railings in ornate cast metal. Small groups of office workers sat around chatting, drinking and smoking at tables and at the shelving against the walls, while they eyed the menu offering microwaved salsa dishes with curly fries. Vinny lit a cigarette and started to feel self-conscious. If he'd been in Thailand alone at a bar he'd soon have had the company of a female or another Western guy chasing women. He'd forgotten how important it was to have company in the West. He looked at his watch. It was 5.30 and he'd left the office at 5pm, almost on the dot. His pint was nearly empty and he started to weigh up weather to fuck off and get the train home. Just as he was about to gulp the last of his beer and leave he saw Mick, the Logistics manager, push his way through the double doors. He had his mobile in one hand and a cigarette in the other and looked like he was sending a text, so was relying on autopilot instead of vision to get him to the bar.

"All right, Mick." Vin was relieved to have a booze buddy.

"Vinny, didn't see you there. How's things?" He looked up from his phone.

"Shite." Honesty was Vinny's Achille's heel a lot of the time.

"Same here, mate. Pint?" Mick was already in his pocket to pay for his drink.

“Aye, it’s Fosters in here.” Vinny finished his pint and put the empty on the bar.

The two colleagues took a seat at one of the high tables in the centre of the bar and perched themselves on high stools. It reminded Vinny of being in Bill Bentley Pub at the airport. He eyed Mick and tried to cover his giggle. Mick wasn’t a handsome guy, a bit taller than Vinny, overweight, same as Vinny, and with a pock-marked face. He was funny though and when he’d had a drink with him and Nigel at lunch a week before he’d enjoyed his dry turn of phrase.

“How’s work going then?” It wasn’t the most exciting topic but Vinny felt like he needed to open up the conversation.

“Fucking awful, man.” Vinny had found a kindred spirit. “They ain’t got a clue about the systems and shite you need to get stuff through the door. There’s people getting stuff they haven’t ordered. People getting invoiced for other people’s orders and people who have ordered gear not getting it. But apart from that every thing’s OK. How’s the wonderful world of Unix?”

“Ah, crap. I need a team to generate leads for us and, on the off-chance that I do find someone who needs a Unix box, I ain’t got a car to go and see ’em in.” He slurped his pint and tapped one of his Thai Marlboro Lights on the table before lighting it.

“So you glad you joined then?” Mick smirked and sipped his pint.

“Aye I can just see it now, flogging an eighty-grand Sun box to Nat West over the phone. ‘Yes, sir, we’ve got those in stock. Would you like two or three?’” He was mimicking the sales patter Charles had formulated. ‘Two.’ He was being the customer now. ‘Sir, if you buy three we’ll give you a free mouse mat and on orders over five hundred pounds there’s a free T-shirt.’ He put the imaginary phone down and shook his head.

Mick laughed.

The doors to the bar opened and in walked Toni, Janet and Amir.

“We’ve got five of them in stock.” Mick hadn’t noticed the others walk into the pub.

“Five of what?” Vinny had lost the thread.

“Sun E-10 000s or summat.” Mick looked nonplussed. Vin was shocked.

“Are you sure?” He couldn’t quite believe what he’d heard. At eighty grand apiece most people ordered from the manufacturer once they’d made a sale rather than holding so much capital.

“That’s what it says on the stock list. I’ll check on Monday.” Mick looked up and saw the others arrive. “Hi guys. You going anywhere near the bar?”

Toni offered to get the drinks in and out of politeness Vinny accepted another pint.

“It’s good of the management to let me know we’re carrying stock. Seeing as I’m meant to be in charge of selling the stuff, like.” Vinny took a long swig of his pint, knowing another was now on its way.

“That normal to keep those things in storage then is it?” asked Mick.

Vin was getting a bit of confidence. Mick had given him the chance to talk about stuff that was precious knowledge to himself. "Well, they need storing properly, like, and 'cos of the cost most people pass the order on to Sun themselves and take their cut off the top rather than holding them in case they don't sell." Vinny shook his head as the drinks and their colleagues arrived.

The presence of ladies made the conversation turn frivolous and Toni started it off in her thinly veiled north Manchester accent. "So, who's got any gossip then?"

Vinny and Mick were busy finishing their pints so they could start on the fresh ones Toni had bought.

"Well, you two are a lot of use, aren't you." Janet had a much more refined tone and appearance than Toni.

Feeling he was required to contribute, Vinny blurted out, "Nigel's a faggot!" hoping it would spark off on an inquiry as to how he knew.

The other four went quiet momentarily and Toni changed topic. "I've heard Ruth made her first sale today."

Janet took that as her lead and started to real off successes and sales by other members of the team. Vinny took that to mean that everyone except him and Mick wear nailing their colours to the Personable mast by concentrating on the positives.

The doors opened again and a tall guy walked in. He was quite good looking with short brown spiked hair and sideburns. He was dressed casually for an evening in the nicer bars in Manchester rather than in suits like most of the drinkers in the bar.

He sauntered over to Amir.

"Hi Jim." Amir's face lit up.

"Hi, love." He kissed Amir gently on the cheek.

Vinny gulped. He looked at his pint. Most people with a bit of decorum wouldn't have made the same *faux pas*, and if they had they'd have had the decency to want the ground to swallow them up. Vinny resigned himself to being branded a bigot and tried to make light of it. "Where we off after here?"

Mick was chuckling. "Dunno, mate."

The girls were trying to hide their disgust.

Amir could see that Vin's face needed saving. "Where does everyone fancy?" Jim could tell he was missing a bit of the conversation.

Eventually the girls relaxed and the six of them headed into an Irish bar that was only a short walk from Del Sol. Mick and Vin felt more at home in the mock spit-and-sawdust environment. As the drinks started to hit empty stomachs the laughter started to flow and Vin could tell his cock-up had been forgiven.

collect your fags

Vinny woke at midday. He felt warmer than he usually did in bed. His first motion was to grab his groin. The buckle of his belt interrupted his hand's journey to his crotch so he had a feel about. Almost fully clothed! He'd gone to bed in his trousers, socks, shirt and tie; that explained the temperature. There were dark clouds in his head and he had to look round to check where he was.

"Fucking hell." He held his head. He'd made it home but was unsure how. Best get up. He moved sideways and stood up.

"Jesus!" Sudden movements weren't a good idea. He steadied himself against the wall. The bathroom was first port of call, then the kitchen. While he was filling the kettle the phone rang. Keith was due at any minute. A quick conversation on the phone clarified his ETA at five minutes.

Bang on time the buzzer sounded and Vinny let him in, still in his shirt and trousers.

"Y'all right?" Keith was wearing that 'I got a shag last night' smile.

"Ask me in an hour." Vin headed for the bathroom. "Actually, make it three," he shouted.

He emerged fifteen minutes later. It only usually took him a minute to shower but he was trying to wash away the hangover.

"You look like you need a line, mate." Keith was smirking.

"I need summat." Vinny shook his head. The shower had washed away some of the alcohol at skin level but down in his stomach and within his cerebrum he was still pissed.

"Fuck me, your eyes are redder than a faggots ring-piece." Keith had a sealer bag half the size of his hand full of cocaine and was racking up four healthy lines on the table.

"Aye, payday last night. Got bladdered with a few from work." Vinny was hunched up in the armchair, shivering.

Keith passed him a rolled up note. " Looks like you had a good night."

Sssscchhhwwwwchh! Vinny devoured the first of his two designated lines.

"Did I tell you I'd booked my flight?" said Keith.

Sssscchhhwwwwchh! Vinny looked up and squeezed his nose, then breathed out. "That's better." He passed the note over to Keith. "Did you get on the same one as me?"

Sschhniit! Keith made light work of the line. "Aye, fourteenth from Manchester." *Sschhniit!*

The pair sat back in their chairs simultaneously, momentarily in limbo as they waited for the cocaine to kick in.

"Fucking needed that, I tell yer." Vinny gave his head a short, distinct shake. A stream of cocaine was starting to make its way from his nostrils to the back of his throat. He was shaking; the central heating was only set for an hour or two at around 7am, and then in the evening from 6. On the weekend, when he forgot to change the settings, daytimes were cold. Vinny shivered again, half from the chill, half because his fatty tissue and internal organs were crying out to be topped up with alcohol. The cocaine was starting to make him shine and feel majestic in his flat. He clasped his hands in his lap as he felt his confidence grow.

"We'll have a good laugh I tell yer," he continued. He could see the pair of them surrounded by Thai women, being pampered and plied with drink.

"Come on. We making a move?" Keith knew if he let Vinny start talking they'd never make it to the match.

"Aye, I'll get my coat."

Vin pushed himself out of the chair. He held his guard like a boxer with a glint in his eye. Three quick punches at an imaginary opponent then a slip of the head to avoid attack and he went bouncing in to the bedroom, fetched his jacket and bounded into the kitchen. A quick glass of water temporarily washed away the acrid taste at the back of his throat. He paused in front of the kitchen mirror. His New York Yankees baseball cap would keep his head warm and he zipped up the front of his Timberland anorak. Today he was streetwise Vinny, not Vinny the salesman.

"Is it all right if I leave this here for a while?" Keith was holding up the bag of coke as Vinny returned to the living room. "'Case there's any trouble at the match." Keith only bothered leaving his market stall on Saturday if there was the chance of a scuffle at the football, and a cup game always threw up that opportunity.

"Yeah no problemo, gringo." Coke made Vinny boisterous.

Keith tapped a small pile out of the bag onto a square of paper on the table and folded it up.

"Just a wrap to keep us going through the afternoon." He smirked and grabbed his keys off the table. It was going to be a long day.

They drove to Horwich in Keith's car and pulled up at a pub near the ground, The Beehive. It was a big building shaped like a barn and decorated in typical English pub style. Match days got crowded and the boozer had plenty of parking spaces, although it meant walking for twenty minutes to the ground. Vinny and Keith got their first pints of the day and sat in a corner, their eyes glazed and their body language arrogant, with their arms spread wide across the seating in the crowded pub.

"So where did you end up last night, Vin?"

"Nowhere special. Just a few boozers in town." He dragged at his cigarette and stared at the cluster of lights above him. He didn't have a clue where he'd been but didn't want to admit it. "You?"

"Just went for a bite to eat with Vicky." Keith gulped at his pint, "The beer's shit in here. Are we walking down the road?" There was nothing wrong with the beer but the drinkers were mainly old men and Keith enjoyed the company of the more boisterous element. Vinny agreed and they headed down the path at the side of the dual carriageway.

Four years ago Bolton had completed the construction of their new all-seater stadium. It was out of town, close to the motorway network and on the edge of a new retail park. As well as being home to the stadium, Middlebrook Retail Park accommodated a host of chain stores, fast-food outlets, bars and around 10,000 car-parking spaces. It had brought much-needed sterling into Horwich but it lacked shelter from the wind and rain.

The pair joined the shoppers at the retail park and walked past the computer store and bowling alley. They arrived at Old Orleans having been buffeted by the gusting wind and rain hitting their faces at 45 degrees. Old Orleans was in a unit in the retail park. A chalkboard normally reserved for menus with HOME SUPPORTERS ONLY written in bold yellow letters on it was chained to one of the steel pillars supporting a glass veranda. Three bouncers stood at the door in black bomber jackets with earpieces and microphones reaching down to their faces. Two policemen in bulletproof vests were engaging them in conversation.

"Afternoon gents."

The smallest of the three doormen pushed the door open for them. Vinny rushed inside. He was dying to get out of the cold. He hovered in the doorway to savour the warmth, and looked around. Old Orleans was like a million and one theme pubs. It was decked out to look like a New Orleans casino/dance hall from the early 1900s. There were mannequins of old black Jazz musicians standing at the doors and by the stairs to the seated areas. The walls were decked with pictures of traditional Mississippi scenes: paddleboats, slaves working the field and famous musicians at their pianos. A hundred and fifty guys between the age of eighteen and forty watched *Football Focus* on a traditional 1920s Mississippi 6-foot TV screen. Vinny did a quick count there was a grand total of eleven men not wearing baseball caps, and maybe twenty were drinking bottles of lager instead of pints. The room was thick with smoke.

Keith scurried past Vinny. He'd been chatting to one of the doormen. "Lager, mate?"

“Aye.” Vinny followed him to the bar and waited as two pints of lager were poured for them by a guy in his late teens. The pair hadn’t spoken on the walk to the ground. Their minds had been focused on getting to the warm pub as quickly as they could. Keith would have driven but the journey would have taken longer in the match-day traffic.

“So what we gonna do in Thailand then?” asked Keith.

Vinny hauled himself onto a barstool. “Ahh, best not to make plans really,” he said nonchalantly. It would be his fifth visit and he knew that even the broadest of outlined plans tended to fall apart in the Land of Delays.

“Are we gonna book anywhere to stay?” Keith looked concerned.

“Nah.” Vinny pushed the peak of his Yankees hat back and ran the palms of his hands down the front of his face. “Get a taxi into town at the airport then head to Patters after a couple of days.”

“What’s Bangkok like?” Keith thought it was a straight question.

Vinny sniggered and shook his head. “It’s hard to describe really.” He tilted his head back and scratched his neck. “It’s a bit of a shock first time you get there, like.”

Keith seemed perplexed. Vinny knew he’d wanted more of a rundown than that but the truth was he didn’t know where to start. “The traffic’s quite bad,” he added in consolation.

Vinny wasn’t being deliberately mysterious, it was just that Bangkok was hard to describe in a couple of sentences, and he was more interested in watching what was happening on the screen at the other end of the pub.

A panel of pundits were sat in a glossy TV studio chatting in front of a big *Football Focus* logo. The frame switched to Steve Ryder in his sheepskin coat. He was sat on a gantry in the Reebok Stadium. To his back the viewers could see the pitch and a half-full Nat Lofthouse stand. A cheer went up in the pub. His words were inaudible over the music wafting through the speakers.

The drinkers were momentarily distracted by a group of twenty guys approaching the door. These guys were obviously from Wimbledon. Nobody knew them and the doormen stalled them at the entrance. A few of the drinkers inside the pub made V signs or the universally recognised clenched fist moving up and down at them as they walked off. Vinny was busy looking at the team sheet that was displayed on the screen.

“So how much money do you reckon I’ll need?” Keith probed.

“Well, we’re there for nineteen days so about a grand and half, two grand, summat like that’ll be about right.” Vinny was still glued to the screen to see what sort of side Wimbledon were fielding.

Keith looked taken aback. “I thought it were meant to be cheap.”

“Aye, well, it is if you go and stay on Khao Sarn with the hippies or get a beach hut in Pha Ngan, like, but we’re off to Pattaya.” Vin felt he could start to elaborate a bit more now that the teams had been shown on telly.

“That where we’re goin’ then?” Keith obviously wanted as much information as he could get. Forewarned is forearmed.

"Yeah, go an' see Jeed." Vinny's already glazed eyes lit up at the thought. "Lend us your mobile a sec."

Vinny scurried off with the phone to the corridor leading to the toilet. It was quiet there. He pulled his wallet out of his back pocket and rummaged around. He'd written Jeed's mobile number on a slip of paper and he keyed in the number excitedly. The beer and cocaine were definitely making him frivolous.

There was a moment's silence followed by a faint ringing tone. It wasn't like the British dialling tone of two rings then a gap, just a series of single, crackly rings.

"*Herroa*." Vinny's heart jumped even though her voice was faint.

"Hello Jeed." Vinny was grinning from ear to ear. He spoke in a higher-pitched voice. A lot of Westerners did that in Thailand. They thought it made them more understandable.

"Hello…" There was a brief silence. Jeed sounded vague and then the penny dropped. "*Winnneeee*. Winnneeee, how are you?" She sounded rapturous.

"*Sabai dee*." A guy was walking down the corridor to the toilet and Vinny covered his face. The man had heard him speaking with a squeaky voice. He started speaking English properly again but slowly. "How are you?"

"Working bar."

Vinny could hear the sound of glasses chinking and a Western guy laughing with his mates. He looked at his watch. It was 2.15, which meant about 9pm in Pattaya.

"Ooh, sorry, honey. You serve drink?" His voice was squeaky again.

"It OK. What you do?" She started to sound clearer.

"I in pub." He left distinct gaps between each word so that she could tell what he was saying. "Today you watch TV. Bolton playing. I near goal. You see me."

"OK, I look for you. When you come Pattaya?"

Vinny could hear the till open and shut at the other end of the line.

"I come December. Send you email. I go now, phone call expensive." He was happy again; he was viewing a mental portrait of her serving drinks and joking with her friends.

"Winny, I mit yoou." Her voice sounded fainter.

"Miss you too, honey. See you soon." He smiled and cut the call.

There was a fresh pint waiting for him at the bar when he got back.

"Cheers, Keith." Vinny's handed back the phone.

"Mind my pint," said Keith. "I'm nipping the bog." He sauntered off, to return a few minutes later rubbing his nose. He inhaled sharply. No points for guessing what he'd been up to. As he pulled up to the bar he slipped his hand in Vinny's jacket pocket.

"Schnaffle there for when you want it." He winked and took a sip of his pint. "So where we gonna stay in Bangkok then?"

"I know a few places on Sukumvit." He corrected himself. "Sukumvit Road. It's where all the bars and that are."

"So what's this Kow Sam place then?" The last line of coke was obviously taking hold as his eyes were boring into Vinny's face.

"Khao Sarn Rd. It's where all the backpackers stay. Full of shitty guesthouses and cheap restaurants. I'll take you down there. It's good for T-shirts an all that." Vinny started to paw the wrap of dust in his pocket. "Just go an' powder me nose."

When Vinny returned Keith was locked in conversation with a guy in his mid-twenties. Vin assumed it was about the revenue stream Keith hadn't told the taxman about, or the police. Vinny minded his own business. The guy scampered off after five minutes and Keith looked at his watch.

"Finish these then go the ground?" Vinny was starting to get eager, though he didn't much like the idea of being exposed to the elements.

"Aye, why not." Keith looked over his shoulder and nodded towards the lad he'd been talking to. "Pemmy over there was just sayin' Wimbledon have brought a couple of hundred lads. They're gonna be on the edge of town around six-thirty, seven. Everyone's meeting in t'Arrers." Keith was starting to look pleased with himself. He was looking forward to engaging the rival fans in a little more than friendly banter. "We off?" he said, gulping the rest of his pint down.

The pair took their seats in the BEN Stand. They were in the second row from the front, about ten feet to the left of the goal.

"Pity we couldn't get in the Lofthouse," said Vinny.

The BEN Stand was designated as the family enclosure where people could take their kids or wives and watch the game without worrying about being surrounded by foul-mouthed yobs who reacted boisterously when goals were scored. The real fans went in the Nat Lofthouse to their left. The BEN also tended to attract quiet a few senior citizens who could sit contentedly without being jostled.

The game started and Bolton were attacking the end opposite to Vinny and Keith. It was a tight game. Bolton pulled out all the stops and pushed hard when they got the ball, but Wimbledon were used to playing Premiership opposition week in week out so their skill level was a notch higher and showed through. In the first half neither side made any great impressions, although Wimbledon had a couple of chances that left Vinny clutching his head in despair.

The second half started and Keith nudged Vinny. He was getting restless. "Just getting a pie, mate. Fancy one?"

"Aye, meat 'n' potato. Cup o' tea'd go down well an' all." Vinny was transfixed. Wimbledon were pushing forward pretty consistently now.

Keith wandered down the concrete stairway ten minutes later with two pies and a flimsy plastic cup of tea from a machine. He started to walk past the seven or eight spectators in Row B that were separating him from his seat. Vinny looked on as he worked his way past people, turning side on in their seats to let him past as he wobbled and swayed in an effort to maintain his balance and keep hold of the pies.

"Fuck me, that was close." He'd been grinning impishly in anticipation of spilling scolding hot tea down a pensioner's front. He passed Vinny his pie and brew just as Wimbledon's number 10 struck a clean shot from just inside the penalty box. It swerved agonisingly through Bolton's defence and was looking like a goal. Vinny winced. The keeper appeared from nowhere as if he was on springs and tipped it over the bar. Most of the Reebok Stadium let out a collective sigh of relief. The shot seemed to strengthen Wimbledon's resolve and during the next half-hour Vinny must have smoked ten cigarettes.

With five minutes to go it was still nil-nil, when suddenly a gap appeared. Xavier Rickets, Bolton's dream boy star player burst through a gap on the right wing and started to hurtle across open territory towards the box. Thirty thousand and two people rose to their feet expectantly and a frantic roar filled the stadium. The thirty thousand and two was made up of the whole of the Nat Lofthouse stand to the right of the terrible twins, the whole of the West Stand to their left, and the terrible two themselves in the BEN. The rest of the BEN sort of mumbled hopefully.

The Wimbledon defence started to close in on Ricketts but his shiny black legs were galloping at an electrifying pace. He was two yards outside the box when out of nowhere a blue shirt slid in and sent him tumbling to the floor. Thirty thousand and two unrepeatable profanities were yelled in unison as Xavier rolled around on the grass in agony clutching his shin. The Wimbledon players' girlfriend would have disagreed with what was suggested by the crowd. With a face like thunder the referee blew his whistle and showed a yellow card to the shamed Wimbledon player.

Xavier recovered quickly and placed the ball for the free kick as a wall of blue shirts formed between him and the goal.

"'Ere, Keith, we can get on the telly." Vinny stood up with his arms spread wide above his head, waving them from side to side. Keith joined him and started punching the air.

"You daft bugger, I can't see!" Vinny felt a prod in his back. The crowd hushed. Vin sat down and turned to the grey-haired old guy behind him to apologise. A wall of sound the volume of the Space Shuttle taking off erupted.

Vinny looked back at the pitch to see the ball bobbling about in the back of the net. Keith was already on his feet jumping up and down like a madman. Vinny joined him to a chorus of tuts and dirty looks from the pensioners and parents surrounding them.

The south stand at the far end of the pitch was silent as the rest of the ground broke into a chorus of 'We love you, Bolton, we do. We love you, Bolton, we do. We love you, Bolton, we do. Oh Bolton, we love you'.

Wimbledon rushed to the centre spot to resume play. They tried desperately for the last seven minutes or so to equalise but Bolton's defence was solid. When the whistle blew for full time Vinny rose to his feet and clapped, smiling at his pride and joy as they circled the pitch applauding the fans.

Vinny and Keith joined the throng slowly leaving the stadium. They walked through the concourse and headed out into the car park.

"Swift one in Orleans while the traffic dies down?" Vinny proffered.

"Aye. Can't be arsed sitting in neutral for an hour." Keith was looking round. His eyes were scanning the territory like a hawk as he looked for opposing fans.

They settled at a table in the window of Orleans, looking out onto the bleak and windswept car park of Middlebrook Retail Park. Night was starting to draw in. They were joined by a couple of guys that Keith and Vinny both knew for their drug habits.

"Me and Vin are off to Thailand at Christmas," said Keith, facing the two guys whilst leaning his back against the window. Vinny was getting friendly with his pint, cuddling it affectionately.

The older of the two smirked. "Lad at work goes twice a year. Fuckin' loves it. It's all he talks about."

"Sounds like someone I know." Keith nodded towards Vinny, who was gazing vacantly through the pane of glass.

"What are the birds like?" the younger of their two companions asked. He had the same taste in baseball caps as Vinny.

Vinny had been brought back to normality by the question. He shook his head and looked at his pint briefly, "They're summat else, kidder. I never fancied Oriental birds, like, till I'd been there, but when you see 'em. Fuckin' 'ell." He gulped at his pint. "These days I can't even look at an English bird."

"How much do they cost?" The questioner sounded like he was trying to work out a budget for a trip of his own. Vinny started to warm to him.

"Well, once you've paid the bar fine it's up to you, like. Usually about a thousand baht." Vinny toyed with the little pleasure parcel in his pocket.

"What's that in English?" The young one was looking eager.

"There's about sixty baht to the pound and the bar fine's between two and five hundred so you're looking around twenty quid all in." Vinny glanced at Keith, who was looking at him in a proud way. His best mate was Mr Well Travelled and their two buddies were obviously impressed.

"What's a bar fine?" the older guy probed.

"Well, you have to pay the bar for taking her away, like, to compensate 'em, sort of thing. Then the money you give her in the morning's hers to keep." Vinny tapped his pocket. "All right having a toot on this, Keith?"

"No problem."

Vinny was out of his chair before Keith had answered him and he headed to the loo to devour some more of the Devil's icing sugar.

He re-emerged minutes later with glazed eyes and a smile on his face.

There was a commotion at the double doors. He could see a line of policemen holding back a group of angry guys trying to force their way in. The bouncers scampered inside, slammed the doors and locked them tight. Keith and their two dubious friends were out of their chairs looking alert and ready for a fight. Vinny joined them and sat at his chair to keep his pint company. The cocaine had made him confident again and he was non-plussed by the commotion. The police appeared to make headway and pushed the guys away.

Outside a straggler had broken away from the fans being herded off. He looked rough and had a psychotic glare in his eyes, as well as a brick in his hand. The brick came flying towards the window. Keith and the two other guys scattered away in a panic, covering their faces. Vinny sat there calmly.

Thud! The brick hit the glass.

"Good job it's toughened glass," said Vinny calmly. He sipped his pint while the other three stared at him in disbelief before joining him back at the table in fits of laughter.

Vinny nonchalantly tossed the wrap of coke back to Keith. "Nearly finished that. Probably enough for one in there."

Keith headed off to the toilets.

A couple more beers each were sipped and Keith offered their two mates a lift back to town.

As they got close to the Three Arrows Keith suggested leaving his car at Vinny's and he agreed.

They pulled up outside his flat. "We getting a bit more C for in the Arrers, Keith?"

"Nah, if it goes off and I get nicked I'm fucked." Keith was careful about getting caught.

The group of four walked the three hundred yards to the Three Arrows in the dark with shoulders hunched up by the cold. As they approached they walked past a line of four police vans.

"Looks like the party's gonna be pooped." Keith was disappointed that the police knew where all the bad boys were congregating.

The Three Arrows was far from the most spectacular pub in the world. It had one main door with a room to the left and a room to the right. The bar in the centre served both rooms. Vinny and Keith went to the left but the other two had spotted some other mates in the room to the right so bade them farewell.

Two pool tables all but filled the room Keith and Vinny had chosen. Vinny headed to the bar and could see that the far room was full of likely lads, as was the poolroom.

Keith headed off to the toilets at the back while Vinny waited to get served. Sheila was serving but had her back to him. She was Sarah's mum.

She was a real tough nut and at nearly eighteen stone she cut a terrifying figure when she was crossed. Vinny waited patiently.

Sarah appeared in front of him. "Oh, hi, Vincent."

Vinny winced as he looked at her. Without make-up she looked awful and far too young to consider tampering with.

"What can I get you?" She looked down in the mouth and avoided eye contact with him.

"Erh, two lagers please, Sarah." Vinny was trying his best to suppress a laugh at the thought of her squirming around underneath Keith.

She stood in front of him pouring two pints of cloudy orange liquid that the brewery had the cheek to pass off as lager.

"Is Keith with you?" She didn't look up as she asked the question.

"Aye, he's about somewhere." He smiled as he looked over his shoulder to scan the room. Stirring things up where possible was a favourite pastime of his. He spotted Keith with his back to the bar sat against one of the pool tables talking to someone sat on the bench seating built into the wall. "He's over there," he said and nodded towards where Keith was chatting. Vinny paid for the drinks and walked over to join his mate.

A thickset half-caste guy was holding court. "That's nothing. Last week Gorey shagged Sheila in the cellar halfway though a lock-in." The three or four people, including Keith, in his audience burst into a raucous fit of laughter.

Vinny passed Keith his pint and felt a bit out of sorts being the only one with a straight face.

"Cheers, Vin. You know Royston, don't you?" Keith nodded towards the half-caste guy. "Just been telling him about Sarah."

Vinny nodded at him. "All right?"

The banter was flying and it was hard to make themselves heard above the noise of 40 or so football hooligans enjoying the crack.

From the presence of the police vans around the corner it was obvious there wasn't going to be trouble, but most people were in a buoyant mood after the result and were happy to take the rise out of one another over several beers.

After about twenty minutes Sarah came round collecting glasses. As she approached Keith and Vin's group they quietened and started to grin impishly. She looked nervous as she got near Keith and avoided his eyes as she picked up the empty glasses stacked on the edge of the pool table.

"Can I have a word Keith," she said, looking sullen.

"Yeah, what is it?" Keith started to blush in front of his tough-guy mates.

"In private." She glared at him and sauntered off towards the door.

Keith took a gulp of his drink and followed her. She'd left the stack of glasses on the bar.

Sarah was stood in the doorway looking anxious.

"What is it?" Keith wanted to keep it short and sweet.

“Have you got some cocaine?” She was holding a cigarette in her left hand next to her face and her right hand was pressed into her left elbow.

“Have you got fifty quid?” Keith looked down into her grey eyes.

“Wait in there. I’ll have to get it from upstairs when me mam’s not looking.” She flicked her ash on the floor and headed off into the other room.

Keith pushed the door open into the pool room and made an exaggerated gesture of pretending to pull his flies up as he headed back across the room to sniggers and laughs from Royston and Vinny.

The pub was starting to empty slowly as Bolton’s group of hooligans headed in twos and threes into town or home to shower and change into smarter clothes for the town-centre pubs and clubs.

Vinny and Keith stayed and chewed the fat with Royston.

Keith looked at his watch and glanced around the room impatiently for Sarah. He wanted to head off. As soon as she’d come up with the money he was going to nip over to Vinny’s to get her a gram before heading into town.

Two men in their early forties walked into the pub. Nobody gave them a second glance. They went to the bar and ordered drinks. Sheila served them and they started chatting to her as if they knew her.

By now Keith had managed to get a seat on the upholstered benching fitted to the wall. The two guys walked over to the pool table and put their pints on the edge. One of them was wearing a winter anorak and he went to stand in front of Keith, who was busy talking to Royston about a mutual acquaintance.

“Keith Rossi?” The guy looked him in the eye sternly.

Keith looked up. “Aye.”

“I’m Detective Constable Davenport.” He flashed his warrant card in front of him.

The colour drained from Keith’s face and the three guys sat by him suddenly went quiet and looked at their feet.

“I believe you are in possession of drugs and would like to search you. If you refuse I may choose to arrest you and conduct a search at the station.” He looked round at his colleague, who nodded in conformation. Vinny was stunned and looked at Keith in panic.

“You’ll not find anything.” Keith shrugged his left shoulder and frowned.

“We can conduct the search outside if you like.” DC Davenport thrust his hands into his pocket.

“Fair enough.” Keith stood up. DC Davenport slipped his hand up the cuff of Keith’s jacket and held onto his wrist as the two coppers and Keith headed out of the pub.

The pub had gone silent and every eye in the room was on three people in particular. The door slammed to and the conversation started again.

Outside on the pavement Keith held his arms out wide. “Get it over with then. You won’t find owt.”

Davenport moved towards him and started to look through his inside pockets. The other guy went behind Keith and removed his wallet from the back of his jeans, which he placed on the floor, and started to pat his legs down. Then he felt up the leg of his jeans and down his socks. Davenport took Keith's mobile from his jacket and held it while he continued to pat him down. Keith looked up into the night sky, expressionless. The second constable passed Keith's wallet to Davenport and he leafed through it and looked at his mobile phone.

"It appears that we've been given misleading information." Davenport had the look of a guy who'd walked into a Mormon meeting room expecting to find strippers. "The landlady of that pub told us you were selling drugs. Do you know why she would have cause to make such an allegation?" He looked Keith squarely in the eye.

"Yeah, 'cos I shagged her daughter and dumped her, and 'cos she's a nasty old boot." He turned his nose up. "Can I go back to my drink?"

"You're free to go now but we'll be keeping an eye out for you."

Keith turned and walked back into the pub. The room went quiet as he strolled over to his seat.

"You're banned," Sheila squawked over the bar.

Keith turned and glared. "Not till I've finished my pint, I ain't."

Keith took his seat next to Royston, who moved uncomfortably away. He'd been sat close before but wanted to put at least a foot between himself and Keith now.

Five minutes previously Keith had been highly regarded, top of the social ladder, wide boy, hustler. Since leaving the room in the company of DC Davenport he'd slid four or five rungs down the rogues' hierarchy. Everyone was anxious not to be associated with him.

"Close call that," said Keith before slurping at his pint.

Royston looked away. Vincent tried to bring his glass to his lips but his hand was shaking vigorously; the half-ounce of pleasure powder that Keith had left in his living room was giving him cause for concern.

"What happened," asked Vinny as he rested his pint on his knee to keep it steady.

"Nowt. Just frisked us. Found fuck-all and did one." Keith was glaring at the bar. Sheila was conveniently tending a customer in the other room.

"Come on. We off?" Keith slipped the last of his beer down his throat. Vinny nodded and they headed out.

"What's the plan?" The pair had just wandered aimlessly for five minutes while Keith was deep in thought. Vinny felt they needed direction.

"Fuck knows, kidder. Need to get my head together." Keith looked over his shoulder. It was the twelfth time in five minutes that he'd done it.

"What's Vicky doing?" Keith needed cheering up.

“She’s gone down south. Summat to do with her mam and dad.” Keith looked at his feet; he was still in a state of shock. “Few cans at yours? Can’t be arsed with town.”

“Aye. Go t’Fosbry Flop an’ get a few transits. Save your money for Christmas.”

They headed for the Co-op and bought a mountain of tinned beer, a bottle of rum and a two-litre bottle of Coke. Keith footed the bill.

Vinny was back home and loading the fridge with beer when Keith’s mobile rang.

“Hiya.” Keith had an unchilled can on his knee and was pulling it open.

“Winnee,” came a faint, soft voice.

“No, it’s Keith, love. Hang on.” He walked into the kitchen. “Some bird asking after yer. Winnee.” He passed the handset to Vinny.

“Hello.” Vinny had almost forgotten that he’d phoned.

“Winnee, it Jeed.” she was sounding exasperated at having spoken to the wrong guy.

“Jeed.” Vinny slammed his can on top of the fridge, “How are you?”

“Jeed goot.” Vinny could hear her friends cackling close by. “ Winnee, I’m see you TV. Bolton winning. Iss goot.”

“Yeah wicked.” after five or six pints and a few lines of coke he was forgetting to put his special accent on. It was nothing to do with worrying about looking a twat in front of Keith.

“Bolton champion. Number one.” her mates had gone quiet now.

“I’m see you T V dancing. Also yo fliend.”

“Vinnie happy *mak mak*.” he raised his can, aiming at his mouth but missing, and spilling a quarter of it down his shirt.

“Winnee, wot yo flend name?” Despite the distance Vinny recognised the flirtatious tone.

“Him Keith.” Vinny glanced towards Keith as he tipped out a hefty pile of Bolivian.

“Ohn think Keith welly handsom.” Jeed had her friends’ welfare high on her list of priorities.

“OK, OK, Ohn want speak with Keith?” Vinny was struggling hold on to the conversation and took the easy option. He passed the phone to Keith.

“Heillo.”

Keith stopped chopping the powder momentarily and glared at Vin.

“Hello.”

“Wass yo name?” a faint but seductive voice probed him.

“Keith.” He sounded disinterested.

“Yoo cum Patteeya, stay my loom?” Ohn sounded frantic.

Keith hit the off button on his phone and placed it on the coffee table. He would have done it forcefully if there hadn’t been a pile of powder that would scatter if he’d slammed it.

“That’s not very nice.” Vinny smirked.

“I need a shag, not phone sex.” Keith pushed a pile of powder round the tabletop with his credit card.

Vinny smiled triumphantly. He’d got under his friend’s skin. Keith was desperate for sex and willing to pay.

“Sounds like you’ve pulled.” The can connected with Vinny’s lips this time.

Ssssshhhhnnnnuuuuffffffffftttt! Keith devoured an enormous line. He sat back in the sofa. “ Who the fuck does that Sheila think she is?” His words were pointed and aggressive. “She’s gonna fucking pay for that, I tell you.” From the nod of Keith’s head, Vinny knew that he meant it.

Keith left at 6am. The fridge was empty and so was the bottle of rum, but his head was full of mental images of Bangkok and Pattaya.

Vinny spent the day lying in bed trying to sleep, but the coke running through his veins only allowed him the odd half-hour slip into slumber.

Around the corner

Monday morning arrived on time, unlike Vinny. The office hushed momentarily as he pushed the door open and headed for his desk. A good weekend of intoxicants had left him looking like the negative of a panda; white with black round the eyes.

Better get this one out of the way, he thought. Mr Unavoidably Delayed headed straight for Sue's office with his metaphorical Yankees cap in his hand. "Hi, Sue." He tried his best to smile as he popped his head round the door. "Sorry I'm late. Overslept." He nodded his head upwards in acceptance of the anticipated admonishment.

"*Aeschew!*" He sneezed a blob of snot onto her floor. Sue looked up from some form or other on her desk and smiled politely, pretending not to notice the mucus that had landed on the carpet.

"OK. Not a problem." She was wearing her best fake smile but couldn't disguise the shake of her head.

Vinny sauntered off to his seat and logged on to his PC. Devoid of energy and motivation he looked blankly at the notes and messages doing the rounds of Personable's email system. All told, it took ten minutes to skim over them and despatch them to the trash file.

Toni tottered towards Sue's office and started smirking at Vinny as she approached him.

"Sobered up then, Vincent?" Trying to make fourteen stone of female look enticing wasn't easy but she gave it her best shot.

"What? Eh…" She'd taken him by surprise. "Oh aye, yeah. Just about." Friday night seemed like a million years ago and her prompt left him trying to piece together the events that had led to him waking fully clothed. Up till that point his mind had been occupied with the events in the Three Arrows. Had Keith become the subject of a surveillance operation? Was he being labelled as an accomplice?

Without Nigel around to supply him with the morning newspaper Vinny was stuck for something to do. He assumed the 'I'm busy' position with his right hand on his mouse, gazing blankly at his screen. The door to Sue's office creaked open and Vinny grabbed at the phone with his left hand.

"Busy, Vincent?" Toni thundered past like a baby elephant.

"What?"

She sniggered and returned to her desk.

After two very slowly made cups of coffee and an extended cigarette break, Vinny headed for the restroom to get some shuteye. There were sometimes newspapers in there as well, which could kill ten minutes. Inside the cubicle Vinny took his position on the throne and picked up the soggy *Metro News* that was left in stands at bus and tram stops for commuters to use for avoiding eye contact. Starting at the front he read about a girl who had been misdiagnosed for the flu when she had leukaemia. He knew Bolton's result would be back page news but he saved the pudding till last.

A 100-watt mental light bulb flooded his dimly lit grey cells with candescence.

"Back on the road in no time," he muttered to himself as he pulled his wallet out of his pocket. The brand.new Merchant's credit card and his cash card had thin crusts of 'Nicaraguan Nightshift' around their edges. Vinny's eye's gleamed as he carefully scraped the edges onto the top of the toilet-roll dispenser. It was amazing how resourceful one could be in a crisis. Cautious of alerting other toilet users to his actions, he scraped his cards against each other with the stealth of a bank robber working the combination of the safe. Cards clean, he licked the edges and the bitter sweetness sparked a tingle in his tongue and a dull, heavy happiness at the back of his eyes. The pile on top of the paper dispenser was hardly enough to wake the dead. If only he'd had Keith's bag with him. His breathing got deeper and heavier as his heart started to race with anticipation. The naughtiness of it all helped. Monday was never a good day for finding notes in his wallet so he carefully tore a square off the *Metro News* and rolled it into a tube. Now for the awkward part. He flushed the toilet and hurriedly tried to vacuum the flakes up his heavily blocked pipes. The small pile appeared to have gone. He removed the tube from his nose and half the original crumbs landed back on the enamel paper holder.

"Bollocks." He sniffed harder, this time leaving all but a couple of specs. They were mopped up with a fingertip and lovingly licked. A quick squeeze of the tip of the nose made him smile. Nothing could throw him now. Powder was power. It took a moment to unbolt the door.

"Always fucking sticks, that door." He glared at fat Geoff, who was staring at the restroom mirror as he rinsed his hands, poker-faced and sullen. Vinny was ignorant of him having heard his motivational manoeuvres and strode confidently back into the office with a renewed sense of purpose.

The phone became attached to his ear as he spent the morning chasing potential business. At 12.30 Toni sauntered over. "What you doin' for lunch, Vincent?"

Her hand was on his desk and she leaned towards him, thrusting her cleavage at his face. Vinny looked up from his screen like a rabbit caught in headlamps. "Fuck me, if you dropped your fags down there you'd need a long piece of string to get 'em back."

"Oi, Vincent Croston. Look at me face, not the girls." She pretended to act offended but was almost purring at Vinny's acknowledgement of her breasts.

"Sorry." He lowered his head and mocked shame.

"Me and Janet are going in Del Sol at one," she offered.

"I'll pop in later." He knew from Friday that she meant twenty-five past.

Once on his lunchbreak, Vinny called at the cash point and wandered round China Town before heading for the bar.

Janet and Toni were sat at the same table they'd occupied on Friday, smoking and chatting like fishwives. Vin got a lemonade and joined them.

"So, you drunken bastard, how did you get home?" Toni blew smoke in Vinny's face.

He paused for effect, rubbed his face and shook his finger at her once. "Still awaiting confirmation on that one. Method of transit as yet unknown."

The pair giggled joyously.

"And could you also explain why when you got in the office you looked like death?" She dragged on her cigarette, adding weight to the grilling. "Then come mid-morning you're as bright as a button?"

"Errrm." He scratched his ear. "Two strong cups of coffee works wonders." A gulp of his drink helped him avoid eye contact. His two bitches gave him a friendly but slightly disapproving look.

"Ooh, you are a rogue." Janet was a little more proper than Toni but still had a playful feminine air about her.

"So what's the gossip then?" He was under the microscope and wanted to deflect the attention.

"Well, Sue's been asking us all about business. Apparently Charles is starting to get impatient." Toni was playing the hierarchical role now. "And the feeling is that Nigel jumped before he was pushed."

"So how do you fit into this?" Vinny wanted to avoid questioning.

"Well, we've both sold stuff, about five grand's worth and she knows us from Meg. So we're OK for the time being." Toni lit another cigarette.

"Just make sure when she asks you next week you've got something that sounds solid," Janet interjected. She was being helpful not authoritative.

"Aye, I'll have something solid for her." He grabbed his crotch and smirked. "Thing is wi' me it takes a while, but when you do get one it's a big 'un." Vinny couldn't have made his reference to sales smuttier if he'd tried.

The conversation in the pub at lunch hadn't pleased Vinny. Personable, if the truth be told, had dropped him in a pile of shit. They'd made grand promises about a big department and the right sort of back-up that he needed, but now there were hints of interrogation and self-justification. A lot of phone calls were made that afternoon and on Tuesday, Wednesday and Thursday.

On Friday morning Vinny walked into the office looking exhausted and stressed. Sleep had been difficult. OK, he didn't want to be working for

Personable, or anyone else in the UK, but he wanted to leave with a chunk of cash in the bank under his own steam, rather than be ushered out after a month without being given a fair crack of the whip.

At his desk he was trying to look busy, but it was difficult. As he put the phone down to the thousandth secretary of the week who'd refused to put him through to the purchasing department, he heard his name.

"Vincent." He looked over his shoulder. Sue was leaning out of her goldfish bowl with her best corporate beam adorning her face. "Have you got a minute?" She held the door open for him.

Without answering he left his chair and walked into her office. He stood in front of her desk with his hands behind his back like a schoolboy who had been summoned to the headmaster to explain why he'd not done his homework for a month.

"Just to let you know…" She was back at her desk. "Your car will be arriving today around two o'clock."

Vinny's heart started to beat normally again and his hands made their way to his pockets.

"Oh great. I can get out and see clients now." He smiled. Travelling with the public on the train was getting him down.

"As well as that, I need to set up a time when we can sit down and do a business review to pass to Charles early next week." Sue looked at him expectantly through an inch of foundation.

Vin sucked his lips and tried not to look worried. "Yeah. Monday should be fine. About eleven?"

"I'll put it in my diary." She blinked and scribbled on her pad.

Shouldn't take long, Vinny thought as he headed back to his desk. How long does it take to say 'fuck all'?

Toni's invitation to the pub at lunch was turned down and Vinny spent an hour wandering round the city centre with his hands thrust deep in his overcoat pockets, looking at the floor and racking his brains as to what he could do get some business in. A twin-decked car trailer fixed to the back of a juggernaught brought delight to the office as it pulled up on Princess Street loaded with VW Golfs. The senior members of the company gathered outside the office, acting suitably grateful to Charles and Personable for delivering them some status. Vinny was non-plussed. His last company car had been a BMW so driving a Golf meant dropping a rung or two on the flash scale. Anyway, material possessions were starting to mean a lot less to him these days.

When he picked up his vehicle, he drove it round the block onto a parking meter and consoled himself that it had a cassette player for him listen to his Hello *Thailand* tape.

The remainder of the afternoon passed uneventfully. Driving home made a pleasant change from joining the throng on the train. His cerebral function was locked onto business.

Keith came round that evening looking down in the mouth. Word about his brush with the law the previous week had spread around Bolton's cocaine clan like wildfire and business had been slow, with all but his most regular customers fearful of walking into a bust or becoming the subject of surveillance. He'd missed the interaction as much as the trade.

"Never mind," Vinny said in consolation. "Five weeks and we'll be surrounded by birds in bikinis pissed out of our heads."

By the end of the evening Keith was well versed in the etiquette of bar fining, showering before sex, spotting a lady boy and paying the right amount in the morning.

On Saturday Keith used his unpopularity as an excuse to win family points and had dinner with Mama and Papa. At 9.30 he rang Vinny, who was sat at home saving cash for the anticipated trip. "All right, Vin. OK if I pop round?"

He arrived at the flat with a big stack of cans and two bottles of red wine to add to the six cans Vinny had already devoured. Acting decent he put the cans in the fridge himself. He entered the living room brandishing a can and tossed a bag of coke across the room into Vinny's lap.

"Fuck me, I thought you'd have stashed that somewhere by now." Vinny held the bag up in his can-free hand and eyed the remainder of the ounce they'd started working on the previous Saturday. There was probably still a good ten grams left.

"Aye, well, if they were serious about nicking me they'd have searched my flat when Sheila dropped me in it. They probably just think it's her being a daft cow." Keith pulled the ring on his can.

He was proving to be a good student. He had remembered all of the previous night's lesson on Thailand etiquette, and this evening he became familiar with how taxi and tuk-tuk drivers would try and fleece you, along with the basic geography of the red-light districts in Bangkok and Pattaya.

At around 1am Keith ordered himself a cab. The pair had shown uncharacteristic restraint on the party powder and were both happily but controllably drunk.

"'Ere, Keith, you couldn't leave as a couple of grams of that, could you?" Vinny begged as Keith gathered his belongings before the taxi arrived. Between lectures on the relative merits and price differences of Nana Plaza and Pat Pong girls, and quiet spells watching *Match of the Day*, Vinny had been hatching a plot to make that vital sale.

"Yeah, no problem." Keith poured a small pile out onto an empty cigarette packet on the coffee table before jumping to the taxi horn when it sounded.

On Monday morning Vinny strolled to the office from a car park on the edge of town, oblivious to the odd looks he was getting from passers by as he muttered incoherently to himself. "*Neung, sawng, sam, sii, ha, hok, jet, pat, kaow, sib. Neung, sawng, sam, sii, ha, hok. Jet pat, kaow...*" The first section on *Hello Thailand* was how to count to ten and it had engrossed him for the whole of the traffic snarled 50-minute journey in from Bolton.

Vinny took to his desk and did his best to look busy. Most of the other staff seemed occupied with trying to get their figures looking respectable for Sue. Vinny had decided to baffle her with jargon. She came from a PC background and knew nothing about Unix. Eleven o'clock came and she was still busy in her office with fat Geoff, who was proudly going into detail about every pack of toner he'd sold in the past ten years. Twelve o'clock came and the pair seemed to be locked in heavy debate. At ten past twelve Vinny was starting to feel hungry when the door opened and Geoff departed for his desk to a "Well done" from Sue.

Vinny felt a pair of eyes in the back of his head. He looked round and could see Sue with her painted-on smile looking his way. "Shall we run through business?"

"Yeah, fine." Vinny decided on the diplomatic approach with regard to the delay. A hastily fabricated list of clients and their projected demand printed on two sheets of A4 was neatly placed on a corner of his desk. He grabbed it and headed into the goldfish bowl.

"So, how's it going?" Sue looked up from her desk as she was typing an email and hit send with her mouse.

"Fine," Vinny lied.

Sue looked back at her screen to check the mail didn't bounce then pushed her mouse away.

"How's business looking?" She clasped her hands together in front of herself on the desk as she leaned forward.

"Well. On the sales front, as you know, nothing yet, but with this level of equipment it does take time." He put the sheets of A4 on her desk.

"Are there sales imminent?" It was the first time he'd seen her without her synthetic smile.

"Well, I've been prospecting very proactively." He avoided her gaze because of the whopper he was about to tell. "And there seems to be a lot of interest in using Personable in future for upgrades from clients I've dealt with in the past." Vinny gulped like an accused murderer in the dock telling the jury he was elsewhere on the night in question.

"I've made a list and broken it down into clients who are currently running Sun Sparc workstations and may want to upgrade to servers in the next six to twelve months." He looked up. "On the list as well, which I emailed you earlier, is a list of clients running the E10, thirty-two way server, who I know are getting higher volumes of traffic and will be likely to need the sixty-four way server with a few more gig soon as well."

Vinny was expecting Sue to be looking in her in box to get the work of fiction he'd sent her, but she was still surveying him as he tried desperately to avoid eye contact.

“So, there’s nothing definite.” The bolt hit him right between the eyes.

“Errm,” he sighed. “No.” Although it wasn’t the answer he wanted to give, he felt relieved at giving an honest one.

“Well, I don’t know if you know but Charles is starting to want to see results and all the other divisions except yours have made sales.” She was homing in on her target and Vinny squirmed in his seat. “When is it you go on holiday?” The change of tack confused him.

“The fourteenth of December.” Two honest answers in one meeting was something of a record for Vin.

“That’s five weeks’ time. We will need to see some sales before you go, or we’ll have to review, well, terminate your position.” Sue leaned back having put her point across and looked at her screen, waiting for Vin to kiss her behind as was the custom.

“OK, will do. No problem. Let you know when I’ve done one.”

He pushed his chair back and left the office. Until then he’d started to feel normal again with a trip to Thailand on the horizon, but the news knocked him back to zero on the happy scale. There was nothing like an ultimatum to increase the awareness and, once back in his chair, Vinny’s eyes darted form desk to desk in the office. Why had she drawn a line in the sand? Who knew about it? He was trying to read their faces. Was anyone trying to move in on his department? He sucked his lips and then looked around again, this time to see if there was anyone within earshot. He picked up the phone, dialled a number quickly and waited for the answer.

“Good morning, Intra Tech,” a bright-sounding receptionist sung into his ear.

Vinny put on his best professional voice. “Hi, can I speak to Graham Hughes, please?”

“I’ll just put you through.”

“Graham Hughes.” The fat little porker sounded out of breath.

“Gray, you fat cunt.” Normal voice now for someone he was pretending to be friends with.

“Hello…” He sounded perplexed. Graham didn’t get many calls and it had been a long time since he’d spoken to Vinny.

“Its Vinny, you bovine ball bag.” Vinny was trying not to snigger. Graham had stopped panting like a puppy. Obviously he’d got his breath back after having to walk to the phone.

“Oh ho, Vincent. Good to hear from you.” He was on his guard now.

“Fancy a pint tomorrow after work?” Vinny offered. “It’s on me.”

“Yeah. Yeah. What time?” Graham sounded like he’d won the lottery. A phone call and an offer of a pint in one day was an oddity.

“’Bout sixish in the Old Monkey.”

“OK, see you there.”

“Don’t tell anyone you’re meeting me,” Vinny asserted.

“OK, six in the Monkey. See you tomorrow,” Graham agreed with secrecy in his tone.

Vinny put the phone down, sucked in the air between his teeth, wiped his nose and rubbed his crotch.

“We’ll soon have you nailed, boyo,” he muttered to himself and looked over his shoulder slyly at Sue in her office.

When Vinny strolled into the Old Monkey on Tuesday, fashionably late at 6.15, Graham was already standing at the bar in his duffle coat, still overweight, and nursing a pint and a cigarette. Graham was employed as a sales co-ordinator at Intra Tech. He was a glorified clerk. If someone was working on a bid he’d put the right bundle of sales literature in the post on behalf of the sales rep, or he’d spend some of his day carrying customer records to and from desks in different departments. General dogsbody would be an apt description really. His appearance made him unsuccessful with women and generally in life, which added to his lack of charisma and charm, and made him one of life’s great dogsbodies. If you ever needed someone to dump on at work, Graham was your man. His only redeeming feature was his reliability, although coupled with a low level of aptitude it didn’t really count for much. Intra Tech kept him on because he didn’t cause trouble and he knew everything that went on.

“Graham. Good to see you.” Vinny smiled like he was wooing a client. That sycophantic long-lost brother smile was plastered across his face. “How’s things?”

“Not bad.” Graham looked up from his pint.

“Got yourself a bird yet?” Straight for the jugular but with a smile it wasn’t too harsh.

“Not yet. How about you?” Graham looked into his pint again.

“Fucking dripping with ’em, mate. Naomi Campbell should be in here any minute. How’s life at Intra Tech?” Vinny ordered a pint and the pair headed for a seat in the corner.

“Do you remember Amy in Admin?” Graham started on his round up of the last two years’ results.

“Blonde one?” Vinny was guessing.

“No, black girl.” Graham slurped at his pint. “She’s been shagging Damian. Got herself promoted to Admin Manager.” Damian was one of the directors.

Vinny let him talk for fifteen minutes or so about who was still there, who wasn’t, how the office had changed and how Manchester City were doing. Vinny had a target he was focusing on.

“How’s Dean getting on?” he quizzed inconsequentially.

“He’s doin’ well.”

Vinny tried not to wince with jealousy at that answer. “Still doin’ the Sun kit?” Vinny avoided eye contact as he focused in on enemy HQ.

"Yeah, he's just sold three E10s to a company in Leeds." Graham could smell treachery. "Top price as well."

Dean was the whiz kid at Intra Tech and had been biting at Vinny's heels when he'd been performing well. He was a typical ruthless salesman and his colleagues revered him. Nobody got in his way.

"How's it going at your place?" Graham was a greedy guy and knew he had information that could help. Why else would Vinny be approaching him? Nobody liked spending time with him unless they wanted something. He'd got used to his unpopularity.

"OK really. Plenty of birds. Don't know what they're doing though." It was Vinny's turn to be the mediocre one.

He slipped a wrap of coke onto the table and pushed it subtly towards Graham, who nearly choked on his drink.

"What's that for?" No one had ever given him anything for free.

"It's a present."

"Aye, but you'll want something for it?" The fat kid was getting nervous now.

"Just some information."

"What like?" Graham looked round anxiously in case they were being watched.

"I need to know next time anyone's got a Sun sale lined up and how much they're quoting." Vinny took the penultimate gulp from his glass. "More of that on receipt of info." He finished his drink stood up and walked out.

Graham was left aghast but trying not to show it through paranoia of prying eyes.

Vinny drove home and learned that *Yin dee thee dai ruu jak khun* meant 'Nice to meet you'.

On Friday the day drew to a close without word from Graham. Vinny knew it would take time to get the information but he didn't want him forgetting. He picked up the phone and dialled.

"Hello, Intra Tech."

"Graham Hughes, please," Vinny said curtly.

"Just putting you through, sir."

There was a short puff and pant before Graham could get his words out. "Graham Hughes."

"Graham, it's Vinny, give us your mobile number." He stared hard down the phone to make himself sound aggressive.

"Yeah, it's 07687 411324." the phone went dead.

Vinny sat in his chair and waited. The office was emptying around him, the 'Personable People' heading home for the weekend. Friday over with, he was left with weeks to keep his job. Instead of four weeks with his feet on the desk he was going to have to do four weeks' full work. He waited until 6pm when the office was empty. By now Graham would be on the bus home. Vinny dialled his mobile number.

"All right, Gray, it's Vin. Just seeing how you've got on with that little project."

"There's nowt doing. Dean's the only one shifting Sun stuff really and he's been away all week." Graham sounded anxious.

"Yeah. When's he back?" Vincent sounded cross.

"Middle of next week."

"You best not be bullin' me. 'Cos I've got some nasty friends who'll do nasty things if you are." Vinny only half meant it but it sounded like he was serious.

"N-n-n-no. I'm not. Wednesday he's back in. I'll see what help he needs then." Graham was audibly scared.

Vinny slammed down the phone, swiftly left the office and called in to Del Sol for a beer with Toni and Janet.

For a week and a half Vinny harassed and harangued virtually every company he could think of who had ever even thought of borrowing a computer, never mind spending half a million quid on the worlds leading Unix machine, but it was all to no avail. Graham had got a reminder call every couple of days but was insistent that Dean had nothing on the go. Vinny was starting to get nervous and was having trouble sleeping. The days were spent churning through endless lists of phone numbers in the hope of finding a buyer, when late in the day on Wednesday the phone rung. It was Graham, out of breath as usual.

"Vincent."

"Graham." Vinny's heart started to pound.

"I've got some news. Meet me tonight." The phone went dead. He had the mystique of *Deep Throat*. Vinny could sense he was enjoying this. Laughing to himself, he dialled Graham's number.

"Graham, you prick." There was good humour in his voice.

"Vince," Graham whispered.

"It's normal etiquette when you meet someone to arrange details like a time and a place. Call me a picky bastard. like."

"OK, six-thirty in the Monkey," said Graham anxiously.

"I'll be reading *The Financial Times* and wearing a pink rosette." Vinny still couldn't contain his snigger as he put the phone down. Looking round the office triumphantly, he rubbed his hands together and tried not to punch the air.

At 6.30 Vinny sauntered into the Old Monkey with a smile and a swagger. Graham was seated in the corner reading a piece on Man City in the *Evening News*. He looked up as Vinny made the universal cup-to-mouth gesture in offer of a drink.

"Lager." Simple answer.

Vinny joined him with two fresh pints. There was a brown envelope on the seat waiting for him.

"Give us the rundown then," said Vinny.

"It's all in there." Graham avoided his gaze and looked unhappy, like he was selling the plan of the D-Day landings to the Germans.

"Yeah but where's it up to?" Vinny picked up the envelope and started to open it.

"Jesus fucking hell!" Graham forced the envelope back onto the seat. Vinny put on a mock sombre frown.

"Sorry, mate."

"Details in there." Graham looked at the door. "Company, buyer, specs, the lot. Dean's got an appointment this Friday to meet the guy and give him a full rundown. Where's me coke?"

"You'll get it when I get a result."

"Got to go. If we get seen I'll be for the chop." Graham left his drink and skulked off.

With the cloak-and-dagger stuff over, Vinny opened up the envelope. There was all the usual glossy stuff and a letter addressed to a guy called John Moston, the Managing Director of some company in Preston called Globe Hop. The letter outlined a rough price guide and why Intra Tech were the best people to buy from, and how their services matched John's needs to just have the equipment dropped off and left alone while his technician's integrated it into his existing network. Sounded perfect. Only problem was the timing. If they were serious, Dean would have it sewn up on the day.

Vinny was the first in the office on Thursday. It was the first time he'd been in there alone. It felt weird.

A machine was manning Globe Hop's phone. During the evening Vinny had managed to read the information Graham had supplied and knew that they were a company selling flights and holiday packages over the web. They were doing well and needed more hardware to support their traffic. Vince made himself a coffee, pacing up and down the kitchen while the kettle boiled. There were some surprised looks on people's faces when they walked in and found Mr Last In, First Out already at his desk.

On his tenth attempt Vinny managed to get a human to pick up the phone at Globe Hop.

"Hi, can I speak to John Moston, please?"

"Ooh, I don't know," an old lady quivered down the phone. "I'm only the cleaner. No one gets here till nine."

Vinny slammed the phone down. It was 8.20.

Nine o'clock on the dot he called again. "Hello, Globe Hop."

"John Moston, please."

"Is he expecting your call, sir?"

"Yes."

"Can I take your name?" She could have been a machine.

"Vincent Croston. Personable Computers."

"Let me check the list." She paused at what Vinny figured was a pretence. "I'm sorry, sir, but John doesn't appear to have you on his list. Can I help?"

"I'm calling to make an appointment regarding the supply of Computer Equipment."

"We already have an established supplier who satisfies our needs, sir," she lied again. "You may leave your number in case that changes."

Vinny started to sound desperate. "Look, I can save John thousands on a purchase he's about to make. Can you please put me through?"

The phone went dead. No wonder Vinny hated Western women. His life was full to the brim of uneducated secretaries saying 'no' to him all day. He preferred have Oriental women saying 'yes'.

"Bollocks." He held his head in his hands and wracked his brains to try and find a way through.

When he looked up he noticed concentric rings forming in his coffee then felt the ground thunder as Toni tiptoed towards Sue's office.

"You all right, Vince?"

"Yeah." He shook his head. "Not really."

"What's up?" She could sense the opportunity to be of help.

"I've got this guy I know wants to buy but I can't get past the rottweiler."

"Give us a minute, I'll sort her out for you." Toni threw her head back and soldiered on towards Sue's office.

When she returned she scribbled Vinny's details on a Post-it note and trundled back to her desk. Vinny was silent. He stared at her desk like a football manager when his team was taking a penalty, as she spoke on the phone.

Moments later, she put the phone down and headed back to Vinny with the Post-it in her hand, looking triumphant.

"Right. He can't see anyone this week. But he's got a spot in his diary on Thursday next week." Vinny's face dropped. "But he's playing golf this Friday afternoon. That's the name of the club." She pressed the sticky paper onto his screen.

Vinny couldn't contain his grin. It wasn't particularly useful information but the fact that she'd managed to get any at all was leeway.

"How did you get through to him?"

"Well, I told the receptionist I'd left my knickers in his car last night and needed to speak to him. Then I asked if I could come and talk to him about office furniture." She purred as she walked back to her desk.

Vinny smirked. He'd seen her outrageous side in the pub and knew she wasn't joking.

It was lunchtime and Vince scratched his face before grabbing his coat and heading outside. Manchester in late November wasn't a sun-drenched place and he strolled round the city centre drawing heavily on his cigarettes (the Thai ones long since finished), wondering how he could turn the knowledge that John would be at Duxbury Gardens Golf Club in Chorley tomorrow into a sale. The Christmas lights cheered him. He thought of being in Pattaya on Christmas Day with Jeed, and the anatomical implications made him stride a little awkwardly.

"Keith." Back in the office Vinny was on the phone.

"Croston, you fat knacker." Vinny could hear the sound of Bolton Market's customers chattering in the background.

"Need a big big favour, mate." He sniffed briefly.

"Yeah, what's that?"

"Can you play golf?" he asked, expecting a negative.

"Does Mother Theresa take it up the arse?"

"All right then." Vin sighed. "Can you stand in a bar and look like you've been playing golf?"

"I can try my best." the signal started to break. "Vin, Vin."

"Bollocks."

Vinny's phone rang.

"Fucking signal's shit in here." Keith was crystal clear now with no background noise. "What is it you want again?"

"I need you to prop up a bar with me tomorrow afternoon in a golf club." Vinny's voice was filled with gravity.

"What is it? Should I get tooled up?"

Vinny chuckled. "Nah, just be a pisspot as usual, can you manage that? I'll fill you in on it tonight."

Vinny and Keith stood at the bar in Duxbury Gardens Golf Club, each wearing a pair of Keith's dad's slacks and V-neck woollen jumpers. Keith was a proud member of the Anglo Italian Friendship League and Vinny was a member of the East Lancashire Cooked Meat Buyers Association, according to the emblems on their knitwear.

Vinny had driven up to Preston on Thursday afternoon and hung about in Globe Hop's car park so that he would recognise the guy who got into the car in the MD's space. He'd briefed Keith on the background and they were waiting for him in the bar so they could subtly grab his ear and usurp Intra Tech and Dean's sales pitch.

An hour and two pints each passed with no sign of John. Although Vinny knew what the guy looked like he really knew nothing about him so he was just going to wing it when he arrived.

Two hours passed and the initial anxiety of pulling a ruse had melted. Now the problem was staying sensible. By 4.30 the pair were as sober as Catholic priests, talking about previous conquests, retired footballers, incarcerated friends and the forthcoming trip.

The bar was only supporting four or five customers when John Moston, bald, tanned and well fed, pushed the double doors open. Vinny recognised him straight away.

"Here's yer man," he whispered to his pint, signalling the arrival of their quarry.

Keith glanced up at John briefly. He was alone.

"Double whisky, no ice," John wheezed through a phlegm-filled throat at the bartender. He was in his early fifties and obviously enjoyed the finer side of life.

Gulp. "Another." He slammed the glass on the table.

"Jeez, I needed that," he gurgled at no one in particular.

Vin sensed an opening. "You on yer own?" He looked over to John.

"Aye, my partner's gone back to the Mrs."

"How'd your round go?" Vin could only just remember they were in a golf club.

"Shite."

Vinny started to snigger. This was a bear with a sore head. "Fucking week of it, I've had. I need my medicine now." The bartender looked at John with one part disdain and two parts worry. He was obviously one of the bigger spenders in the bar, but that didn't always make you the best customer in polite establishments.

John turned and started to eye Vinny and Keith. They'd made contact and weren't members he recognised. To him that probably meant he hadn't upset them before.

"You blokes want a drink?" he gurgled through his trachea.

Vinny's eyes lit up. "Aye, two lagers please, mate."

While the barman obliged, John pulled a stool up to the dynamic duo so he could share with them his misfortune over the previous seven days.

"So, you two been members long?" Not that he was interested, just an opener before a whinge.

Vinny was grinning from ear to ear. It wasn't meant to be this easy.

"Just joined." He smiled with his full face, not just the Personable sycophantic lip smile.

"Three years I've been here now. Might not renew though this time. Sick of the place."

Vinny read that more as the place being sick of him judging by his moaning and the pace he'd put his first two double whiskies down.

"Do you want a drink?" Keith proffered.

"Aye, lager now I've warmed my throat up." John pushed away his empty tumbler.

The barman obediently poured a pint of lager, which John grasped before he'd had chance to place it on the bar. He gulped down over a third in one go.

Vinny was starting to like this guy, a true pisspot, a kindred spirit.

Keith remembered the matter in hand even if Vinny was letting his emotions get in the way. "So what is it you do?"

John let out a short, high-pitched fart. "I'm Managing Director of a travel company." He gulped another third of his pint and belched.

"Anyone we know?" Vinny was back on the scent.

"Globe Hop." He looked at the remaining third of a pint and decided not to take a sip for fear of looking greedy.

"I've heard of them. Aren't they in Blackburn?" That was a deliberate mistake from Vin to keep him talking.

"Nah, Preston." He swelled with pride. "I've got a hundred bloodhounds flogging flights and packages over the phone."

Keith and Vin nodded in approval.

"Must be stressful," Keith empathised.

"Is when your PA walks out on you."

"What?" Vinny sounded shocked.

"PA walked out yesterday morning. I've been, err, ahem, treating her more like a lady than a PA the last two months and she just ups and leaves." He gulped at the last of his beer.

"My round." Vinny was concealing a giggle, remembering Toni's words.

"Phone's not stopped ringing, and then to top it all I've got some wide-boy salesman telling me to fork out over half a million on updating my computer system."

Vin could sense his cue but Keith took it for him while he was waiting for the drinks.

"Vinny here flogs computers, don't you?"

"Fucking shop's shut, mate. Birthday." He did his best to look disinterested.

"Birthday! You'll be having a drink then?" John looked like a helmsman taking the rudder.

"The thought had crossed my mind."

"Aye, well, put your money away and get chasers with them three pints." John reached for his wallet in his back pocket.

The barman shook his head and poured out three whiskies as well.

The afternoon turned into early evening and Keith and Vinny took John's advice and agreed never to employ a Pakistani. They also wholeheartedly vowed never to marry a woman who dyed her hair, or to have kids. When informed that all southerners were homosexual, they professed that they were already aware of that fact, and in mind of John's instructions they promised to try and remember never to drink with Scousers.

They also consumed half a gram of cocaine each during a series of visits to the lavatories in order to keep pace with John's drinking, and shared a taxi to a pub down the road with him where his carcass was welcome only because it housed his wallet.

By the end of the evening they'd had a curry forced down their necks, been told that they were, "Good blokes, you two," by a nineteen-stone barrel of beer with a pulse. And Vinny had secured a meeting, "On Wednesday when I've sobered up," on the proviso that he wouldn't, "Team up with my ex wife to try and rob me," the way Intra Tech had done.

On Monday Vinny spoke to the credit-control department at work and had Globe Hop checked out. They were good for a lot of credit. John, despite his grouchy approach to life, had built a very good business running at around £30 million a year. No wonder he didn't mind buying a pint. Vinny was starting to get anxious now. He only had two weeks remaining in work to get a sale done and John was his only hope; if this one didn't come off he'd be in deep deep trouble.

On Wednesday Vinny skipped the office, telling Sue that the meet was at 9.30.

"Best to go straight there." His nerves were showing through when he spoke to her without smiling.

When he arrived in Globe Hop's office in Preston ten minutes early at 10.50 he was shitting himself. A lot depended on this meeting going well.

Sitting in his car he eyed himself in the vanity mirror on the back of the driver's sun visor. He straightened his tie and patted down his hair. It was his little good-luck ritual and he performed it subconsciously before every business meeting.

Waiting in reception he took in his surroundings. The receptionist had buzzed through to John and offered Vinny a drink while he waited. It was a well-furnished place with expensive leather settees, and a sleek black coffee table housed a host of travel-industry publications. Vinny eyed the plaques behind the receptionist (a temp, he'd guessed) showing Globe Hop to be reseller of the year for a variety of airlines. He sipped at his coffee as John appeared from around a corner. He'd managed to force his less-than-slender frame into a suit and was puffing and wheezing at the effort of having to walk in a straight line on a level surface.

"Ah, Mr Croston." He extended his hand for Vinny to shake from the seated position on the sofa.

"John, how are you?" Vinny beamed and took up the offer to exchange handshakes.

"Surviving. We'll pop through to my office." John wiped his nose across the back of his hand and led Vinny through his empire. His office was decked out similarly to Personable's, banks of desks with women wearing headsets constantly making bookings for Mr and Mrs Customer's next trip abroad.

Once inside his private office, a pretty nondescript affair with a computer on a desk and big leather chair, John took the initiative.

"Right, don't give me any bullshit. I need an E10, there's the spec." He pushed a piece of paper across his desk to Vinny. "My IT manager wants two of the buggers but I'm too tight fisted. Don't give me any bollocks about installation or maintenance, my IT man can do all that. I pay the bastard enough."

"What price did Intra Tech quote you?" Vinny looked up from the piece of paper in his hand.

"Six hundred." John tapped the desk with a pen.

Vinny sucked his lips and frowned. "Six hundred grand is about the standard price. Because you have to be a Sun-authorised dealer. You need to stick to a price structure otherwise they remove your licence."

John gave him that 'don't bullshit me' look that gritty Lancastrian businessmen practice every time they pass a mirror to save them negotiating verbally.

"I think we could get it down to five-fifty, but we'd need to shorten the payment terms to a week rather than twenty-eight days because of the discount." Vinny looked at him expectantly.

It was John's turn to suck his lips. "Five hundred."

"Five-twenty?" Vinny returned the volley expecting the game to carry on.

"Done." John fixed him with a glare that meant 'fuck me about and I'll kill you'.

Vinny smirked, "Right you are then, five hundred and twenty grand, payment within seven days of delivery. I can write out a purchase order now. Once you've signed it I'll speak to the guys at the warehouse. When can you take delivery?"

"I could take delivery today, but my IT man's not around. I won't sign now, I want to read the small print. I don't believe in credit. You'll get a BACs transfer when it gets here." John wheezed and looked down. It was a sad moment for him. Agreeing to part with over half a million quid was never easy, no matter how much money you made.

"Thing is." Vinny could taste blood. "We've got a big sales team, and 'cos we keep 'em in stock if someone sells the last one I might not be able to honour the price." Vin wiped his mouth to hide the lie. "We have got a cooling down period of a week. If you read anything in the purchase agreement and warranty you don't like, you can pull out."

John looked unimpressed.

"If you sign now I can have the warehouse guys put barbed wire round one so it's yours, and we'll deliver once you tell me your satisfied with the terms." It was his last gasp.

"Go and wait in reception. I'll read it and let you know." John turned his pen into an imaginary cigar and took a puff.

Vinny sat down on the leather sofa in reception with his hands clasped and held low between his knees for ten minutes. John was leafing through the purchase agreement he'd left him. He paced to and fro across the reception area, much to the amusement of the temp manning the phone for five minutes. Leaning on the doorframe outside he sucked three cigarettes down to the butt.

Back in reception he drank four cups of water and leafed hurriedly through two travel-industry magazines. Fuck, this was bad for his nerves. Everything depended on that fat swine signing.

Outside, he lit his fourth cigarette in 25 minutes and resigned himself to failure. He was halfway through it, considering throwing himself off the top of a Pattaya hotel on the last day of his holiday rather than return home to unemployment, when he heard the aluminium-framed smoked-glass door creak open.

"Thought you'd buggered off, lad." John's shiny crown was poking out of the gap in the double doors.

"Just, errm, getting a bit of fresh air." He hid the cigarette behind his back as he exhaled a lungful of white smoke.

"Come in and warm your arse in my office. You look like a tramp, lad." John was smiling.

Vinny was still expending nervous energy at the rate a rapist would waiting for the jury to return. He sat down opposite John Moston at his desk.

"Right. I'm a tight bastard but I know a good deal when I see one." He was warming to Vinny. "And any bloke who can match me drink for drink's worth a chance. So I've signed."

Vinny's heart rate surged momentarily then dropped back to normal. His breathing slowed. During the wait his heart and lungs had been racing. He was lost for words.

"We'd been planning this for six months and your terms are same as Intra Tech's. But you've beat 'em on price so we'll go with you." He handed the counterfoil of the carbon copied purchase order to Vinny with his signature on it.

Speechless again he looked at it and tugged at the paper to make sure it was real.

"Cat got your tongue, lad?" John growled at him.

"Yeah. Errm, I mean no, yeah." Vin felt light headed as if he were about to faint. He loosened his tie. "Thanks, I'll give you a delivery date."

Vincent clutched the paper and headed out of the office. It was the best he could to stop himself from breaking into a sprint. Now he knew what it must have been like for the 1966 World Cup squad.

In the car park Vinny could hardly contain himself. With a small amount of skulduggery and a little help from his friend, he'd hit the jackpot, providing Fatty Moston didn't invoke the cooling-down clause.

Walking to his car the nerves in Vinny's hands and feet started to jangle. Once inside he ground his teeth hard and with a clenched fist slowly, very slowly, punched the steering wheel.

It took him ten minutes and three attempts to get his key in the ignition. The drive back to Manchester was surreal, like he was anaesthetised or on that rape drug, where you were only half aware of what was going on. On the motorway a Ford in the outside lane beeped long and angrily as he swerved into its path. The brush with automotive death brought him back to his senses. It made him more aware, although he was still in endorphin oblivion.

Once back in the office he trod across the carpet carefully to Sue's cubbyhole. The pile of the blue carpet seemed richer than usual. Meekly he knocked on her door.

"Hi, Vince. Good meeting?" She was looking anxious. He couldn't read her face. Did she want him to have made a sale or was she hoping she could sack him?

"Think so." He was half playing with her, half still unconvinced that it would all go through.

"What do you mean?" She looked concerned.

"Well, he's signed up for an E10 but there's still the seven-day cool-down to cover." He couldn't bear to look at her.

"Well done." She put her pen down. "What price?"

"Five-twenty." He shrugged in mock disappointment. "Bit off the list price, like, but still a sale."

"Great, excellent, well done." She started to hover in the chair. Vinny's nasal receptors noticed a familiar musky feminine smell.

"I've got the purchase order here." the counterfoil had become crumpled. It had been kissed more than once on the motorway. He flattened it out on the desk in front of her. She picked it up and eyed all the detail. Everything in order, she grasped her pen and signed it quickly. Sue was as anxious as Vinny to get the business.

"Hand that in to Mick and he'll sort out the delivery." she passed the slip back across her desk to Vinny.

He turned and ran, well, walked really but he just didn't feel comfortable in her presence. It was a defiant salute he'd provided her with and he smiled with immense pride as he sauntered over to Mick.

"All right, geezer?" He wiped his mouth. The excitement was making him salivate like a hungry dog. "Stick that in the in tray. Make sure it's fucking there a week today." He stressed the 'fucking' and headed out of the door.

By the time Janet and Toni joined him in Del Sol at 5pm he was almost asleep on the bar. Sue was to their rear in her fur-collared overcoat and her patent black handbag. Happy, groggy and incoherent, it took Vinny every ounce of spiritual energy to utter the magic word, "Pint," and then hug Toni for getting through to John in the first place.

After a while Vinny attempted the upright position on his bar stool, lit the wrong end of a cigarette, burped and muttered, "Taxi." He could well have told Toni and Janet he loved them but his memory of that was vague. When he tried to prize himself from the stool and head for the door Toni pushed him back into his chair while Janet called for a cab on her mobile.

Vinny woke with his torso on the futon. He undressed and clambered into bed.

The following days before the delivery date were agonisingly slow in passing and Vinny had more than one pint during the lunch hours. Manchester was full of Christmas shoppers during the daytime and it went dark at four o'clock. As well as nervously hoping that Fatty Moston didn't cancel, Vince managed to get a couple of grand's worth of travellers cheques on his credit card, along with some currency and three weeks' worth of travel insurance. The day before the delivery date Vinny rung Pete Jensen in Pattaya, he wrote down some numbers on a sheet of paper and then typed them up on his PC and printed them off on Personable headed paper.

When the arrival day came, Vinny went along with the delivery van to do his bit on the customer-service front.

The IT manager, a pimply young geek who'd reached his mid-thirties, was ecstatic when the tailgait of the truck dropped to reveal a box the size of a washing machine with the Sun Microsystems logo emblazoned on it. When the lift at the back of the van lowered it to within touching distance he ran to embrace it like a proud father holding his newborn.

"Fucking surprised he's not got his camcorder for posterity," John grunted disapprovingly, looking at his Head of Systems.

"Need your moniker on the delivery note and cash-transfer document before we can officially let you have it," Vincent insisted before the deliverymen wheeled it indoors.

"Aye, just nip in reception, lad," Moston huffed. With only a cursory glance, he scrawled his name nonchalantly on the papers Vinny produced for him.

"Drink," the big spender insisted.

"Why not." Vinny smiled and put his hand out to be shaken.

"You're paying." His fat suntanned, greasy paw almost wrenched Vinny's arm out of its socket.

The afternoon in the pub was painful. Vinny didn't like the guy in all honesty; kept him out of the office though. Personable's *de facto* salesman of the month drove home very carefully after six beers and looked in his mirror constantly in case of police behind him.

On Thursday Sue made a fuss of him when he arrived at eleven o'clock. Vinny had been to the doctors. He'd planned to pretend he was having difficulty sleeping to get sedatives for the plane, but after the last couple of weeks' coming and going he wasn't lying.

Vin put the finishing touches to his packing on Thursday night. He'd learned over the years not to overdo it on trips to Thailand: three pairs of trousers, five or six shirts, a couple of pairs of shorts and a few T-shirts was usually enough, along with toiletries and his CD Walkman with portable speakers and a couple of pairs of shoes. It all fitted neatly into a Reebok sports bag. Had to remain loyal to Bolton, didn't he?

While Vinny opened a can of beer before bed the phone rang. It was Keith.

"Waheeeey. Vinny, how are you?"

"Not ser bad. Yourself?" He was tired and ready for bed.

"Fuckin' wicked. Buzzin'. Can't wait, man. Over the moon. Packed and everything." Keith sounded like an eight-year-old running down the stairs at seven o'clock in the morning on Christmas Day.

"Yeah, should be a good laugh. What time you pickin' us up on Sat'day?" Vinny wasn't over excited. He felt more like a five-day commuter heading home for the weekend after his week's toil in London.

"'Bout nine-thirty."

"See you then, then. Don't forget your pyjamas."

On Friday Vinny went for a drink after work with some of the staff.

long time

When Keith pulled up at Vinny's on Saturday morning he was dressed and ready for the off. Toni sat beside him on the sofa sipping a cup of coffee. The pair had avoided eye contact since crawling out of bed.

Vinny heard the horn beep.

"That'll be Keith. He can drop you at the station." Vinny looked up coyly, expecting an answer. Toni just grabbed her handbag.

"Right, well, I'll see you New Year then," she huffed.

"Yeah. I'll look forward to it," Vinny lied.

He grabbed his bag and she followed him out. Before leaving, Vinny had a quick run round. All the windows were shut and locked. The heating was off. He looked around his living room. The sum of his life's achievements lay before him: a telly, a video, a few CDs and a hi-fi.

"Arrgh. Fuck yers." He shook his head and pulled the door shut.

When he reached the car he could see Keith in the driver's seat with his sunglasses on. His younger brother was on the passenger's side ready to drive the car back from the airport.

Toni trotted into the street and jumped in the car.

"OK dropping Toni off at the station, mate?" Vinny could see in the mirror that Keith was smirking.

The four of them drove into the centre of Bolton in silence.

When Toni shut the door behind her at the railway station the car filled with the raucous laughter of three irreverent males.

"What the fuck was that?" Keith had to raise his voice to be heard above he chorus of Vinny and his brother.

"She's rolling a fag with her arse while she walks." Keith's brother pointed at her rear end as she walked into the station.

"Lovely personality," said Vinny, rolling out the old excuse.

"Aye, she looks it," said Keith with an unforgiving look.

Tears were almost rolling down Vinny's cheeks. "Woulda been bad manners not to give her a Christmas present. Mind you, I burned me arse on the lightbulb doin' it."

"I've heard she's got her own postcode," Keith dropped in.

On the way to the airport the three ran through a list of polite explanations for her physique, including a healthy appetite, a salad allergy and a desire not to conform to stereotypical media images.

They waved Rich, Keith's younger but near-identical brother, goodbye and headed for the check-in.

The pair dropped their luggage on the conveyor and bade it farewell while having their tickets and passports checked and confirmed on the computer. Keith flirted with the check-in lady; Vinny decided to wait till Bangkok.

"So what do we do now?" Keith looked at the stubs of paper in his hand mournfully. They had cost him 700 quid.

"Bar." Vinny steered him through the shops towards the departure lounge.

"How long's the flight?" Keith probed. Vinny knew he was in for a barrage of questions and was preparing to make interrogation easier with alcohol.

"'Bout eleven hours once we've changed in Amsterdam." Vinny looked at his watch and was surveying the concessions in the airport mall.

"Fuck, what are you supposed to do?" Keith had been told a few times about the length of the flight but the reality of spending eleven tedious hours in the same seat was beginning to hit home.

"Cunning plan." Vin produced the blister strip of sleeping pills he'd got on prescription and waved them under Keith's nose. "Any road, gotta get some johnnies in Boots. Thai brand are shite and last thing you want's a split un."

The till girl blushed as Vinny paid for three packs of a dozen condoms, and avoided his eyes as she hurriedly packed them in a semi-translucent carrier bag.

Ahemm! Vinny coughed politely. "Can I have the receipt in case they don't work?"

Keith covered his mouth to hide the laugh while the girl's blush grew deeper.

Vinny and Keith strolled past hoards of travellers, business and leisure, through Passport Control, through security and into the departure hall, with Vinny displaying to the world the Durex logo through the white of the Boots bag. His carrier raised an eyebrow at the x-ray machine and a smirk when he placed it on the bar nearest the departure gate.

"My round. I owe you one for the golf club."

Five gulped pints each later and their flight was called. Vinny was flushed from the beer.

It took an hour and a half to get to Schipol and the pair legged it out of the departure area to the mall full of shops and bars to carry on drinking and get their last fix of nicotine for eleven hours. They had to show their passports again to get back to the gate and were merry and airborne in no time.

With the ascent over the meal was served. The beauty of the Dutch hostesses stunned Keith; Vinny's mind was elsewhere. Full of airline fare, Vinny ordered two Jack Daniels with Coke and passed Keith a sleeping pill. Down the hatch.

"We'll be there before you know it, kidder," said Vinny.

Keith was looking worried.

"What's buggin' yer, man?" Vince was his guide and his friend's welfare was a high priority.

"I've never really liked Chinky birds. Will I find one I fancy?"

Vinny put his best bedside manner on. "Well… There's quite a few of them, like. Chances are one'll catch your eye along the way."

"But I've never paid for sex!" Keith's head slipped forward.

Vinny laughed, looking at the big-time drug dealer shitting himself at going to see a brass. He ordered another JD and gulped it down quick as his own sedative took hold.

Vinny woke. The seat next to him was empty. He looked at his watch it said 5 o'clock. Did it mean morning or night? He looked at the TV screen. The white writing said, LOCAL TIME AT DESTINATION 12:07, ESTIMATED ARRIVAL TIME 13:52. Vin felt odd. He was expecting to be ecstatic, but somehow he just felt normal. The noise of the lock on the toilet door down the aisle being unbolted caught his ear. Keith emerged and wandered down the aisle looking bog-eyed.

"Mornin'" Vinny looked up from adjusting his watch.

"Fuckin' is as well, innit." Keith was trying his best to be articulate.

"Soon be there, sunshine." Vin chirpily took on the parental role before heading to the bog.

The landing was smooth. Having a quick wash and crap, a drink and a play with the headset helped pass the last hour and three quarters. The plane eased to a halt. Vinny rested and smiled to himself before unbuckling his belt. All around him passengers were clambering out, banging their heads and generally getting stressed. Keith looked at Vinny and saw a level of serenity in his face he'd only seen once before, on his grandma's corpse in the open casket. A hint of Bangkok's warmth had seeped into the cabin. Our heroes headed down the aisle. Vinny took pole position with his bag of rubber lifesavers in his grasp. He paused at the door. He didn't even notice the hostess wishing him a pleasant stay. He took a single step onto the platform. Bangkok's humid hand gently caressed his neck and he closed his eyes. It stroked down his neckline like a sensuous lover waiting for her returning soldier before brushing against him in her negligee. "You're home, darling. I love you," she whispered. Vinny spread his arms, johnnies in hand like a condor.

"Fucking hell, Vinny, there's folk tryna gerrof!" Keith squawked, ruining the moment.

"Sorry, ark." Vinny headed down the steps.

Inside the shuttle bus to the terminal he could see Keith on his tail. He was being embraced by a lady as well, only the woman welcoming him hadn't been the gentle slender beauty that had greeted Vince. Keith was being straddled by a nineteen-stone miner's wife from Wigan. On an E. Sweat was pouring off him. He was wearing the gravest of frowns and pulling at the shirt that had become instantly soaked to his chest.

No point hiding the laugh; this was treat number one for Keith.

"It's a bit fucking warm," said Keith once he found safety next to Vinny.

"Thought you Itai's were used to a bit of heat." Vinny looked over his shoulder at some guy's four-foot wife.

"'M only half fucking Itai though, arn I?" Keith protested.

The shuttle bus docked and the pair were inside Don Muang. They walked up a gantry and onto a marble-floored corridor.

Vinny breathed in. The warm musty smell that tingled the nostrils for the first few days in Krung Thep made him smile.

"What's that smell?" Keith's nose was turned up in disgust.

"Bangkok." Vinny slapped him on the back. "Lovely, innit."

Vinny smiled at the AMAZING THAILAND banner on the wall as the pair's trainers squeaked on thc marble floor.

Keith saw his first real Thai in a blue quasi-military uniform stood with his back to the wall doing nothing. The guy was your average Joe, dark skinned, mid-forties, five-foot two without an ounce of fat on him. Keith was transfixed, eyeing him head to toe. He walked into the back of a fat bloke.

"They're not like Chinks, are they," Keith gasped. "More half paki crossed with a miniature chink."

Vinny nodded his head and headed for the flat-roofed brown greenhouse down the way where a group of nicotine addicts were fending off the painful detox.

The pair filled their lungs with tar and headed into the corridor. Keith was struggling to keep pace with Vin. They walked for what seemed like a mile to Passport Control.

A long line of farangs stood sort of patiently at each of the four manned desks. It was a good profile of Thailand's 10,000 weekly visitors. Eighty per cent were male. Youngish guys in groups of four stood around in knee-length shorts and bright T-shirts, looking like surf-dude rebels heading for the islands; guys in semi-business dress stood on their own next to briefcases; there were guys in their early fifties heading for Pattaya, slacks, short-sleeved shirt and bum-bag wedged under their massive beer guts. It was the Pattaya uniform. There were guys like Vinny and Keith as well waiting impatiently to pass through, grab their luggage and find heaven behind a curtain.

The pair reached the front of the queue. Vinny passed his documents to the guy in the brown uniform. It was the same one who'd stamped his papers every time he'd entered or left the country. He didn't look up. He didn't smile. There was no, "Good to see you, Vince. There's a happy hour at Pink Panther tonight," just a sullen glare at the passport, a quick check of the entry card he'd filled in, a couple of stamps and a staple. He hadn't even noticed the bag of Durex Vinny had rested on the desk.

Just thirty days' entry graciously granted to the Kingdom of Thailand.

Keith waited anxiously behind the worn red line on the floor. The guy looked up and stretched out his hand. Keith shuffled forward and waited for his visa to be granted.

The pair headed down the stairs to the luggage hall, grabbing a trolley on the way.

"All right, our kid?" Vinny was in the driving seat.

"Yeah. 'S a bit cooler in 'ere." Keith was looking at the stamp on his passport and leafing through the useless bits of paper he'd collected on his journey. There were a couple of bags that looked similar to theirs cruising along the rubber flaps of the conveyor. They'd been thrown on haphazardly by the handling staff. It took ten minutes for theirs to arrive and Vinny hauled the trolley round for the dash through the customs post. Two guys manned the desk. Vinny had always wondered why these guys were fatter than your average Thai. No hassles. The new arrivals looked at them with a touch of paranoia, but their angst was replied with a broad, warm, genuine smile that said, "Go and get all that Western sadness sucked out of you through the pipe at the top of your legs."

They headed through the brown glass double doors into the arrival hall.

"Jeez." Keith was stunned. "Fuuuuckin' 'ell!" The cacophony of chattering Asians hit him. Vinny smiled.

Smell plus noise equals Bangkok. Inside the airport it was only half the equation. They'd landed. Vinny headed out of the pen fenced by chrome railings towards the left-hand exit. He looked over his shoulder. Keith was bewildered, looking left then right, then turning and repeating the neck exercise.

"Keith." Vinny had to raise his voice to get his buddy's attention.

They walked through the gap in the railings and past the hoards of chaperones waiting for visitors, signs in hand for MR AND MRS REILLY NEWPORT and hundreds of others like them.

They forced their way out of the building, past bodies that only reached shoulder height, and that was when the heat hit them, and the noise. The Bangkok traffic was deafening. Even Vinny started to sweat. After a cigarette each they headed for the queue at the taxi stand.

Keith minded the trolley while Vinny got the chit for an official ride.

"*Sukumvit*."

The girl pulled out a ticket and stamped it without looking up and Vinny jumped into the road where 100 yellow and green and 80 red and blue taxi's waited to ferry people down town. The drivers stood around in pairs, shirtsleeves rolled up, looking tough, hot and dark.

Vinny approached a group of three of them with his chit in one hand. The guy just pointed over his shoulder at a taxi driver pushing his car slowly forward, both hands on the boot and smiling at the throng of passengers. The guy spotted Vinny and his smilegrew; only half of the front of his upper jaw was filled with teeth. He beckoned when he saw the chit and ran to put on the handbrake.

"Keith, you nobhead." It was the second time he'd had to raise his voice. "What you doin'?"

Keith was standing in front of the ticket booth, transfixed. The girl hadn't seen him. His hands were by his side and his eyes seemed glazed.

"Keith," Vinny shouted again and finally got his attention. "We're in 'ere."

Keith picked up the two sports bags and winced under their weight. Vinny trotted over to join him while the driver opened the boot. The effort was pushing beads of sweat out of Keith's skin. Vinny hopped into the front.

Keith looked drained when he joined them. He was still careening to get a glimpse of the ticket girl.

"Got a sweat-on, matey?" Vinny was smirking at Keith's enchantment with his first Thai sweetheart.

"That bird at the desk was fit as a butcher's dog." He had been stunned for about the third time in an hour.

Vinny laughed. "Didn't notice her. Anyway, thought you didn't like Chinky birds."

Vince directed his attention to the driver. "*Sukumvit Soi Nueng*."

The driver nodded and pulled into the traffic. Keith's gaze caught a traffic cop in his skin-tight brown uniform, five-foot two (the national average), with his face covered by sunglasses, smog mask and his golden motorcycle helmet. His white-gloved hands were gyrating as he guided the traffic. He could have been a well-designed robot showing barely any human traits.

"Where the fuck have you bought me?" Keith inadvertently spat a lipful of sweat onto Vinny's neck.

"Caught you off guard, has it?" Vinny was smiling. He felt like Scaramanger watching Roger Moore trapped in the maze of mirrors on his island, only with less deadly intentions.

"There's plenty more surprises, kidder, don't worry." Vinny turned to the driver. "OK for cigalette?"

Keith spent the hour in the taxi in stunned silence, weighing up the offbeat new world around him. The mass of traffic, the concrete ramps, the tower blocks, all of which seemed to be TO LET, and the advertising billboards. His only words were, "Why do you have to pay for the road?" when they hit the expressway.

Vinny spent the journey down town explaining to the driver that they were from Manchester (easier than Bolton), that he liked Thai lady (very sexy iss goot), that he had a girlfriend in Pattaya and that David Beckham was a *katoey*.

They eventually headed off the expressway by descended a ramp and were joined at the traffic lights by a herd of guys on 100cc motorbikes wearing flip-flops and acrylic waistcoats with Thai writing on them.

Here the contrasts began to show. To the left were the makings of a shantytown: tin shacks, broken-down pick-up trucks, shoeless kids kicking a ball, food stalls. A hundred yards away was the Landmark Hotel, glistening and sparkling in the sun.

They turned left onto Soi 1 and drove slowly in the heat past cheap hotels, restaurants and hairdressers.

"*Leeo Kwa*," said Vinny, showing off what he'd learned on the tape. The driver obeyed and turned right down a side street.

"Stop, Stop."

The driver ground to a halt. They'd arrived at Sara Inn, Vinny's Bangkok billet on his last couple of trips. "Wait here, our kid."

Vince hopped out of the cab and strolled up the concrete ramp to the entrance area. He strolled into reception, and the owner – a smiling, beautiful (for a 40-year-old), brown-skinned lady – was sat at the desk. Was she smiling because she recognised him or because she always smiled?

"Hello." Her voice was soft and warm.

"*Sawasdee krap*." Vince was on friendly territory.

"You hap leserwayshaarn?" Her eyes were big and expectant.

"No. No. Not have reservation. Need two room. Sawng room." Vin was leaning on the counter.

The lady sucked her lips. "Solly, sah. Hotel full."

"Shit," Vince cursed under his breath. He looked over his shoulder and could see the driver helping Keith haul their bags out of the boot.

"OK, you know where have loom? Room?" His mispronunciation was kicking in quickly.

"You know Nana Inn? Soi Thlee." She pointed out of the door.

Vinny shook his head. Sweat was forming on his brow.

"OK, Soi thlee, turn lept. Hap loom." She nodded confidently and handed him an address card for the Nana Inn. "Same familee."

A relieved smile cracked on Vinny's face. "Same owner. OK, good."

"*Khop khun krap*." He raised his thumb before heading out.

"*Khop khun kaa*," she sung back to him.

Vin walked out with a contented smile on his face. Dealing with helpful Thais was always a pleasure.

Keith looked up.

"No luck, kidder. Full up." Vinny was checking the address on the card he'd been given.

"You what?" Keith looked panic stricken. He was on the other side of the world in the strangest of strange countries and the hotel was full. They were going to have to sleep on the street and be buggered and robbed by tramps with AIDS and God knows what else.

"No worries. Uncle Vince find solution." He held up the card. "We just need t'nip round the corner."

"*Rua pai, Soi Sam*," he said to the driver.

They hauled the bags back in the boot of the cab and headed through the gleaming archway under the towering Bumramgrad Hospital.

"You can nip in there after for the lady-boy op." Vinny nodded towards the entrance.

"Yeah." Keith was intrigued.

"It's a snip at two thousand dollars." Vinny giggled.

"Owwrrrrgh." Keith winced and held onto his crotch in fear.

The taxi took them past the immaculately dressed guards, and onto the pristine private road that took them to Soi 3. The driver was careful; the sleeping policemen could ruin his suspension. At the junction with Soi 3 they stopped. A traffic guard had held his hand to halt them.

"*Leeo Sai.*" Turn left, Vince ordered the cabbie.

He shook his head. "Cannot." He pointed at the stream of traffic headed towards Sukumvit. "Von Vay."

"OK, stop." Vinny looked in the mirror and saw a couple of cars backing up behind them. "How much?"

"I've already paid the man," Keith interjected.

The driver inched to the side. Vinny grabbed his bag of condoms from the dashboard and the two hopped out. The boot was already unfastened and they hastily grabbed their bags and set them down on the pavement. Vin tapped the window, raised his thumb in thanks and the pair headed down the road. They strained under the weight of their bags and felt awkward pushing through diners sat at rows of worn plywood tables of a pavement restaurant. Vinny could see the big white sign hanging off a wall ahead with NANA INN written in big pink letters.

A glass-fronted building was their safe haven from fumes, beggars and heat. In the window there was a small fountain carved out of marble. Four ornate figures supported a brown marble ball twice the size of a basketball, and jets of water rotated it. The pair stopped for a second and eyed it.

"All right that, innit." Keith was impressed.

"Let's put a shift on, get down the boozer." Vinny could already taste the beer.

They pushed the double doors and almost tripped down the steps. A guy in a red bellboy jacket held the door for them and smiled, pointing with his hand to the reception desk.

The reception area was at least air conditioned. Their shoes squeaked on the black marble floor as they hauled their bags to the desk. A girl in her twenties sat at reception. The chair she was on was low. An older guy in her forties – her dad probably – was sat in the corner watching over proceedings.

"Hello, sah," said the girl, looking up at them with big, round, doe-like eyes. "You want loom?"

"Two rooms, please," said Vinny.

"Foh how many nigh, please, sah?" She looked down at her check-in book.

"Two, maybe three." Vinny shrugged his shoulders. How long was a piece of string?

"For one nigh, one thousan two hunled baht." She placed two check-in forms on the desk.

"Have discount?" Vinny chanced.

"OK, pay now, one thousan baht." She pushed the forms towards them.

"OK." Vinny smiled.

They sorted out the forms, handed over their credit cards, had their passports examined and signed the credit card chits. The girl handed two keys attached to two big brass tags to the bellboy. He reached for the guys' bags but Keith stopped him from picking his up.

"Don't be so fucking paranoid," Vinny instructed. "He aint robbin' yer."

Keith backed down. The young guy wasn't fazed by the weight of the two bags that these well-built Westerners had struggled with, and he led them to the lift and their rooms. He opened up 405 for Vinny, 407 for Keith and held his hand out. Keith reached in his wallet and placed a hundred-baht note in his hand. Vinny winced. The guy smiled and walked off silently.

"Quick shower then out, ark?" Vinny nodded in anticipation.

"Aye," agreed Keith.

The two doors shut in unison.

"Yes!" Vinny threw six quick uppercuts in the air. He clapped his hands. "C'mon!"

The room seemed decent enough. Nice big bed, wardrobe, dresser, bedside table and a few lamps. He flicked the light on in the bathroom, stepped inside and turned on the shower. Home and dry. Now the fun could start.

It took Vinny twelve minutes to shower, shave, put in some contact lenses, deodorise, dress in white canvass trousers, a black short-sleeved shirt and spray some aftershave on. He slipped on his trainers and headed out of the door.

"Keith, you nonce." He knocked once then pushed the door open.

Keith had a towel round his waist and was in front of the mirror with a pot of hair wax, carefully picking at strands of hair and moving them a millimetre or so to one side.

"Jesus Christ." Vinny put his hands on his hips.

"What's the Basil Brush?" Keith straightened his back like a peacock showing his fan and eyed himself carefully in the mirror.

"Listen, the birds ain't too fussed what y'look like." Vince moved the pack of cigarettes from his left to right hand. "But I'm dying of thirst. Get a shift on. I'll be in reception." Vinny looked round the room. Like the nancy boy he was he'd hung some shirts neatly in the wardrobe and placed all his toiletries in line on the dresser. Vinny shook his head and walked off.

When Keith eventually arrived in reception he looked like a fashion model in brand-new Armani silk shirt, his hair slicked back, sunglasses, perfectly creased white linen trousers and espadrilles.

Vinny whistled. “Ooooh. Sexy maaan.”

The pair hit the road and were welcomed by a chorus of horns beeping, motorbikes with unsilenced exhausts and tuk-tuks, tuk-tucking. The dry heat hit them. They started off down Soi 3 towards Sukumvit and the smell of fish sauce, garlic and chilli invaded their nostrils as they pushed their way through the roadside restaurant.

“What’s this place?” Keith asked as they passed Bamboo, a large wooden-fronted bar with its name spelled in crooked yellow letters and tall thin bushes masking it from the street.

“Bamboo,” Vinny elaborated.

Keith stretched his neck to look inside.

“We’ll call in for some breakfast tomorrow.” Vinny’s sights were set on Nana.

Keith looked to his left and saw the grand, tall white building of The Grace Hotel with its ramp and collection of taxis at the front. Ahead he could see The Landmark and The Nana Hotel. Keith had to quicken his pace to stay level with Vinny who was walking like a man possessed. Was Nana magnetic? Did Vinny have some secret lemming-like instinct to home in on the place?

They reached the end of Soi 3 and waited at the crossing. The traffic stopped and the pair jumped onto the zebra crossing. They walked down the middle of the black and white stripes when a motorbike almost hit them. Vinny panicked and performed a freaky dance to evade the collision, to the amusement of two young girls walking arm in arm safely a yard downstream of the crossing. Alive, they made it to the other side and congregated with the rest of the faithful facing Nana, wedged into the gap that gained them access to Sukumvit and the sacred ground beyond.

Keith looked up. “What’s that?” He pointed to the concrete platform resting on concrete ramps that stretched to his left and right as far as the eye could see.

“Skytrain. BTS. Fucking godsend for getting about on.”

The throng of worshippers got thicker but wave after wave of taxi, motorbike and tuk-tuk kept flowing down the road. The traffic stopped, and after their near-death experience the pair crossed a yard off the crossing rather than on it, along with most of the other pedestrians. The far carriageway was at a halt as well so they didn’t hover long on the central reservation.

Safely over Sukumvit, Vinny heaved a sigh of relief. He was beginning to sweat. He looked round at Keith and smiled. The 35 minutes he’d spent preening himself had gone to waste. Drenched in sweat and with his neatly combed hair forced to obey gravity by his perspiration, he was no different to anyone else.

The policeman in the traffic box didn't look up from his paper to say hello to Vince. Miserable git, thought Vinny, he'd bought him a beer once.

A mass of humanity was swarming in all directions. Mecca was always busy and they pushed their way through the crowds of bar girls proudly displaying new mobile phones, fat beneficiaries and cleavage or thigh – sometimes all four.

"Keith. Over 'ere." Vinny had forged ahead but Keith was stuck in a logjam and looked unsure of how to push his way through. Vinny gestured towards the Nana Hotel… Well, the bar built into the frontage called Golden.

Vinny stepped into the road and looked up at the sign above the walkway to Nirvana. NANA ENTERTAINMENT PLAZA. The sign was past its best and he briefly made a polite wai gesture.

"Sir, you wan' tuk-tuk?" a poorly fed pock-marked guy insisted. "Go massard, hap sexy girl."

Vinny ignored him. Keith was still bringing up the rear, delayed by everyone that passed in front of him. The same tuk-tuk driver that had pitched Vinny grabbed his attention and was assaulting his senses with a barrage of incomprehensible offers. Vinny had to retrace his tracks and grab his buddy by the arm in an effort to retrieve him from the grasps of the nuisance.

"Fuck off," Vinny suggested.

The guy looked at him blankly.

"What was he on about?" Keith looked perplexed.

"You'll get a lot of shit like that," Vinny elaborated. "They can tell you're straight off the plane."

The pair finally made it to the safety of Golden Beer Bar, a haven filled with groups of guys sat round circular tables drinking, chatting, laughing and flirting with the waitresses. Vince and Keith chose seats on the barrier that separated the dipsomaniac males from the masses.

"It's a top bar to sit and watch the world go by in, this one." Vinny paused and joined Keith in eyeing the diverse sample of Soi Nana's permanent and temporary patrons swarming to and fro.

A small girl in her early twenties approached them. She had her shiny black hair tied in a ponytail and wore a white blouse and black skirt. It singled her out as a waitress.

"Hello, sah. You wan' some dlink?" She had her pad at the ready.

"What y'avin', Keith?" Vinny was lighting a cigarette.

"Pint."

"Yer best stickin' to the bottles out 'ere, mate," Vin advised.

"Err. Carlsberg."

"*Sawng* Carlsberg, please," Vin instructed the waitress.

She returned moments later with two bottles of Carlsberg in polystyrene sleeves, an ashtray and a small bowl of nuts on a tray. Great care was taken to place them neatly in front the happy drinkers. She wrote out a chit and placed the bill in the plastic pot on the shelving the pair were leaning their elbows on.

Keith was transfixed by a group of three girls sat on the opposite side of road on the edge of the pavement, gracefully painting and decorating bamboo umbrellas to sell to gullible drunks or sober culture vultures later in the day. Vinny's mind was on other things; he was scanning the bar, or rather the ladies who worked in the bar, on a more recreational remit than just serving drinks.

He felt the prod of a finger in the wad of fat he'd carefully built up to protect his kidneys from impact wounds, and he looked round.

"Hello Wincent." A slender brown hand was offered for him to shake, which he gladly accepted.

"Aarn." He smiled and moved forward, gently pressing his cheek against hers.

"This is Aarn," said Vinny as Keith eyed her up and down. "Aarn, this my friend number one. Keith."

She smiled and offered her hand to Keith, which he gratefully accepted.

"You want drink?" Vinny offered. He knew she wouldn't refuse; it was her job.

"Sank you. *Nam som*." She pulled a free stool up and perched herself daintily between Vinny and Keith.

A waitress had miraculously arrived and obediently scurried off to the bar to return moments later carrying a glass of orange, and the menu Vinny had ordered.

Aarn smiled politely as Vinny stroked her leg.

Keith was dumbstruck. "Fuck me, she's fit as fuck," he muttered under his breath to his buddy.

Vinny laughed. "So, your starting to appreciate kitchen sinks then?"

"You speak too fast. I'm not understan'." Aarn looked paranoid for a moment.

"Keith say Aarn *sooway*." He stroked her leg again in reassurance. "*Sooway mak*."

She looked down coyly as she sipped her drink through a straw, while Vinny eyed the menu. Keith did his best to try and look like he was watching the world go by, but was attempting to catch sly glimpses of the delectable creature between them.

"You wanna try some of the food 'ere, kidder?" Vinny asked Keith.

"Might as well." Keith took a swig of his beer. "They go quick these bottles." He eyed the nearly empty green vessel.

"Aarn want *aharn*?" asked Vinny.

"Is OK. Have eaten," she replied with a polite smile.

"You can get for us *laarb nuen*, *laarb kai* and *sawng* Carlsberg." Vinny pointed the order out on the menu in case he'd mispronounced, and Aarn scurried away to the bar.

"Who's that then?" Keith was showing more than a passing interest.

“Shagged her a while back. Think it was the second time I came here.” Vinny drained his beer.

“Decent by your standards that, Vin.”

“Aye, had better shags but she’s decent lookin’ an a right nice girl, like. I try and make a point of saying hello when I pass through.”

Aarn returned from the bar with two fresh bottles of beer and took the empties out of the cooling sleeves and put the fresh ones in, turning the bottles neatly so the labels faced the two boozers. “Food come soon.” She took another sip of her drink.

Vinny pointed with his bottle towards the entrance to Nana Plaza across the road. “We’re off over there later. Nana Plaza.”

“I can read the sign,” said Keith indignantly.

“It’s sex maniacs’ Mecca. Perverts’ paradise,” Vinny elaborated. “If you can’t find a bird you like in there it’s time to hang your boots up.”

“It looks pretty busy,” Keith replied.

“There must be over five thousand birds in that gaff.” Vinny looked over his shoulder. A waiter in a bellhop’s uniform from the Nana Hotel was carrying a tray with two plates on it. “Food’s here.”

The waiter placed the two metal plates and the cutlery politely on the shelving and then presented a vinyl book containing the bill to Vinny. Vinny looked at the damage, pulled a few notes out of his wallet and placed them in the book. The waiter bowed politely. He came back moments later offering a small amount of change but Vinny waved to dismiss it.

“What’s this then?” Keith prodded the mass of mince that lay on a single lettuce leaf.

“*Laarb.*” Vinny dug in a forkful and swallowed. “Fucking delicious.”

“Yeah, but what’s in it?” Keith looked apprehensive.

“It’s, err, minced meat with chillis an’ onions an’ shit.” Vin gulped another forkful. “Give it a whirl.”

Keith dug and gingerly took a mouthful. He chewed a minute then swallowed. Vinny was watching him as he took another mouthful. Halfway through chewing he turned bright red and grabbed at his beer. “Fuck me, that’s hot.”

Vinny and Aarn were in fits of laughter. Aarn grabbed a napkin from the table next to them and wiped at Keith’s mouth.

“Is good you like spicy, no?” She rubbed his back gently.

“Yeah, but not that hot.” Sweat was pouring from his brow. “You trynna fuckin’ poison me ’ere, Croston?”

“Yer get used to it.” Vinny was merrily working away at his.

The pair worked their way through the food and another beer to wash it down, Keith eating in fits and starts, interspersed with gulps of beer and a wipe of his brow. By the end of the meal there was a mountain of paper napkins soaked in Keith’s sweat flapping in the breeze from the electric fans that were dotted round the bar.

Vinny paid the drinks bill, kissed Aarn gently on the cheek and the pair headed across the road. As they walked under the entrance sign, Keith's eyes were everywhere, staring unbelievably at every one of the dozens of petite girls milling around. Vinny forged on and led the way to the first bar in the middle of the courtyard. PHARAOHS the rustic brown lettering on the edge of the roof informed them. They had to work their way round a mass of parked motorcycles to get in the entrance, where two young girls greeted them. Pharaohs differed from Golden slightly in layout and size but mainly in the apparent ratios. There were probably seven customers at the most but over twenty-five girls. A group of around ten of them who were huddled in a corner started joking and laughing loudly in Thai when Vin and Keith walked in. After a while the fuss died down and they reverted to their pastimes of laughing and chatting among themselves, or flirting with the customers for drinks or the chance to be bar fined.

The smaller of the two girls that greeted them showed them to some chairs at the corner of the bar. They were below a fan, which didn't stop Keith from sweating, while Vinny ordered another *sawng* Carlsberg.

The beers hadn't arrived when a slender young beauty decided to introduce herself to Keith. She boogied over from the group of girls she was chatting to and gently flicked Keith's earlobe. Keith was startled and turned his head quickly to meet the big brown eyes boring into his. She giggled at his reaction and quickly his shock turned to a smile.

"Hello," she purred, confident of her charms.

"Fuckin' 'ell. Y'all right?" He was dumbstruck.

She giggled at the expression on his face. Vinny looked on in admiration. He didn't need to ask if Keith was getting to like Bangkok.

"Wassyonem?" her arm was on his shoulder now.

"Vin, I think you're gonna have t' interpret for us." Keith was captivated.

"I think she wants to know your name," Vinny explained.

"My name's Keith, love." He grabbed at his bottle as soon as the beer arrived. "What's yours?"

It was the ladies turn to look confused now. Keith wasn't used to making himself understood.

Vinny stepped in. "*Pu chai chu* Keith, *phom chu* Vinny. *Khun chu aria*?"

A look of comprehension landed on the girl's face. "Oh. Yo nem Kees, him Winny. My nem Dtom. Nite to meet you."

She held out her hand for Keith to shake and he obliged.

"Fuck me, are they all this direct?" Keith was excited by her boldness.

Vinny smirked. "She's taken the subtle approach, kidder."

"Winnneeeee!" The pair looked round to see who was shouting. In the middle of the bar was a small girl in her early twenties. Her round face and soft brown skin seemed to be glowing. There was a look of delight on her face as she recognised an old customer and she did her best to trot gracefully in her four-inch platform-soled boots across the bar.

"Nid. Good to see you." Vinny threw his arms open as she paced towards him and hugged then kissed him.

"Oh, so happy." She kissed him again. "My fliend say she see you but I not beeleef."

"Keith, this is Nid." Vinny looked over at his friend. In the time it had taken for Nid to say hello, Dtom had managed to wedge herself between Keith's legs and was launching a full-on assault on him, gently stroking the buttons on his chest. Keith looked content with his arm gently cradling her back.

"You want Cola?" Vinny asked Nid.

"OK." She was getting the eye of the girl behind the bar and a Coke was on the table with the chit in the pot in a second. Vinny looked over to Keith to see if his hostess was thirsty but could see that a small glass of Cola was in her hand already.

"You all right there, lad?"

"Not ser bad." Keith had to stretch his neck to be seen round the side of Dtom's head.

"Lookin' after yer, is she?"

"Aye, she is that, all right." He strained to straighten his back. "Got a fuckin' boner already."

Vinny laughed and eyed Dtom's shapely behind through her almost opaque white trousers, and nodded in approval.

"We'll sup these an' move on." Vinny couldn't let his mate be suckered by the first girl that said hello to him.

"Aye. Just let the swelling go down first." He gently eased Dtom off his leg and she took the cue to go back to talk to her friends. Not without kissing him sweetly on the neck first though. Keith blushed.

"Welcome to Bangkok." Vinny raised his bottle.

"Cheers," Keith replied.

"*Chok dee.*" Nid obeyed etiquette and chinked Vinny's then Keith's bottle with her glass.

"What's this '*chok dee*' bollocks?"

"*Chok dee*. Means good luck, cheers type o' thing." Vinny started to view his surroundings. He could see that Keith had been doing the same and had eyed the bars and curtained doorways below neon signs displaying words like RAINBOW 2 and SPIRITHOUSE. They had occupied his pupils for a while when he noticed the big golden shrine to the left of the entrance, shrouded in garlands of flowers and incense sticks. A girl dressed in black was standing in front of it with her hands clasped, holding burning incense sticks and praying to the shrine.

"See that all the time," Vinny pointed out. "Prayin' for good luck, like. It's mad as fuck. They're proper religious. Give it half an hour she'll be bollock naked on stage with a dildo up her arse and come midnight she'll be gettin' spit roasted by two Krauts."

"We off?" Keith knocked the last of his beer back.

"Aye, sort the bill out for us, Nid."

Nid grabbed the collection of chits in the pot and did her stilt act in her boots towards the bar.

"Keith. Word o' warnin'," Vinny interrupted as Keith feasted his eyes on a young girl in the next bar.

"Yer, what?"

"When yer see a bell in the bar, never ever ring it."

"Why?" Keith was only half listening.

"Tradition, like. You've gotta buy everyone a drink."

Keith made a note of it as Nid returned.

"Thlee hundled eighty baht."

Keith had his wallet at the ready. "I'll get these."

"Jesus." Vinny shook his head.

"What's up?".

"Don't go flashing that much lucre about." Vinny looked concerned.

Keith closed his wallet, quickly grabbing a purple five-hundred baht note and placing it on the tray.

"Keep the change."

Vin shook his head again. "I'm gonna have to have a word with you. We off in one of the go-gos?"

"I need to nip back to the hotel." Keith looked apologetic and combed his hair back with his hand.

"Aye, leave that fuckin' money in t'safe. How much is there?"

"'Bout three hundred quid."

The pair headed back to the hotel. They waited patiently for an eternity at the Sukumvit crossing and made their way down Soi 3 to the Nana Inn while Vinny explained to Keith that, while he might have a lot of money on him now, he'd have an empty wallet when he woke up.

"Why, will I get mugged?" Keith felt like the alien he was.

"You'll enjoy it more than a muggin', but they'll 'ave it off you all the same," Vin felt obliged to explain. "Anyway, what we goin' back to the hotel for?"

"Wait an' see."

Back at base camp Keith got his room key.

"I'll wait 'ere an' ave a bevy," said Vinny, heading to the small white bar in the reception hall.

"Come up in five minutes." Keith scurried off.

Vinny stood and sipped his beer while he wondered what was going on. He gave him seven instead of five minutes and took the lift up to the fourth floor. He knocked on the door.

"It's open," Keith's muffled voice explained.

Vinny walked in and could faintly smell freshly digested and defecated food from inside the bathroom.

“Fuckin’ ’ell, Keith. They’ve got bogs in the bars, mate. You could have had a crap in one of them.” He shook his head, bemused at his mate’s eccentricity.

“Aye.” He flushed the toilet and buckled his belt noisily then opened the door grinning. “But it wouldn’t have been much fun.” He grabbed Vince and showed him into the bathroom.

“*Voila!*” He smiled and pointed with the palm of his hand to a dark brown log sat serenely in the centre of the white enamel bath. “Exhibit A.”

Vinny held his head in his hands. “I know Asia can be a bit rustic at times but you didn’t have to lay a cable in the bath.”

Keith smirked. “All will become clear, my dear Hastings.” he put on his best Inspector Poirot accent. He turned on the shower and guided the jet at the offensive-looking turd. “You see, my fine English chum…” Keith loved play acting. “We ’ave what appears to be a simple lump of turd. But look as ze water ’elps it disintegrate.” He was trying his best to keep a straight face and maintain the Poirot voice. “Ah, *voila.*” He leaned into the bath and thrust his fingers into the melting brown mound, then held what he’d collected under the shower. “An ’Enry ze Eighth of ze finest Zorro.”

It was Vinny’s turn to look shocked. “I ’ope it’s good shit.”

“Fuckin’ scared the life out of me when we passed customs, that did,” stated Keith as he looked on proudly at the knotted condom in his hand.

“They machine gun drug smugglers ’ere, you know.” Vinny was starting to look serious. OK, he liked a toot now and then but getting caught with drugs in Thailand was serious. The prisons weren’t nice and the powers that be would take their time speaking to your embassy.

Keith quickly cut the condom open and spilt a small pile of powder on the dresser. He put the rest in a sealer bag he’d brought especially for the job. In no time he’d turned the mound into two lines and a rolled-up a note his went up his nostril. He passed Vinny the note. Vince shook his head. He didn’t fell comfortable with it but, never one to be a stick in the mud, he devoured the coke anyway. Keith placed the sealer in his shirt pocket and motioned for the door.

“Nah, Keith. You don’t wanna get caught with that shit out here. Seriously.” He sniffed and fingered his nose.

“Wassup? They won’t have a clue.” Keith looked nonchalant.

“Nah, trust me, kidder. Do another here and save it till later.”

Keith conceded and, with two lines of coke inside them, they headed out of the hotel.

“We back to that Nana Plaza gaff then?” Keith enquired. “I reckon that Dtom fancies me.”

Vinny smiled at Keith’s naivety. “Nah, I’ll take you down Soi Cowboy, kidder.”

“All right.” The coke was giving Keith an air of confidence.

Vinny flagged down a taxi and the driver headed down Sukumvit towards Soi 21. He dropped them off at what looked like a massive set of road works.

"Where the fuck 'ave you brought me?" Keith asked.

"Jus' have to nip through here." Vinny pointed through the road works.

They scurried across the road, dodging through traffic, and headed through the temporary barriers. Keith's face lit up as he saw the sight before him: a road 200 yards long decked out on either side with bars displaying names in neon like SHADOW, LONG GUN and RAWHIDE.

"My favourite part, this one, kidder." Vinny looked proudly down the street like an architect viewing one of his own creations. "At Nana they just want your dollars. 'Ere's a lot more laid back."

Keith's eye's bulged as he saw hoards of girls standing around outside the bars and in groups on the streets, giggling, scurrying to and fro and waving and calling out to punters.

They entered the street and Vinny pointed towards TILAC, it's pink neon sign flashing brightly above the two curtains that secreted the delights within from the world.

"Get us a seat an' a bevy in there, Keith. I've gotta go and get some fags." Vinny pushed Keith towards Tilac and walked up the road. Keith pulled the curtain back and headed inside anxiously.

Vinny shook his head. It was fun showing a virgin round town. Quickly he nipped into Toy Bar on the opposite side of the road. He had a surprise in store for Keith. Inside the door he stopped and surveyed the room in front of him until he found his quarry, an older lady in a suit who was stood at the bar. He approached her trying to look polite. "You Mamasan?" he enquired.

"Yes." she smiled.

"I come here one hour with my friend. When I go you have lady take care of him, OK?" He nodded in anticipation.

"OK, no problem." She nodded and smiled.

"How much?"

"Two lady, three lady?"

"Err. three lady." Fuck it, give the cunt a treat, Vinny thought.

"Nine hundled." She held up nine fingers in case he didn't understand.

Vinny pulled a 1,000-baht note from his wallet, placed it on the bar and raised his hand to say 'forget the change'.

He headed back towards Tilac to make sure Keith was OK. He was almost inside when he remembered the cigarettes and back peddled to a general store wedged between go-go bars that sold everything a happy whore could take home.

Back in Tilac Vinny popped his head through the curtain and peered around. He was trying his best not to smile mischievously at the plans he'd laid down for his mate.

Keith was wedged in the seat built into the front wall of the room between the two entrances; he was being entertained by two petite little temptresses in bikinis and thigh-length boots.

"Alright, kidder?" Vinny smiled and Keith looked up.

"Aye, yer beer's here."

"Nok." Vince pointed to the girl to Keith's right with her hair in bunches.

"Hello. Winny." She smiled and waved.

"Fuck me, Vince, do you know every single girl in Bangkok?" Keith looked pissed off that Vinny was acquainted with his new discovery.

Vinny ignored his mate's jibe . "How are you?"

"*Sabai. Sabai.*" She giggled cutely.

"I not recognise your hair." Vinny pointed at her pigtails.

"Is sexy, you like?" She pawed at them seductively and wiggled her behind on the seat.

"Oooh, very sexy." Vin squeezed into the seating and slurped at his beer.

"How do I get this one home with me, Vinny?" Keith had his arm round Nok, who was sipping at the Cola Keith had bought her.

"Just pay the bar." Vince was struggling to open the first soft pack of cigarettes he'd had in a while. "Top shag, that one, as well."

Keith's face dropped. "You mean you've been there already?"

"Aye." Vin smiled fondly at the memory. "Got her an' her mate together in a short-time gaff round the corner."

"Orrgh." The beer in Keith's mouth started to taste sour. "That's put me right off, that 'as."

Vinny shook his head. "I've a feeling she may have slept with more than one bloke in her lifetime, kidder. You can't get too fussy, mate."

He turned his attention to the bigger of the two stages that filled the floor at Tilac. A host of bikini-clad beauties was crammed into the platform surrounded by chrome bars, doing their best to catch the attention of the mainly European but occasionally Japanese and Arabic punters that sat transfixed by the ladies. Tacky techno music that Western ten-year-olds annoyed their parents with was pounding out of the speakers, and the lows in the music were filled with laughter and chatter.

Vinny looked at his watch. It was eight o'clock.

"So, what do reckon to yer first go-go then?" Vinny had to shout to be heard above the din.

"Ye what?" was Keith's response.

"I said, what do you reckon to yer first…" A gorgeous young creature with dyed blonde hair pushed round the table in front of Keith and sat on his knee. He smiled as he smelt her scent and ran his hand along her thigh.

"What was that?" Keith popped his head over her shoulder cheekily.

"Forget it."

The pair spent the next 40 minutes being pawed and mauled by a host of scantily clad women. With their egos suitably inflated Vinny dragged Keith out. He winced at the size of the bill. There were over eight Colas at 100 baht apiece, along with six beers.

"Fuck it. It's only money," he muttered to himself.

Keith looked down in the mouth as they crossed the road. "I was enjoying myself then, you cunt."

Vinny ignored him and pointed to Toy Bar. He pushed the heavy wooden door open and winked at Mamasan while Keith brought up the rear. She shepherded them into a seat and the two surveyed the surroundings. It was a dimly lit place with raised seating down one side and a bar down the other. There were fake flames dotted around the bar in tall ornamental torches. The flame effect was made from long triangular pieces of cloth being blown upwards and illuminated by a bulb. Vinny could see Mamasan chatting to a group of four girls at the bar and she soon manouevred them over to the two guys, the braver of them heading straight for Keith and resting her hand on his knee.

"Sah, you want dlink?"

Vinny butted in. "*Sawng* Carlsberg, *sawng* whisky *lippo*."

She scurried to the bar as two girls came and smooched their way onto Keith's lap.

The drinks arrived and Keith started to look anxious. The girls were getting very friendly. Vinny took a drink of his beer and looked at his watch. "Shit," he exclaimed in mock shock. "I'm meant to meet an old mate at half eight." he took another quick swig of his beer.

"He'll wait," Keith managed to mumble through the pair of lips that were being planted on his own.

"Nah." Vinny put on a look of urgency. "Catch us up when you've finished them drinks. I'll be in a bar called The Ship. Turn right out of here, then turn right at the top, it's about a hundred yards."

Keith tried to protest but was being pinned to the chair by three girls. Vinny dashed out of the bar, leaving Keith panic stricken.

When Keith eventually pushed open the door to The Ship he looked bewildered, drained and disorientated. He eyed his surroundings in shock. It was like stepping through a time tunnel that had taken him home; the place looked a typical English country pub.

"Keith," Vinny called out. The old guy Vinny was talking to at the table looked up and Vinny slipped a piece of paper in his back pocket.

"You fuckin' wanker." Keith shook his head, not knowing weather to smile or cry.

"Welcome to Thailand," Vinny chirped. "Get a beer and sit down." Vinny carried on talking in hushed tones to the gent while Keith was at the bar. When he arrived at their table Vinny looked up. "Keith, this is Pete Jensen, an old mate of my dad's. Pete, this is Keith." Vinny sat back so the pair could shake hands. “It’s Keith’s first time in Thailand. I left him in the capable hands of the ladies from Toy Bar for a while.” Vinny lit a fag.

“Aah. That’ll explain the satiated look on his face.” Pete laughed and took a drag of a cigarette.

Keith eyed the guy suspiciously. He was in his late-fifties at a guess. He had thinning white hair combed back from his forehead. His white striped shirt, which was the sort old guys always wore, was rolled up at the sleeves and the top three buttons were undone to show a tanned chest covered with wisps of white hair. For some reason he looked dodgy to Keith; he couldn’t decide if he was a paedophile pervert or some sort of villain hooked into the triads? He felt anxious.

“I just thought I’d say hello, wish him happy Christmas from my dad, like,” Vinny explained.

Keith knew he was lying.

“So how is old England these days?” croaked Pete with a hint of a cockney accent.

“It’s still north of France. You don’t see white dogshit anymore and they’ve got two-pound coins these days,” Vinny chirped and the three of them burst into laughter. Keith’s was a nervous laugh and Vinny and Pete seemed to be laughing at something more private.

“Oh, I do miss old England,” Pete continued through his shabby vocal chords. “Them gorgeous chunky Birmin’ham girls with their chips and brown ale.” He sighed as a distant look formed in his eyes. “There was one special one called Laura.” Pete paused and sucked his lips while Vin and Keith listened intently. “I wonder if they ever found her corpse.”

The pair burst out laughing.

“Me and Keith are ’avin’ a night on the town, Pete. Fancy taggin’ along?” Vinny offered.

“Ooh no.” Pete shook his head. “I couldn’t do that. The wife’d ’ave me guts for garters.”

Vinny looked disappointed.

“I’ll have to go now, lads. My tea’s getting cold.” Pete finished his drink and stood up.

“You seem like a nice chap, Keith. Let me give you my card. If you need help with financial matters give me a call.” He took a business card from his shirt pocket, placed it on the table and was gone.

“Who the fuck’s that, Vinny?” Keith seemed angry and looked his mate right in the eye.

“Mate o’ my dad’s.” He swigged his beer and avoided eye contact.

“Don’t bullshit me.” Keith read the business card. “Pete Jensen. Consultant. Stringent Global Finance.” It had his email address and a couple of phone numbers on it.

“Like I said, mate o’ my old fella’s.” Vinny still wasn’t convincing.

“You better not be dragging me into no dodgy shit out here.” Keith put the card in his pocket.

“How was Toy Bar?” Vinny changed the subject.

“Fuck me. Just after you left…” Keith paused for effect. “I was looking at the trophies the rugby team had won, and one of the birds sat on me knee pulls me kecks down, don’t she, then another appears with a cushion that she holds in front of me, and all three of ’em weigh in, sucking and pulling till I shot me duff.”

Vinny laughed. “It was my treat. Only wish I could have seen your face.”

“Fuckin’ summat else, that, I tell yer.” Keith shook his head and finished his beer.

“We off?”

The terrible twosome headed back down Soi Cowboy. Vinny pointed out Wet Lips bar as they passed. “See that joint there?” he said. “They call it Wet Lips, ’cos at the start of the evenin’ all the birds line up outside in short skirts an’ one of the punters gets to throw his beer down the line trynna soak their muffs, like.” He looked at his watch. It was nine thirty. “ We’ll nip in here for a couple.”

He steered Keith into Long Gun. “One of the best gaffs in town, this. You need to get in early or you can’t get a seat.”

They pushed the curtain aside and entered the den. Seemingly like all the other bars on the street it was dimly lit. There was a rectangular stage in the middle of the room with the obligatory chrome poles reaching to the ceiling. On either side of the stage there was tiered seating, and at the far end was a bar. Virtually all the seats were full. Three lithe young girls were on stage wearing cut-down denim shorts that nearly hid their underwear, small improvised dark green smock tops with frayed hems that reached to just above their nipples and cowboy hats. They were gyrating provocatively to ‘Hotel California’, which belted out of the speakers to drown the drinkers’ chat, and massaging their own erogenous zones to the delight of the crowd.

A girl who was, surprisingly, clad in garments that preserved her modesty grabbed Keith, guided him to a seat at the edge of the stage and took his drinks order. Vinny joined him and squeezed in next to a plump American guy in his forties wearing a tennis shirt and outdated spectacles. The beers arrived and the pair sat transfixed as one of the darlings stood with her legs spread wide facing the opposite wall, rubbing her crotch within eight inches of the pair whilst holding onto a pole with her spare hand. Vinny felt a presence over his right shoulder. He could feel warmth.

“Hello,” a soft, polite voice said.

He looked round and saw a hand stretched out for him to shake. It was paler than a lot of the usual girls. As he took the hand and shook the owner winked and made a clicking sound with her mouth.

What your name?” She smiled and her face invited Vinny to cuddle her.

"Vince. My name Vince. This my friend Keith." He pointed at the carcass next to him that was staring at the performer's crotch. She writhed within inches of Vin's face and he pulled an imaginary pubic hair from between his front teeth.

His new friend giggled.

"Can sit here?" She clasped his arm and pointed to a gap in the tier of seating at the back.

"OK." Vin grabbed his beer and nudged Keith. "Get a pew up the back, kidder. Bit more room."

The pair edged their way through the crowd and Vinny's new companion sat next to them.

"What's your name?" Vinny enquired.

"Gess." She smiled and winked again, making the same clicking sound with her mouth.

"Gess." Vinny imitated the wink and click but didn't get it right. "Is nice name."

The girl giggled and covered her hand with her mouth. She wore a blue grey dress that buttoned down the front in camouflage print, and leather boots to below the knee.

Keith's eye's were fixed on the goings on on stage but Vinny's heart was fluttering.

"You want drink?" he offered.

"Sank you." She kissed his cheek and nattered to a waitress in Thai. A small glass of Coke arrived.

"You work in Bangkok?" She stroked his hand.

"No, no, holiday." he was flattered.

"Where you come from?"

Vin started to feel light headed. "England, Manchester," he explained.

"Gess like Iingland." She sipped at her drink and smiled. "Gess go high school, learn speak Iinglit."

"Wow." Vinny put his best shocked look on. "You not need. Speak English good already."

She smiled. "*Puk wan*."

"Not *puk wan*. You speak good." Vinny turned to Keith. "What do you reckon o' this one?"

"Payin' more attention to that one," said Keith, pointing to the stage where a stunner was sat in the splits massaging her exposed breasts.

"Keith like lady."

"Her name Hom," said Gess.

"Hom." He nudged Keith. " She's called Hom, that one. Wanna see if she's free?"

Keith gulped. "Fuckin' too right."

"Gess. My friend like Hom. You ask Mamasan she go with Keith?" Vinny liked acting as the intermediary.

"OK." Gess got up and strolled over to the old lady by the door, waving quickly to one of the customers on her way. She spoke to Mamasan for a moment then made her way back.

"Sorry." She looked glum. "Mamasan say Hom hab cutomer alleddy."

"*Mai phen rai*," Vinny shrugged. "I pay bar for you?"

She clucked and jumped an inch off the floor in delight then leaned over and kissed him.

"*Tow rai*?" he asked.

"Four hundled baht." She sipped at her drink while she watched Vinny reach in his wallet for a 500-baht note.

"I come back one minute." She smiled, winked and clicked again before prancing off to the bar.

"Could do with another line, me." Keith was slurring at Vinny. He wasn't used to drinking without narcotics to stabilise him.

"Pop back in a bit. I've just bar fined her." Vinny looked proud as he sipped his drink. "That one you wanted has gone."

Keith looked around for another recipient of his DNA.

Gess seemed to be gone for a while. She'd disappeared through a door at the side of the bar. When she remerged she was wearing a denim jacket over her dress and had a beige canvass bag over her shoulder. She stopped and spoke to a girl standing at the bar in her underwear then headed back to Vinny. Instead of sitting next to him she sat on his knee and tucked her bag under the seat. As she wriggled on Vinny's leg he could feel her warmth and he slipped his arm around her. She leaned forward and nudged Keith, who was swaying in the breeze.

"My frien' say you sexy man." She pointed at the girl she'd conversed with moments earlier.

"Nah." Keith shook his head and emptied his beer. "We off?"

Keith was following his urges, as many people did in Bangkok, but for the time being his were for narcotics rather than nipples.

They jumped in a cab and headed back down Sukumvit towards the hotel, dropping Gess off at the petrol station at the junction of Soi Nana. Vinny pressed 200 baht into her hand for a drink. "Meet you ten minutes in Big Dog."

"How do you know she won't do a runner?" Keith asked suspiciously.

"She's waiting for pay day."

The taxi weaved down Soi 1 and underneath the hospital, dropping them twenty yards from base camp. Keith was out the door and down the road before Vinny had a chance to place two crumpled twenty-baht notes in the driver's hand. He shook his head as he walked down the street. "Boy, that kid's got a problem," he muttered.

Vinny took the lift to the fourth floor and headed for Keith's room. He tried the handle but it was locked. A snorting sound came from within and he heard footsteps approach the door and the click of the handle turning.

"What took you?" Keith's eye's were glazed.

Vinny squeezed in the room as Keith didn't open the door too wide in case anyone saw him. There were three lines of coke on the dresser and some dust where a fourth one had been. Keith passed Vinny a tubular note. He devoured one of the lines and Keith cleaned away another then passed the note back to Vin, who swept up half the line and returned the note to Keith.

"You finish that, I only want a touch."

Keith obliged.

They headed back on the street and Vinny trailed behind Keith who was nonchalant but accelerated in his stride. Vinny was worried. What could you do to look straight when you were coked up? He'd have put on sunglasses to cover his eyes but it went dark in Bangkok at 7.30pm in December, and it was 10.30 now. A light bulb lit in his head. Get pissed, he thought. They'd never guess.

Gess was sat quietly at a table in Big Dogs, the first bar at the entrance to Nana Plaza. She was drinking a glass of orange. Vinny smiled at his lady for the night and she returned the gesture. He was relieved to arrive there safely, especially after the heart-stopping moment when the policeman in the traffic box had looked up from his paper.

Gess looked into his eyes then looked away. Vince could tell he'd been bubbled.

The waitress arrived and Vinny ordered two beers and two whiskies. He gulped down his spirit and wiped his mouth. Keith did the same but showered the table with it.

"What the fuck's that?" His mouth was turned up in disgust.

"Mekong." Vinny laughed along with Gess at Keith's reaction.

"'Slike fuckin' Jay's Fluid, that." He gulped his beer to take away the taste.

"Yer get used to it." Vinny slipped his arm round Gess and squeezed her.

Keith was craning his neck like an owl; he'd almost managed a full 360. He spotted an old guy in his sixties with a paunch, thin grey hair and a young girl no older than eighteen with her arm linked in his. The guy was wheezing as he walked gingerly through the crowd of lascivious drunks traipsing along the street.

"Fuckin' 'ell." He tapped Vinny with his bottle. "Have a butchers at that. Old enough to be 'er granddad."

"What's the problem?" Vinny shrugged.

"Turns yer stomach." Keith looked disgusted.

"She's happy, he's happy. She gets paid. He gets a drain-off. No problem."

Gess looked over her shoulder to see what the fuss was about but couldn't see anything out of the ordinary.

"I mean, where the fuck's a guy like that gonna get a shag in Europe apart from in an old folks' home? Might as well enjoy his pension," Vinny explained.

"Aye. But it just don't look right, does it?" Keith protested.

"Get used to all sorts 'ere." Vinny pointed with his bottle to another similarly aged guy strolling out with a taller, more elegant creature with perfect breasts and glamorous make-up. "That one there's a geezer."

Keith looked stunned. "Fuck off."

"Aye. Stands out a mile." Vince looked to Gess for confirmation.

She looked round. "OK, yes." She IDd the same couple. "This one *katoey*."

Keith shook his head in amazement. "Don't anyone warn 'em?"

"'E might like it," Vinny continued.

"What…" Keith's look of amazement became more and more pronounced. "You mean, he chose to go with a geezer?"

"Yeah, some blokes prefer 'em." Vinny was straight as a die; Keith could read it in his face.

Gess had a confused look on her face. They were talking quickly and she couldn't get the drift of the conversation. Vinny stepped in and explained politely, "Keith first time in Thailand, he not see *katoey* before."

She nodded in comprehension. "Yes. In Thailand many lady man."

Vinny pointed at a spot in the middle of her chest. She looked down and he flicked his finger gently onto her nose.

"*Ting tong*," she protested and the pair fell about laughing like teenagers.

"Sha' we go an' see if that Dtom's still around? Fit as fuck, 'er," Keith suggested. He was starting to feel like a gooseberry.

"Yeah, if yer want."

Keith looked over his shoulder at a girl who was serving a drink at the next table. "Although I could 'ave found an alternative 'ere. She's not a bloke, is she?"

He'd soon put his disgust to one side.

The girl could tell she was being talked about and offered her hand to Keith. "*Sawasdee ka*."

He looked confused. "What she say?"

"She say hello," Gess explained.

"Oh, right. *Sawasdee ka*," Keith replied, thinking he'd picked up the lingo.

The three fell about laughing, leaving Keith feeling self-conscious. "What's ser funny?"

Gess interjected and touched his arm. "Lady say *sawasdee ka* is good. Man no say. Man say *sawasdee krap*."

Keith nodded, pretending to understand. "Ooooh. OK. *Sawasdee krap*."

She smiled and shook his hand.

"Fuckin' all right, that one, Keith. Fancy part exin' it?"

"Fuck that, she's mine tonight." He put his arm round her. "You want drink?"

She nodded her head and scampered off to the bar.

When she returned Gess had nipped to the toilet so Vinny could eye her up properly without getting elbowed in the ribs. She was short and looked quite young, maybe nineteen, twenty. Her skin was a lovely coffee-brown colour and she'd dyed her hair in blonde streaks. Her outfit consisted of dark brown flared combat trousers that covered her platform-soled boots, a figure-hugging white T-shirt with a plunging neck and an army-style belt. Pity she was only four-foot eleven. Eighteen inches taller and she could have been on the catwalk. Vinny tried to keep his swoon to a minimum.

The happy foursome drank, chatted and cuddled while watching the world go by.

Keith paid his first bar fine and smiled proudly while Vinny patted his back and insisted he downed a whisky to celebrate. At around 1am Keith suggested a change of scene.

"Where you want go?" he asked Gess.

"Up to you," she replied.

Vin looked at Keith's new acquisition, who shrugged her shoulders. "You want go disco?" he asked the two girls.

They both nodded.

"I'll 'ave a bit o' that," Keith agreed.

"OK. We go Nana Disco." He rubbed his legs and jumped out of his chair. They sorted the bill out and headed over the road.

"Where we off to, Vin?" Keith was happy and curious.

"Nirvana, mate," Vin philosophised. "The closest thing to heaven on earth."

"Yeah, but what is it?"

"Is Disco. Is good," Gess explained. She started to bob her head in anticipation of the music.

They strolled across the car park of the Nana Hotel, and through the walkway inside the building, which housed some shuttered shop fronts closed for the evening and spillover chairs from the coffee shop. At the end of the indoor parade was a queue of girls, waiting while two uniformed guys shone their torches on something the girls were pulling out of their bags.

"Just wait here a sec, Keith," said Vinny. "Let the birds go in first." He leaned against a pillar. The beer was starting to affect his balance.

"What's up?" Keith didn't want his belle to leave his side.

"They check the birds' ID to make sure they're not underage." Vinny swayed in the breeze. Keith was starting to wobble a bit as well.

Their partners disappeared inside the door after queuing for a moment and the guys followed. As they approached the door the *thud thud thud* of poppy European dance music started to waft towards them. They strolled past a line of girls waiting to be allowed entry and stamped on the hand as being of legitimate age, and pushed through the doorway.

Keith stopped and looked at the sign above the door: ANGELS. He followed Vinny inside and his mouth fell wide open. It was a medium-sized nightclub, no different to any other, with dark walls, the odd mirror, a few tables, two bars, a dance floor and a DJ booth, but Keith was dumbstruck. It was full, packed, heaving with women. There was the odd bloke sat about or stood at the bar, but all told there must have been 500 women in the place, talking, laughing, dancing or drinking, and there were more queuing to get in. He forgot himself. He forgot Vinny. He forgot the blonde from Big Dogs. He stood on the spot with his hands in his pockets in amazement. Time stood still as he spotted woman after woman after woman, all unattached and all worth a seeing-to. He wondered where to start. A guy pushed past him and brought him out of his coma.

Where's Croston? he thought as hc surveyed the scene without avail. He started to walk, aimlessly. His legs seemed too frightened to move and he took tiny ginger steps. As he approached the crowd gathered at the bar he noticed Gess and his own purchase stood waiting politely. He scanned the bar and saw Vin chatting to a bloke as one of the barmaids was placed drinks in front of him. Keith leaned over and grabbed a bottle of Carlsberg that had his name written on it in invisible ink. He overheard Vince's conversation.

"So you reckon it's the Grace after hours then?"

"Few Arabs knockin' abart but 's alright, like," a cockney drawl replied.

Vinny pulled away from the bar with his handful of drinks and headed to where Keith had joined the girls. He handed out the bottles and took a swig of his own.

Keith was only just beginning to manage words and couldn't keep his eyes on the same woman for longer than two seconds before another stunner entered his field.

"What the fuck is this place?" He sounded exasperated.

"Nana Disco." Vinny didn't flinch.

"Where did all the birds come from?"

"Isaan."

in the afternoon

Tap. Tap. Tap.

"Fuck off."

"Hahaha … Keith."

"Fuckin' 'ell."

Vinny heard the unmistakeable bumps of a guy with a hangover looking for his underpants. A few irregular footsteps later he heard the catch on the door being jangled. The door opened slowly.

Gess and Vinny saw a very ill man with his underpants on inside out.

The remnants of Keith turned and went back to bed. A corpse was hidden under the duvet. They walked carefully through the door. There were clothes and discarded condoms scattered across the floor. Vinny had to watch where he stepped and Gess hovered in the doorway.

"We're off in Bamboo for summat to eat," Vinny said gently. "Take it you won't be there for an hour or so."

"Time is it?" a zombie groaned.

"'Bout half one." Vinny started tiptoeing out.

"In a bit," someone croaked.

Vinny wiped the last piece of sausage around the plate to soak up the remains of egg yolk and ketchup. As he chewed the last of his English breakfast he saw a geriatric in a 27-year-old's body stand in the doorway and look round the bar through his sunglasses. Vinny sipped at his coffee and waited to see how long it would take before he recognised him. After scanning the bar twice Keith made eye contact and shambled like a cripple across the floor to where Vinny sat at the bar.

"Mornin', dickhead." Vinny smiled as he lit a fag.

"Fffffeeewwwww." Keith shook his head and turned up his top lip.

"How's it goin'?"

Keith didn't respond. He grabbed at a stool and very cautiously pulled himself onto it.

The barmaid looked at him but Vinny waved her down to stop her asking a question that might offend, like, "Would you like anything?"

Keith folded his hands on the bar and laid his head on top of them.

The barmaid looked at Vinny. Vinny carefully mouthed the word '*mau*' and mimicked a bottle at his mouth.

Vinny sipped his coffee and finished his cigarette. He poked Keith in the ribs gently and his head rose.

"Wanna drink, kidder?"

Keith straightened up slowly. "Aye. Get us a brew."

"Two coffee." Vin held two fingers up for the barmaid.

The wreck was holding onto the bar with both hands and shaking his head.

When the coffees arrived Keith tried to pick his up but dropped it back in the saucer, spilling nearly a third of it in the process. He shook his hands a second later from the delayed reaction of the heat. The barmaid giggled to herself.

After a few sips of coffee, Frankenstein seemed to come to life. "Got any fags?" Vinny tossed a fresh pack of Marlboro Lights across. Keith lit one and inhaled. The nicotine and caffeine started to bring him out of his dream. "Fuck me, I've felt better in my time." Keith took off his shades and wiped his hands with his face.

The barmaid tossed him a small plastic packet the size of a Mars bar.

"What's this?" He pawed it suspiciously.

"Open it up." Vinny nodded him on.

Carefully he pulled at the serrated plastic seal and looked inside, then pulled out a cool, damp towel. He didn't need telling what to do with it and placed it on his face. It sat for a second then he rubbed it across his forehead, cheeks and down the back of his neck. It chilled him and made him smile. The barmaid smiled coyly and looked down. She was glad to have helped.

"Praise the Lord for small fuckin' mercies, eh." He crumpled it up and passed it to the barmaid. "Thank you."

"Joinin' the land of the livin', are ye?" Vinny felt a bit braver now.

"Aye. Could do with a line though."

Vinny winced and shook his head. He put his finger on his lips and looked round.

"Sorry, mate." Keith shook his head. "What time did you leave that Nana Disco thing?"

"Not a clue." Vinny shrugged his shoulders.

"That's when I left." Keith perked up and chuckled. He eyed the menu. "Can I have bacon on toast, love?" He took a final drag of the cigarette before stubbing it out. "Fuck, I can see why you like the place."

Vinny chuckled. "It has it's advantages. How was that bird?"

Keith shook his head again and a distant look moved across his face. He looked to the heavens for inspiration. "Mate…" He sighed. "I don't know what to say." Again he paused, trying to find the words. "I ain't 'ad lovin' like that since I were a babe in arms. Can't fuckin' describe it."

"So she was average then?"

Keith started to chuckle to himself. It was a chuckle that lasted intermittently until his bacon sandwich arrived, and for a while after he'd finished it.

"'Air o' the dog?" Vinny suggested.

"Could bring us round, that."

"What was her name?"

"You know, I forgot to ask."

"You fuckin' heartless bastard," Vinny jibed. "Poor girl gave you 'er cherry and you didn't even ask her name."

Keith shook his head with a grave look of disagreement. "That was no first-timer, that one."

"How much did yer give her?" Vin quizzed.

"Think it was about three thousand."

Vinny placed his beer on the bar and shook his head.

"What's up?"

Vinny was wearing a heavy frown. "Suppose it's my fault, mate. Should've warned yer, never give 'em more than fifteen hundred. She's spanked yer arse there."

"That was one thing she didn't get round to actually." Keith's first full-on seeing-to from a Thai had left him in good form and he giggled. "We poppin' back the 'otel for a livener?"

They paid the bill and headed back to Keith's room. A line each brought them both back to life. It made their bodies tingle. Vinny sat on the edge of the bed and laid back on his elbows.

Keith padded over to the TV and flicked it on. The Eastern version of MTV was showing and two young trendy-looking Japanese guys speaking near perfect English were trying to enthuse about an Oasis video they were about to play.

"Fuck me, we've come all this way just to watch two lads from Burnage." Keith shook his head.

"What you wanna do today?" Vince asked.

"Fuck knows. What is there to do?"

"Dunno, have a look at a few temples, go down the Grand Palace, day trip to the floating market. It's up to you." Vinny shrugged his shoulders. "Or we could just get pissed and shag a few birds."

Keith pretended to chew it over for a minute and stroked his chin. "The gettin' pissed and shaggin' sounds good to me."

People don't actually plan to spend all day on the piss in Bangkok but that's how it usually turns out.

"Deal." Vinny extended his hand and they shook on it. "Just need to get some cash out. Blew through a hundred quid last night."

Vinny nipped next door to his room to get his wad of traveller's cheques and his passport. He'd dressed in Bangkok daytime attire, his old faithful combat shorts, a polo shirt and his Reeboks. Keith waited in reception. They handed in their keys and ventured forth unto the breach.

Between 11am and 3 or 4pm the Bangkok heat was stifling. They walked slowly so as not to break sweat but it didn't work.

"What happened to that bird of yours?"

"Fucked off after we came in your room. Didn't want owt to eat," Vin replied.

"Any good?"

"Not bad," Vin pondered for a moment. "Right nice girl though. You get some giving you loads of cock an' bull that they love yers and then blag all your money. She just said she had to go to English classes and tottered off once I'd paid her."

"Yeah."

"Might see her again tonight," Vinny added.

Keith couldn't help laughing. "I thought that Jean in Pattaya was your only true love."

"Oh yeah, yeah. Jeed's great," Vin insisted. "But yer can't walk through an orchard without plucking a few apples."

The pair ran the gauntlet of the Sukumvit crossing and made it onto Soi Nana alive.

"Where we off?" Keith enquired.

"Golden, Pharaohs, Big Dogs, up to you."

"I fancy seein' if that Dtom's about."

"Pharaohs it is. I've just gotta cash a cheque." Vinny reached in his side pocket for his cheques and passport and headed to the kiosk by the entrance of Nana.

When Vinny arrived at the near deserted Pharaoh's, Dtom had already joined Keith. She was stroking his back and nursing the small Cola he'd bought her.

The plaza wasn't the mêlée it had been the night before. Bars were beginning to open up. Some were still shut and most of the drinkers in those that were open were in shorts and looking hungover.

Keith passed him a beer and Vinny looked round. Nid was behind the bar putting bottles from a crate into the chilled display cabinet. She stood up, smiled and waved, then bent back down to carry on with the job.

"Works like a fuckin' slave, that one," Vinny pointed out to Keith. "She's 'ere from eleven in t'morning till two the next morning."

"Ehh." Keith looked up. He seemed more interested in the contents of Dtom's blouse.

Vinny laughed.

"Me and Dtom are just poppin' to the hotel for half an hour." Keith mopped his brow.

Dtom scurried off to the bar with some rolled-up notes in her hand.

"Like a dog wi' two dicks, you are." Vinny shook his head.

“Aye, see yers in an hour.” Keith’s hand got clasped and pulled by a slender dark beauty.

“I’ll be in Golden,” Vinny shouted as Keith was dragged off to bed by the money-mad moma.

Vin finished his beer and strolled out of Pharaohs. The collection of motorbikes that blocked the entrance in the evening was absent and Vin stood with his hands on his hips weighing up the world around him. He let the sun soak his face for a moment and it helped wash away the memory of England, Bolton, work and Toni. He smiled to himself. Last night had been wonderful, trouble free, carefree: gorgeous food, beer, narcotics and a beautiful girl. His best mate was well on his way to becoming hooked on Siam’s delights and the sun was shining. This was what life was about.

Vinny strolled down Soi Nana. He chose to walk in the gutter rather than on the pavement; it saved bumping into people. He didn’t really know where he was going but just felt motion in his legs so obeyed it. Thirty yards into his trundle he saw a shop front over the road. It was pretty nondescript and you couldn’t see inside because the blinds were down but the lettering gave him an idea: INTERNET, OVERSEA CALL, PHOTOCOPY, TRANSLATION. A tuk tuk had to swerve to avoid hitting him as he zeroed in on his target. He pushed the door open and felt the calming waft of an air conditioner. The room was full of PCs perched on desks and Western guys tapping away quietly in front of the screens. The floor was tiled in beige squares and the whole place was an oasis of serenity against the noise and fumes outside.

A dark-skinned girl was sat at a desk in the corner and she looked up from the paperback she was reading. She pressed the book down to keep her page and scurried over to a free desk with her arm outstretched, motioning for Vinny to take a seat. He pulled up a swivel chair and logged onto his account. There was a message from Jeed.

Vinny Tilac,

Where are you? You tell arrive in Thailand on 15 but I not know where you are. Tell me please your name hotel and I’m get taxi. Miss you too much and love you also.

Jeed

It warmed his heart and he smiled. He felt a stirring in his loins and he had to rub his crotch to try and shift it. Words didn’t seem important for a moment, he just stared at the screen and Jeed’s face seemed to appear through it. A bit like the image of Christ on the shroud of Turin, except it was highly unlikely there'd be any sort of virgin birth where Vinny was involved. He hit reply.

Jeed Honey,

Vinny in Bangkok. I'm staying with Keith in hotel. Keith want to look at Bangkok before we come to Pattaya. We come to Pattaya soon. Maybe Tuesday, maybe Wednesday, I telephone you before come and I'll meet you in the bar.

Keith likes Bangkok but I want him to be careful because I think he is turning into a butterfly.

See you soon Tilac,

Vince.

The PC's were slower than the ones he was used to at work so once he'd hit send he had to wait a while to get the confirmation of message. He pushed back the chair and headed for the desk in the corner. The girl looked up from her book and pressed a button on one of the seven or eight stopwatches on the desk and looked at the time on it.

"Fipty baht." she smiled at Vinny.

He dug into his pocket, pulled out some crumpled notes and coins and placed three dog-eared blue twenty-baht notes on the desk. She counted them carefully and opened a drawer in the desk. She picked up a ten-baht coin but Vinny shook his hand.

"*Mai pehn rai*," he insisted.

"*Khop khun ka*," she sung softly to him.

"*Khop khun krap chok dee*." He waved as he headed out of the door.

Thai women were wonderful. Even the non-bar girls had a warmth and gentleness that no Western woman could match. Vinny walked next door and took a seat in Golden. The heat was getting to him and the girl who brought him a bottle of Sprite and a glass full of ice also brought him a cooling towel in a plastic packet to wipe away the grime and heat. He'd chosen a seat inside the bar rather than at the railing where he'd sat the previous night with Keith. The shade made life easier and he could look at the TV screen in the corner. ESPN Sports was showing, a worldwide channel that showed European football. A few pundits were chatting about forthcoming fixtures. Arsenal versus Liverpool was going to be televised in the next few days, which seemed important but Vinny wasn't too bothered. He was more concerned as to how Bolton had performed on Saturday. With the excitement of being home in Thailand on Sunday and because he had been on a plane for the best part of Saturday he'd forgotten to check how they'd got on. He looked round the bar. There were a few guys sat around in pairs or with a lady, most of them in their fifties or overweight, most of them both. A guy sat near him was fixed to the screen. He was older than Vin, maybe forty, and dressed like one of the backpackers they'd seen at the airport. The screen was showing highlights and he cheered audibly when Roy Keene put one in the net for Man United.

Vinny took his chance. "Y'all right, mate?"

The guy warmed to Vinny's northern accent. "Magic, kidder, magic. Yerself?"

"Fair t'middlin'." He picked up his glass and the pot with his chit in it. "Mind if I join yer?"

"If you want."

Vinny shuffled over. "How's United getting on?"

"Just highlights, mate, but they're two up at Everton on 'ere. Three-one, I think, was final score." Unusual for a United fan – he actually had a Manchester accent.

Vinny turned to the screen and feigned interest in the world's favourite football team, or the worlds most hated if you supported anyone else. "Who scored?"

"Keene got two, Beckham free kick, the other." He sipped his beer. "Been 'ere long?"

"Nah, just landed yesterday," Vince replied. "You?"

"Been 'ere three days. I were meant to be on a flight t'Patong at midday but got too pissed last night." For a man who'd just missed a plane he didn't look too worried.

Vinny chuckled. "Off to Pattaya in a day or two meet my bird."

"So you've been here before then?"

"Yeah. Think it's me fourth or fifth trip. I'm starting to lose count."

"Gets under your skin, dunnit," the guy went on. "Been coming here two or three times a year for about ten years now. First time it blew my mind an' I ain't looked back since."

"I know, yeah." Vin had found a kindred spirit. "It's me mate's first time. We've been here twenty-four hours. He got sucked and wanked by three birds in Toy Bar last night, got a long-time from Big Dogs and he's just off on a short-time. Five birds in twenty-four hours. Normally takes twelve months to get through that many."

The guy nearly choked on his drink laughing. "Do you reckon 'e's enjoyin' it?"

"Not 'ad chance to ask."

The pair laughed. They carried on chatting for a while. Vinny looked at his watch. It was 3.30. Keith had been gone double the half hour he'd mentioned so he started to look round in case he wandered past. No sign.

"Do you know how Bolton got on at the weekend?" he asked Dave. He'd elicited the guy's name earlier.

"Drew one apiece wi' Wolves."

Vinny winced. Wouldn't do their title chances any favours. He saw Keith looking feeble as he mounted the steps at the side of the bar.

"Keith," he shouted.

Keith looked round.

"There he is lookin' lost and saddle sore." Vinny pointed him out to Dave.

Keith wandered over and pulled up a chair.

"Keith, this is Dave, he's from Salford."

"All right, Keith?"

"Could do with a beer," Keith panted. "What's up, Vinny, not drinkin'?"

Three beers arrived and within minutes they had disappeared. Keith seemed to get on with Dave, as did Vinny. They sat and took the piss out of one another in a lighthearted way, suggested doing obscene things to every woman that passed within ten feet of them and generally behaved like true degenerates.

Come 6 o'clock they'd run up a heavy bill and were finding it difficult to stay upright in their chairs.

"I can feel the powder calling," Keith whispered to Vinny.

Dave overheard and his eyes darted to Vinny's.

Vinny looked worried and pretended not to hear.

Keith's guard was down. "We're poppin' back the 'otel for a line, kidder. Wanna tag along?"

"You don't need to ask twice." Dave put his drink down and paid the bill.

Back in Keith's room Vinny felt uncomfortable. He knew the penalties for drugs in Thailand and was even more cautious about showing them to a guy he'd known little more than two hours. Keith racked up six lines. Two each and a hush fell while it took effect.

Dave started the conversation freefall. "What you two doin' tonight?"

"Thought I'd show Keith Pat Pong," Vinny stuttered.

"Getting' pissed and shaggin,'" Keith uttered in the same instant.

Dave laughed.

"Need a shower and put some clean kecks on," Vinny spat.

"Freshen up and change my shirt." Again Keith spoke in time with Vince.

"Are you two fuckin' twins?"

The three of them burst out laughing.

"Another line?" Keith offered.

Two heads nodded in unison.

'Another line' turned into three or four by the time Vinny and Keith had washed, changed and emptied Keith's mini-bar with Dave's help. They'd also commandeered him into coming to Pat Pong with them.

Keith held the bag of cocaine up before they left the room. There was about a gram left.

They wandered out of the hotel looking shabby. Dave commented on the statue that had grabbed the pair's attention when they'd arrived, saying how quaint it looked, then capped off his comment with, "D'you reckon that receptionist takes it up the shitter?"

The three were in raptures when they got in the taxi. The driver looked uncomfortable ferrying three wasted, obnoxious degenerates around. They wove through the streets of Bangkok. The traffic was still heavy even though it was 8 o'clock. A lot of time had elapsed in Keith's room.

When they hit Surriwong the traffic ground to a standstill. It was a mass of bumper plates, headlights, car horns and motorbikes bearing down at breakneck speed between the taxis.

They seemed to be in neutral outside a bar where two beautiful hostesses in evening gowns waited, smiling. Keith was distracted by them.

"How about that gaff?"

Vinny and Dave stretched their necks to look at it.

"Nah," Vinny turned his nose up. "Japanese gaff, innit."

Dave nodded. "Never let us in."

"Why's that?" Keith asked.

"They have Jap-only bars round 'ere. Look at the writing on the sign," Dave explained and pointed to the Japanese characters on the front.

"An' if they did it'd cost an arm an' a leg," Vinny continued.

The car still didn't move.

"Fuck it, let's walk." Dave threw the driver a few notes and jumped out of the front passenger seat onto the pavement.

Vin and Keith joined him. They weaved in and out of tourists and vendors all going they're own way.

"'Ere we go." Dave started to edge across the pavement ready to cross the four lanes of gridlocked traffic that made up Surriwong. He'd seen the sign for KFC that signalled the beginning of Pat Pong.

The three of them weaved in and out of the traffic and finally made it over the road, with only two near collisions with motorbikes between them. The coke was forcing their eyes gently out of their sockets.

"Where first?" Vinny asked. It was aimed more at Dave than Keith. He obviously knew the layout.

"Little Devils ?" Dave suggested.

"Aye. Saves yer gettin' knee deep in tourists," Vinny agreed.

"What is this place?" Keith's eyes were all over the show, both from curiosity and cocaine.

"Pat Pong." Vin turned his head to address Keith and walked into a middle-aged Western woman with her husband. "Sorry, love. It's the best-known red-light, but these days it's full o' tourists and the birds try and gouge yer."

They pushed through the crowds to the door. A young guy in a white shirt and black bow tie stood smiling.

"Hello, sir. Welcome. Beautiful girl. No…" They went inside in spite of his sales pitch.

The cocaine made them surge rather than stroll and they rushed into a free seat. It was a go-go bar. Keith was beginning to get the gist of things and was no longer gobsmacked by the bevy of beauties dancing on stage. Before the drinks had been ordered five girls were on top of them begging for Cola drinks and kissing their necks.

"Bit full on, this gaff," Keith wheezed as he eased one off his knee and placed her feet first on the floor.

"Tell us about it." Another who's looks suggested she may have been in the business more than six months or so was rubbing the somewhat deflated contents of her bikini top on Vinny's ear while stroking his crotch with her hand.

As soon as the drinks arrived Vinny nudged Dave and said, "Sup these and fuck off, they're too heavy."

It only took three 'Fuck offs' each for their welcoming committee to disperse empty handed and lynch the next wretched soul through the door.

They drank up quick and headed out the door. The bill was twice what it would have been in Nana but they couldn't be bothered arguing.

"Used to be all right, that gaff," Vinny moaned to Dave.

"Like anywhere though, innit. They change."

"I saw a couple of stunners in there," Keith protested. He wouldn't have minded hanging on.

"Aye, but the hassle's not worth it, man." Dave was on a mission. He forged on up Pat Pong's second road like his radar was guiding him. He came to a junction and stopped. Batman and Robin arrived a second later, sweating under the atmospheric weight on their shoulders.

Dave's eyes darted from bar to bar.

"One in 'ere." It wasn't a question, more a directive. He pointed to a hole in the wall, nothing special, just a bar with music playing and a few girls hanging around.

Dave took the lead ordring three Carlsbergs. Then he looked over his shoulder. "All right, Alan?" He nodded to a big guy sat in the corner nursing a beer.

The guy looked at him for a second before it registered. "David, how are you?"

Dave turned and took the couple of steps required to cover the width of the bar to shake the guy's hand.

At the bar Vinny and Keith were sweating profusely. The girl behind the bar was viewing them with caution. Thais could read you like a book, especially the ones in the bars. When they started working in the bar they couldn't speak your language and it was easier to read your bodies. Keith and Vinny's eyes spoke volumes.

Dave sauntered back to the two friends. "That's Alan, that. He owns this place."

Vinny and Keith raised their bottles to him. "Evenin', Alan," they said in unison.

"Evenin', lads," he purred in a soft Geordie accent.

"Proper nice guy, he is, real gent. Do you know any of the Kings group o' bars, Vinny?"

"Do they do the shows?"

"Nah, just normal go-gos"

"I could do with taking Keith to see a show, like, show him the sights. First time and all that."

"Yeah, if you want."

Keith nodded. He was being guided and didn't know one way or the other.

They supped up and left after bidding farewell to Alan.

After cutting through the Soi that joined Pat Pong Rd 2 to Pat Pong Rd 1 they had more problems to contend with. Despite being no less ugly than its sister, Pat Pong 1 was jam packed with stalls selling everything under the moon that could be faked. Designer T-shirts, watches, sunglasses, bags, caps, jeans, you name it, if it was branded, they'd faked it. The welcome staff were a little keener to earn their commission than in other parts of town.

Every five yards or so they were stopped. "Hello, sir, you want see show? No cover charge. Pussy fuck banana. Man fuck pussy on stage. Pussy blow balloon."

Keith couldn't believe his ears. Middle-aged Western couples walked along with stiff upper lips pretending not to be intrigued. Occasionally they'd stop by a stall and innocently toy with a shirt or ornament, trying to catch a glimpse of what was going on behind the curtain but scurrying away when the welcome staff caught their eye. If it hadn't been so busy it would have been funny.

Dave was leading the way Keith got waylaid; he was looking at a sign of marvels on offer. Vinny could sense they were missing a defender. He looked around.

"Keith."

Keith shuffled up to him.

"Fuckin' sign there says LADY FUCK MOTORBIKE. Is that right?"

Vinny started to laugh. "Wouldn't put it past 'em."

Dave stopped at a doorway where a girl who looked too young to be out on her own was holding a sign listing FUCK SHOW GOOD and LADY BREAK BOTTLE WITH PUSSY, among the delights in store within.

"Might as well grace this one with our presence," Dave suggested.

They mounted a set of stairs and were greeted by two slender, heavily made-up creatures who guided them to seats in front of a large stage.

Three beers arrived at Dave's behest and Keith stared at two slightly jaded, bored-looking ladies pulling long strings of flowers out of the part of their body normally reserved for intercourse.

Vinny nudged Keith and nodded to the girls on stage. "All environmentalists, this lot."

"Yeah"

"Terrible conditions for photosynthesis where them flowers 'ave been planted."

Keith spat out a mouthful of beer as he laughed.

Keith remained transfixed but Vinny and Dave were looking round to see what the talent was like. There didn't seem to be many customers and there were guys in dinner suits stood around staring at the threesome at the bar.

"Don't look kosher, this, to me," Vinny muttered to Dave.

"Same here."

The girls on stage trotted off to a faint round of applause. A lady well over 40 approached with a bowl.

"Sir. Tip for show." Keith delved in his wallet for some money and dropped a note in the bowl. She approached Vinny.

"*Mai ow krap*." He held his hand up. She glared at him for a moment then moved onto Dave. Same answer, same glare before moving off.

A bikini approached Keith and stood behind him. She started to massage his back. He straightened up and groaned as he felt a strong pair of hands working at the knotted muscles in his back.

"Fuck me. Lovely, that." Keith's eyes rolled half shut as the tension oozed out of him.

Vinny fell silent for a moment.

"Come on, sup these, we're off."

It brought Keith round. Vinny checked the bill and nudged Dave. He eyed it and shook his head. Reluctantly they paid the 250 baht each and headed out of the door. Suddenly four men in dinner suits appeared to be blocking them.

"Money for show." The biggest guy at the front held his hand out.

Vinny started to shake. Keith didn't see anything out of the ordinary and went for his wallet.

"Nah, kidder, we ain't payin'," Vinny whispered.

Dave was at the front. "OK, OK. Money for show *rua pai poliit*."

The guy stood aside and let them through.

Vinny sighed and Keith wondered what all the fuss was about.

"How d'yer get us out o' that one, Dave?" Vinny was admiring their new mate.

"Said we'd go the police." He headed into the throng.

Dave was waiting outside a bar when Laurel and Hardy caught up with him. "We in 'ere?" he asked.

Vinny looked up at the sign: KINGS CASTLE 3. "Might as well."
Keith rubbed his back, grinning. "That bird had lovely strong hands."
"It weren't a bird." Vinny looked him in the eye.
Keith's face dropped and he turned a shade paler.
"Don't worry, mate, there's many a man made that mistake."
Vinny winked. "Least you didn't shag it."
They headed into the bar. Dave sat facing the stage, eyeing the dancers.
"I just need a slash," said Vinny. "Get us a Carlsberg." He headed towards the toilet sign at the back of the room, leaving Keith and Dave agog at the women on stage.
Vinny returned from the loos looking concerned. There were beers at the table but he didn't touch his.
"It's fuckin' great, this place," Keith muttered to Vinny out of the corner of his mouth. Vinny gulped his beer and looked at the floor.
Dave was sat with his arm round a dancer, stroking her bare leg.
"Why didn't you bring us 'ere before, Vince?" Keith was looking longingly at one of the performers on stage. "All the other bars the birds 'ave small tits. This one seems to 'ave collected all the ones with decent knockers." He swigged his beer and winked at the one who'd caught his eye.
"Does that not tell yer summat?" Vinny coughed. Bangkok was starting to get in his chest.
"What d'yer mean?"
"They're all false tits. Work it out."
Keith's jaw opened slowly. "Fuck off."
"No bullshit."
"Blokes."
"Every last one of 'em."
"I'll warn Dave." Keith nudged him on the arm. "Dave."
Dave removed his tongue from 'Boy George's' mouth. "What?" He pecked George's lips.
Keith leaned forward and whispered, "Dave, that's a geezer." He leaned back so that George wouldn't know he'd blown his cover.
"Oh aye, yeah. Prefer 'em." He squeezed George round the shoulder and smiled at him lovingly.
Keith dropped his beer, shoved the table out of the way and bolted out of the door like a kidnapped priest having the blind took off him in a brothel.
Vinny started to laugh and looked over to Dave. "First timers. Y'know what they're like."
Dave pushed his cheek affectionately against his loved one's. "Don't matter," he mouthed quietly.
"Cheers for the bevvies." Vinny stood up.
"Cheers for the powder."
"Enjoy yourself." Vinny strolled out the door, smirking.

Out on the street Keith was stood a safe distance away, shaking. Vinny laughed.

"Where the fuck have you brought me?" He looked like he was going to hit him.

"Pat Pong." Vinny walked towards him with his hands in his pockets. He looked at the floor then back up at Keith, smiling.

"Get me the fuck out of here." Keith was raising his voice and the stallholders eyed him cautiously.

"Head down there, get a cab." Vinny motioned back towards Surriwong Road and started walking at a leisurely pace. He was enjoying seeing Keith in a state of shock.

Keith surged ahead through the crowd like a ferret. Vince could see him like a slalom skier ducking and weaving through the tiniest of gaps between people. He finally caught up with him at Surriwong, Keith fretting frantically as he tried to flag down a taxi.

"Fancy getting a tuk tuk?"

"I've had enough fuckin' new experiences for one night." Keith was turning blue in the face.

Vinny nodded to a bloke leaning against a stall who was watching Keith and trying to work out what the madman was doing. "Taxi?"

"OK." He nodded.

"Keith, got one sorted." he beckoned for his friend to follow him and trotted off behind the guy to a parked taxi.

Once they were on the road Keith heaved a sigh of relief. "Thank fuck we're away from there."

"Shit you up, did it, lad?"

"Fuck me. I need a line, a beer and a bird with a proper fanny, not summat made out a plastiscine."

"Think we can manage that." Vinny lit a cigarette and offered the driver one.

"How could you tell they were blokes?" Keith was still stunned.

"Ahh. There's certain giveaway signs." Vin loved playing him along.

"What like?"

"Well, when I saw one tuckin' his bollocks into his bikini in the bogs it gave the game away."

Keith needed a very big line to set him straight. They got in a cab to Tilac and sat in the same seat as the night before. Two whiskies each cleared away any anxiety that remained. Vinny thought he'd do the decent thing, and passed the blonde one that had sat on his knee the night before over to Keith. She was probably the best-looking girl in the bar. She touched his nose and smiled. Her eyes sucked him in and he was safe again.

Vinny nipped over the road to Long Gun to see if Gess was around. Mamasan said she'd gone home sick. Likely story. He trudged back to Tilac morosely; she'd seemed quite nice. Would've been OK for a few nights before hooking up with Jeed. Keith was getting closer to the blonde as Vinny sipped at a drink. Go-go lovers often had spells when they would talk to their best mate's back, and Vinny was going through one of them. He nipped to the toilet and stood at the urinal, which was filled to the brim with disinfectant balls and slices of lime. Two of the girls were stood in front of the mirrors, nattering away in what sounded like Thai – but it could have been Lao or Khmer – while they adjusted their bikinis and unclipped and adjusted their hair. The urine had a magical power that unleashed the scent of lime and Vinny swooned as his second-hand Carlsberg unlocked the aroma from within the porcelain.

"Ooooh, iss biig." One of the girls was looking at Vinny's 'action man' as he released his liquid.

"Ow," the other one yelped as she joined her friend to inspect Vinny's best mate. "Too biig. Cannot boom boom. Hurting. Te he he he he." She pointed and the pair ran off.

Vinny shook off the droplets and smirked to himself. It was worth the 700 quid airfare just for that moment.

Keith was sat alone now.

"Where's blondie?"

"Getting changed." Keith stretched his arms across the backrest of the seats like a King in front of his harem.

"What's the bar fine?"

"Four hundred." Keith was starting to sound like a veteran. Thirty-six hours ago he'd been a callow Westerner who'd never paid for sex. Reclined like a regular Don Juan in front of his admirers you could have been forgiven for thinking he'd been a habitual bar finer for years.

"Fuckin' shocked me, that Dave geezer." Keith shook his head.

"Takes all sorts, mate. All sorts."

"D'yer reckon we'll see 'im again?"

"Doubt it. Anyway, we're off down Pattaya tomorrow."

The happy threesome wandered out of Tilac. Vinny needed a partner for the evening; Keith's new attachment was very attentive so Vinny didn't get much conversation out of him.

They got a cab back to Nana Plaza. Keith suggested a few in Big Dogs but Vinny explained it might not be a good idea. However, it was too late. Keith had already forged ahead and taken up residence with his living love toy in the middle of the bar. Vinny joined them while they waited to get served. The bar was busy and Keith saw last night's conquest stood by herself in a corner satisfying her lust for nicotine. He waved to her, and she scowled and looked out of the bar into the Plaza.

"Bit off with me tonight," he mentioned to Vince.

"Aye. Told yers not to come in 'ere," Vinny huffed.

"What's 'er problem?" Keith seemed bemused.

“You’ve made ’er lose face,” Vinny explained. He was a little embarrassed at Keith’s fau pax, not to mention anxious about having to fight off jealous bar girls.

“How come?”

“You’ve brought another bird in the bar. It’s like tellin’ her and ’er mates she’s no good.”

“Best go somewhere else then, aint we.”

They upped and left. With nowt to sup up and no bill to pay they headed into the heart of the Plaza and drank at a bar for an hour. Keith headed off to the hotel before everything closed down. He was obviously keen to get some shuteye before the arduous trip east the next day.

Vinny had not only his own reputation to think of, but that of degenerates right across the world. Imagine spending a night in Bangkok alone, he thought. Unthinkable. He moved from go-go to go-go in search of someone to rest his beer gut on and share his halitosis with in the quiet of Room 407, Nana Inn, Sukumvit, Soi 3. It wasn’t as easy as it might have sounded. Christmas drew in the punters, all competing for the intimate space of the best-looking bar girls. Vinny was no longer blessed with that wide-eyed glare that guys wore on their first two trips, which said, “Fuck me, a room with twenty women in bikinis. I’ll pay anything for the one with the tattoo to sleep with me.” It could be a handy piece of equipment. The bar girls’ radars bleeped at every newbie that walked through the door. “First timer heading through. Treat him nice, 5,000 baht.” A phrase rang in his ears snatched from an overheard conversation between two guys at a bar. “*Farang roo mak mai dee*.” ‘Foreigner who knows too much, no good. We can’t have him over, knows the score.’

He tried every last one: Pretty Lady, Rainbow 2, Cathouse, Spirithouse, G Spot, Hollywood. In some he’d stop for a beer, spot a decent one and seethe when she went to sit with a fat bloke. Occasionally he’d be approached, buy the girl a drink then give her the once over; maybe her skin would be a bit blotchy, sometimes it was stretch marks or maybe the tits weren’t big enough. He headed out of one nondescript place to extend his search when all around lights came on. The government had started a crackdown and everywhere in Nana was shutting at two. A mass of couples emptied out towards the street. If Noris McWerter had been there he’d have been able to record the highest number of couples mismatched on height and girth gathered in one place. He stumbled out, half carried by the wave of humanity. The cocaine wasn’t going to let him sleep. Might as well head home and stare at the ceiling and save himself for Jeed.

The throng was heading in different directions and he headed towards his hotel.

While he was hovering at the entrance of Nana a tuk tuk was stuck in the traffic. A bird was sat in it. She looked the spitting image of Vicky. Vinny’s jaw dropped as he eyed her and started to head her way. She had a red dress and sunglasses on and was accompanied by a Thai guy in smart Western clothes. The tuk tuk was round the corner in a flash.

Nah. Vinny shook his head. Can't be, he told himself. "A bird with a tan and dark hair in Bangkok. Must be millions of 'em," he muttered and reminded himself to wind Keith up tomorrow.

On Soi Nana there was a barbeque with a dark-skinned guy selling skewers of meat cooked over charcoal for ten baht a throw. The smell of the chilli and garlic marinade charmed his nostrils and he decided to stop and try a couple.

"*Nee aria?*" He pointed to a pile of uncooked meat on sticks.

"Pork." The guy smiled as he wrapped up some freshly grilled ones for a big European bloke in glasses.

"And this?"

"Chicken."

"OK, one pork, one chicken." He thrust his hands in his pockets and hovered uncomfortably, trying to find a safe eddy in the human cascade around him. A girl with her hair dyed brown and sunglasses resting on her forehead was standing next to the grill looking at some of the skewers being cooked. She was holding something wrapped in newspaper and picking little nibbles from within occasionally. Vinny noticed the pair of half coconut shells she had under her V-neck T-shirt. He looked at his meat starting to spit. He looked back at her tits. She looked up from her supper and smiled.

"You like Buddha?" She held up the amulet nestling in the valley and giggled.

Vinny started to salivate. The food had little to do with it.

"Hunglee?" she purred and offered him her supper.

He wandered over and smiled. He looked in the wrapped-up newspaper and pulled out a skewer. She smiled. It was half nibbled already.

"You can. Iss goot." Vinny sunk in his gnashers with his neck extended. He didn't want fat dripping down his neck or to stand in her space. She giggled again.

Vinny put his neck on the line. "You come my room?"

"Yes." She looked around.

"How much?"

"Two thoussaarn baht." She pushed more food at him.

"Oooh, expensive. Cannot." Vinny sighed. She looked down.

"One thousand," Vinny offered.

"OK." She smiled, nodded and put her hand round his elbow.

Who said romance was dead?

do you remember when?

"Croston, you faggot."

"Uuuurgh."

"Hey yoou, Clot ton faegort."

"Eh."

Vinny stumbled out of bed. He tripped over two empty bottles of beer on his way to the door.

"All right, Vince?" Keith was sparkling like a new pin with his blonde on his arm in the doorway.

Vinny rubbed his face.

The blonde giggled and covered her mouth with her hand.

Vinny wheezed and coughed pushing his chest out.

"Bamboo?" Keith enquired.

"Half hour." Vinny shut the door. He heard two people walking away and one high-pitched laugh. With his head in his hands he traced his steps back to last night. He remembered Noi; she'd fucked off after a while. Cocaine did funny things to a man's hydraulics. First you felt like you wanted to and it worked. Then you felt like you didn't want to and it still worked. After that it stopped of its own accord. Then you felt like you wanted to again and it half worked then you gave up. Vinny's giving-up point had arrived when he was knelt behind her. She was on all fours and he was inspecting a mole on her back. She'd looked stunning with her clothes on but the sub T-shirt inspection had revealed stretch marks. When she'd come back from the shower and dropped the towel Vinny could see the ISO inspector in the corner with his clipboard frowning and shaking his head. "Sorry, madam, got to stamp you as being post-gestational. Only safe for use after thirty Carlsberg."

As soon as gravity had become more important than fluid pressure in the evenings dynamics, she had picked up her mobile and started to text someone. Boyfriend probably. She'd dressed, collected her 1,000 and let the door close itself behind her.

Anyway, with the important part of last night's events available for immediate recall Vinny showered, put on his trusty shorts and headed for

Bamboo. He stood at the door, much the same way Keith had done yesterday, only he wasn't feeling as bad. Bamboo was quite a spacious bar by Bangkok standards. Six pool tables and a stage for bands gave it a more casual feel than a lot of the pokier establishments closer to Nana, where floor space was at a premium. A cursory glanced located his partner; he was in the same corner Vinny had occupied the day before.

"Morning." Vinny smiled at Keith. "*Sabai dee mai?*" he asked his partner. He pulled up a stool and eyed the laminated menu.

"*Sabai mak*," purred the blonde as she lifted her head an inch off Keith's arm.

Vinny ordered some breakfast and sat back.

"Kees. I go pi pi loom," his assistant purred and headed off to the ladies.

Keith eyed her behind as she waddled away. He shook his head twice then started to nod. "Top top top top shag, that, our kid."

"Did you get her name this time?"

"Aye, Nan." He was trying his best not to look self-satisfied. "What d'you gerrup to?"

"Picked one up outside Nana after last orders." Vinny drew on hs cigarette.

"Yeah?" Keith looked interested. "Any good?"

"Nah. Couldn't get a proper bugle on with all that coke. She fucked off after 'alf an hour."

"Ppheewww," Keith empathised.

"Still, no chance of any kip, like. So I fucked off down The Grace."

"What's it like?"

"Grotty room, full to the brim. Fucked off when I seen some Arab get stabbed."

Keith shook his head.

"So I went back the hotel an' emptied the mini-bar."

Nan tottered across the floor back to Keith. She sped up when she got near him and kissed his cheek.

"Hello, Nan." He hugged her softly.

"Hello, Kees." She clasped his arm.

Vinny shook his head. Mr ladies' man was smitten within two days of landing in the Orient.

"Ready for Patters today, our kid?" Vinny was eager to see Jeed.

"She wants come with us." Keith tapped his arm.

Vinny shook his head. He ate his food and paid the bill. The threesome headed back to the hotel. Nan made no sign of doing the decent thing and disappearing; she just clung to Keith like a limpet.

Nana Inn has a travel agency attached to it. They headed inside before going to their rooms. The girl who had checked them in was sat behind a desk. There was a Finnair calendar on the wall behind her. She was tapping some figures into a calculator and looked up. “One minni, please.” She carried on tapping. “OK, sir,” she said when she’d finished. “Can help you?”

“Can you get us an ’otel down Patters?”

She frowned.

“Sorry.” Vin cleared his throat. “Hotel, Pattaya, for me my friend.”

“Yes, sir. Pattaya velly furr. Iss Chlitmat.”

Vinny’s face dropped. “No hotel?”

“Yes, sir, hotel but espensif.”

“How much?”

“One thoussarn two hunlet baht.” She looked down at some paperwork.

Vinny let out a sigh of relief. “Is OK. Two room.”

“Sah, you pay now. I giff liseet. You hap lesserwaysharn.”

The two threw over their credit cards. A quick phone call, a tap on the credit-card machine and two signatures, and the pair were booked into Town in Town.

“Sah you wan hotel minibut ? It leap fipe pm?”

“Nah, we get taxi.”

Simple – the two were booked into a top hotel.

They headed off to their rooms. Vinny phoned Jeed who squealed with delight when he told her his arrival was imminent.

In the lift down, Nan was whining that Keith hadn’t decided to take her with them. They stood on the street outside and flagged down a taxi. After a bit of barter Vinny managed to secure the fare for a thousand. He could have got it lower but couldn’t be arsed arguing.

As they pulled off, Nan stood on the street and the tears were dripping from her eyes. Keith craned his neck. “I shoulda brought ’er with us.”

“Don’t worry, kidder. She’ll be cryin’ the same tears for Gunter tomorrer when ’e comes Patteyer.”

Keith got his first proper taste of Bangkok traffic. When you came in from the airport it was a clear run across the Express Roads to Sukumvit and the rest of their travel had been restricted to the evenings. They headed onto Sukumvit Road. The traffic moved for a while. Then it ground to a halt. The horns were setting the beat and unregulated exhausts provided the melody. They were in the shadow of the concrete platform that was home to the Skytrain.

“Look at that cunt there.” Keith pointed out of the window. He’d spotted a motorbike weaving its way through the traffic. Thais used 100cc Hondas as cargo carriers. The one that had raised Keith’s eyebrows was being used to ferry the driver’s seven-year-old son (no helmet, just shorts and flip-flops) and a washing machine. The machine was strapped onto the seat with flimsy looking string and the son sat between the driver and the handle bars swinging his legs without a care in the world.

Keith shook his head and lit a fag.

They passed the white marble-faced expanse of the Emporium shopping centre.

After twenty minutes of stopping and starting they reached the Bang Na intersection and joined the highway heading east. The road opened up quite quickly and before long they were out of Bangkok.

The last two days had taken their toll on the Bacchanalian Brothers and they were both feeling drowsy. Keith was looking out of the window at the dried grass and derelict buildings.

Bangkok was weird. It was like being off your head. The heat, pollution and waves of humanity ran you down like a depressant, but the lights, the life, the smiles and your libido kept a man going like a stimulant. Now Bangkok was behind them there was little stimulus to keep them alert and the pair started to nod off.

"Keith."

"Uhh."

"Fuckin' sure I saw that Vicky bird last night."

"Naaah." Keith's head dropped. His eyes were shut and he was gone.

Vinny sat back and shut his eyes. Jeed's face was painted inside his eyelids.

It was hard to say when either of them woke. They probably drifted in and out of sleep for the duration of the journey.

The sign said Pattaya 20 Kilometres when Keith whined like a nine-year-old, "Are we nearly there yet?"

On the outskirts of Pattaya the driver had to stop and ask a motorbike taxi the way to the hotel. Vinny was looking round trying to get his bearings. Most parts of Pattaya were identical. Even frequent visitors found it hard to get their grid when they first landed.

After driving aimlessly and doing a circle of the one-way system the taxi driver found his bearings. They trundled slowly up the dusty concrete roadway of Moo 9. Town in Town peered down on Vinny and Keith like a Gulliver weighing up two Lilliputs. The guard at the barrier nodded to the driver and let them through.

"Bit of all right, this gaff," said Keith as he eyed their new home.

Vinny didn't reply. He just stared up the gleaming blue-glass colossus in front of them. There was a marble porch at the front of the building and to the right were some hedges and gardens. A coach load of Japanese tourists in sun visors and golf clothes were congregating at the steps, all carrying their sensible luggage and cameras. Vinny looked concerned when he saw them. On his previous stays in Pattaya he'd stayed in guesthouses full of degenerate Europeans visiting Thailand for the same reasons as himself.

"Not sure about this gaff, Keith," he frowned.

"Looks pretty smart to me."

"Aye, might be dodgy about us bringing birds back."

The driver was paid off and departed, and they headed with their bags into the reception area. It was high ceilinged and marble floored. The reception desk was hidden away in a corner behind some neatly arranged sofas. Another group of Japanese, or possibly Korean, tourists in sensible clothes were stood listening intently to their guide who was speaking authoritatively about the bottle of water he held in his hand.

Vinny wasn't used to opulence. It didn't suit him. It reminded him that he was an underachiever.

The reception desk was well staffed. One of the uniformed pretties took the chit off Vinny and gave the guys a form each to complete, and asked for their passports. They filled in the usual stuff – name, date of birth, passport number, hometown, and profession.

"What you puttin' down as yer profession, Keith?"

"Arsonist."

Vinny giggled. "I'm an evangelical preacher."

They slid their forms over and the girl gave them their keys. Vinny leaned on the desk and watched her intently as she scribbled some notes and smiled. She had a tiny little mole on the left-hand side of her nose. Her posture in the chair was perfect and she had the figure and skin of a twenty-year-old who didn't overeat or fill her body with intoxicants. Keith seemed agitated; he was hopping from foot to foot and eyeing the lift.

She passed them back their passports and smiled.

"Fuckin' 'urry up, Vin, I'm touchin' cloth." Keith had a look of urgency on his face.

They hit the up button on the lift.

"If it don't get 'ere soon I'm bount shit me keks." Keith was standing tense and upright.

The lift arrived and the two hauled their bags in.

"What room you in?"

Keith looked skyward as if he was in prayer. "Eleven eleven."

"Twelve nine, me." Vinny was looking at the floor. "No fuckin' about, like. I need to go an' meet Jeed sharpish."

The lift stopped at the eleventh floor and Keith started pushing at the door before it opened. When it did he was gone in a flash.

Vinny laughed. He got to his room and pushed the door open and pulled his bag in, pleasantly surprised. It was nicely decked out. The beige carpet was thick and clean. The furnishings weren't worn, the light switches were up to date, there were no exposed wires. He could have been in Europe. The room was rectangular and a curtain jutted into the floor at an angle at the far end. He pulled it back to reveal a patio door and a small concrete balcony. Vinny slid the door back and looked over Pattaya Bay. The sun was three quarters of its way to the horizon on his right, the sea was clear blue and Pattaya, warts and all, lay in front of him. He breathed in the air and stretched his arms.

His watch said 5.15. Fuck it! He showered, changed and jogged down to Keith's room and tapped on the door. A shirtless Keith opened the door looking pale and drained.

"Y' right?"

"Just get a shirt on."

"Look a bit pale, kidder."

"Yeah, just shat my body weight." He rummaged in his bag and pulled out a shirt.

Keith had stopped bothering spending hours preening himself so they headed out in good time. At reception the girl with the mole took their keys. She was eyeing a dog-eared English/Thai dictionary and seemed worried when Keith put his key on the desk.

"There y'are, Keith. She's looking up 'arsonist' in the dictionary." He nudged him and they headed out the door.

The Moo or Road leading to the hotel was lined with a few quiet shops, restaurants, a karaoke bar and a launderette. It was pretty much deserted as they walked down to Central Road. Parts of Pattaya could be pretty unappealing, especially away from the entertainment section, and Central Road fitted the description. It was a wide road lined with shops selling motorbikes, motorbike spares, the odd empty bar or restaurant and clothes too small to fit a Westerner. Gangs of motorcyclists seemed to be racing each other up and down either carriageway as the sun started to set.

"Need to flag down a cab, our kid." Vinny had his hands on his hips and was looking up and down the road. He spotted a pick-up truck and waved.

"We're in 'ere." Vinny jumped in the street.

"That a taxi?"

"Aye, baht bus." Vinny strolled down to the driver. "OK." He nodded.

The pair hopped in the back and joined two girls chatting in Thai who were sat on the vinyl bench seating and holding onto the rails in the ceiling. With the crunch of a grinding gear lever they lurched into the traffic.

Keith looked through the glassless sides and eyed up the world around him. They turned left onto 2nd Rd where, instead of shops, there were open-sided bars advertising Thai and European food underneath signs provided by breweries. Some of the signs were English, some were German and there was the occasional shop but the emphasis had changed – this was Fun Town.

Vinny was leaning forward anxiously when he saw the Prince Hotel to his left. He rung the bell on the frame and the driver pulled up. Keith and Vinny hopped out and the amorous one passed the driver a few notes. They headed down the narrow walkway of Soi 7 and were surrounded by small open-sided bars staffed by smiling girls serving drinks for guys playing Connect 4 and Jenga. When the ladies of the bars saw Vinny trying to look cool and halt the urge to sprint to Tommy Bar with Keith by his side, the chorus of cat calls started.

"Oooh, handsom maarn. Welcome, please. Hab sum dlink, hab ladee."

A girl from one of the bars hopped down the concrete steps, grinning broadly, and linked arms with Keith. She walked with him for a pace or two then tried to drag him back to her workplace. Keith stopped and tried to unleash himself but she put up a fight. He had to yank his arm and up the pace to catch Vinny.

As they approached Tommy, one of the girls who was playing Connect 4 with a fat guy in black shirt and shorts noticed Vinny.

Her jaw dropped she turned from the game and started screaming, "Jeeeeeed. Jeeeeeed."

All hell broke loose among the five girls behind the bar. Vinny's face lit up and he glanced at another bar coyly. He saw Jeed turn from the far side of the bar. She didn't seem to smile in the moment he caught her face and she ducked under the bar. Vinny started to feel light headed, then the brown girl he'd been pining for, clad in white and orange, tore towards him at the speed of light. She threw herself at him from the raised concrete platform that housed the complex of bars and landed with her arms around his neck. Vinny was in heaven. All around the reunion had become the centre of attention. Jeed pecked him on the lips. He looked down at her deep brown eyes and she kissed him again. The kiss seemed to last forever as her small pointed tongue cleaned the inside of his lips and tingled against his gums.

Keith laughed and took a stool next to the fat guy at the bar, who was watching Chonburi Amateur Operatic's version of *An Officer and a Gentleman*.

"You must be Keith." His broad Geordie accent was welcoming.

"Yeah." Keith was shocked. "'Ow d'yer know?"

"'Eard nowt for the last week an' 'alf off Jeed but Vinny an' Keith from Bol'on." His Connect Four partner was back at the okey. Fat bloke dropped a disk. She laughed, pointed at three yellows in a row and plopped in another to make four.

The lovers' embrace was starting to slacken off a little. Jeed had made him stiffen and his hardness rubbed against the warmth in her glowing white jeans. Vinny was flushed. He felt like rifling her there and then. Jeed took his hand and dragged him to the bar. She pulled out a stool and guided Vinny on, then squeezed herself in front and rubbed her behind into his crotch.

Fat Geordie had noticed Vinny's protrusion.

"Got somewhere to 'ang yer 'at now, Jeed." He laughed and extended a chubby hand to Vinny. "I'm Stez."

Vinny had his arms wrapped around Jeed and was nibbling her ear. He looked up and accepted the hand. "All right I'm—"

"I know who y' fuck'n both are." He smiled. "Jeed's told w's all about yer."

Two beers had arrived on the bar.

"You wan' dlink?" Vinny whispered in Jeed's ear.

She turned and brushed her wet lips against his and yabbered in Thai at Stez's Connect 4 friend. A third beer arrived as Vinny stroked Jeed's long straight hair; he moved his head so he could admire her face from the side.

A thin guy in his early thirties wearing a faded blue Fred Perry T-shirt waded through the crowd. His cropped brown hair stood an inch or two above the throng of merrymakers assembled round the cluster of bars.

"There's mi mate Paul." Stez started to chuckle. "'E's add the Ertha Kitts last two days."

Paul arrived and stood next to Stez. He was wearing grey cotton jogging shorts and training shoes with socks.

"How's yer hoop?" Stez enquired.

"S'like two halves of a lemon." Paul looked distressed. "Bin scared of fartin' all day."

"This is Vinny an' Keith." Stez nodded towards the pair at his side.

"Woy. Nice to meet yer, lads." His accent was Geordie like his pal's.

Paul extended his hand and Keith shook; Vinny wasn't paying much attention. "Suit yerself, y'amorous get."

Vinny looked up from Jeed's neck. "Oh, sorry, mate." He held his hand and shook.

Keith got a warm glow from these guys. Geordies had that effect. Keith decided to make conversation. He had a funny feeling Vinny's tongue might be tied up for a while.

"'Ow long yer been 'ere?"

"'Bout ten days now." Stez rubbed his chin.

"'Ow long yer stayin'?"

Paul and Stez looked at each other.

"Dannaa," Paul offered.

"Got enough money for aboot six months, like." Stez plucked some grime for his nostril. "Unless w' get some more work before."

"Why what d'yer do?"

"Wa work on planes, like." Stez started a new game of Connect 4. "Just done nine months in Saudi."

"Same length a time as givin' birth, only ten times more fuckin' painful," Paul added.

"Aye, so wa bin supp'n an' tupp'n till wa forget."

Keith was warming to them more by the minute. Vinny and Jeed hugged and kissed while Keith listened to the aeronauts' antics and joined in with his own story about Dave in Pat Pong.

An attractive-looking girl appeared. She was small. Unlike most Thai girls her dark hair was wavy. She had paler skin than most and her face had a striking likeness to Diana Ross. Her nipples were fat and stood out boldly through the fabric of her lime-green dress.

Paul nudged Stez, who hadn't noticed her. Stez called out to her in Thai. She looked, smiled and trotted over to him. It took a quick wriggle to squeeze her in front of him while she placed her handbag on the bar.

Stez cleared his throat. He raised his hands daintily and placed both his thumbs and forefingers round her nipples and started to twiddle. Through his lips he mimicked the oscillations of a radio being tuned, broke in with a small crackle and put on a mock BBC accent. "Lundy four, gusting to Fairisle three, Fastnet Easterly four, Finnnistere six. Rockall tits, Dogger one thousand baht, Arsole extra." He raised his right buttock and farted. "Strong gusts expected."

Anyone English in earshot was laughing and Stez looked round to soak up the adulation.

He looked back down at the job in hand and put the voice on again. "That was the shipping forecast from the Met Office, and now on four The Archers. Lah dah dah dah dah dah daaaaaah, lah dah dah dah daaaaah da."

There were smiles and laughter all around and Vinny looked at Keith with a glint in his eye. The Thais didn't really understand but laughed along anyway.

Stez bought his wireless a drink and she squeezed her way out to stand round the other side of the bar.

With the mini Footlights Review finished, Stez turned to Paul. "Finish these and shoot off, eh?"

"Aye, just gotta nip an' 'ave a Clifton." He put his beer back on the bar and rushed off.

"What's a Clifton?" Keith was curious to learn of this mystical Siamese ritual.

"It's a colliery near Nottingham," Stez elaborated.

"Ehy?" Keith was bemused.

"Rhymin' slang." Stez was playing him on. "Clifton Pit."

Vinny had been listening in and sniggered along with Keith. Guys who spent time abroad tended to build up their own vernacular and when they explained it to you it meant they were your mates. When they didn't, it was because they wanted to exclude you.

Stez finished his beer. "We're off. Getting' fed an' watered. But if yer fancy a Don Revvie later we'll be down Paris about nine."

It was an invite aimed at Keith.

"That down Soi Diamond?" Vinny ventured.

"Aye, yeah. Paris A Go Go." Stez walked off with Paul.

Vinny finally got a chance to introduce Jeed to Keith. She held out her hand and when he shook she smiled. "Nite to miit yoou." She turned back to her man. "Winny, look." Jeed pointed at the pillar in the middle of the bar. "Iss Bolton Wonder shirt." She turned and kissed Vinny again.

"Wow." It was a bit grimier than when he'd given it to her in October but the sentiment was more important than the presentation.

"Beefor man come. Hiim welly *mau* and say Bolton no goot." Jeed shook her head. "Him say him flom Balackapoo and try make fiya."

"Where him from?" Vinny was confused.

"Balackapoo."

Vinny looked at Keith confused for a second, then it dawned on him.

"Ohh. Blackpool," he corrected her.

"Yes. Balackapool." Jeed gave the thumbs up. "And try make fiya." She mimicked the sparking of a cigarette lighter. "So Jeed boxing him. He not come back." She punched Vinny playfully on the nose.

Vinny looked over to Keith. "Apparently some gimp from Blackpool tried torchin' mi shirt so Jeed stuck one on 'im." Vin hugged her tight.

"Typical Blackpool getting worked over by a bird." Keith laughed. "Bit 'ungry, mate, fancy getting a nose bag?"

"Jeed. Me Keith go get food. You want come?" He stared his love in the face.

"Yes." Another kiss made him smile. Keith was starting to feel a bit of a gooseberry.

"OK, we go Rosie?" Vinny let go as Jeed went to get her bag. "We'll go t' Rosie O' Grady's round the corner, kidder. Top notch."

They paid the bill and hopped into the street. Jeed linked arms with Vinny and walked along happily, swinging her fake Louis Vuiton handbag as she went. They strolled slowly through the crowds and motorbikes. Jeed got the odd glance from single men starting on their night's mission.

The three of them arrived at Rosie O' Grady's on Soi 8. The restaurant was a little incongruous in its surroundings. It was an Irish place surrounded by the makeshift looking bars that typified North Pattaya. There was a terraced section elevated from the road and fenced off by an oak-spindled barrier and the indoors was sectioned off by hardwood panelling and windows with lace curtains and the Guinness logo emblazoned across the glass.

"Outside or in?" Vinny directed the question at both his accomplices.

"Outside seems decent enough," Keith offered.

They wandered to a table and pulled out the chairs. A waiter approached and asked if they wanted drinks.

Keith was starting to get comfortable in his Asian surroundings and took the lead. "Errm. *Song* Carlsberg and, err, Jeed, you want dlink?" He'd even started to mispronounce.

"Hab Carlseberk." She smiled at Keith.

"OK, three Carlsberg." Keith sat back feeling proud of himself.

Jeed squeezed Vinny's leg and leaned closer to him to whisper in his ear. "Honey. I'm not wan' you dlink too muts. Tonigh' make good boom boom, OK?"

Vinny turned to her. "OK, yes."

"Plomit?" She looked expectantly into his eyes.

“OK, Vinny plomise. For Jeed can do.” He winked at her and tried not to blush.

Vinny and Jeed leafed through the menu. Keith was distracted; his eyes were drifting up and down the road focusing on the ladies either hanging off bar stools or sauntering up and down the street to their place of work.

Jeed nudged Vin. “Kees always looking. Him look ladee. Not hab ladee for sleep.”

Vinny sniggered. “Yer’ve bin sussed, our kid.”

“Eh ?” He looked back at Vin.

“Jeed thinks your butterfly,” Vin elaborated.

“What’s butterfly?” Keith looked worried.

“Isss man hab many ladeee,” Jeed poked at him playfully.

“In two day Keith have six lady,” Vinny half whispered to keep Keith in on the fun.

“Wow.” Jeed acted shocked. “Kees no butterfly.” She shook her head. “Helicopter.”

The three burst into laughter as the waiter arrived with the drinks. He looked paranoid as he walked into their fun.

“Now OK you can order food?” He looked each one of them in the eye sternley.

Jeed jabbered something in Thai and he noted it down.

Vinny looked quickly at the menu. “I’ll have the roast beef dinner, please.” He looked over to Keith. “Well worth a try, that one.”

“Yeah, make that two.”

The waiter headed to the kitchen.

“Aah, Kees, tonigh’ you wan’ ladee?” Jeed enquired politely.

“Probably.” He was taken aback by her directness.

“My flen Ohn, she see Kees TV, football wiss Winny. Say Kees hansom maarn.”

“I think she’s trying to set you up with her mate,” Vinny explained.

“Ohn wery sexy. Make good boom boom for you,” Jeed added.

What a sales pitch. Keith didn’t know where to look.

“Maybe Keith look lady. If like, OK, if not, no problem.” Vinny was trying not to make the commitment too strong. Just because you viewed a property didn’t mean you wanted to put in an offer.

“OK, I look,” Keith promised.

The first round of beers were nearly finished when the food arrived so Keith ordered another three. Vinny felt his leg being squeezed as Jeed heard the word beer.

The smell of roast beef and gravy filled the air and something a little more aromatic came from the pot that was placed on Jeed’s mat.

Vinny and Keith dove straight into theirs while Jeed was more reserved. She took the lid off her ceramic pot and prodded the contents and sniffed. She looked disappointed and put the lid back on. Vinny noticed something was up.

"Is OK?" he enquired.

"Ziss, they make for *farang*. Not spicy. Jeed wan' spicy. *Pet mak*." She took her napkin off her lap and put it back on the table.

The waiter noticed the commotion and crept over to the table. Jeed jabbered at him in Thai and he scurried off, returning a moment later with some chopped chillies in a dish. Jeed spooned them in and scowled at him. The waiter smiled like waiters always did to ease away the problems.

"Fuckin' bang on, this, Vincent." Keith was wolfing his down as if he'd not been fed for a week.

"Aye. Bit of English is good for t'stomach now an' then," Vinny managed to gurgle between mouthfuls.

Halfway through his plateful Keith burped and smiled at Jeed apologetically. "Fuckin' stuffed." He sat back, wheezed and pulled at his belt before burping again.

Vinny smirked. "Same 'ere, mate." He pushed his plate away. "All that ale ruins yer stomach."

The pair lit cigarettes in unison. Jeed carried on eating politely.

With cigarettes over, Keith started to eye the street again. His glare was occasionally met with a smile and a wave.

Jeed finished her dish after insisting Vinny tried some.

"You tly, iss goot." She held out her porcelain spoon. "Ziss chickaen ant coconut ant chilli."

Vin smiled as drops spilled out of his mouth. "Is good," he complimented her on her choice. "Delicious. *Aroi mak*."

They paid the bill and hopped out onto the street. Keith looked at his watch. It was 8 o'clock. They had an hour to kill before meeting Stez and Paul.

"We get taxi Walking Street?" Vinny suggested to Jeed. "That's where that Paris gaff is," he added for Keith's benefit.

They headed down onto Beach Road and flagged down a baht bus full of revellers on their way to South Pattaya. Vinny and Jeed were arm in arm and gazing longingly into each others eyes while Keith weighed up his surroundings. He saw the thin strip of sand that claimed to be Pattaya Beach, the palm trees and promenade. There were a few boats in the bay bobbing in the waves and wearing lights like trinkets. The Beach Rd, as ever, was crowded with baht buses, scooters and Harley Davidson lookalikes being ridden by fat guys accompanied by girls less than half their size. Inland of the beach and the promenade was an assortment of bars, restaurants and vendors, and the road was crowded with tourists heading in different directions but all with the same final destination – drunken oblivion in the arms of a hired honey. They passed the almost grandiose stairway leading to the Royal Garden Plaza, which housed typical Siamese establishments like KFC and a Timberland outlet.

"'Ere, Keith." Vinny pointed over his shoulder. "Pattayaland Soi 2, that."

"Looks like Vegas." Keith had seen the collection of neon signs like EMERGENCY with it's red cross and ALL GIRLS with its flashing female outline lighting the street.

"Aye. A lot o' folk stick money in slots down there but very rarely get owt back." Vinny smirked. "'Cept for the odd rash."

They'd passed Pattaya's highest concentration of go-go bars. They passed a host of stalls and bars and eventually came to a corner where the carriageway veered off to the left and the traffic ground to a halt.

"Our stop, this, Keith." Vinny let go of the railing in the roof of the van and hopped out. Keith and Jeed followed him.

"My shout." Keith scurried off to pay the driver.

The three bustled across the road and were soon on the pedestrianised extension of Beach Rd known as Walking Street. The ingenious Thais had managed to line either side of this section with money-making ventures, most of them involving filling the patrons with alcohol and allowing them to leave with a new friend, but some selling keepsakes, sportswear, pharmaceuticals or tailored clothes.

"Want to have a look round before we go in Paris?" Vinny offered.

"Might as well." Keith was taking it all in.

They strolled through the crowds, Vinny and Jeed hand in hand, and Keith people watching. In this part of town there were the omnipresent single guys in groups from all over the world but, unlike Nana and Cowboy, there seemed to be youngish Western couples parading up and down as well.

Keith noticed a boxing ring in one of the bars. "We 'avin' a butchers in 'ere?"

They passed an escalator, wandered into the bar and took a seat close to the ring.

Jeed ordered three beers and they settled back. It was still quite warm and the rest was much needed.

A waitress approached with a tray and three beers.

"Keith, go an' 'ave a look at that bar we've just passed near the escalator." Vinny pointed to where they'd just come from.

"Iss goot. Hab sexy girl," Jeed added and smiled as she grabbed Vinny's arm.

"Best not be a wind up, this, Vince." Keith knew it was but played along. He got up and walked out, returning thirty seconds later.

"You like?" Jeed squeaked.

"Fuckin' *Katoeys* 'r' Us, that one." Keith smirked. Today he was ambivalent, yesterday he'd found it abhorrent. "I still can't work out why folk choose Lilly Savage when there's proper birds around."

"Jeed hab flend *katoey*," she added. "Him nite ladee."

"Why do they do it?" Keith was looked puzzled.

"Can make money," Jeed explained.

"Eeurrgh." Keith screwed up his face. "'Ave yer bits lobbed off so yer can sleep wi' fat Germans."

"'S a good earner," Vinny protested. "Thought o' doin' it myself."

"Croston. That's put me off my beer, that 'as." Keith shivered and put his bottle down.

Vinny laughed.

There was activity in the boxing ring. Rough-looking guys in nylon shorts with Thai writing emblazoned on the front occupied two of the corners. They were chatting to their seconds standing outside the ring. A weird wailing music punctuated with dull beats and the odd cymbal started to pipe out of the speakers attached to pillars at the corner of the bar, and the fighters started to circle the ring. After a full circuit they headed to the centre and sat on their heels with their knees spread wide and started to pray to the heavens. Occasionally they'd look down and bow to the floor then look up and wave their arms and start praying again. When the ceremony finished they returned to their corners and the music stopped.

The referee entered the ring in his striped black shirt and pulled the fighters to the centre.

"Who's yer money on?" Keith was offering Vin a sportsman's bet.

Vinny weighed up the fighters for a moment. "Well…" He stroked his chin. "Red corner looks leaner." He swigged at his beer. "But blue's got the height advantage." He sucked his lips.

Keith looked in respect at the self-appointed Thai boxing aficionado.

"So it'll be the one the bookies 'ave told not to take a dive." Vinny laughed at his own joke.

Keith settled back to watch the two guys in the ring beat each other round the head with the parts of the body soccer players normally use for playing keep-ups, while Vinny and Jeed pawed each other and laughed and giggled like the lovebirds they were.

The fighters put on a good display of theatrical knockdowns and recoveries which had the crowd gasping. When the fight finished the referee held up the hand of the guy in the red corner. The fighters left the ring and toured the bar as punters pushed currency into their gloved hands.

Keith looked at his watch. "Tryin' another?"

Vinny stretched himself up out of his chair. "Aye, if yer want."

They wandered around and found a bar that looked onto the street where they could watch the world go by. At 8.55 they headed off to Soi Diamond. It was a street off Walking Street that was home to a number of beer and go-go bars, including Paris Super A Go Go, where they'd promised to meet the Geordies.

"Shall we have one outside while we wait for 'em?" Vinny suggested.

"Let us nip in and 'ave a look first." Keith tottered off and popped his head behind the curtained entrance to Paris and returned moments later to the bar opposite where Vinny sat stroking Jeed's knee.

“No sign of ’em.” Keith looked at his watch. He thought Jeed was nice but was quiet impressed by the number of mating opportunities on offer in Pattaya and didn’t want to spend his first night with a couple.

The bar they’d chosen to sit at was staffed by three ladies who joked and giggled happily amongst themselves while the trio tucked into their drinks. One of them noticed that Keith seemed to be left out of the proceedings. She nipped under the counter and picked up a girl no more than ten years old who was sat at the end of the bar watching the world go by, and led her by the hand to Keith and lifted her onto a stool next to him. The girl looked into his face with big brown innocent eyes.

Keith gulped and turned a shade paler. “’Ere, Vin. Tell her I ain’t into no paedo nonsense.”

Vin and Jeed looked up from each other’s eyes. The girl’s mum was reaching over the bar.

“Can play game.” She straightened her back and produced a wooden box containing the pieces of a Jenga set.

Keith heaved a sigh of relief and Vinny and Jeed became two opposite poles of a magnet again.

The girl’s mother set the game up and Keith was well on his way to his third successive defeat when Paul and Stez arrived. It was 9.30.

“Sorry wah late.” Stez was reddened at the effort of having to walk 80 yards from the start of Walking Street. “Paul’s ma said he couldn’t play out till his room wa tidy.”

“Nah, bollocks man,” Paul protested. “Wa had ter wait while fatty ’ere did ’is forty minutes daily on the magical penis-extendin’ vacuum.”

Keith chortled along with his new mates. Paul ordered beers for the pair.

“I’ll just nip in Paris for a sec.” He toddled off.

When he was out of earshot Paul explained, “He’s been after fuckin’ one called Nom from in there, like, but she keeps blankin’ ’im. I’ve been windin’ ’im up sayin’ ’e’s too fat.”

Stez returned moments later shrugging the layers of fat above his shoulder up around the layers of fat round his neck. “Some cunt’s ’ad ’er already.”

“Be that Garmun cunt with herpes again,” Paul goaded him.

“Aye, aye.” Stez needed to divert the attention from himself. “Grab a look at Antony an’ Cleopatra there.”

He nodded at Vinny and Jeed chewing each other’s faces.

“Looks like yer on the toon wi’ us pair th’night, Keith.” Stez had made light work of his bottle. “Happy a Go Go next, is it?”

Keith drank up. He felt a bit awkward about being in a new town with two guys he’d never met before and a bit sly on Vinny leaving him alone.

Vinny didn’t mind. He said he’d catch them up but didn’t mean it. He didn’t finish his drink and neither did Jeed; they paid the bill and got a taxi back to Town in Town.

Inside the lift to the twelfth floor they embraced and kissed until the bell signalled the arrival at their destination. Once safe inside Vinny's room, they kissed long and passionately, Jeed's pointed tongue exploring every corner of his mouth. She pushed him onto the bed and pulled at the buttons of his trousers. She pulled them down as far as his shoes and looked hungrily at his delight popping out of the top of his boxer shorts. Vinny decided to do the decent thing and lifted the hem of Jeed's orange T-shirt. She lifted her arms obligingly. Vinny's eyes lit up at the sight of her perfect brown mounds and her heavy brown nipples. She giggled and covered them with her hands.

"Honey," she sighed. "Showa. Must hab showa."

Vinny's perfect woman grabbed him by the hand and dragged him to the bathroom. She turned the water on and tested the heat with her hand, then pushed him against the sink unit and helped him off with his polo shirt. Vinny crossed his arms and stood staring at Jeed proudly as she pulled a towel from the rack on the wall and placed it daintily on the floor. She turned, pulled the waistband on his boxer shorts and looked inside smiling, then pulled his shorts down. They snagged at his knees and Vinny had to unfold his arms and balance as he stepped out of them.

"Iss goot. Welly bic." She looked down at Vinny's populator, grabbed it gently at the base as it pointed to the ceiling and guided him into the shower. Jeed nipped out of the bathroom. Vincent stood in the shower with his back facing the jet. He let the warm water run down the top of his shoulder and his spine. He threw his head back and let shower soak his hair. The bathroom door opened and Jeed returned with a towel wrapped round her body.

Vinny pulled back the plastic curtain. "Ooooh, sexy girl."

She turned and winked; she was looking through the complimentary hotel hygiene products. Vinny watched in admiration then let the shower curtain secrete him.

It seemed like a lifetime before she eventually pulled back the curtain and tiptoed in to join Vinny. She'd managed to find the transparent shower cap and tuck most of her hair into it. She stood back from the jet and Vinny smiled as he eyed the body he'd longed for for so long, and he moved to one side to let the jet wet her. She flinched as the warm jet hit her chest then shut her eyes and moved closer into the stream to wash her face. Vinny hugged her and the warm water formed a river between their bodies. He felt her shower cap rub against his chest then pulled away to kiss her.

That was enough of the shower for Vinny. Fuck getting soaped up; on with the festivities. He scrambled out of the shower and had to steady himself while he looked for a towel. The amount of alcohol consumed that evening hadn't been vast but was enough that manoeuvres required a little attention. He retired to the bed with a towel round his waist, lit a cigarette and folded his legs as he sat upright against the headboard. The remote control for the TV was on the bedside table so he tried flicking on the set but only managed to get a blue screen and some piped music.

"Fuck it." He removed the towel and climbed under the sheets and blanket that were tightly tucked into the bed.

Jeed took a while to finish in the bathroom. When she opened the door she was wearing a towel again and tossed her long sleek hair. Despite the shower cap it had got damp and in the artificial light it was more her natural black than the brown she coloured it. She blew him a kiss and took the unopened packet of condoms Vin had unpacked and left on the dresser, and climbed on top of him. He smiled and stubbed out his cigarette. Jeed put the packet on the bedside unit then held his face gently with both hands.

"I'm miss you too muts," she whispered and kissed his forehead.

Vinny was almost moved to tears. "Honey, England no good." He kissed her cheek. She lowered her head and kissed him softly with her moist lips, slipped the towel off and pulled the sheets back so she could join him.

Vinny was standing proud and it crushed against his stomach when she hugged him tight and kissed his neck while gently flicking his nipples. With a gentle push Vin moved her onto her side and kissed her while he rubbed his trembling hand along the top of her leg and her hip. Jeed kissed his nipple and let her other hand wander slowly down his body. Vinny closed his eyes momentarily and smiled in satisfaction then opened his eyes and looked down. Jeed's head was on his stomach and her soft brown hand was starting to stroke the tip of his manhood. He closed his eyes again; his senses started to awaken as Jeed stroked his favourite limb and gently kissed his navel. Vinny's breathing was beginning to intensify and he glanced at Jeed's crown and gently pushed her head a little lower as he felt her hand at the base of his rod, then the moistness from her mouth mingled with the damp he'd produced himself and he felt her sucking his tip gently and softly while she teased his shaft with her hand. Vincent's head sunk deeper into the pillow and his eyes rolled as he looked to the heavens through his eyelids. He was in a state of sedated elation that dampened his breathing and dulled the nerves in all but one part of his body.

"Hhhpphhhewww … that's heaven," he whispered softly and stroked her ear with his hand.

His hand pulled at her head. He didn't want her to stop but he wanted to see the face he'd dreamed of every night in England. She looked up and crawled up his body and held her head softly against his. There was so much Vinny wanted to say but he was speechless.

She sat astride his stomach and he raised his hands to softly massage the small firm breasts he'd missed so badly, then moved his hands slowly down her sides and held her hips gently. She wriggled slightly and the warmth and fur from her crotch lubricated his stomach. Jeed leaned over to the bedside table and grabbed at the condom packet. She tugged at the cellophane wrapper with her teeth and pulled out the purple foil casing of a sheath. She tapped him gently on the nose with it and giggled.

"Win happee?" She kissed his forehead.

“Vin happy,” he confirmed as he felt her take him in hand again.

He closed his eyes and heard the rip of the foil, then felt two slender hands working the lubricated rubber down his pole.

He heard the sheets rustle and Jeed was astride him again. Using her left hand she steadied his manhood and positioned herself above him. His tip felt the warmth of her entrance and he looked her in the face. She was gazing into his eyes.

Jeed’s hands touched his shoulders and she pushed herself down onto him slowly while she threw her head back. Her inner warmth was like an oven and as she reached the base she started to quiver and groan. She moved back up slowly and pushed herself down, this time with stronger shudders. She had to use her right hand to steady herself against his leg then started to move and shudder in a spiral motion, pumping and squeezing while moaning and whispering to herself.

Vin was starting to feel guilty about his laziness so helped by thrusting from beneath. She started to pant and gasp louder. “Aah, aah, aaaaah.”

She stopped and looked at Vinny with a fire in her eyes then manoeuvred herself sideways without letting him escape. Vinny followed her lead and edged his way on top of her as she lay back, gasping at the effort of taking his length. He pushed harder and faster while he steadied himself on the knees at his side for what seemed like an age until he exploded and felt his semen streaming out of his tip. Mission accomplished he lay flat against his love and softly tasted her breathe, then looked up at her eyes. She kissed the top of his head and they pulled into each other. Vinny smiled a happy smile. He was back where he wanted to be, with the woman he’d pined for in the cold and rain. She kissed his chest.

two girls

It was three o'clock in the morning when Keith knocked on Vinny's door and walked in without waiting for an answer. There were six used condoms on the floor and one part-used one delaying Vince's dream of fatherhood. Jeed dismounted quick as a flash and wrapped herself in the sheet, hiding her face from the onlookers. Keith had two ladies he'd paid to massage his ego and other more tangible parts of his persona in tow. He was staggering about looked glassy eyed as he tramped in, pulling one girl by the hand while the other trailed behind weighing up the room.

Keith stood on a condom and it made him wobble.

"Watch yerself, dickhead." Vinny tugged the sheet to cover his dignity. "Yer can trace what's in them back to William the Conqueror."

The girl whose hand he was holding tittered and covered her hand at Keith's clumsiness.

"Fuckin' Pattayar's brilliant," Keith slurred as he wrapped his arms round the more attentive of his two attendants and looked over her shoulder at Vinny in bed.

The girl jabbered in Thai at Jeed, who groaned and replied with a faint, "*Mak mak*," though she refused to reveal her face from under the sheet.

"You make many boom boom," girl number one said, pointing at Vinny and smiling.

"Aye." He stroked Jeed through the sheet. "*Khun chu aria*."

"Jaib." She smiled again.

"Nice to meet you, Jaib." Vin plucked a cigarette from the bedside and looked at girl number two. She was looking at a framed picture by the door, uninterested by the world around her. Vinny tried to catch her gaze to ask her name as well but couldn't so dismissed it.

"Eh, Stez an' Paul are a right good laugh," Keith managed to articulate.

"They seem it." Vinny was trying not to laugh at Keith's condition.

"Been chuckin' tequila down mi neck all night, the cunts." He started to slump forward onto Jaib. She pushed back to straighten him up. "Sha' we 'ave party?"

Vinny shook his head. "Have one tomorrow."

"Miserable twat." Jaib started to pull Keith out of the door. "I tell yer what, Vin… fuckin' Pattayar's brilliant."

The door slammed shut. Vinny rocked Jeed gently and she pulled away the sheet covering her face.

"I'm hear Kees speaking. Him dlunk." She rubbed her eyes and put her arm across Vinny.

He stubbed out his cigarette then padded across the room to lock the door and switch off the light. He lost his footing on a condom as well, then snuggled up to Jeed and tried to sleep. It took a lot of time staring into the darkness before he managed it.

When Vinny woke it was around midday. It made a pleasant change not having a steaming hangover or the headache he usually got from cocaine. He looked to his side and saw Jeed staring up at him. She smiled and kissed his cheek then moved her leg over his. With it being morning his compass was facing north; the softness and warmth of Jeed's lower half increased the polarity. She moved her body downward and her breast stroking against his stomach made him ache. While she tried to inflate his stomach through his pennywhistle, he lay back and considered what to have for breakfast. Last night's efforts had left Vince devoid of bodily fluids and Jeed's efforts ended disappointingly. It was still a better way to start the morning than pressing snooze three times then wandering out into the cold and dark of Bolton.

Vinny smoked a cigarette while his sweetheart showered. She returned from the bathroom wrapped in a big white towel, looking edible. When she took the chair in front of the dresser Vinny stood behind her, put his arms around her shoulders and stared at her face in the mirror. This was more than lust. Every move she made made him smile as she picked up bits of make-up and applied them to her face.

"Now I here I take care of you long time, honey." Vinny kissed her cheek.

"No," Jeed frowned. "Jeed take care for Winny goot."

She dabbed on some lipstick. Vinny kissed her cheek again. Bending to be at her level was stiffening his back so he straightened up. The sun was shining directly into the room. The sliding balcony door was stiff but moved with a decent pull.

The twelfth floor was about 200 feet above ground and a strong breeze buffeted Vinny's ears as he walked onto the balcony in his shorts. He felt the sun start to scorch his skin as he looked out over the bay. A glance down made him step backwards quickly. The floor seemed to move when he looked at it. Then he remembered he didn't like heights. After a moment of sweating he decided to move forward to the rail again but looked forward instead of down this time. He didn't feel as comfortable now he knew how far away the floor was. Concentrating on the sea half a mile away was a safer option. A small boat on the bay was occupying his view when he thought he heard panting down below. A gust of wind howled in his ears and it went, then he heard the panting again – it was faint but definite.

"Ugh, Ugh, Ugh."

Vinny put his vertigo to one side and chanced a look over the railings. Below him to the left he cold just make out a brown pair of hands on the railings and a flock of black hair rocking forwards and backwards. The angle made it awkward but there was definitely someone enjoying a bit of 'al fresco'.

"Fuck me." He shook his head. Then it registered. "Keith, is that you?"

"Aye. 'Ow's it goin'?" Keith grunted.

"Not ser bad." Vinny laughed. "You're a dirty cunt, you know that?"

"Just thought I'd take in the view." He gasped as the flock of hair kept nipping backwards and forwards. "If I'd known you were awake I'd a come up an' 'ad a brew."

Vinny stepped back inside. Jeed had managed to dress. "Jeed," he beckoned. "Look."

She had a hairband in her mouth and walked across the room barefoot as she pulled back her hair. She stepped outside and the sun and the wind made her screw up her face. Vinny put his arm round her and guided her to the edge, and pointed to where Keith was misbehaving.

"Look. Is Keith, he boom boom."

Jeed stared for a moment then stepped back, shaking her head. "Iss clazy. *Pii baa.*" She tapped Vinny's forehead.

The volume of the groans had started to take on a noticeably higher volume so Vinny shouted out, "You've got a bit louder, our kid."

"Aye," Keith hollered into the wind. "'S 'cos I've stuck me thumb up 'er arse."

With that Vinny shook his head, laughed, rubbed his face and led Jeed back into the bedroom.

Jeed was still playing with her hair.

"I have shower. We go have breakfast?" Vinny suggested.

She kissed him and nodded.

They sat on plastic chairs under a tarpaulin roof at one of the restaurants on Moo 9 and shared a bowl of rice soup with pork. Vinny watched proudly as Jeed daintily spooned in her food.

"What we do today?" Vinny enquired.

"Today Jeed work in bar for apternoon," she sighed. "You come hab some dlink?"

"OK, yes. But I want take Keith to massage." Vinny looked away.

Jeed frowned. "You wan' butterfly me?"

"No, honey. You number one." Vinny put on his best amorous voice. "I take Keith. Not for me."

"Ok." Jeed stuck out her bottom lip.

Vinny knocked on Keith's door.

"'Ang on a sec." Vinny heard Keith approach the door. "Y'all right, mate?"

Keith was fully dressed in shorts, sandals and a striped polo shirt. Jaib was sat on the side of his bed counting a few notes.

"Not three bad, our kid." Vinny nodded a hello at Jaib. "Where's t'other un?"

"'Kin' slag." Keith shook his head.

"What's up?" Vin was puzzled.

"Seen the fuckin' mess she made?" Keith pulled back the sheets and pointed to a big red blotch on the bed.

"Ah. Liverpool home fixture." Vince smirked.

"Aye. If I'd wanted red sauce I'd 'ave got a bottle of ketchup, wouldn' I? Sent 'er 'ome wi' five hundred." Keith sucked his lips.

"Win some, yer lose some," Vinny sympathised. "Any road, make yerself lively. I've got a treat in store."

Keith looked surprised. "What sort o' thing?"

Vin shook his head. "That'd be telling."

They headed out into the sun after cashing up a hundred pounds' worth of baht each at reception. Jaib got on the back of a motorbike taxi and waved goodbye when they reached Central Rd.

"Fuckin' good sport, that one, I tell yer." Keith shook his head to conceal his wickedness.

"Yeah," Vinny interrupted. "I noticed."

"No." Keith took on a serious tone. "It's like she proper enjoys 'er job."

Vinny hailed down a passing baht bus and asked the driver to drop them at Big C. There was an older lady in the back with some fruit in plastic bags who got off further down the road.

Keith looked confused. He was eyeing up all the bars they passed to see which one was his surprise.

"C'mon, kidder, what's it all about?" Keith started getting anxious.

They pulled up outside the Big C shopping centre, straight out of middle-class America. It was a glass-fronted mall with banners advertising shopping concessions and ice-cream shops. The tacky sign on a pole gave it that extra special gaudy edge.

"Aw, fuck. If I'd wanted shoppin' I'd a said," Keith moaned.

"Nah, mate. Got it wrong." Vinny steered his pal back the way they'd come.

They headed round the side of a grandiose Portuguese-style building with virginal white balustrades around the roof. The sign gave something away. A white orb housing light bulbs named the building SABAI DEE above a picture of a perfectly formed lady in a bikini.

They walked across the car park, half of which was in the open and half beneath the building. Vinny led Keith up a small set of steps and through a door with OPEN written in marker pen on a luminous orange piece of card.

The narrow corridor carpeted brown with white walls opened up into an entrance area. In front Keith could see a space. It looked like a newly refurbished working-men's club, with tables and chairs and a bar with the shutters down. A young guy dressed like a snooker player clicked his feet together and bowed, holding his arm out to a table for the pair to take, and Vinny rushed ahead and sat back smiling. As Keith got closer he noticed the glass and took more of a diagonal to see what was behind.

"Fuck me!" Keith put his hand on his forehead.

Vinny started to laugh. Keith shook his head while he stood rooted to the spot.

Behind the glass was a sight that would bring any man to his knees. There were over a hundred ladies – and yes, ladies was the correct term – clad in evening dresses and perfectly made up, chattering and eyeing Vinny and Keith as the only customers in the place.

Keith walked towards the table where Vinny reclined in his seat smoking a freshly lit cigarette.

"What's up, kid?" Vinny exhaled with a self-satisfied grin. "Took yer by surprise?"

Keith had to take his seat gingerly. The shock of over a hundred women was too much for him. They all wore badges with numbers on and virtually every one was trying to grab their attention with a wave a smile or just a seductive blink of the eyes.

The half-Italian one remembered to keep his cool. He licked his teeth. "So, errrr… what's the script 'ere then?"

"Pick one an' away yer go." Vinny liked stating the obvious.

"I've not 'ad mi breakfast yet," Keith protested.

"Why, y'ungry?"

"Well, I can put it to one side for a minute." Keith was eyeing the four or five tiers of ladies in front of him.

The welcome guy approached politely with a menu. "Some drinks, sir?"

"Just a coffee," Vin requested.

"Errrm, beer. No, coffee. Errrrm, Cola." Keith had never been good at decisions.

The bloke took his time returning with two cups of coffee and a cola on the tray. Keith was intently scanning the rows but couldn't find fault in any of the temptresses, let alone pick one he wanted above the others. Vinny noticed the extra coffee and had to explain in sign language and broken Th/English that he only wanted one.

The guy returned with an altered chit. "Er, sir, you can choose lady?" He looked them both in the face, wearing the same expression he'd worn when he had taken the drinks orders.

Vinny turned up his nose and passed the guy's glare over to Keith.

"Yer not 'avin a do?" Keith seemed disappointed.

"Jeed drained the life out o' me las' night." he avoided his glare.

The pressure was on Keith. “Thirty-four.”

The guy nodded. He strolled off to the wall that separated Sabai Dee’s delights from view as people enter, and spoke into an intercom. ‘Thirty-four’ smiled at the status having her number called gave her among her piers, picked up her make-up bag and took her line out, being careful not to tread on toes or hems.

Keith stood as she appeared through a door and walked over. She smiled and took his hand. He smiled and looked into her eyes. She smiled again.

“’Iya.” Keith looked her down from head to toe.

She smiled again and held out her hand for him to take. The black silk dress that hugged her figure and finished halfway down her calves was breathtaking. So was she.

“What’s yer name?” Keith was floating an inch above the carpet.

Another smile. She guided him back towards the entrance and took a side door up some stairs onto a corridor like the one that housed 1111 in his hotel.

‘Thirty-four’ pushed one of the doors open and took Keith into a room. It was half bedroom with a kingsize bed, armchair and dresser, the other half swimming baths, shower room with non-slip tiles, a triple-sized bath and an inflatable lilo propped up next to the shower.

She guided him into the armchair.

“One thousan’ baht for massard.” Her voice was nearly undetectable.

Keith reached in his back pocket, pulled out a crisp new 1,000-baht note and placed it on the dresser.

Surprisingly enough, she smiled and took hold of the note. “Dlink?” she squeaked.

“Cola,” Keith whispered, following the protocol she’d set.

She slipped off her shoes, hovered over to the bath, turned on the taps then hovered out of the room. A couple of minutes later she returned with a waiter carrying a Cola on a tray.

She walked over to the bath and added some foam, and motioned with her arms for Keith to take off his top. He put down the cigarette he’d lit and stood up. She grabbed the hem of his T-shirt and helped him off with it then pulled both pairs of shorts down to the floor. She bent down and lifted each foot out of the crumpled cloth round his ankles.

Keith wanted to sit back down in the armchair but was scared of leaving a skid mark. She walked over to the door, unzipped the back of her dress and hung it on a hook. Keith eyed her back: she was perfect, no fat, a hint of muscle beneath the skin but nothing too rippling, and curved hips that just invited you to rest your hands on them. She slipped out of the thong she was wearing and turned to face Keith, smiling as usual and coyly covering her breasts with her arms. Like a nymph she skipped to the bath and squatted next to the three-man bowl of foam. She tested the water with her hand and stirred it a touch then beckoned Keith. He looked down at his crotch, ready for the main event. Purely out of politeness he joined her next to the bath. She half stood up, took his hand and placed her own hand behind his calf, gently pushing it towards the bath. Keith lifted his leg and dipped his toe in. It was perfect, warm enough to be hot but not hot enough to be uncomfortable. She'd managed to beat him in without making a splash, held his hand while he hauled his second foot inside then cradled his back and gently eased him down into the corner. As she sat down opposite him Keith got his first glimpse of her flawless orbs crowned with brown cherries. His bottom jaw slowly obeyed gravity – he was mesmerised. In all his life he'd never seen such perfection. Instinctively he leaned forward and slowly caressed them. He was like a schoolboy being offered the FA Cup to hold. Yes, they were real. She giggled coyly and turned to get a sponge from the cradle at the side of the bath, managing to do it without moving her breasts a millimetre away from his fingertips.

Carefully she dipped the sponge in the suds then started to tenderly wipe the soles of his feet, then carefully between his toes. Keith shut his eyes and slowly tilted his head back. When she reached his ankles he opened his eyes and she seemed to know he'd done it because she smiled again.

Rossi was expecting her to work her way up his legs with the sponge but she pushed his knees apart and placed herself against his torso.

She smelt clean. It could have been perfume, it could have been soap or moisturiser, but whatever it was it smelt heavenly. The tap was still running lightly. She placed a small bowl in the flow then dipped her sponge in it and wiped back his hair from the side of his head, then mopped his face. Keith smiled and shut his eyes. A spongeful of water cascaded on top of his crown and it made him jerk and open his eyes. Guess what – she was smiling. He smiled back and gently took hold of her breasts again. The whole experience was making him tremble. He let go and lay back as she softly bathed his torso, then went back down to his feet and worked her way sensually to his waist. Keith had been waiting for this moment and opened his eyes as she reached his tent pole.

Bitch. She stroked it once then hopped out of the bath. He was rock hard and forced his lips together to stop him cursing.

The suds ran down her body and made her look like a statue in the rain. She took the lilo from the wall and put it on the floor, then took the bowl she'd used to wet his hair and scooped up suds and warm water then poured them on the inflatable bed. It took three or four bowls before she walked over to Keith and took his hand. He stood up in the bath and bravely risked getting out with her help. She guided him over to the mattress where she lay him down on his front. A non-slip tiled floor had never looked so good. Keith felt a firm pair of hands massage his calves; not a heavy massage, nice and light. Then he felt it at the back of his thighs. After a set of fingertips scampered across his buttocks, the hands massaged his lower back. A set of thighs bridged his buttocks as the hands worked up his back. Keith felt his lady's undercarriage lower onto his behind and a warm soft crop of pubic hair nestled into his crack. The hands moved up his shoulders and he felt his lower neck being worked. The undercarriage on his backside was starting to circulate and the fat of his buttocks felt a warm, oily lubrication. He was sure he felt nipples on his shoulder blades, then he didn't, then the full breasts pressed into his back. After the tingle of the initial contact had subsided Keith sighed. It couldn't get better than this, could it? The crotch started to circle on his behind then the breasts started to circle in his back, clockwise like the crotch but out of sync. Keith couldn't keep his eyes open. His breathing got heavier. Parts of his body that hadn't been known to experience delight were experiencing it now.

Keith's numerical Venus worked her breasts down his back. The pleasure level was reaching unsurpassed heights; he was motionless. She moved down his body and, as her breasts caressed his buttocks, Keith spasmed. Then she cooled him by gently blowing on his cheeks. Lightly she removed her body from his. Keith was in a natural state of opiation. Then he felt her undercarriage gently lower onto the top of his back and her warm, softly furred, moist crotch started to circle gently on the top of his neck. It was too much. Pleasure and pain were the same sensation and when you held your finger in a flame for too long you couldn't help but pull it out. Keith bucked his back. She knew what it meant and dropped the intensity of the pleasure she was providing. Once she'd worked her way down, she turned Keith onto his back and repeated the process on the front of his torso. She worked her way head first, then breasts and crotch, up his body from his feet, pausing to kiss his manhood and tease it with her breasts. When his shudders got too intense she eased off, like an expert interrogator torturing her victim to extract information – she knew when she was going too far. After tits first feet to head, it was tits first neck to body as Keith lay on his back. Keith whimpered through the full treatment and was stuck for where to move as her haven brushed his nose.

She let him recover then pulled him, gently as ever, by the hand and offered him a towel before leading him onto the bed.

"Two thousan' baht for sekt," she purred.

Keith nodded. His jaws were clenched together. A condom appeared from nowhere. Some semen appeared from somewhere else seconds after her warmth enveloped him. Keith lay back, drained. He couldn't speak or think or open his eyes. It took ten minutes for him to lift his eyelids. She helped him dress and thin out his wallet then guided him gently downstairs.

Vinny looked up from the *Pattaya Mail* he was reading when Keith returned. There were five cigarette butts in the ashtray.

Vinny smiled as he saw Keith. His friend's face was expressionless and he was walking bolt upright. 'Thirty-four' scampered back through the door to the goldfish bowl.

When he'd been at school Vinny had been shown a video about a Japanese prisoner-of-war camp in History. It showed the faces of the guys who'd suffered torturous conditions for years. They were bewildered by freedom. Keith was the same. He didn't seem to recognise Vinny. The world was in soft focus.

"Your face is a picture, man." Vinny slapped him on the back.

Keith didn't flinch, or answer. He just followed him out of the door.

The pair were 300 yards down the road before Keith stopped in his tracks, held his head and proclaimed, "I tell you, man, that's the closest to heaven I'll ever fuckin' get."

Vinny sniggered to himself.

"How long was I gone for?" Keith was looking at the floor.

"'Bout an hour," Vinny answered.

Keith shook his head and looked to the sky. Vinny smiled a sly smile. There was no better feeling than corrupting a mate, and he owed Keith one for getting him into cocaine. It had only taken four days to take the wholesome gleam off Keith.

"So do yer mind payin' for sex now?" he probed innocently.

"Phhew." Keith chuckled. "I did at first, but fuck me. 'S worth every penny."

"How would you feel if Sarah turned up an' tried draggin' yer to bed?" Vinny asked.

Keith almost choked on his cigarette and looked Vinny in the face. "Be like drivin' a Lada after yer've 'ad a Porche for six months."

Keith slapped Vinny on the back and pulled him into his shoulder. "I tell yer, I weren't sure about comin' over 'ere, but fuck me, I don't know if I'll be able t'shag an English bird again."

"'S bin fun watchin' yer learn." Vinny took Keith's arm from off his shoulder. "See down there?" He pointed to the street to their right.

"Yeah."

"Soi 6."

"What is it?" Keith followed the way Vin was looking.

"Whole street lined with short-time bars an' massage parlours," he explained.

"Yeah?" Keith's eyes lit up.

"You get guys tryin' to work their way from top to bottom in one day."

Keith started doing mental calculations. "How many bars are there?"

"Dunno. Fifteen, twenty, summat like that." Vinny shrugged.

"Could be good for Chris'mas day, that."

"Jeed'd chop mi nob off if she found out, like, but not a bad way t'spend fifteen thousand if you've got it spare."

They turned down Soi 7 and ran the gauntlet of girls hungry for the next meal. It was only three in the afternoon but they still got howled and shrieked at and offered all manner of relief.

"Fuck me," said Keith. "I know 'ow The Beatles felt when they got off that plane in New York." He craned his neck in response to a girl shouting, "Hey, Mister Iiinglant. My pusseee wan' meet yooo."

"You wanna teach 'em a bit o' your patter from t'market, lad," Vinny suggested. He put on a mock Cockney accent. "Getch yer titwanks. Getch yer titwanks. Only four quid a dozen. Fresh from Isaarn today."

They called in at Tommy Bar and ordered beers. Jeed wasn't around. The girl who served them tried to explain where she was but her English wasn't too good. Keith nipped into a small restaurant come bar further down the road and asked them to bring him up a cooked breakfast.

Jeed turned up while Keith was eating. She'd been shopping at one of the stalls on Beach Road and bought herself a new top, which she showed off by holding it against herself and doing a little sexy dance for Vinny before kissing him gently on the ear.

"Wass yoo do today?" They'd been apart for about two and a half hours but it felt like an age.

"I take Keith *Sabai Dee*."

"OK," she frowned. "You hab massard?" She tried not to look concerned but was watching him for the slightest flinch.

Vinny curled up his nose quickly. "Nah. Jeed only lady."

She smiled and kissed his ear again. "Goot. Jeed no wan' butterfly."

"I no butterfly."

"OK, you butterfly me, I cut him off." She made a playful move to cut Vinny's pride from between his legs with an imaginary pair of scissors.

Vinny pushed back on his stool and would have fallen off if she hadn't caught him and kissed his mouth.

Keith finished his breakfast and put the plate to one side.

"Today you hab massard?" Jeed was pushing her face forward and smiling broadly into his.

"Pphhow." He shook his head. "Yes, very good massage."

"My flend Ohn can massard fo' you." Jeed started nodding in the hope he'd follow suit. " Ohn say Kees haandsom maarn."

"'Ere y'are, Keith. Tring to set yers up with 'er mate." Vinny nodded and raised his thumb. Vinny was starting to play the part a lot of frequent visitors played, and help the girls get along with customers. Sometimes it involved guiding the guy's attention towards her, sometimes they'd interpret for the pair, some went to the length of writing emails and helping them concoct heart-wrenching stories in the hope that the guy would transfer half his savings to her bank account. In Vinny's case it was more a bit of fun.

The two Geordies turned up. Stez was wearing glasses today and smiled a big toothy grin as he arrived at Tommy Bar and saluted all within before mounting the concrete lip to take his stool.

"Mornin', suthnas." He smiled at Vinny, Jeed and Keith.

Vinny looked up. "First time I've been called a southerner."

"Aye, anywhere south o' Middlesbru's Cockney in my book." He toasted them with his first beer.

"See laughin' boy's still alive," Paul butted in.

The pair started laughing. Keith started to look worried.

"Make it 'ome OK, did yers?" Paul smiled at him.

"Fuckin' made it into my room while I was on t'nest. Cunt," Vinny chirped up.

"So you found the 'otel then?" Stez enquired.

"Errr…" Keith sucked his teeth. "The exact details are a bit vague, like, but I woke up in the right bed."

"Last we seen yers, yer coul'n't find yer arse wi' both 'ands," quipped Stez. "Same again tonight?"

"Not if there's tequila's involved," Keith protested.

"What's up wi' yers, man?" Stez tried to look offended. "We's only had fourteen each."

Vinny was playing the besotted and had his arm around Jeed. "Honey, I need make phone call," he whispered.

Jeed reached in her bag and pulled out her mobile phone.

"No, no." Vinny shook his head. "Overseas call, expensive."

"You get phone card from shop. I come wiss you." Jeed put her mobile back in the bag.

They headed hand in hand down onto Beach Road and joined the throngs going slowly about their business. Western women stopped at stalls to eye up ornaments and held up the flow of humanity. After pushing and shoving their way through the populous, Jeed pulled Vinny by the hand up the steps to the Royal Garden Plaza and guided him into a shop selling mobile phones and cards. He bought one worth 3,00 baht and unwrapped the cellophane sleeve.

"Can use outside." Jeed pointed to the street and pulled him out of the marbled complex. She pointed to a phone attached to the concrete wall of the building next to the plaza; it was shielded from the world by a plastic hood.

Vinny made a beeline for it and put the card in the slot. He looked round at the goings on around him and reached in his wallet and produced a business card. Jeed stood a couple of yards away waiting with her handbag clasped in both hands in front of her knees. Vince looked at the card, dialled a number then waited. He looked at the card again and tapped in six more digits then waited, took another look at the card and tapped a digit, waited a second then tapped in another number. He looked at the sky and stared at a cloud for a second then looked at the floor. He put the receiver back in the cradle, brushed his hair back and scratched his head. He wiped his face and ran through the process again. He paused after the numbers had been punched in cursed, slamming the phone in the cradle and kicking the wall. Jeed was watching and he walked over to her with a pained expression on his face. She clasped his arm.

"Winny OK?"

"Yes," he lied. "Just have problem."

"Wass ploblem?" She looked him in the eye.

Vinny looked over his shoulder, then ahead, then to his side.

"Only small problem. Not worry."

Jeed could feel him shaking. As they walked back to the bar his eyes were darting around every three seconds and he was sweating more than he normally would.

When they got back to Tommy Bar a girl was perched on a chair, pinning plastic gold-coloured bunting to the edge of the roof with HAPPY CHRISTMAS printed on it in red.

Vinny looked at it and shook his head.

Keith, Stez and Paul were laughing at a joke.

Vinny pulled up a stool next to Keith and Jeed joined him. She jabbered something in Thai to the girl behind the bar and a cooling cloth in a packet arrived on the Formica. Jeed unwrapped it and wiped Vinny's brow while he looked at the floor.

"'S up, kidder?" Keith didn't see Vinny out of sorts very often.

"Nowt." Vinny clenched his teeth and frowned.

Keith made a tactical withdrawal from the questioning. He'd seen Vinny like that a couple of times before when he'd first got to know him and Kerry had cropped up in conversation. The Geordies piped down for a minute as well. Vinny swigged at his beer and stared into space. Jeed sat at his side in silence.

The awkward silence spread across the bar. Stez and Paul went to play pool in another bar close by and, after half an hour of wandering what was up with Vinny, Keith joined them.

When he returned Jeed was sat alone smoking a cigarette.

"Jeed, where's Vinny gone?" His spirits had been lifted a little by the Geordie's playfulness but he was still concerned about his mate.

"He go telephone," she sighed. "Kees, I'm sink Winny aflaid. Why him aflaid?"

Keith shrugged his shoulders.

When Vinny returned ten minutes later his demeanour hadn't improved. He stood at the bar silently and swigged his beer. When he put it back on the bar his hand was shaking visibly, as it was when he lit a cigarette a moment later.

A girl appeared in front of Keith. "Hello."

"Hello," he replied.

She was a taller than Jeed with a slightly fuller figure. Her hair was cut in a bob and the point of her chin lined her face up perfectly.

"What's your name?" Keith had got used to the protocol.

"Ohn."

"Aarh." Keith put his cigarette in his mouth and offered his hand.

She giggled and shook his hand. "You Kees. Nite to miit yoo."

“You wan’ play gem?” She produced a Connect 4 set.

“OK.” Keith smiled and nodded.

Keith spent an hour or so getting beaten soundly at the simple game. Ohn smiled and giggled and flirted with Keith. Vinny disappeared with the phone card twice and came back looking ashen. In between visits he was gulping down beer like it was his last day on the planet and adding in large shots of whiskey for good measure. He was starting to look drunk; he was spilling beer down his shirt and swaying on his stool. Jeed sat beside him and rested her head on his shoulder. She looked worried. It was not that unusual a sight. Farang’s in Pattaya often decided not to go home. They came on holiday, found heaven on earth and debauched until their credit cards were stretched to the limit. Then they extended the limit and carried on drinking until the day came when they had no access to funds and it hit the fan. They would sit at a bar, drunk, snarling at the world with a little brown creature at their side trying to screw the last 500 baht out of them.

The sun started to set. Stez and Paul returned from playing pool. Keith decided to pull out of the Connect 4 tournament and chat with his new mates. They gave Vinny a wide berth conversationally. They’d been around long enough to know when not to prod a bear.

‘Shipping Forecast’ arrived. Today she was wearing jeans and a white top.

Vinny piped up, “Eh, Shipping Forecast.” He couldn’t have sounded more like a drunk if he’d tried.

Keith, Stez and Paul shuffled in embarrassment but Vinny didn’t pick up on it.

“Come in handy at Christmas,” he slurred.

The three amigos looked over.

“How’s that?” Keith saved his face.

“Queen’s speech.” He giggled to himself and slumped on the bar.

The amigo’s laughed nervously.

Jeed hugged him.

Paul and Stez agreed to meet Keith at Paris a Gogo at 9pm and disappeared.

Vinny sat up from the bar and started drumming the top with his hands. He smiled a drunken smile and kissed Jeed on the lips.

“Keef, we getting some fodder?” Vinny’s lips didn’t quite move in sync with his words.

“Might as well.”

They headed off to Rosie’s. Vinny was managing to get well over half the food he picked up with his fork into his mouth. Occasionally he slurred something, Jeed would rub his leg and Keith would nod.

They walked down to Beach Rd to jump on a baht bus back to the hotel. Keith wanted to get showered and changed. Vinny was going to stay in his room with Jeed.

In the cab Vinny glared at a 50-year-old guy sat opposite. "What you lookin' at nobhead," he said with a sneer.

The guy shrugged his shoulders. Jeed tightened her grip on his arm. Keith avoided the glare of the other passengers.

"C'mon, what yer starin' at?" Vinny snapped.

He looked away. Keith was getting uptight. They approached the Royal Plaza shopping centre. Vinny rang the buzzer, which signalled the driver to pull up.

Keith shook his head; Vinny was getting out of control. He'd never seen him like this before and he was worried. Vinny had that look in his eye like he was going to kill someone, and Keith didn't want to end up in a Thai police station trying to bail him out.

Vinny hopped out of the back of the bus, barged his way through the pedestrians and headed for the phone. He took out the business card again and dialled the number, then waited, then pressed in more numbers. The baht bus had pulled away. Keith and Jeed stood at the bottom of the steps looking on anxiously. Vinny slammed the phone against the wall. Keith winced as his mate staggered back through the crowd.

"'S up, Vin?" Keith wore a concerned look on his face.

Vinny slumped on the bottom step.

"'S nowt." He held his head in his hands and stared at the floor.

Jeed sat next to him and put her arm round him as Keith looked around uncomfortably.

Three minutes staring at the floor brought him round enough for Jeed to grab his hand and lead him into the road for a taxi. When they finally pulled up at the hotel Vinny was silent. He remained silent as they got in the lift.

"Can yer say what all this is about?" Keith enquired.

"Nah."

"See yer tomorrow then," said Keith as he got out at level eleven.

When Vinny got in his room he headed for the phone. Jeed took it from his hand and undid his trousers. She had him stripped in no time. He stumbled into the bathroom. Jeed's silky soft hands and lips couldn't make him stand to attention. He lay staring at the ceiling then got a bottle of beer from the fridge. Again he reached for the phone but Jeed's hand pulled him away.

"Wincent," she sobbed. "Why you angly?"

"Not angry." The ceiling was getting a hole burned into it.

"Why you cannot tell?" She rested her head on his shoulder.

He shook his head.

Jeed wrapped herself in a towel and went over to the dresser where she'd left her handbag, and started rummaging inside. Vinny swayed over to the fridge and got another bottle of beer. He put on a pair of shorts and sat on the end of the bed. Jeed turned from the dresser with something in her hand and smiled her cheeky smile. It lifted Vinny. She held something in her hand for him to inspect. He took what she held out to him. It was a small cellophane package stuffed with dark green, compressed ganja. Vin opened the packet and the rich aroma wafted towards his nostrils. He put his nose into the bag.

"Wow." He looked startled. "Strong."

He passed her back the package; she'd already laid out some cigarette papers. Vinny lay back on the bed and watched her from behind as she neatly rolled and creased the paper and foliage. She turned and smiled then popped the cone in her mouth. The dark of her skin made the paper seem whiter than white. Sat against the headboard she patted the space next to herself, and Vinny crawled up the bed to join her.

Jeed lit the joint while Vinny nestled his head on her shoulder.

"I not know you smoke ganja," Vinny whispered.

Just the act of opening the bag had helped lower the frantic index.

"Jeed smoke when angly." She exhaled the sweet, earthy smoke. "Make peaceful."

She passed Vinny the joint and the ashtray. He took a chug. There wasn't much tobacco in it. He smoked half of what Jeed had passed him and returned it to sender. His mouth started to dry. He coughed halfheartedly and looked up at the ceiling. His world and its occupants flashed before him as Jeed's hand stroked his head.

Sue's face flashed in front of him then turned into Toni. Charles Grantwell appeared wearing a suit the same blue as the carpet in the Personable office and the logo on the breast. John Moston looked over his shoulder and they pointed at him in unison, frowning. Vinny laughed. Jeed carried on stroking his head. Eventually his eyelids started to feel heavy. A dark kaleidoscope of pastel translucents replaced the beige of the ceiling. He heard voices, some strange, some familiar.

When the audiovisuals faded he looked up. The lights were on. Jeed kissed his cheek. He looked at his watch – it was midnight. His mouth felt like the Sahara. Jeed got him another beer. The night blurred. Somewhere in the dream a guy who looked like Keith walked in smiling and treading the carpet softly. Vinny smiled back and passed him the glowing ember of a joint. He felt Jeed's lips kiss the crown of his head.

Keith packed off his companion at 12.30. He though it best to check on Vinny. Jeed let him in and dashed back into the bathroom. There was still a faint aroma of herb in the room. Vinny walked back in from the balcony with Jeed's mobile pressed to his ear. He was listening to a man's voice at the other end.

"So two, three more days till it comes through then," he estimated.

The man at the other end started talking.

"Right. I'll bell you when it's sorted." Vinny pressed a button to cut the call. He shook his head and wiped away the sin from his face with his hand. "'Ere, sorry about yesterday, Keith. Heads up my arse about summat." Vinny's eyes were a deep shade of red.

"Iiss OK. No ploblem," Keith mocked like an an Isaan temptress.

Jeed nipped out of the bathroom, grabbed her clothes and dashed back in.

"What's on today's itinerary then?" Keith enquired.

"Fuckin' 'ell, thinkin'." Vinny frowned at the responsibility of planning. "Can't do that at the moment."

They headed down to Tommy Bar and got some breakfast. Jeed headed off to get a change of clothes. Stez and Paul arrived looking chirpy; they were standoffish when they saw Vince tucking into his 'Full English'.

"Sorry about yesterday, lads," he said, looking up from his plate.

"Aye, well…" Stez philosophised. "I've bin an arse mysel' more than once, like."

"Aye, like that funny phase yer went through," Paul interrupted. "Between the age o' one an' thorty-five."

The four laughed as Jeed reappeared in fresh clothes.

They whiled away the afternoon but the guys trod carefully with Vinny. A few beers were dispatched with but Vinny only played with his. He nipped off to the phone once and came back looking jumpy but he had almost returned to normal.

Keith bar fined Ohn. The double couple went back to the hotel and left Paul and Stez to trawl Pattaya's go-go bars alone.

They decided to sit in Vinny's room and smoke some of Jeed's grass. The guys leaned on the railings of the balcony and gazed out over the bay. Jeed and Ohn huddled together gossiping while they rolled a spliff at the dressing table.

"Tell yer summat, Vin, I can see why folks like it so much 'ere. Ever thought of comin' livin' over 'ere?"

Vinny took a drag on his cigarette, flicked it in an ark into the breeze and sucked his lips. "It'd be sayin' then."

"What's goin' on, all the phone calls and goin' off yer 'ead yesterday?" Keith made it sound simple.

"Like I said, it'd be sayin'." Vinny left Keith on the balcony while he inspected the work in progress.

When the first joint was built Jeed lit it and passed it to Vinny. He toked on it a couple of times and took it out on the balcony to Keith, then sat on the end of the bed. Keith came inside a minute later. His eyes were already glazed and he passed the joint to Ohn before taking a reclined posture in the armchair next to the dresser. Another joint came his way after ten minutes and he passed it on after taking a couple of drags.

"Fancy nippin' down the go-gos and getting pissed?" Vinny chirped.

Keith's headed nodded forward and his eyelids fluttered downwards.

"Keith," Vinny stabbed.

"Wwwow." Keith shook his head. "Lead in mi boots."

Keith's chin hovered about an inch above his chest for most of the night. Thai grass was a lot stronger than the strains in Europe. Ohn dragged him to bed around midnight.

After Vinny and Keith had had their night smoking ganja, things settled into a rhythm for a couple of days. They rose about the same time, went to the bar together, had a few beers with Paul and Stez in the afternoon and went separate ways in the evening. Keith went out on the town. Vinny went for some food and a quiet drink with Jeed. Vinny still nipped off to make his phone calls but everyone stopped taking any notice of it.

On the second night Vinny was lying in bed with Jeed when Keith knocked on his door. He was swaying in the breeze, holding a four-foot teddy bear, and a girl in her early twenties had her arm linked in his.

"Been at the tequila again?" Vinny looked unimpressed.

"'Ow can yer tell?" Keith slurred and put his arm round his lady.

"Just a wild guess." Vinny rubbed his crotch.

With only one arm holding the teddy it slipped out of his grasp and he struggled bending and keeping his balance while he picked it up. His girl tugged at his arm and dragged him off to bed.

the best things

Vinny dragged Keith out of bed at the ungodly hour of 1pm.

Keith didn't look clever in the taxi down to North Pattaya; he never had looked clever but today he was worse than normal.

"What 'appened to your bird?" Vinny had been surprised that's Keith's hired hand hadn't been around when he roused him.

"Fucked off at half four." He looked at the floor and half coughed, half wretched. "Said she had t'go see 'er mam an' dad."

"Shoulda gone with 'er. Meet the folks," Vinny poked, then paused for a moment. "I must say, you've got great taste in teddy bears." Vinny sniggered and jabbed Keith in the ribs.

Keith shook his head as he looked at the floor of the taxi. "Nine hundred bastard baht that cost."

Vinny laughed. "Bet she took it straight back the stall when she left."

"I can still taste fuckin' tequila, man," were his last comprehensible words before his eyes were rocked shut buy the sway of the taxi.

They opened a minute later and he proudly announced, "I fancy knockin' fuck outta summat down the Ray Parlour."

Jeed hadn't arrived at the bar when Vinny and Keith took their seats. Ohn was wiping the bar. She scowled at Keith. In the two nights since he'd slept with her, news had reached her ears that he'd had another two ladies. Bad form. Ladies didn't like butterflies. If Keith had had his wits about him he'd have felt the vibes but he was too hung over to notice.

Stez and Paul arrived looking fresh as daisies and started laughing when they saw Keith.

"I see Ollie Reid's alive." Paul nodded over to where Keith was staring at the bar top.

"Fuckin' that pissed last night 'e were dancin' on the stage in Vixens." Stez giggled to himself. "We've renamed 'im Keith a Go-Go."

The three chuckled. Keith had trouble telling what was going on.

"Daft cunt turned up in my room at three o'clock with a four-foot teddy." Vinny smirked.

"Ohh fuck," Stez wheezed through a cigarette. "Theodore Roosevelt."

"Did yer pay twelve 'undred baht to shag a cuddly toy last night, Keith?" Paul enquired.

Keith looked up from the bar top. "Cunts."

His three teasers burst out laughing.

Vinny looked at his watch. "Just got t'go—"

"Make a phone call," Stez interrupted. He was still cynical of Vinny, having seen him lose the plot before.

Twelve minutes later Vinny returned. He walked up Soi 7 sweating and red faced. Maybe walk is the wrong phrase; he was quickstepping, half running, half walking. And he was grinning from ear to ear.

Keith was still slumped at the bar. Vinny hopped up the concrete ledge, grabbed him on the love handles and started shaking him.

"Wake up, yer cunt, it's Christmas today, mate," Vinny almost shouting.

Stez and Paul looked at one another, confused. They frowned as if he'd finally lost his grip.

"'S only the twenty second, yer daft cunt," Paul shouted.

"I know but technically…" Vinny squirmed like he had a rabbit under his shirt.

Keith rose from his headrest. "'S goin' on?"

"Christmas." Vinny reached behind the bar and rang on the bell.

The three girls behind the bar started to beam ecstatically and ran to the fridge to get the most expensive drinks they could find. The two other drinkers perched in the far corner ordered beers.

"Seein' as it's Christmas I'll 'ave a Babycham." Stez said.

"Make that two," Paul chipped in.

Even Ohn was smiling. The girl serving Paul and Stez looked confused.

"Carlsberg'll do pet," Stez said with a resigned smile.

Keith wondered what was going on and why a drink had arrived in front of him. He was starting to come round but the bell ringing caused a commotion that took him by surprise.

"It aint Christmas for another three days yet." Keith looked at the date on his watch and scratched his head.

"It's come early for me," Vinny beamed. "There any o' that coke left?"

"Well, I was savin' it for New Year, like." Keith looked at his drink and blushed. He was embarrassed at Vinny's frivolity.

"C'mon, when Jeed gets 'ere we'll go back the hotel an' I'll explain." Vinny hugged him.

The fuss from Vinny's campanology died down but he was still grinning from ear to ear. Jeed trotted down the street swinging her handbag and smiled the smile she always smiled for Vinny. It made him melt. He smooched over to her, hugged her, lifted her off her feet and then span her round in his arms. When he let go she was unsteady on her feet and he dragged her to the bar.

"Honey, you have champagne?".

Jeed shook her head.

"Today Vinny make big money. No have to work. No go home to England. You can get champagne for bar?"

Jeed's eyes got bigger. She kissed him but looked confused. Like Keith and the Geordies, she wasn't sure what to make of it. She nattered in Thai to one of the girls and took a tissue from her handbag.

"OK, can get no problem." She wiped her eyes with the tissue and smiled.

"Why Jeed crying?" Vinny put his arm round her.

She kissed him. "Happy you not go home."

"C'mon, we tuckin' into that yak back at ours then?" Vinny spurred Keith into action.

Keith obeyed but was ashen. This couldn't be right.

They found a baht bus. It had a few passengers in it. Vince remained tight lipped with his arm round Jeed. Keith sat upright and his hands gripped the seating either side of his legs. He looked into the distance. The driver had dropped all the passengers off by the time they'd got to Walking Street.

Keith relaxed and stretched out. "So what's the fuckin' script 'ere, man?"

"Just become a millionaire." Vinny smiled smugly.

"What?" Keith squawked in disbelief.

"Millionaire," Vinny repeated.

Jeed was looking up at him.

"Fuck off."

"Straight up," Vinny nodded, looked him in the eye, and he hugged Jeed closer to him.

"Bit out of the blue." Keith was nearly lost for words. "How come?"

Vinny scratched his ear. "Well, you know that fat cunt we met at the golf club?"

"Yeah."

"An' I sold him a computer worth half a mill?"

"Yeah."

"Switched the invoice, didn't I."

"You what?"

"Aye. Switched the fuckin' invoice. Payment gone in today."

"Fuck me!" Keith laughed and looked at the ceiling.

"Won't they catch up on it through the bank?"

"Nah. With the help of my good friend Pete Jensen it's sitting tight in Switzerland," Vinny explained with self-satisfaction plastered across his face- "So I've now got a grand total of one million, two hundred and twenty-seven thousand, two hundred and fourteen Swiss Francs to my name."

"Are you bullin' me?" Keith looked suspicious.

Vin sucked his lips and shook his head.

Keith shook his head as well.

Let's go out

They got back to the hotel. Vinny ordered champagne to be sent to his room when he picked up his keys. They got in the lift and Keith got out first to get the Latin American Livener.

In Vinny's room Jeed hugged him and looked up at him. She looked normal; Vinny expected her to look ecstatic.

"Hey, honey, today we happy." Vinny lifted her in a hug.

Jeed smiled but it dropped off. "I'm worry." She looked away.

She wasn't the only one worried. "Why worry?"

"You take money, poliit come for you. Take you monkey house." She frowned and hugged him.

She'd touched a nerve. Vinny had received a caution for shoplifting when he was seventeen. Other than that he'd never been in trouble with the law. The thought of prison made him shake. He hugged her tighter and rested his chin on her head. His only venture into criminality since robbing a bottle of brandy from Tesco had been the odd visit to a knocking shop, a bit of weed, the coke Keith threw at him and a parking ticket. He took a deep breath and sighed with his eyes shut.

"Jeed, I can buy bar in Pattaya, you can work."

She flung herself on top of him and thrust her tongue down his throat.

There was a quiet knock on the door. Vinny opened it to see a bellboy stood wearing the serious face bellboys always wore. He held out a tray with a bottle, a bucket and three glasses. Vin took it off him and set it on the table. Keith arrived as Vinny was signing the chit.

Vinny poured out the Moet into three glasses and raised a toast. "To John Moston and Personable Computers." He swigged at his bubbly. "*Chok dee.*"

"*Chok dee*," Jeed and Keith chorused.

"Line," said Vinny, grinning.

Keith chucked a sealer bag with a small amount of powder in it on the dresser. "'S all there is left."

"Better than nowt." Vinny emptied the contents onto the wooden surface and cut away three thin lines from the pile. He had a note ready rolled and devoured his. Keith did likewise.

"Jeed, you want try cocaine?" Vinny held out the note for her.

"OK, I not take before but try one time." She grabbed at the paper and leaned over the line, looking uncomfortable with a note in her nostril. She used one hand to hold the note in place and another to block up her other nostril, then inhaled slowly, following the trace. Halfway through she stopped, looked up, smiled and went down again to finish clearing the powder, this time with more ease. Job done, she returned to upright and a spec of white powder fell out of her nostril. She sniffed and smiled then stood motionless waiting for the world to explode, then went and sat in the armchair.

Vinny and Keith watched intently and awaited a reaction. It was always fun watching someone do something naughty for the first time.

"Iiss no working," Jeed piped.

"Must wait one minute," Keith explained.

"Can feel in nose." Jeed rubbed the tip of her hooter.

"More champers." Vinny refilled the three glasses.

"OK, now Jeed can feel." She'd slipped further down into the chair with her hands clasped on her belly and her legs crossed and outstretched.

Vinny smiled proudly at his partner. She smiled back, confident and intoxicated.

"Jeed number one." Vinny raised his thumb.

"Yes," she nodded. "Jeed number one. OK, two hundlet per cent. Also Winny number one."

She paused for a moment. "We hab more cocaine?"

Keith and Vinny laughed and slapped their knees.

"I thought you only want try one time." Vinny feigned indignation.

"OK, yes, but just *nid noi*." Jeed pursed her lips and narrowed her eyes.

"OK, little bit can have." Keith had started to pick up on the lingo.

Vinny offered to do the honours and craftily chopped out a fat one for himself and two finer ones with the remainder. Jeed cleaned hers up a lot quicker this time.

Vinny lay on the bed with his hands behind his head and smiled. His eyes, his shoulders, his cheeks, his hands and his ears were tingling.

"Fuck me, I'm a millionaire." He sat up and looked at Keith.

"What you gonna do?" Keith was smiling nervously.

"Gotta go to Switzerland for a day or two to clear up details, then back 'ere on a false passport." Vinny had it all mapped out.

"Gonna stay in Patters?"

"Eventually, like, but I wanna go an' lie low for a bit till the fuss dies down. Where we can go stay for six month, Jeed?"

"I not know. Maybe can go place hab flend." Jeed smiled like a lottery winner and shrugged.

"Oh. The Old Bill might want to ask a few questions when yer get 'ome." Vinny forced an apologetic smile at Keith.

"Aye, the thought had crossed my mind," Keith said with a frown.

"They won't know what I've done till about the seventh of Jan when the invoice flags up," Vinny carried on. " Maybe longer knowin' how shit Personable are."

"Might cause a few problems that, kidder," Keith sucked his lips and finished off the last of his champagne.

"Aye, we can sort the story out later." Vinny dismissed the comment and got on the phone to reception for more champagne.

Keith padded out of the door looking worried and signalled that he was just nipping to his room. He returned before the second bottle of champagne arrived, looking tortured.

"What we doin' the rest o' today?" Keith queried.

"Thought we'd try and get some more gear and call it big one. Not often you get six zeros in your bank account." Vinny stroked Jeed's leg as she tapped in some numbers in her phone. "Jeed's gettin' on the blower to see if she can sort summat out for us."

Jeed got a dialling tone and held the phone to her ear. She paced round the room, nattered away in Thai for a moment then took the phone away from her ear and covered the mouthpiece with her finger.

"You want can get E or cockai?" she asked Vinny.

"How much?"

A flurry of Thai flew across the airwaves and Jeed looked up from the phone. "For E iss one thoussarn, cockai also one thoussarn."

Vinny sucked his lips. "Two coke, six Es."

Jeed relayed the order down the phone, waited then laughed and terminated the call.

"Will come hotel half an hour." She blew him a kiss, joined him on the end of the bed and hugged him.

Vinny could feel the Little General start to stir. He grabbed her by the hand. "Just wanna talk to Jeed in private."

He dragged her into the bathroom.

Keith looked through the book of CDs Vinny had on the dresser. The portable speakers attached to Vinny's Walkman were making the Ministry of Sound CD it was playing sound tinny. He fancied a change. The door knocked and he took it on himself to open it. The bellboy was waiting with a bucket of champagne.

"One minute." he smiled. "Vinny."

Keith pushed the door of the bathroom. Jeed was leaning against the vanity unit, her trousers were bellow her hips, and Keith could see the white of her thong above the waistband. Vinny was pushed up close behind her and his shorts were undone.

Keith covered his eyes and let the door shut. "Champers is 'ere."

Vinny scampered out, flushed in the middle of doing up his flies, and signed for the champagne. The bellboy's blush was showing through, despite the darkness of his skin.

Vinny's second signature of the day was irregular but still resembled his own.

"Tuck into that, our kid. Just gotta help Jeed wi' summat." He disappeared back into the bathroom.

Keith poured out a glass of champagne for himself and carried on looking for a new CD. When Vinny emerged The Fun Loving Criminals were telling people to 'Stick 'em up, punk.'

"I just 'ave stuck it up," quipped Vinny as he buttoned his shorts.

"Din't tek yer long." Keith highlighted the fact that Vinny had been gone four minutes.

"It were just a quick poke," Vinny explained semi-apologetically.

Jeed's phone started to ring on the dresser. Like most Thai girls, they couldn't just leave it in the casing they get when they'd bought it. She'd personalised it – not the way Europeans did with their favourite football team or something tasteful; it was a purple-backed *Snow White* scene. She'd put the pendant from some Christmas-cracker necklace through the slot designed for a wristband. It made her seem younger than her years – maybe that's why they did it.

She scampered out of the bathroom with her jeans pulled up and fastened, and picked up the phone. "Herrow."

A female voice jabbered back in Thai.

"*Nueng sawng soon kaew*," Jeed replied. "*La gawn ka*." She hit the 'off' button. "My fleind iss comink. Hab ya E ant ya cok."

Vinny rubbed his hands together. "All the comforts of home, kidder."

He winked at Keith and poured out some champagne for himself and Jeed.

People usually got a bit anxious when waiting for drugs, but Vinny was happy. The small amount of cocaine he'd had was keeping his dopamine levels high but there were natural causes coming into play. The success of the scam he'd been half thinking about since he'd met Jenson on his last trip had him on top of the world. It was like he was on a never-ending bungee rope; he'd been in freefall since 2.30 that afternoon when the Charter Bank of Switzerland had confirmed that he was rich. So here he was in a posh hotel, drinking champagne with his best mate and the bird he loved, and with narcotics in the lift on the way to room 1209.

The beak and pills arrived. A small girl in an anorak and sunglasses knocked on the door. She looked carefully before stepping into the room and shuffled in with her shoulders hunched. Vinny didn't ask her name, he just smirked. She looked like a mini version of one of those comedy Scouse or Manc drug dealers you used to see at raves in the late eighties. Paranoid and shady, they told the whole world they were selling drugs through inadvertent body language.

Once she was sure the CIA weren't hiding in the mini-bar, she lifted up her sunglasses. Her figure had made a part of Keith's anatomy move upwards as well.

"OK, haff piew ant cocai." She rummaged in the breast pocket of her anorak and placed a sealer bag on the dresser.

Vinny looked over, eyed the six little brown circular concoctions and two oblongs of folded magazine paper. The wraps were the objective. He fished one out and unravelled it. There was a meagre amount of powder in it and he told Jeed it was too expensive. With a bit of tooing and froing they managed to get an extra wrap of coke thrown in for the price.

Miss Nice disappeared with her glasses down and 6,000 baht in her pocket, not before peeping out of the door in case the police had arrived.

Vinny massed the cocaine together in one wrap once they'd all had a line.

"Hundred quid for a half a gram an' six pills." He shook his head.

"More fuckin' talc than beak in that." Keith echoed Vinny's dissapointment.

In the back of the baht bus down to Tommy Bar, Keith was avoiding Vinny's glare.

"What's up, man?" Vinny asked.

There was no one else in the taxi.

"It's givin' me grief, this." Keith looked at the blackened steel floor of the cab.

"Nah, man." Vinny was full of *joi de vivre*. "Just say you 'ad no idea. I've worked it all out. No problem."

Keith sucked his lips. "Thing is, mate. Got summat on the go myself."

"Won't make a difference takin' 'ome a few moody T-shirts, like." Vinny sat back and swigged at the champagne bottle he'd brought from the room.

"Nah, man. More than that." Keith looked his friend in the eye.

"What is it?"

"You'll find out today." Keith stared over his shoulder into the road. "An old friend's turning up."

"Who?" Vinny was swaggering like it was a joke. "Not Sheila from t'Arrers?"

Keith started to laugh and wiped his face to regain seriousness. "You know who it is."

Vinny tried to wrack his brain but shook his head.

They hopped out of the cab and Vinny left the empty bottle by a lamppost.

When they reached Soi 7 Stez and Paul were sat at the bar like it was just another day in paradise.

"C'mon, man, yer can't keep us guessing. Who is it?" Vinny whinged.

Keith was looking serious. He eyed the two Geordies. "We'll 'ave a chat somewhere private."

They grabbed two beers and walked down the road. It was a struggle getting through the motorbike guys who were congregated at the junction of Soi 7 and Beach Rd. They crossed the ten foot concrete promenade and Keith hauled himself onto the storm break that separated Pattaya Beach and the contents of the Gulf of Thailand from the tarmac on Beach Rd.

Vinny struggled down and looked out to sea. The pair sat staring into the lowering sun and banged their heels like schoolboys at Tenby waiting for the boats to come in.

"So what's the score?" Vinny slugged at his beer.

It wasn't the quietest place in the world. The beach itself was jam packed with holidaymakers on deck chairs worshiping the Siam Sun God.

"'Ard to say." Keith furrowed his brow, looking for a start point.

"Well, who's gonna be 'ere?" Vinny was intrigued as much as anything else.

"Vicky."

"What?"

"Vicky."

"'Ave you heard that sayin' about coal and Newcastle?" Vinny looked at his best mate, confused.

"Bit more to it than that, like." Keith rested his bottle on the ledge and wiped his face.

"Keep us waitin' if yer want." Vinny mopped some sweat off his brow.

"Well," Keith half sighed. "She's got me smugglin' a bird back."

"Yer what?"

"Yeah." Keith crossed his left leg over his right. "I'm getting wed in a couple o' days."

"Fuck off."

"Aye. Soon as I get 'er 'ome she fucks off an' starts work in a brass house in Stockport." Keith looked over his shoulder.

"Fuck me." Vinny rubbed his face. "'Ow's it all come about?"

Keith laughed. "Well, she introduced me to some guys. Cockneys, like. Proper heavyweight villains. I mean proper." Keith pulled a fag packet out of his pocket and lit it. "Some oriental bloke as well. Paid for the flight. Give us some spends. More when I get 'er 'ome."

"How much?"

"Five grand all told."

"Fuck that." Vinny looked at the floor. "I'll pay 'em off and you can stay out 'ere wi' me."

"Nah," Keith snapped. "They went to great lengths to explain it'd cost me more than a few quid if I fucked up."

"Fuckin' 'ell." Vinny stared into the sun. "Shoulda said, man. I'd have cut yers into my deal."

Four month's ago Vinny was a washed up salesman who couldn't pay for a pint on Friday night. Now he was a half-million fraudster and his mate was trafficking humans.

"So why's Vicky showin' up?" Vinny dropped his empty to the floor.

"She said to let 'er know if owt untoward 'appened. Wants to speak to yers. I were gonna aff to tell yer soon any road." Keith looked him in the face.

"Aye, well, least we'll 'ave a stag do for yer." Vinny patted him on the back. "Back to the bar?"

They ran the gauntlet of teatime traffic. Before they reached Tommy Bar Vinny fielded one more question.

"What made yer do it?"

"Doin' more coke than I was sellin'."

It had been a day of revelations. Neither party knew whose had been the biggest.

The Geordies were conspicuous by their absence; they'd probably gone to get a bite to eat. Vinny and Keith had been in each other's pockets for six days and conversation was starting to run low. The shock factor played a part in the silence as well. Jeed sat on Vinny's lap. Keith looked over his shoulder occasionally, as did Vinny. In Keith's case it was because he was awaiting the arrival of Vicky, in Vin's it was down to paranoia.

He gave Jeed a squeeze. "Honey, we go shopping."

She kissed him and hopped off his knee.

"Just nippin' down Beach Road for a min." Vinny patted Keith's flank before trotting down to the main road hand in hand with Jeed.

They battled through the melee of people forcing their way between the stalls.

"Honey, where we go?" Jeed sounded excited.

"We look can buy clothes."

Vinny homed in on his target. About 200 yards from Soi 7 was a stall propped against the concrete fencing that marked the edge of a German restaurant. A small, dark-skinned guy sat next to his stock peeling some fruit, and gave Jeed the once-over. Obviously impressed with what he saw, he said something in Thai but Jeed didn't take up the thread. She held Vinny's hand and waited while he weighed up the guy's cash crop packed onto the table and stacked onto a board leaning against the restaurant wall. They were hats, mainly baseball but some the cricket type, made of cotton with a brim all the way round. He also sold a few woollen bob hats; well, he stocked them at least. Quite who would buy a woolly hat in a country where the lowest daytime temperature was 18 degrees C was a mystery to Vinny but he didn't bother mentioning it to the guy.

Vinny eyed a few of them. The Thais were good at imitating things and the Nike, Adidas, Reebok and sports-club logo's emblazoned on the front of the headgear could easily pass as the real thing. Vinny tried on a white Nike baseball cap and eyed himself in a shaving mirror tied to a metal pole. The stall owner had fitted it on a stand that propped up the tarpaulin and protected his living from the elements. The cap didn't suit him so he put it back untidily and the owner leaned over to refold it and place it neatly in line with the rest of his merchandise. Vinny saw a dark blue denim cricket hat with the New York Yankees logo embroidered on it and tried it on. He looked at himself in the mirror and turned it on his head so the logo 'NY' was dead centre. He smiled and looked at Jeed.

"You like?"

"Wery sexy." She pulled her arm tighter onto his and pursed her lips.

"You want hat?"

Jeed shook her head.

"*Tow rai?*" Vinny asked the vendor.

"Fibe hundled." He hardly looked up from the fruit he was slicing.

"*Mai ow*. Two hundred," Vinny retorted.

"Cannot. Iss good plite. Fibe hundled." he looked indignant at Vinny's offer.

Jeed attacked him with an aggressive flurry in Thai.

He shook his head, sulking. "OK, two fipty."

Vinny reached in his back pocket for his wallet but Jeed gave the guy a heavy scowl. Vinny sensed another shot being played and stalled the retrieval of his pocket book.

"OK, OK, two hundled." The guy looked mortally wounded.

Vinny passed over the notes and the guy shooed the pair away as he folded two red 100-baht notes and placed them in his pocket.

Vinny smirked as they headed back the way they'd come.

"Honey, you want some clothes?"

He didn't hear a reply but felt a pull on his arm and looked down to see a beam on Jeed's face that made the early-evening dusk disappear.

As they approached the steps to the Royal Plaza shopping centre Jeed dragged Vinny off to the right and headed for a stall. Vinny soon started to regret his generous offer, not because of the expense but the time. He blinked and imagined himself prowling the stalls at midnight without having bought Jeed anything as she tried on the 10,000th blouse.

He got off lightly. Next to the phone where Vinny had received his good news a stall had appeared selling ladies clothes. Jeed looked at a couple of items, held them against herself and in less than ten minutes they were walking arm in arm back to Tommy Bar with Jeed clasping a carrier bag containing an orange vest top with a small cartoon logo on the front and a pair of blue denim hot pants.

When loves young dream arrived back at base camp Keith was sat next to Vicky. The tropical heat left a fine veneer of sweat on the parts uncovered by her plain white cotton dress. She had sunglasses pushed back onto her temple and was sipping a clear fizzy drink with ice and lime through a straw out of a tall glass. An Oriental, probably a Thai man, was sat next to her. He looked like he was in his forties but Thais aged better than Europeans so it was hard to tell. He had a pock-marked face and was smoking a cigarette, which had obviously come from the slightly worn but unmistakably English gold-coloured Benson and Hedges packet in front of him. The guy looked menacing. Vinny didn't have much trouble imagining him holding some terrified miscreant's hand on a table and bringing the edge of a meat cleaver down on his little finger in remittance for a gambling debt. The girl behind the bar was eyeing him cautiously and when he caught her glare he smiled proudly.

Vinny gave him a wide berth as he was walked behind him to take a seat next to Keith.

"Arlight, Vick?" Vinny put on his best smile to cover the jangle of nerves Mr Triad had given him.

"Hi, Vincent." She looked sideways at him but didn't smile.

"Who's yer friend?" Vinny took the bull by the horns.

"Eddie," the guy answered.

Vinny had expected a Thai name and a Thai accent. He had one but not the other.

"Nice to meet you." Vinny looked away from him. Eddie's eye contact made him nervous.

Eddie raised his glass.

"We're going for something to eat soon, Vincent. Would you like to come?" Vicky's question was rhetorical.

"Might as well." Vinny was staring at a distant point far out in the bay.

His own secret had made him anxious for a while but it was his own gig. Apart from the banking arrangements that Jensen had made, no one else was involved. How was he supposed to know he'd thrown a spanner in an international vice gang's machine? His legs were trembling.

"I'm just nippin' to the bog." Vinny trotted off to the toilet block that served the drinkers at the group of bars at the bottom of Soi 7.

When he returned there was a dark patch near the left pocket of his shorts. Vicky was out of her chair with her handbag over her shoulder. She looked at the damp spot and started to smile. Eddie and Keith finished their drinks and moved away from the bar.

"OK if Jeed comes?" Vinny directed the question at Vicky.

"If you want." Vicky smiled and linked arms with Keith.

The group of five headed down onto Beach Road and turned right. As you went away from Walking Street and against the flow of traffic, the pavements got less crowded and there were gaps between the bars. The brim of Vinny's new hat was restricting his view so he took it off and folded the brim upwards. He looked round at Keith.

"Fuck me, you look like Jimmeny Cricket."

“Cheers, man.” Vinny felt dejected. He’d bought the hat to try and disguise his face but it seemed like it was generating more attention than it was diverting.

They arrived at a large open-sided bar. Vicky guided them in and they worked their way past tables of drinkers. It took Vinny a moment to realise that the pretty serving girls in white plimsolls, skirts and T-shirts weren’t actually girls.

“’Kin ’ell, they’re all cock in a frock, these,” Vinny announced to the group.

Vicky scowled at him.

“You’d never guess, would yer.” Keith smiled.

After passing through the bar complex they reached a pool area. It wasn’t a swimming pool, more of an indoor pond, dark water with lilies growing in it and a small artificial stream cascading into it at one end. There were three or four Oriental-looking guys – not Thai, maybe Japanese – sat round the edge with short fishing rods trying to catch their supper. The pool area gave way to another space filled with tables. It was populated mainly by Japanese guys either sat in groups of two or three, drinking, chatting or eyeing up the ladyboys, or alone with a ladyboy playing hostess at their table.

Vicky grabbed the attention of one of the waitresses who was scurrying to the kitchen with an order, and started chatting. He or she, depending on how much you’d had to drink, pointed at an empty table in the middle of the floor. Vicky led the way and took a seat at the head of the table.

“So has Keith been caught out by a ladyboy yet, Vince?” Vicky grinned.

“Nah.” Vinny fixed her with a stare. “Got his old mate lookin’ after ’im.”

“Too right,” Keith agreed as a particularly convincing one approached Vicky to start taking orders. “Mind you, late at night you could be forgiven…”

Vinny gulped. Talk about U-turns. He looked down at the menu to hide his blush.

Behind them was a platform bordered by a cane barrier. An older *katoey* with age lines showing through her foundation and dressed in an evening gown was miming to a soft, haunting Thai love song that wafted across the diners through speakers. A Japanese guy in round glasses and golfing gear was coaxed to join the singer by Johnnie Walker. Johnnie’s a great guy; he helped people overcome shyness, although sometimes his sense of fun got in the way, and tripped and pushed his mate to make him look unsteady. He was having a field day with this bloke. Unperturbed by the lack of an invite, the Jap smooched up to the singer, put his arm around her waist and started crooning along with her. The Thais, if nothing else, were tolerant, and the performer was doing her best to tolerate him.

Drinks arrived and the waitress stood patiently while the nefarious friends eyed the menu.

Eventually she disappeared with an order and Vicky sipped at her vodka and soda.

"So tell me about your little windfall." Vicky was staring at Vince along with Eddie.

Vinny sucked his lips.

"It's OK, you can talk here, no problems."

Vinny took his hat off, rested it on the table and ruffled his hair.

"Simple really. Switched the invoice. Half a mil in my account instead o' work's." He sipped his beer.

He could feel Eddie's eye's burning his face.

"Really?" Vicky smiled as her eyes widened. "Where's the account?"

Vinny paused and shook his head. He didn't want to answer. He looked at Eddie sat opposite him and saw the glare of a psychopath. "Switzerland."

"Won't the police trace it?" Vicky continued.

Vinny started to shake. "Nah, got another account under a moody name, just transfer it all in cash, Frank's your auntie."

"Right." His interrogator sounded a little unconvinced of the simplicity of it all. "When will the police realise it's gone through?"

"'Bout the sixth o' Jan, summat like that. Depends when the accounts people start back and look at the invoices."

"Who set up the accounts for you?" She seemed a little more relaxed.

"Can't say."

Eddie picked up his steak knife.

"A bloke called Jensen I met in Bulldog," Vinny spat through the sweat dripping down his face.

The food started to arrive.

"And will the police want to talk to Keith?"

"All's he did was come wi' me when I buttered the customer up."

A waitress placed Vinny's steak in front of him. "I need a Barry White." Vinny ran towards the door marked TOILET as he heard giggles from the table.

He returned a few minutes later wiping his nose and smiling, with a fine glaze on his eyes. Eddie was chatting in Thai on his mobile phone.

Keith looked up from his food. Since Vicky had turned up he'd been acting like an obedient employee in the presence of the MD, not uttering a word out of place, and smiling or frowning with her. Vinny got a jealous sideways glance when Keith saw him rubbing his nose.

Eddie cut his phone call and turned to Vicky. "OK, no problem." He chewed his lips then tucked into his food.

Vicky started to wear a more relaxed expression. "Everything seems OK." She aimed the comment at Vinny. "We were worried your little escapade might alert the police, but the Thai authorities don't know anything about it."

Keith looked relieved once the comment had been made as well.

"How do you know?" Vinny sounded shocked.

"I hab friend poliit. Him tell me good infomayshon," Eddie elaborated.

Vinny didn't like this situation one bit. "M'off back t'bar," he muttered as he pushed his plate away.

"Chuck us a line first, mate," Keith chirped.

"No, no, stay, my friend. Drink whisky," Eddie insisted.

Jeed looked Eddie in the face. She was obviously fearful of the guy.

"Your ghafliend velly nite," Eddie added, smiling at her with enough slime to grease down Don King's hair.

Jeed avoided his gaze uncomfortably.

Vinny tossed the wrap of coke nonchalantly across the table to Keith. Eddie didn't look like the sort of guy who took rejection well. Eddie had finished his meal and was ordering a bottle of Johnny from one of the silicon-enhanced serving maids.

Keith's return from powdering his nose coincided with the arrival of a bottle of Black Label. More out of fear than politeness or generosity, Vinny offered the wrap to Eddie.

"Not take druk," he scowled. "Only whisky."

He poured out a tumbler for Vinny then himself. He pushed the bottle into the middle of the table for the others to help themselves. He fixed Vinny with a steely glare. "Thiis man Jensen…" He separated the two syllables in Jensen. "He gib you ploblem, I kill him."

Eddie chinked his glass with Vinny's and gulped down the contents then retrieved the bottle from Keith who was pouring himself a nip.

It didn't take the six of them long to get halfway through the bottle. Eddie and Vinny had the lion's share of it while Jeed and Keith had the odd sip and Vicky abstained.

"I need to go an' get showered and changed." Vinny looked at his watch. It was 9 o'clock and an oil slick of darkness had engulfed the restaurant.

"That's OK." Vicky sounded relieved. "I need to discuss a few things with Eddie."

She gave Eddie the sort of look wives give their husbands at dinner parties when they were drunk and had let slip with things she'd rather he didn't. Eddie was haunched over his glass, circling the potent brown liquid and smiling lovingly as it sploshed up the sides of the glass.

Vinny, Jeed and Keith stood up to leave.

"Bright and early on Thursday, Keith," Vicky ordered. "And looking smart. We don't want to disappoint the bride now, do we?"

With his hat back on and cooled by the breeze from across the bay, they waited for a taxi at the side of the road. "Bit much, that Eddie geezer." He shielded his lighter from the wind as he lit a cigarette.

"That's the guy I met with Vick and them Cockneys." Keith spotted a baht bus so they decided to go flag it down.

They got back to the hotel, showered changed and had a line or two each.

Jeed wore the clothes Vinny had just bought her and stood in reception as the two happy felons cashed more travellers' cheques.

When they turned to head out of the door, she had her back to them. She'd commandeered Vinny's new hat. It was a bit too big but it added to her cuteness. The shorts left little to the imagination, outlining her behind like a peach. A third of an inch of tender brown flesh poked out of the bottom and Vinny and Keith smiled together as it caught their eye.

"I can see why you robbed a million Francs now." If they hadn't been in a town with a quarter of a million available women Keith would have been jealous.

"Aye. Well, I need somewhere t'park my bike, don't I?" Vinny smirked with self-satisfaction.

In the taxi that took them back towards Tommy Bar, Keith explained that Vicky had organised the wedding at some place upcountry for Christmas day, and that he was going to spend a week with his new wife (whose name he still didn't know) having photos taken and getting to know her to authenticate the visa application, although the majority of the paperwork had already been given the green light in return for a bundle of notes.

The two Geordies were just finishing their drinks before heading towards South Pattaya's go-go bars when our hero's arrived, so they tagged along with them and formed the sort of group that people had to dodge as they walked down Walking Street.

"Dollhouse first?" Stez suggested.

Nobody objected so they tramped past the escalators leading to Marine disco, turned into the bar with the boxing ring where they'd drunk on the first night and headed through the curtained door in the back wall that was the entrance to Dollhouse. Vinny stopped and smiled when he was through the doorway. Dollhouse was new in Pattaya; they already had a bar in Bangkok and were bringing consumerism to prostitution. Maybe one day they'd have the same market profile as McDonalds with a concession in every town centre and airport across the world. The interior alone set it apart from the competition. Most of the time when punters went in a go-go bar the décor was the last thing on their minds and the owners knew that. The carpets were usually matted with chewing gum, the mirrors chipped and the chrome plate flaking off the poles the dancers used for support. Dollhouse was brand spanking new. The pile of the carpet shifted satisfyingly when you trod on it, the poles gleamed and the seats were as comfy as the ones in a new multiplex cinema. The mamasan looked more like a head croupier than the head of a whorehouse. She wore a smart suit and her youthfulness had been exchanged for some loose skin that she kept under her chin. 'Hotel California' by the Eagles was blaring out of the speakers as she guided the Croston Five to one of the tiers of seats that surrounded the revolving stage where five girls in black briefs and black bodices were actually enjoying dancing for the crowd. Vinny's new bank balance made him the leader; he sat with Jeed and Keith to his right and the Geordies to his left. A demure waitress with sticky-out ears and tied-back hair took the drinks orders and tottered off. Keith was eyeing up the dancers as the revolving stage took them in and out of sight. Vinny stroked Jeed's bare leg while he watched a group of guys throwing tiny little missiles that landed on the floor with a loud crack to a chorus of laughs from the girls. The Geordies were locked in unintelligible conversation and Vinny's world was just fine.

The waitress returned with five bottles of beer on a silver tray. She struggled to balance it on her right hand while using her left to steady it.

They were taking their opening swigs of beer when Stez pointed and proclaimed, "Woy, it's Noi."

"Another one of Stez's 'opefuls," Paul explained.

"It's the tequila girl, she's lovely," Stez said with proud grin.

Vinny spotted the apple of Stez's eye and, to be honest, he could see the attraction. She was dressed in silver: silver shorts and a silver top, styled like a cowboy's denim shirt without sleeves, and knee-length black suede boots. Unlike most Thai women she had sizeable breasts. Her coffee-coloured skin was standard issue. She wore a wide toothy grin on a wide happy face, and with her hair in bunches she looked like fun. She saw Stez and waved, then walked across the neutral space with her hands in her belt, mocking a gunslinger approaching a duel. But with the wiggle of her hips and the hint of cleavage, it wasn't her bullets that you had to be afraid of.

She squeezed in front of Stez and kissed his cheek. Vinny got a close-up of her belt. Crafted out of black leather and steel studs, it housed a number of dangerous weapons, the most lethal being a bottle of tequila. The other pouches held shot glasses, slices of limes and a salt cellar.

"'Avin' a tequila, man?" Stez insisted.

"Looks like it," Vinny agreed.

"Keith," Stez checked.

Keith screwed up his face in disgust for a minute then lightened. "Aye. Only the one though." He looked to the heavens for mercy.

"Six." Stez held up six fingers for Noi.

She counted the Croston five. "Only fibe."

"One for you," Stez insisted.

She nodded reluctantly and did the honours. Five tequilas went down five hatches. Jeed seemed unfamiliar with the process and watched the rest of the team before following protocol, but not without a little wretch and a screw of the face.

"Another," was Stez's next edict.

After five or six the conversation and laughter was flowing and Noi was pouring without prompt.

"Jeed go toilet." Her head had been resting on Vinny's arm and when she looked up her pupils seemed to stray from their normal central point.

Vinny moved sideways and embedded his knees in Stez's fleshy legs to let her get past. He smiled as he saw her dodge invisible cones on the way to the rest room.

"Looks a bit lubricated there, man." Stez nodded towards Jeed's backside as she pushed the toilet door.

"Aye." Vinny's eyes glistened with fondness. "Top bird though."

"Y' wanna be careful, man," Stez said as Vinny knocked back lucky number seven. "Never get to close to a Thai bird. Always ends in shite."

"Nah." Vinny defended his credibility and Jeed's honour. "Not paid her a penny yet."

"Aye, well, she seems all right." Stez pulled back. "Just 'ave a look at Stickman before you do owt stupid."

"Oh yeah. Keeps me goin' when I'm at 'ome. Know all the shite about payin' for 'er dad's sick buffalo an' that." Vinny put both their minds to rest.

Jeed swayed her way back to them looking seasick. She nearly tripped over Paul's feet as number eight was being poured out.

Noi offered Jeed a shot. "Cannot." She held up her hand in refusal, "Winny, Jeed dlunk." She clasped both her arms round his right one and nestled her face in the flab that should've been a tricep.

"What's yer 'otel like?" There was nothing like a few tequilas to kindle a friendship and it was working for Stez and Vinny.

"All right, like," Vinny nodded. "Few Japs but they're no bother."

"There's a few Spinal Taps at our gaff," Stez replied.

"Winny." With a tug of Vin's arm Jeed stopped the conversation going any further.

"Yeah?"

"Winny, I'm tiyad, want saleep." She held onto his arm, obviously not reacting well to the tequila.

"OK, OK, no problem." Vinny stroked her hand.

"Time for emergency medication." He directed the comment towards Stez as he fished in his shirt pocket. "Stez." Vinny did his best to look inconspicuous. "Send Noi over t'bar so she don't see."

Stez gave Noi some instructions in Thai and she happily trotted to the bar. Vinny hastily fished a pill out of his bag of tricks popped it in Jeed's mouth. He held a bottle of beer to her mouth and she took a swig without raising from the half-supine position she was in.

"OK, honey, soon be dancing." Vinny stroked her arm again.

Stez tried not to look too inquisitive. "What's them?"

"Es."

"Gary Abletts?"

"Aye."

"Have y'any more, like?" The fat Geordie wheezed with anticipation.

"Enough for us three." Vinny motioned his head towards the closer of his friends. "I'll ask Jeed when she comes round though."

Noi was starting to look unsteady and the tequilas had been abandoned for beer.

"Here you are though, mate." Vinny was feeling generous. He rummaged in his shirt. "Toot on that'll keep yer goin'," and he pressed the precious wrap of coke into Stez's hand.

Stez took a few gulps on his beer before heading off to the loo.

Keith was transfixed by a dancer on the stage. When Vinny saw what he was looking at he was glad that Jeed was half asleep. She was, even by go-go standards, extremely good looking. She wore a silver band round her upper arm; it was like the banister of a spiral staircase, and covered a tattoo. Like Noi, she was well stacked. Her hair was crimped and when she smiled she showed a stud in her tongue.

Keith noticed she'd got Vinny's attention. "I'm bount barfine that one."

"I'll sneak in yer room and 'ave a slide on it myself when Jeed's akip." Vinny still had eyes in his head.

Stez emerged from the toilet door at the far side of the bar wiping his nose. Keith beckoned to the mamasan.

Stez squeezed himself between Vinny and Paul. "Sorry 'bout this, man."

"Whassup?"

"Errm… bit of an accident, like." Stez sucked his lips. "Your gear's down the bog."

"Fffffuck!" Vinny's hand covered his face. "You're windin' me up, man."

"Straight up."

Vinny shook his head and looked into the middle distance scowling. Jeed had started to wake and kissed his neck. Losing your toot was never easy but in a country where it was scarce on a night when you were celebrating it was bad news.

Keith was in conference with Mamasan. She nodded and walked over to the stage. She tapped the special one on her boot mid dance. Her response was to hop off stage and engage the mamasan in conversation. Miss Wonderful glanced once at Keith and hopped back on stage while Mamasan went and stood a safe distance from Keith.

Vinny had been watching proceedings. "Take that as a 'no' then."

Keith looked over with a smile and look of mock rejection. "Musn't like the look o' my mates."

The pair sniggered.

"We off down the road then?" Paul made himself heard for the first time since they'd arrived in the place.

"Aye. Lerrus barfine Noi first though." Stez's eyes were starting to glint from the line he'd taken.

"Noi. Noi, check bin." He had to raise his voice to be heard above the soft metal.

Noi had shifted herself a couple of yards and had her back turned as she watched a commotion at the other side of the stage. She turned and smiled at Stez. He nattered with her in Thai. She smiled again.

“OK, yes.” Noi couldn’t conceal her glee; she totted up the slips that had accumulated in the pot in front of them and showed Stez the final sum.

“Fuck me, I wanted the bill, not your phone number.” Stez showed Vinny the slip.

“Six thousand, two hundred and forty.” Vinny took the paper off him and looked again to be sure.

“Forty eigh’ takeela ant twelp beeya,” Noi explained.

“I’ll get it.” Vinny reached for his wallet.

“Nah, it’s mine.” Stez put his hand across Vinny.

“’Ad a bit o’ luck, mate. My treat,” Vinny insisted.

“All right, halves,” Stez conceded.

They threw some notes at Noi.

“Keep the change,” Stez added.

They headed out of the door and started to make their way through the boxing bar.

“Sorry ’boot the gear, like,” Stez apologised.

“’S all right, man.” Vinny feigned nonchalance.

“Yer daft cunt.” Stez burst out laughing and slipped the wrap in Vinny’s shirt pocket. “ Your face were a picture, man.”

“Bastard!” Vinny smiled. “Where we off?”

“Staw Baw,” Paul butted in.

“Where’s Star Bar?” Vinny asked.

“Just down the road,” Stez explained.

Jeed tugged at Vinny’s arm. “Honey, we go dancing.” She seemed to have shaken off the tequila.

They walked back down Walking Street and wove their way through the crowds.

Paul was the first one in Star Bar. It cornered Walking Street and one of the Sois leading off it; typical of tourist bars in Thailand, it was open sided with vinyl seats and a bar in the corner. The five gathered round a low bamboo table and shuffled their seats so they could all fit comfortably. Jeed sat on Vinny’s knee and rocked backwards and forwards to the Brit pop in the CD player. They sat and drank and took the piss out of passers by. The pair that got the most attention and a disgusted reaction was a couple, one half male caucasian, 50 plus, grey haired and over 19 stone, the other half a slender Thai male in his early 20s wearing a cap-sleeved T-shirt and white jeans. The old guy had his arm round the boy’s waist and the rent boy had his hand on the man’s shoulder. Croston and his buddies cursed the guy.

Stez’s voice was the loudest. “Knocks yer sick that, dunnit.”

“Aye, poor cunt,” Paul empathised. “’Avin’ to sell your arse to a young Thai bloke.”

The group congratulated Paul on his efforts.

“Jeed.” Vinny squeezed his tilac’s waist.

She turned, gazed into his eyes and kissed him.

"Jeed, you can get E for Stez?" he whispered.

"Yes. My fliend go Maleen." She brushed his hair back from his forehead and kissed it.

"Stez." Vinny raised his voice.

Stez had turned away and was sharing a joke with Paul.

"Stez." Vinny grabbed his leg. "Sorted, kidder. Jeed's mate'll 'ave some Abletts in t'Marine."

"Shit 'ot."

"Talkin' o' which..." Vinny eased Jeed off his leg and struggled out of his seat. "I go toilet."

Star Bar wasn't furnished with the luxury of a convenience; desperate drinkers had to use a public bog around the corner. The cluster of bars proved a tough challenge for Vince, mainly due to the staff. Jeed's rocking motion on his knee had raised more than his spirits and the girls spotted it a mile off, or maybe they could just smell money.

"Hey, Mister Sexy," a voice rung out. "You want whisky?"

It was unusual not to get offered sex. Vinny turned and saw the owner of the voice amid a group of four girls hanging over a bar top and smiling at him. Her vocal chords were bigger than her breasts. Vinny waved out of politeness. It was returned by whoops and a chorus of unrecognisable comments and laughs.

Vinny spotted his mark, wedged between two beer bars, a doorway flanked by two whitewashed walls with a black sign saying TOILET. A man in police uniform stood outside. Vinny tried not to gulp; he'd intended to use the visit for chemical inspiration rather than defecation. Bollocks. He'd made his approach and backing off now would look suspicious. He grabbed one of the neatly folded sections of toilet roll off the rusty-legged picnic table next to the door, and threw a couple of coins in the basket. The lady that should have manned the toll was away, probably gossiping.

The smell inside the door was less than pleasant. Vinny pushed open a door to a cubicle and held his breath. The brown tiles on the floor had a slimy feel underfoot and felt like they were home to the full spectrum of the world's unfriendly bacteria. There was a transitional zone on the bottom of the walls where the colour graded up from the brown of the floor through a yellow and beige until two feet from floor level the walls were an almost brilliant white. Vinny decided not to sit on the throne. It didn't have a seat and the porcelain had strange speckles on it. With the local plod outside fannying around with cocaine and making snorting sounds didn't seem like a good idea either. He pulled four of the pills out of the sealer bag, popped one in his mouth and had a piss. The cocaine had the same effect on his old fellow that the cold had back home.

With a pill under his tongue he headed back to Star Bar, avoiding the policeman's gaze as he left the loo. At the table he grabbed his bottle and swallowed the pill.

Paul had been joined by one of the serving girls, who sat on the arm of his chair sipping a Cola. She was a touch older than the usual bar girl and taller, possibly half farang, with a fine figure and a smile that set Vinny alight. He couldn't look for too long. Jeed was on her mobile phone but within sussing distance.

Vinny leaned over to Stez, popped a pill in his hand and winked. Stez winked back and discreetly swallowed the contraband.

"Keith." Vinny nudged his mate.

"What?" Keith was slurring.

Vinny pushed a tablet into his hand.

"Uh, cheers." Keith was less than careful about necking his.

"Pass that down to Paul." Vinny passed Keith another one.

"Where we off next?" Vinny enquired. "Marine?"

"Nah, need a bird first," Keith objected. "Pop in Happy. There's one caught my eye last night."

"Sounds all right that, Happy then Marine." Stez's face was starting to glow.

They headed up the side of Star Bar towards Happy a Go-Go and pushed through the door. An usher stopped them from going further inside and counted heads – six in all including Paul's new acquisition. He looked round the bar for a space where six people could sit. Six pairs of eyes did the same; it didn't look good. Happy was a popular bar and getting a seat wasn't always easy.

"Fuck this, I'll see yers in Marine." Vinny took it on himself to make the usher's job easier.

"Same 'ere, man." Paul grabbed his accomplice by the hand. "Catch yers later."

The four of them headed back onto Walking Street and up the escalator between the boxing bar and Peppermint Katoey Bar into Marine Disco. At the top of the escalator Vinny started to feel light headed. They turned left through the darkened foyer with low seating against the wall. Jeed pushed the double doors open into the disco where European techno music was blaring out of the speakers. The floor was crowded with revellers cavorting to the tunes. It could have been mistaken for a nightclub in the UK, except the average age of the guys was 30 plus rather than 20 plus and all the women were Asian. It was a degree or two warmer than outside and the atmosphere carried a wave of humidity. The aroma of testosterone revealed its origin to be armpit rather than atmospheric. Just a couple of notches too loud, the music made their ears buzz and the bass reverberated through the floor.

The bar nearest the door was packed and Vinny pointed to the one at the far side of the dance floor. Jeed led the way through the throng and bobbed her head and wiggled her bum in time with the music as she did so. A couple of shoulders were bumped on the way through but they made it and squeezed through the large upholstered blocks people were using as seats or podiums near the bar.

Paul and Vinny leaned on the bar top. It was in need of a wipe. Vinny felt his elbows soaking in the spillage as he tried to get the tender's attention. They were behind the line of speakers so being heard was easier now.

"What your Mrs 'avin'?" Vinny asked.

"Bacardi Breezer." Paul offered Vinny a smoke.

"Flavour?"

"They're not arsed so long as it's got the label on the front."

Vinny smirked. He eventually managed to get the attention of the barman. Going by the décor and music being played, he should have been wearing a T-shirt with an art-house MARINE logo on it, with his hair gelled into spikes, but he was clad in white shirt and bow tie, and wore the po-faced expression of a waiter in an expensive restaurant. He placed three Carlsberg and a Breezer on the counter Vinny handed over 500 baht. The barman shook his head and held up six fingers. Vinny felt a rush of blood to his head. His knees weakened and the barman slipped out of focus. "What the fuck's he on about?" he asked Paul.

"Needs another 'undred."

"That pills just hit me, I'm fucked." Vinny felt a rush of chemical happiness fill his face and arms.

Paul threw a note over the bar.

"Top lad, you are, man." Vinny hugged Paul, rubbing sweat onto his shirt. Only seconds before, he'd avoided burning his face with the cigarette in his hand.

Vinny swayed over to Jeed, who was stood at the edge of the dance floor. The wiggle of her bum was more pronounced and she was waving clenched fists forward in time with the music.

Vinny kissed her on the cheek. It put her off her step and she threw her arms round him. Vinny pulled back and passed her a bottle. Paul took a seat on the block next to his hired hand as they watched the goings on. Vinny and Jeed danced in synch and matched each other's movements almost telepathically. An onlooker would have been forgiven for thinking it was choreographed. After ten minutes Paul barged past. His teeth were clenched and his eyes were popping out, beads of sweat dripping down his forehead. He joined the throng on the dance floor and started punching out with alternate hands and nodding his head.

"Paul," Vinny shouted but it wasn't heard. "Paul!"

Paul turned and grinned an evil grin through his teeth.

"Got you, that one, 'as it?" Vinny beamed.

"Fuckin' wicked, man. Fuckin' wicked." He held out a hand for Vinny, who clenched it with both his hands, homeboy style.

"Top notch." Vinny slapped his hand and let go.

Paul raised a thumb and winked at Jeed. It made her behind move faster. Paul turned back to the dance floor and let the chemicals do their job. Vinny was eyeing the doors, keen not to miss Stez and Keith's return. A couple of people entered. He moved back and stood on one of the blocks behind him, dancing a little less vigorously and continually eyeing the entrance. He saw Stez's unmistakeable outline enter the arena and survey the club. Vinny started to wave. Keith appeared behind him and his eyes darted manically across the room. Stez looked across, raised his hand to acknowledge Vinny and headed his way. By the time they'd pushed their way through the crowd Vinny had stepped back onto the floor. Stez looked agitated and his cheeks were red.

"Just the ticket, them pills," he nodded to Vinny. "Drink?"

"Usual, get Jeed one an' all," Vinny replied.

Noi was between Stez and Keith. She'd changed out of her tequila outfit into jeans and a T-shirt; it took the gloss off her appeal. She smiled at Vinny and tottered to the block where Paul's new friend was sat, and started nattering like she knew her.

"Y' all right, Keith?" Vinny smiled at his best mate.

Keith rubbed his head. "Mashed."

"No bird?"

"Nah, find summat in 'ere." He glared at Vinny. "Fuckin' pill's heavy, man." He stood on the spot grinding his teeth and sweating. Stez returned with a handful of bottles and dispensed them among his friends. Keith took his and headed into the crowd in search of a woman.

"Where's Jeed?" Stez had to raise his voice above the music.

Vinny looked round. "Fuck knows." When he looked again he saw her ten feet away talking to the girl who'd delivered the narcotics earlier. She'd lost the anorak and her sunglasses were folded into the neck of her T-shirt. The pair were giggling and joking. Vinny pointed. "Over there. That's her mate with the pills."

Stez wandered over and started talking to the girl; Vinny watched what was happening. A guy stood at the bar was staring at Jeed; his eyes spoke volumes about his thoughts. Vinny had to hold himself back from going on the attack before smiling to himself proudly that she was his. The transaction that took place between Stez and Jeed's friend was done with impunity and he returned smiling, followed by Jeed and her amigo.

A light bulb lit in Vinny's mind. "Jeed, your friend like Keith?"

Jeed shook her head; she rose on her toes and shouted in Vinny's ear, "She hab boyflend."

Vinny nodded. Setting his mate up with a drug dealer would have been a coup worth attempting but sometimes things just didn't work out.

"I've got them pills back you give me an' Paul," Stez billowed in Vinny's ear.

"Nip to t'bogs an' give 'em us there," Vinny replied.

The two headed across the floor to the toilet in the corner. As they crossed the dance floor Vinny noticed a guy in a blue polo shirt with England written across the front in white letters and a George's cross on it. He was handing some pills to another guy. He didn't seem too bothered who might be watching. They entered a corridor where boxes of Carlsberg were stacked against the wall, then through a door into the men's room. It stank. The walls and floor were covered with magnolia tiles, and the guys using the facility trod carefully for fear of slipping on the blend of beer, piss and cigarette ash that smothered the floor.

"Might as well 'ave a line, eh." Vinny nodded towards one of the cubicles.

The pair squeezed themselves in.

Stez popped two pills in Vinny's shirt pocket. "Returns."

"Cheers."

Stez was a big guy and there was very little space in the box. Vinny was pressed right against him and tried to edge himself towards the cistern but it wasn't happening. The pair laughed.

"I'll wait outside." Stez shuffled out.

The lights inside the toilets were a shock to Vinny's system and he was still in the throws of his first pill. He had to take his time and his hand shook as he ran the note along the line on the toilet seat. It had taken him a while to wipe it dry with paper. He stood, looked at the ceiling, breathed in, smiled to himself and racked up another line for himself.

Halfway through there was a rap on the door. He panicked and finished it quickly.

"Fuckin' 'ell, get a shift on, folk think I'm takin' rent in 'ere, man," came Stez's muffled voice.

Vinny laughed to himself and unbolted the door. Stez was standing in his way, grinning. There was a quick rub of palms and Vinny waited in the room. He faced a row of backs emptying bladders, extolling the virtues of prostitution and Asian women. The bad air was making him more light headed and he splashed his face with cold water in front of the mirror. He thanked the Lord that Jeed was with him because his facial contortions would have frightened a dalek.

Stez emerged from the toilet, trying not to look suspicious, and returned the wrap to Vinny.

When they got back to their corner, the gang of girls were nattering and giggling. Paul stood at the bar and Keith was standing alone, looking for women as Vinny passed him he slipped a pill in his hand. It was meant for safekeeping but Keith swallowed it straightaway. After a quick soft drink Vinny headed to the dance floor. Keith edged closer to him and the pair hugged each other and started waving their arms like maniacs. Stez bounced over, making the floorboards shake, and the three of them scared people off with their overenthusiastic efforts. Vinny looked over to Jeed. She was smiling proudly. She ventured through the crowd and an amorous look crossed Vinny's visage.

He didn't notice the tall, thickset, blond-haired guy's eyes light up as Jeed ventured through the writhing bodies. But he did see him tag onto her and slap her behind three feet away from him. Vinny saw red. No thoughts, just actions. He struck out with his right hand and connected with the guy's jaw. The guy blinked; Vinny was no heavyweight. Vinny struck again, this time with his left. His heart was pounding; and the guy was big but nobody touched his sweetheart.

Blondie shook his head and raised his right hand. From nowhere a fist hit him flush on the chin. It was Stez's. The guy staggered back then moved forward to fight back. The bottle in Keith's hand landed on his nose. In the instant that Keith's foot connected with the back of his knee, knocking him off balance again, Stez's left hit him in the eye socket and he dropped to the floor. Blood appeared on the varnished wood. Keith kicked his lower back. Vinny ran forward to hand out more punishment but the guy staggered to his feet and held up his palms. Vinny backed off as the guy headed for the door.

"Fuckin' gimp." Jeed hugged his torso and pressed her face into his chest. Twenty pairs of eyes pierced him and they headed to the bar. The crowd closed behind them and by the time Stez pulled up next to them the incident had been dismissed with a laugh.

"We gettin' a seat?" Stez offered.

"Aye, fuck it."

"There's a few up there." Vinny pointed to the far end of the club. "I'll ga'n get Paul."

The seats on the elevated floor gave the six of them a good vantage point over the club. They sat round a table, letting the adrenalin subside.

"Where's Keith?" Paul enquired.

"Fuck knows," Vin answered. "Just dropped another pill so he's probably bayin' at the moon somewhere."

"You're jokin'."

"Nah, just necked it before."

"I'm fuckin' spangled off one." The surprise in Paul's voice wasn't hard to detect.

"You'll see 'im foamin' at the mouth on all fours in a corner somewhere." Said Stez with a chuckle, his whole body rocking. "Fuck me, there 'e is."

His fat paw pointed to the middle of the dance floor. Keith was stood among the crowd, unaware of his movements or whereabouts. His neck was craned and his eyes, now the size of golf balls, gazed at the lighting rig in the ceiling. He stumbled back and forth a pace or two without taking his gaze away from the visuals in the roof.

"I'm the urban spaceman, baby, I've got speed. I've got everything you need." Stez laughed as he sung.

The guys joined him in laughing. There was nothing like an inebriate to cheer people up. The girls smiled politely. They didn't get the joke.

"I'm see you boxing." Paul's companion made a start with Vinny. She held her fists up and mocked fighting.

Vin covered his face in embarrassment, then smiled. "*Khun chu aria?*"

"Lek." She smiled and held out her hand.

"Nice to meet you, Lek," said Vinny, taking her hand.

"Don't go getting fresh now, Lek, 'e might hit yer," Paul butted in.

The group chatted and laughed. Occasionally they'd check on Keith's whereabouts and point him out when they saw him stumble into the back of someone.

When the pills started to subside Vinny felt he needed sustenance. He had two pills left and, fishing one out, he broke it in his teeth and popped the other half in Jeed's mouth. He swigged his beer and lit a cigarette. As he put his lighter on the table the music changed to a slow number and the house lights came on. "Shit." He shook his head.

Illuminated, the club took on a different face. In the dark it was hypnotic and rhythmic, exciting and uplifting. In the light it was worn and ageing. A flotilla of bodies sailed to the exit across a sea of empty bottles and cigarette packets. A few bodies remained and tried to spot friends or took the last chance to grab a partner before heading home.

Among the wreckage Vinny spotted Keith with a woman clinging to him.

"Fuck me, look at that." He pointed the pair out to the rest of the table.

Despite the distance, the males in the party could tell she was no 'Page 3' girl. Her face lacked the usual youthful glow of energetic bar girls.

Keith spotted his family and dragged her towards them. His feet were unsteady and his eyes looked like their sockets had shrunk; his partner got uglier as they got closer. She was pock marked and dull skinned. Her hair was straggly and she carried a lot of loose skin.

"All right, man?" Vinny greeted him.

Keith nodded and snarled. It wasn't aggression, just the concoction. "Off to the hotel, man. You comin'?" Keith was vacant.

"I'll catch yers up." Vinny kept a straight face until Keith had turned and left.

"I can't wait till tomorrer." Stez finished his last drop of beer. "We off down Tony's?"

They headed out of the club. In the entrance hall Jeed spotted her drug-dealer friend and skipped over to chat with her. Vinny hung on while the others headed out. 'Miss Nice', or Na as it turned out, was with the guy Vinny had seen selling pills earlier.

"Honey." Jeed gave Vinny the type of smile he could never refuse. "We go Boom wis Na?"

"What's Boom?"

"Iss diisco."

"OK."

At the bottom of the elevator Vinny looked around for Paul and Stez but they'd gone. Na and her bloke had started walking towards the beach road. Vinny and Jeed followed. When they reached the end of Walking Street, Na and her boyfriend were on a scooter. Na jabbered something in Thai and waved, and they zoomed off. Jeed took Vinny by the hand to a group of guys sat around on motorbikes. She chatted to the guy who seemed to be in charge and winked at Vinny. She hopped on a scooter and another guy beckoned Vinny. It had been a while since he'd used a motorbike taxi and he was anxious at first, but once they were up and running he was fine. He relaxed his body and went with the flow. Jeed looked over her shoulder from the scooter in front. She smiled and poked out her tongue. The warm night air washed over Vinny's face and ruffled his hair as the tarmac zoomed by below him. He inhaled and smiled at freedom.

They left the town of Pattaya. Vinny didn't know where he was. The distance between whitewashed buildings increased and they climbed up a hill. A few yards away he could see a small group of people congregated, and the taxi slowed. It stopped next to Jeed, Na and her boyfriend. Vinny hopped off and passed the driver a note; he smiled and headed home.

Jeed linked arms with Vinny and kissed him.

"All right, mate," the guy in the England top nodded to Vinny.

"Not ser bad," Vinny replied.

They walked into the door of a small building. The large glass front was blacked out.

Next to a 'hole in the wall' bar was a DJ playing trance on a pair of decks. The room itself was small; about the size of a large living room. High, narrow tables jutted down one of the sidewalls and at the far end was a sofa. The floor space was filled by twenty, maybe thirty people, the vast majority of them Thai and nearly all male, dancing to the music under a mirror ball. They weren't all dressed as men, and the ones who weren't in dresses looked camp. Vinny gulped.

"Beer?" the English guy enquired.

"Carlsberg," Vinny said and took a seat.

Jeed and Na took to the dance floor and the guy pulled up with two bottles.

"What's your name?"

"Jamie." he had a Cockney drawl.

The guy seemed inoffensive and amiable. He was in his twenties with the confident but relaxed aura of a guy with no worries.

"So you must be Vince."

Vinny nodded.

"Na's Jeed's mate. Told me she was goin' soft about some northern bloke."

"Aye. She's got me where it hurts." Vinny smiled.

"Good sort, Jeed is." Jamie passed him a cigarette. "She don't go with customers or nothing. How long you stayin' for?"

"Looks indefinite at the moment."

"Fancy a line?"

Vinny didn't hang about giving his answer and they headed to the only toilet at the back of the room. Once the ceremony was over Jamie headed out.

"Just 'avin' a slash first, mate." Vinny excused himself as Jamie left.

When Vinny walked out with an empty bladder he crossed the floor to the table. One of the bigger, camper guys stood in his way, winked and stroked his chest. Vinny gulped for the second time in half an hour. He dodged round him, looking pale. Jeed and Na had pulled up at the table.

"Honey, we go hotel?" Vinny put on his lost-boy look.

Jamie giggled. He'd seen what had happened.

Jeed was unaware and sulked. She was enjoying chatting with Na.

"Na and Jamie come also." Sleep was a while off yet and Vinny liked the pair so was happy to invite them.

They headed outside. Jamie sat on his scooter, revving the engine while they waited for a scooter taxi to turn up. They saw headlights coming up the hill. Jamie's eyes widened as they got closer.

"Stay cool, man," He looked at Na, who moved close and sat on the edge of the seat.

Vinny looked up to see a police pick-up truck. The pill and wrap in his pocket made his heart thump. The back of the van was full of policemen sat on the edges. Vinny sat on a fence pole and looked at the floor while he smoked a cigarette. Three policemen went into the club, and a fourth stood outside while voices echoed out of his radio; he spoke back to them occasionally. After three agonising minutes the policemen re-emerged with a guy in their midst. They all climbed in the van and drove off.

"Faarck me!" Jamie breathed a sigh of relief. "Close call, that."

whacked up

After the previous night's incident at Boom, Jamie and Na had come back to the hotel for a line and a beer. Jamie had explained that in return for greasing the right palms he'd been allowed to sell drugs in Marine for the last two years. At a thousand baht a pill, he was by no means short of cash. They made their excuses after a while leaving Vinny and Jeed to embark on an abortive attempt at sex.

Vinny woke from his semi-slumber. They'd not drawn the curtains and the sun hurt his eyes. He wiped his face. A layer of toxin-rich grease covered his skin. He looked at the ceiling, then his watch, then Jeed. She hadn't really been to sleep either. Vinny made another abortive attempt at sex then opted for a shower. They dressed and rang Keith on the hotel phone; he was in the throws of passion and agreed to meet them at the bar 'in a bit'.

When Vinny and Jeed got to the bar, Stez and Paul were in residence. Today they nursed soft drinks instead of beers.

"Mornin'," Paul greeted Vinny and Jeed.

Vinny looked at his watch. "It fuckin' is as well, innit."

"Where's Keith?"

"With 'is bird," Vinny replied.

"Fuck me, 'e's seen 'er in the light o' day without throwin' up?" Stez sounded amazed.

"Oh fuck." Vinny rubbed his face with his hand., "I forgot about that. Godzilla's baby sister."

"Aye, Medusa." Stez was off. "I hope there wa' no milk in the fridge."

The three chuckled. After a bit of banter Keith sauntered down Soi 7 and the three guys at the bar had never been more pleased to see him. They caught him grabbing a glance at one of the girls in a bar further up the road before lighting a cigarette and pulling up a stool at Tommy Bar.

"Mornin', Keith." Paul and Vinny smiled as Stez greeted him. "Black coffee, is it?"

The three started giggling at their own joke.

"What's up?" Keith looked paranoid.

"You should know." Stez smiled to himself. "With that genetically modified giraffe you 'ad last night."

"Aye, the super virus," Paul added to Vinny's titters.

"Hey, she was all right." Keith protested his innocence. "She 'ad a fit arse. Like the cover of that Gilly Cooper book."

"What, 'Riders'?" Vinny chipped in.

"Aye," Keith said, trying to save face.

"She 'ad a face like Lester Piggott though," replied Stez, cutting him dead.

Keith rested his head on the bar and when he raised it he was bright red. "Fuckin' bastards."

"I've just gotta nip an' sort a few things out." Vinny collected his cigarettes and hopped off his stool.

"I'll come with yers." Keith needed to escape the mocking Geordies.

Once they were out of earshot Keith opened up. "Man, I'm worried as fuck."

"What, about the wedding?" Vinny enquired.

"Nah, man." Keith wore a grave expression. "Worse than that."

Paranoia hit Vinny and visions of Interpol and prison cells flashed before him. "What?"

"Didn't rubber up last night." Keith looked like a schoolboy who'd not done his homework.

"How come?"

"Tried getting' one on but was too leathered," Keith gulped.

"No big deal, that, man," said Vinny, unphased. " Happens all the time. If you do get a dose, antibiotics'll sort it out."

"You reckon?" Keith was relieved.

"Aye," Vinny continued. "Happened to me a couple o' times, no problems."

"That's a weight off me mind," Keith sighed.

"It's more the worry that fucks people up than owt else," Vinny elaborated. "No point ruinin' your last day of freedom over a simple slip-up."

"It were better than rubberin'," Keith reassured himself.

Tourists got lackadaisical in Thailand and convinced themselves that HIV didn't exist.

By now they were on Beach Rd. Soi 6, the home of the blow'job bar was on their right. Thoughts of his last day of freedom, regardless of his marriage being nothing more than a piece of paper, were clouding Keith's mind.

"I'm just poppin' up 'ere." Keith veered off.

Vinny carried on down the Beach Rd until he found a travel agents. He needed to get himself on a flight to Zurich to sort out the money he'd swindled.

Half an hour later he walked out booked onto a Swiss Air flight to Zurich on Boxing Day.

“That’s outbound sorted out,” he whispered to himself. “Now for the return.”

He stuffed the ticket stub in the pocket of his shorts and headed back the way he’d come. Halfway back to Soi 7 he pulled into another travel agents. A girl was sat behind a desk talking in Thai down the phone.

She looked up as Vinny walked towards her and covered the mouthpiece on the handset. “One minni, please.” She finished off her conversation. “Hello, sah.” She smiled. “I can help?”

“Errm…” Vinny looked at the floor. “I need a flight from Zurich to Bangkok.”

He gave her the dates and she clattered a few keys on her computer and scanned the screen while Vinny looked at a poster with the silhouette of a kangaroo on it bidding him to ‘Discover Sydney’.

“Ye,s sir, hab fly you wan. Your name, please.” she didn’t look up from her screen.

“Vinny…” Vinny caught himself on. “Shit, fuck, shit. I mean James. Mr Bradley, James Bradley.”

The girl didn’t bat an eyelid and passed him a scrap of paper and a pen. “Can spell for me, please.”

He wrote out ‘James Bradley’ on the piece of paper and passed it back to her, clicked a few more keys.

“Sir, now you can pay tawenty-one thousan, fibe hunlet baht?”

Vinny rummaged in his back pocket. There were some bits of paper and a couple of cards. He piled them on the desk in front of him and pulled out the blue Barclaycard. He was about to give it to the girl when he spotted his own name on it, Vincent Croston, and he started to blush.

“Err, OK, sorry. This card not have credit. I have to get money, come back.” He headed for the door looking flustered, then looked over his shoulder. “What time you close?”

“Fibe o’clock.”

Vinny blustered out of the shop, aiming generally for a cash machine whilst having a mild neurotic tremor, hoping the girl hadn’t spotted his real name on his credit card. He spotted a yellow Thai Farmers bank cash machine built into the wall of a Seven Eleven store and tried withdrawing the cash, to be told the machine was out of order. He headed towards Soi 7 and saw Stez and Paul hunched over their elbows, burping and gurgling at each other in Tommy Bar.

“Seen Keith, lads ?”

“Doon Soi 6, a think, came back for a breather then went back for more aboot half hour ago.”

Vinny ordered a drink, took a gulp, looked at his watch and headed off to find an ATM that worked.

Without too much effort he got the ticket in the name of Jim Bradley, and went back to the room to stash it safely along with both his passports in his suitcase.

He'd planned to wander round a few bars with Jeed but when he saw her walk out of the bathroom with a towel wrapped round her he made other plans for the evening.

Vinny and Jeed were woken the next morning by a strident knock on the door; the knock of a man with a firm hand.

Vinny opened the door to find an unusually sober Keith. He had the eyes of a man who'd slept without drink, the walk of a man who'd run the marathon and the smile of a man who'd won the lottery.

"Shagged six birds yesterday." Keith rubbed his chest and looked round the room like a triumphant general. "And now I'm off to get married."

"All right, man, good luck." Vinny shook his right hand and patted his shoulder with his left. "I'll be back myself soon, give you a bell and that."

They both sniffed and turned, making their parting as manly and unemotional as possible. Vinny pulled the door shut and climbed back onto his bed. He tried to sleep. His eyelids felt heavy but didn't want to shut them, so he rolled on his side. Jeed was fast asleep. He touched her hip and rocked her but she didn't wake. Vinny lay back, looked at the ceiling and rubbed his lower pelvis. He tried to shut his eyes again and farted, then lifted the edge of the sheet to smell it. He looked at his watch. It said 9.40 am. An hour later his watch said 9.50 and after another hour of scratching his genitals, kissing Jeed's neck and trying to pick the gunk out from under his toenails, his watch said 10.02. Vinny scratched his head, jumped out of bed, dressed and paced around the room.

He decided to have a rummage in Jeed's handbag until he found her bag of grass and a crumpled packet of blue Rizla papers, then fabricated a crude but functional joint, which he smoked while he constructed another, which again he smoked then lay down.

At 1.20pm the phone on the bedside table rang and a hesitant Oriental voice asked if he was Mr Croston and explained that there was a Mr Peter in reception waiting to see him.

Vinny showered and put the same clothes back on, then ambled down to reception. Pete Jensen was waiting for him on a wicker sofa. The refined surroundings of Town in Town hotel did nothing to dilute his larcenous air. He looked the same as he'd looked in The Ship; a gnarled old fraudster with reseeding hair, loose skin under his chin and bags under his eyes.

"All right, Vinny?"

Vinny could feel his eyes bulging from the two joints he'd smoked earlier. "Not too bad, Pete. You?"

"Fine, fine." Jensen put his fag in the ashtray he was hunched over and leaned back. "You all set then? Got everything organised?"

His croaking cockney lilt hinted at years of misdemeanour. Vinny nodded and Jensen pulled two sheets of printed A4 out of a leather document wallet.

"I've give you the bank details before, but I'm giving you them again in case you've forgot. There's the address and number of the bank the money's in, there's the one you're transferring it to, there's the one you're putting my commission in. It's 50,000 Swiss Francs."

Vinny went to pick up the papers and felt Jensen's claw grip at his wrist. "No fucking about. You piss me off on this deal and, as they said in that film, 'retribution will be swift and decisive'."

Vinny started to shake. He looked Pete in the eye; his pupils had a purposeful glaze. Vinny nodded and felt pain in his wrist.

"That clear?"

"Yes, Pete," Vinny's voice quivered. "Perfectly."

He felt the grip on his wrist loosen and cold sweat drip down his brow. He lifted the first sheet and saw '50,000' in high-point size lettering and the name of a hotel beneath it. "Oh, and I've recommended a hotel you can stay in as well. It's OK, cheap by Zurich's standards and short taxi fares from where you need to be. How you feeling about it all then?"

"To be honest, I'm brickin' it." Vinny's frown eased but not much.

"Take a few valium, you'll be OK." Pete flicked his ash in the ashtray and momentarily looked concerned for Vinny's well being. "And don't forget to pay that facking money into my account or you'll never see that young lady of mine again. Oh, and happy Christmas for tomorrow"

Vinny nodded, folded the paper and ordered a drink of soda. Pete shook his hand and walked out into the sunshine.

When Vinny got in the taxi for the airport on Boxing Day he had a small rucksack and was wearing jeans, a shirt and trainers, with a jumper tied round his waist. In the back pocket of his jeans he had his ticket to Zurich and passport in the name of Vinny Croston, and his wallet. In his rucksack he had an acrylic-knit bob hat with a logo that looked almost like the Nike swoosh on it that Jeed had bought him, a small bag of toiletries and a passport and ticket from Zurich to Bangkok in the name of James Bradley, which were wrapped in a used shopping bag along with the two sheets of paper Pete Jensen had given him on Christmas Eve.

In the front pockets of his jeans he had some Thai money, one and a half packets of Malrboro Lights, a torn half-empty packet of immodium, two disposable cigarette lighters, a Thai-brand nasal inhaler, a tin the size of a ten pence coin containing insect balm, some small flakes of tobacco, two blister strips of valium and a blister strip of xanax, which the pharmacist said would be good for sleeping on the aeroplane. He also had a hangover.

Bangkok Airport smelt musty and after check-in Vinny headed straight to Bill Bentley pub, where they hadn't changed the décor, menu, staff or prices since October. The guy that brought him each of his nine bottles of beer had a more affectionate attitude towards him than he'd had in October. Maybe it was because he wasn't with a girl from Isaan or maybe it was because he appeared to be single.

An hour before take-off Vinny walked to Passport Control and waited in line smelling of Carlsberg and needing the toilet. He got stamped out of Thailand, headed for the toilet, then the smokers' cabin and, finally, to his aeroplane.

Cramped in his economy class seat, with his luggage in the overhead locker, he reached into his pocket, pulled out a blister strip, popped a pill out and threw it into his mouth without looking at the packet, folded his arms and shut his eyes. An indeterminate amount of time later he realised that the drinks trolley and the food trolley had passed and he hadn't taken a meal and hadn't slept, so he rummaged in his back pocket, pulled out another blister strip, popped another pill out, swallowed and ordered a Jack Daniel's and Coke off a passing hostess. The ice bumped against his front teeth as he downed the drink in one, and he swirled the remaining cubes round in the plastic glass before putting it down on the fold-out table. He crossed his arms again and shut his eyes. After that the plane jerked and rolled a bit. He felt tired but not overly, then he realised he was waking up. There was a TV screen in the roof space above the aisle nearest to him showing a schematic of an aeroplane crossing the middle bit of the Persian Gulf. He felt 90 per cent awake now so delved in his pocket and pulled out the blister strips again. This time he looked carefully to see that he got the one with Xanax written on it. He swallowed one of the pills and shut his eyes again. Twenty minutes later he realised he still wasn't asleep so he took a pill from each blister strip, swallowed them and shut his eyes again.

Vinny was in a nice sleep when he felt a push on his shoulder. He opened his eye and saw a well made-up woman in her thirties wearing a uniform. She spoke to him in a European language that he couldn't understand.

"Fuck off." He tightened the fold of his arms, shut his eyes and turned his shoulder to her.

"Oh, you are English." Her accent was feminine and aggressive.

"I've told you fuck off."

"But, sir, I cannot do that. We have landed in Zurich and you must get off the aeroplane."

"Oh, sorry, man." Vinny rubbed his eyes, stood up and headed down the aisle.

His legs hadn't turned to jelly but someone had interfered with them. The bones were solid enough to hold him upright but not as rigid as usual. Some of the calcium had been replaced with syrup, which gave his stride a resonant boing. It was nice and he smiled. A lot.

"Excuse me, sir," came the voice of the sexy commandant woman again. "I think you have forgotten your luggage."

Vinny turned round. She was holding his bag out for him. He grabbed it, slung it over his shoulder and headed down the empty aisle for the exits, bumping the seats with his thighs as he went.

Zurich Airport's architecture was modern and minimalist. It had plain walls in pastel colours and corridors with high ceilings leading to big rooms with carousels and mounted booths where men and women with strong jaw lines wearing dark uniforms and an air of Teutonic efficiency looked at your passport and waved you through. Vinny was in a daze as he wandered through and pulled on the sweater he had round his waist when he thought he was clear of Customs.

He followed a sign saying EXIT and glided rather than walked through a pair of dark brown, smoked glass doors onto a concreted concourse, where he rummaged for a cigarette, lit it and smoked it as gradually the coldness of the air began to permeate his skeletal structure. Vinny wasn't sure what time of day it was. He was sort of awake, the sky was dark and gloomy but there was activity that suggested it was daytime. He followed a sign with a picture of a car and the word TAXI on it. He found an ordered waiting area and saw a couple of cars waiting; large German sedans with a small TAXI sign on the top of them and some writing on the side panels. He got in the first one in line and looked at the driver. He had an inordinately large nose and looked as if he was from somewhere halfway between Pakistan and North Africa. He wore an Adidas tracksuit top, an identity badge on a chain and kept clearing his throat. He didn't look like he knew or cared if it was day or night, and started to trundle off down the slip road. He pushed a button on the console that lowered his window and spat a chestful of phlegmy fluid onto the door of a passing Mercedes then headed towards a dual carriageway that was signposted for Zurich. Vinny looked the guy in the face but his eyes were glued to the road.

"So where you taking me, man?"

The driver wound the window down again, cleared his throat, spat into the road and wound the window back up. Vinny rummaged in his bag and pulled out the package with his new passport and bank details. He showed it to the driver, who put it on the steering wheel and read the hotel address that Jensen had given Vinny for what seemed like ten minutes, unperturbed by the traffic in the other lanes. Then he nonchalantly veered off to his right across two lanes of traffic for a turn-off.

Vinny thought about panicking but decided against it. He'd grown accustomed to Thai taxi drivers by now so this was nothing to worry about. He had vague memories of driving down roads with greying snow piled up at the sides and some steep hills in the middle distance covered in white snow but very little recall of much more of the journey until he felt a nudge on the arm to wake him up. When he looked up he saw a brown-glass door set in a mid-coloured marble wall with the word UBERKIPPEN or something similar in steel letters above the door.

The driver pointed to the meter and the red LED numbers, which didn't register on Vinny's brain but danced in time with the throb of the engine. Vinny checked his wallet but only had Thai money. He wasn't sure which language the driver spoke so told him in Thai that he had no money and waved a near empty wallet at him. The driver showed him a digital machine displaying the Visa logo, so Vinny paid with his credit card and staggered into the lobby of the Zurich Fraudhotel.

Check-in was a muddled affair and after a couple of signatures and extraneous chits and bits of paper, Vinny was in a clean but slightly dated room with a mini-bar, which he started to empty wine first. Some time later he woke on the bed with his clothes on, a damp patch in his trousers and an assortment of empty alcohol vessels on the floor.

His head felt cloudy and there was a needle of pain burrowing its way from his left sinus to his right. He picked up the phone on the bedside table, hit zero and waited for the concierge to answer.

"Hello."

"Hiya, I thought I asked for a wake-up call."

"I am sorry, sir, we have no record of this."

"Oh right, well, what time and day is it ?"

"Sir, today is Sunday. It is six o'clock, sir."

"Morning or night?"

"It is six o'clock in the morning. Would you like breakfast, sir?"

Vinny put the receiver down but missed the cradle, pressed his hands on his forehead and shut his eyes.

Four hours later an English man with no coat on wearing a fake Nike bob hat and smelling of piss bought a new pairs of jeans, two pairs of underpants, a warm fleece-lined jacket, three pairs of socks and two T-shirts in the first department store he found open in the centre of Zurich on Sunday.

At 1pm he ate in the hotel restaurant; he was the only one there and the décor made it feel like a staff canteen in a large design agency. After eating he retired to his room where the mini-bar had been refilled and the TV was showing MTV, an adult channel free of charge and some Swiss soap operas.

He woke at around midnight, this time wearing the hotel dressing gown and surrounded by empty bottles. He found a sleeping pill and woke again at around 7am feeling groggy but cheerful. He dressed and went to the restaurant/cafeteria and walked along the buffet with a tray, picking up items of food whilst avoiding eye contact with the assortment of international business travellers who were making him paranoid by ignoring him. Each croissant and knob of butter, each slice of ham and cup of coffee he tried to acquire made him nervous. His hand shook at every serving hatch, and when he thought he heard a man in a suit mention Personable Computers he put his tray hastily to one side and bolted for his room, his tray crashing to the tiled floor behind him.

Vinny's hand was shaking like a cup finalists knee by the time he made it to his room. He swallowed two Valium. When he looked at his collection of blister strips he noticed that he had three sleepers and five anti-shakers left. He swallowed another valium and lay down.

When he felt like moving again it was 9.45am. He took his bag and the remaining pills, walked out of the hotel and stood on the pavement, unaware of his surroundings and trying to focus on the traffic and spot a car that looked like a taxi. The purity and coldness of the Alpine air burned his lungs and felt like it was starting to dislodge some of the tar that had built up over the years. He waited a while. When he saw a taxi it didn't stop, so he went back into the hotel and asked a faceless male receptionist to order him one.

Finally in the taxi, Vinny gave the driver the paper Jensen had given him and pointed at the address of the first bank. The journey was the first chance Vinny had to take in the sights of Zurich. It was similar to Manchester in some ways. The ornate bits were older, nicer and more ornate than the ones in Manchester, and the newer, more modern areas were older and more tired looking than the ones in Manchester. The taxi drove along the edge of a square and pulled up at a building that looked more like the dole office in Bolton than a bank but the driver pointed at it. Vinny paid using his credit card, left the car and walked towards the glass doors of the bank, which were locked. There was an intercom with keypad on the side wall and the doors were lettered CHARTER BANK OF ZURICH, with an ornate, almost papal logo underneath. He pressed the buzzer and heard somebody speak in that same language again.

"Err, I'm the MD of Personable Computers, Vinny Croston. I've got an appointment with the manager." He stumbled over the words.

"Then you must come inside," the voice told him and a buzzer sounded.

Inside looked plusher than outside. The carpet was a rich, almost regal blue and moved under his feet while he walked, but the place didn't look like a bank. He walked down a short corridor, at the end of which was a security desk.

"I'm, er, here to see the manager. My name is Mr Croston, from Personable Computers."

The guard pointed to some seats behind him. Vinny started to feel strange; not nervous as he'd expected and not light headed. But when he started to walk towards the seats he felt like his head was in setting concrete and his legs were in a strong wind. He sat on a seat covered in blue fabric that felt robust and utilitarian as well as springy and flamboyant. From the seat he could see round a corner. There was a room that looked like a standard but unstaffed bank. There were two glass-fronted kiosks that looked like the standard ones in banks where you transact with tellers, and two doors with keypad locks on them and a red LED panel above them, one showing the number '1' and the next with the number '2'. Vinny got a cup of water from the machine next to him and started to feel anxious. He swallowed another valium.

The wait was unpleasant. The fluorescent strip lights were a shade too bright and there was a harsh throbbing sound that filled his ears. At first the noise wasn't too bad, just a gentle hum in the background from a source he couldn't identify like a heater or fan or aircon unit, but the longer he waited the louder the hum hummed and throbbed until he had to hold his hand over his ears. He'd had his eyes shut for what seemed like forever when he felt a tap on his shoulder. The security guard was pointing at the door which displayed LED '2', the number flashing. Vinny did a valium-induced forward moonwalk to the door and let himself in. There was a desk with a PC and a small money-counting machine on it, and high-backed Chesterfields on either side. There was another door in the far wall and a man sat behind the desk. Vinny sat down and the man looked up from some papers in front of him. He looked like a newsreader. He wore a well-ironed white shirt without cufflinks and a grey and burgundy striped tie. He looked young but the lighting highlighted strands of grey hair.

"Hello, you are Mr Croston?" His diction had textbook perfection that identified him as a non-native English speaker.

"Yes." Vinny blinked. The man changed in appearance in Vinny's blink. He now looked old with lines in his face but with jet-black hair. Viscous sweat tried to force its way out of Vinny's forehead.

"I have spoken to Mr Jensen, your agent. He tells me you would like to close your account with us." The man stared at Vinny and looked like the young, slightly greying version of himself again.

Vinny started to tremble. The sweat became liquid and poured out of his forehead. He nodded.

"I have prepared the documentation for you." A hint of a Germanic accent started to appear, "First of all in Swiss, which you must sign, and in English for your reference."

He pushed some papers over to Vinny: two sheets, both with that papal-looking logo on top, the first in Swiss with some number and the second in English with some numbers. The fluorescent lighting started to intensify the thrub of the heater or air conditioner, increased in volume and the type started to blur. Vinny reached in his pocket and popped a valium in his mouth.

"Can you explain them, please?"

"There was a transfer to your account of one million, two hundred and twenty-seven thousand, two hundred and fourteen Francs." He pointed at the first number on the sheet. "You want to close the account before the balance has been there for six months, so you incur a one per cent charge, which is this." He pointed to the second number on the sheet. "So now when you sign here we will give you one million, two hundred and fourteen thousand, nine hundred and forty-one Francs."

"Say that again."

"There was a transfer—"

"No, the bit about the one per cent charge." Vinny was in a valium haze but not that deep a trance.

"It is a standard clause." The bank employee was starting to sound more French than German and looking like his older persona. "It is outlined in our banking terms of business. We cannot change this clause. You can wait six months if you like."

"What's one per cent of half a million?" Vinny needed a cigarette.

"5,000." He sounded even more French.

"Get me the cash. I'll sign."

"First I must cheque your identity."

Vinny tossed his passport onto the desk.

The man spoke in Swiss to somebody on the telephone got up, took Vinny's passport and walked out of the door at the back of the room.

Vinny felt blank. The time that elapsed before the banking officer returned was minimised by the valium. The man walked back into the room looking like his young self, smiling. A woman followed pushing a trolley with a metal case painted enamel grey on it.

The woman put the tray on the desk and Vinny looked at her backside as she wheeled the empty trolley back out. It was wider than a Thai woman's but flatter. The man had a sheet of paper that he pushed towards Vinny before lifting the lid of the metal case, which had a disappointingly small amount of banknotes in it.

"Is that it?"

"I know it looks like a small amount." He became French and apologetic. "There are twelve bundles of one hundred thousand Francs." He picked up a bundle the thickness of a short novel. "These are thousand-Franc notes and there is one hundred in each bundle."

He wafted the bundle, which was clasped with an inch-wide paper bind containing simple black type – 100 x 1,000 100,000 – in front of Vinny. "You can count them if you like."

Vinny thought he could see his heart beat through the sweatshirt he was wearing. He could certainly hear it. He tried to act cool. "Can if you want, like."

The man put the bundle in a counting machine and pressed a button. The readout said '100,000'. Vinny nodded and put the bundle in his bag.

They repeated the process twelve times. Each time Vinny looked at the purple notes displaying the number '1000' and the austere-looking old bloke, and his grin grew with each bundle that ended up in his bag. His anxiousness soon turned to exuberance. With the bundles done there was a smaller collection of notes, which Vinny went to pocket, but he pulled out a 100-Franc note and smiled.

He felt a mass of dopamine build up behind his eyes, which made them roll. "Can I go now?"

"Yes, of course." The man tapped a few numbers on the keyboard of the PC.

Vinny pushed a 100-Franc note across the desk to the man. "You and your Mrs have a nice night out on me."

"But, sir, I cannot accept gratuity."

Vinny ignored him, grinned, jumped up from the chair and punched the air. He shouted, "Yes!" then went for the door, pulled it open onto his face and knocked himself straight out.

He came round with the woman who had pushed the trolley cradling his neck and holding an icepack on his forehead. The room swam for a moment and he realised what he was supposed to be doing. He took the icepack off her, picked his bag up and headed out of the door without an apology.

"But Mr Croston," came the man's voice.

"What?"

"You've forgotten your passport."

"It's OK, I don't need it anymore." Vinny grabbed it anyway and bustled his way out of the bank with half a million quid minus one per cent in Swiss Francs in his bag.

On the street he managed to flag a taxi. He showed the driver the address of the second bank. The driver nodded, switched the meter on, took his foot off the clutch and drove fifteen yards to the first corner. He turned right and pulled over, pointing at a building with BANQUE DU COMMERRCE SUIS written on it. He pointed at the meter and Vinny gave him a ten-Franc note. The driver gave him some change and Vinny alighted and floated towards the door.

The paying-in part of the transaction was easy. BCS was just like any normal bank. Vinny paid the Swiss equivalent of 50,000 pounds into an account named as Peter Jensen's and the remainder into one named as James Bradley's. He was given a cash and Visa card in the name of James Bradley, which he signed for before walking out of the bank.

Smiling, he took a taxi to the airport and bragged to the driver, who looked liked he might have been an escaped Nazi who had fled over the border when the Reich collapsed.

Vinny smiled at him. "You OK, man?"

"I am fine. How are you ?" His accent was the French end of Swiss and he wore a shirt and a pale blue tie.

"Superb, man, superb." Vinny wound the window down and leaned his right elbow out. "Just got half a million in the bank, my old son. Never felt better."

"Oh, so you are using our Banghemis and you are a criminal." The driver couldn't conceal the disapproving shake of his head.

"Well, er, yes, kind of looks like it, I suppose."

“Switzerland is such a beautiful country but it is blighted by this. We are used by criminals from across the world. Sometimes I am ashamed to be Swiss.”

Vinny clammed up. They drove to the airport in silence.

After checking in with no luggage as James Bradley, Vinny had an amble round the duty-free section. He was about to head for the departure gate after a coffee and a look at some European football on TV in the bar when he remembered his passport. He wandered to the newsagent/bookstore, headed for the ‘business’ section took a cursory glance at the passport that had served him as Vinny Croston for the last five years and hid it behind a stack of books on ‘management accounting in the European community’.

there are places

As Vinny approached Thailand's Passport Control he started to sweat. He got an overwhelming urge to run away, not to any specific destination, just away. Somewhere with a corner he could cower in would be ideal. As he entered the small quadrant where the officials checked the passports he gulped, looked at the floor and carried on walking, trying his best not to look sideways.

Once he was back in the simple corridor he held his head and brushed his hair back from his forehead.

"Fuck. C'mon, man." He looked up and saw a smoke room.

He took a seat alongside the other smokers and looked at the floor. Sweat poured out of him like a freshly wrung sponge. When he raised his head he could tell the colour had drained from his face. He crossed his arms and hugged himself tight. Vinny felt like he was in Greenland not Thailand but the sweat still oozed out of him. The cigarette he took from his shirt pocket was damp, but it calmed his nerves. He half smoked another and dipped it out in the sand of the ashtray before closing his eyes, counting to ten, clenching his teeth and heading out to face officialdom. It was the first time his passport had been under any type of scrutiny. This was the really make or break. Those twenty yards around the corner seemed longer than the Paris–Dakar Rally. He walked into the tiled square feeling faint and joined a queue in front of one of the desks. A group of officials stood chatting in front of the glass-fronted immigration office to his right. They were talking about him; he knew it. Vinny looked straight ahead, sweat pouring down his neck; he daren't look sideways so he looked straight at the back of the man in front. The queue was moving at an agonisingly slow pace. Vinny could feel his heart pounding in his ears and hear his own breath. He could sense the people around him. He wondered which ones had been planted by the authorities to mingle with passengers and spot fraudsters. After what seemed like about fourteen months it was his turn at the desk. The officer eyed his passport, looked at the 'Non-Immigrant Class B' stamp that Jensen had managed to procure for him, stamped a page and passed him back his repo documentation and looked at the guy behind him. Vinny grabbed his passport and flew off down the stairs without looking back and stood like a whippet in a trap by the luggage conveyer waiting to collect his bag. When it arrived he grabbed it and sped through Customs and out into the departure hall.

He ran outside and lit a cigarette. He needed to get away in case they changed their minds about him. Where the fuck was Jeed?

"I'll turn left when I get through the doors," he'd told her.

Perhaps she was in on it. Maybe she'd decided to tell immigration he was on a false passport for a backhander and they were waiting until he was firmly on Thai soil. His eyes met then darted away from every passer by. He dashed out of the main doors and parked himself on a row of plastic seats and tried to stop his right hand shaking by holding it with his left. The cigarette helped calm him and, as the sun shone in his face again, he relaxed. He spread his arms wide on the seats next to him and smiled. Four days of Swiss efficiency had got him accustomed to things happening on time. The solar energy reminded him where he was, and to just sit and wait maybe an hour or so for Jeed to turn up. He shut his eyes.

"Winnee!" Jeed trotted as quickly as her heels would let her down the pavement towards him carrying a bag full of clothes and make-up.

She had her bag over her shoulder and her short black skirt stopped him looking at her smile for too long.

Unabashed by the activity in his shorts, Vinny stood and embraced her. She jumped into his arms and saturated him with a kiss. He spun her round and landed her on the floor to hug her again.

"Happee Noo Year." She kissed him again.

Vinny had almost forgotten.

"Happy New Year. We get taxi?" With her hand in his the illegitimacy of his existence washed away.

She nodded behind a thinly veiled smile.

They got a taxi at the stand and directed the driver to the Asia Hotel.

Vinny looked at Jeed. "Fuck me, I bricked it goin' through Customs."

She looked up at him, bemused.

"I need a drink. Have y'any whisky?"

"Jeed no hab wiskee."

He realised he'd started speaking quickly again and reminded himself to slow down.

When they arrived the lavish entrance hall impressed Vinny; the bellboy that took his bag added a touch of elegance to the place. The parking lot at the front was full of limousines rather than taxis, and there were too many Mercedes badges for him to count. They had a stretch limo as well; Vinny eyed it for a moment wondering how it managed in Bangkok's gridlock.

They sauntered up to the desk while Vinny looked in wonder at the reception area. 'Reception' was an understatement. It was the size of a shopping mall, with marble floors, chandeliers and staff in pristine uniforms. The majestic marble desk was over 30 yards long and the staff behind it were immaculately preened.

Vinny approached the desk. It took a while for anyone to approach him, which furrowed his brow.

"Yes, sir. Can I help?" The guy didn't crack a smile.

"I have reservation." Vinny slipped back into plain English.

"Your name?"

"Vin, errr, Jim Bradley." He gulped.

"Passpor', please?" The guy held his hand out.

Close call, that one, he thought. Vinny filled out the forms, still anxious at the inspection of his imitation ID.

"You hab cledi' car, sir?" Vin rummaged in his wallet and passed over his latest piece of plastic.

The guy ran it through the machine and gave him a chit to sign. Vinny closed his eyes while he signed it as Jim. The receptionist passed the bellboy a key on a large brass fob. The bellboy nodded for Vinny to follow him. He took Jeed's hand and started to follow. Within a second he was alongside the bag carrier and within three he was ahead of him so he slowed down. Not one to be left standing, the bellboy upped his pace to keep with Vinny. The combination of adjusted tempos resulted in the bellboy speeding ahead to the far end of the foyer. He stood and snarled as Vinny and Jeed sauntered along to meet him.

In the lift he avoided eye contact with the pair. They weren't the type of guests he approved of. It wasn't that he didn't like Westerners, but a Westerner with a whore…

The room was nice. The bellboy left with 50 baht in his pocket.

Vinny and Jeed did what couples do when they've been apart for a week.

At 8 o'clock Vinny hugged her tighter and kissed the top of her head. She looked up with her doe eyes and smiled.

"Honey, where we go?" asked Vinny.

"Where you wan' go?" she replied.

"Where you want go?"

"Up to you." She straightened in the bed and lit a cigarette.

Vinny did likewise. "OK, errrm. We go Las Vegas."

She looked up at him.

"Errrm, OK, Paris." He hugged her and looked down. She was sulking.

"We stay Thailand. Wisa no can get."

Vinny felt embarrassed at his childishness.

"OK, we can't stay Pattaya. Where in Thailand? Ubon?"

Jeed shook her head. "Ubon good for farang is not."

The idea of in laws didn't really appeal to Vinny either.

Hhhhhhmmm, Vinny thought to himself.

Being honest, he hadn't given the matter too much thought. Pattaya was going to have to be given a wide berth for a few months at least, until the fuss died down, as would most major tourist destinations; Vinny needed a measure of anonymity.

"OK, we think about it. You want champagne?"

It must have been the first time since he was sixteen that Vinny had stayed in on New Year's Eve. He had everything he wanted so it didn't matter.

When he woke Vinny kissed Jeed's forehead. She groaned and hugged him. Vinny got out of bed and walked over to the window. He looked out over the grimy half of Bangkok. Below him were slums and ramshackle buildings separated by dusty streets cluttered with old motorbikes, stray dogs and capering kids.

What a beautiful sight, he thought as the sun tried to force its way through the rising morning smog.

Jeed rubbed her eyes and padded over to him wrapped in a towel. She kissed his neck. "Honey, what we do today."

"Tonight I meet Keith." He paused and looked into the distance. "You want go shopping?"

She almost knocked him to the floor as she jumped up and wrapped her legs around him before thrusting her hips energetically into his. Playfully he threw her onto the bed before diving in for his breakfast.

Showered and dressed, they stood on the Sky Train heading towards Siam Square. The BTS, as the Sky Train was known, offered clean air and a sanitised yellow and grey capsule for commuters to travel through Bangkok in. The passengers were more respectable than the type found at ground level and some of the suited businesswomen threw an odd unnoticed disapproving glance at the two lovebirds.

"We still not decide where to go." Vinny looked down towards Jeed as he held onto the grey handrail.

"Iss up to you, I say," she replied.

"I want go Ko Samui, but think no good. Too many farang," Vinny explained, waiting for another suggestion.

"You wan' go Ko Pha Ngan?" Jeed offered.

"What Ko Pha Ngan like?" Vinny hopped out of the sliding doors as they pulled into Siam Square.

"My fliend go." Jeed joined him and looked up and down the clean concrete platform to get her bearings. "She say it hab beatifur beat ant Furr Moon Diisco."

"Wow. Nice beach?"

"Yes. Can get boat flom Ko Samui." Jeed clasped his hand and guided him with the flow of humanity down some concrete steps. "You want we go?"

"OK, we go in few days," Vinny nodded, pleased that he had a plan.

They worked their way through the labyrinth of walkways and staircases that wound it's way from the Sky Train alighting points to various sides of Siam Square, the focal point of the city's traffic. The square itself was flanked by a number of glorious glass and steel shopping malls.

Down at street level the heat was strong. The pavements were awash with moneyed Thais, mainly female and under the age of 30, looking chaste in groups of four as they scurried to and from shops gossiping and giggling.

They headed up the steps to the Siam Centre and Vinny got the urge to jump in the fountain to cool down.

Inside the centre they wandered up and down the escalators. Jeed squeezed Vinny's hand tight when he bought her some perfume, and kissed him once they'd left the shop. They wandered past hi-fi shops and furniture outlets. They passed a few boutiques with nothing spectacular in the window. After 40 minutes of window shopping they stumbled across the Armani outlet. Vinny stood at the doorway and looked in. It had been a while since he'd been able to afford Armani. Jeed didn't notice and tugged at his hand, but Vinny stood fast.

"We look in here." He strode in.

The shop smelt expensive. A couple of elegant but arrogant sales staff glided between the racks of neatly folded garments while they oozed refinement. One of them gave Vinny and Jeed a sideways glance while Vinny fingered some T-shirts. The cotton felt soft and superior. Vinny pulled one off the shelf and held it against him. It was really nothing special, just a plain T-shirt with a logo on the breast, but Jeed nodded her approval. Vinny noticed the assistant sneering at him.

"Fuck it, I'll 'ave four of them." Vinny threw it over his arm and picked out the same garment in grey, blue and white to go with the black one he was holding.

The act of earmarking four garments gave Vinny a rush of adrenaline; he gave the guy the four T-shirts to hold.

"You want some clothes?" he asked Jeed.

She skipped with delight and ran over to the ladies' side of the store.

When the girl at the check-in finally totted up the pile of jeans, shirts, shorts, blouses, sandals, T-shirts and other odds and ends that the pair had accumulated, she hit 'total' on the till. The glowing red digits read 107,100 baht; Vin let out a sigh of shock. A quick mental calculation put the total at around 1,700 quid. For a moment he thought about putting some of the clobber back but that would have meant a loss of face in front of the shop staff, and Jeed. He looked away as he passed over Jim Bradley's credit card and tried not to look at the amount when he signed the chit.

On the Sky Train Jeed was as proud as punch. She held Vinny's arm tightly and her head swelled as two office girls looked enviously at the collection of freshly sealed Armani bags at the pairs' feet. Vinny was proud of his purchases as well and mentally raised a glass to John Moston. He started doing some arithmetic.

Fuck. The magnitude of the amount struck home. If he spent like that every day he'd be skint in less than a year.

When they got back to the hotel room Jeed pushed him onto the bed and undid his shorts. She performed the most satisfying felatio he'd ever received.

Vinny dosed off. When he woke Jeed was singing in the shower. He looked at his watch.

"Shit." His watch read 7.15.

He was supposed to meet Keith at 7.30 down Khao Sarn Rd for a farewell drink.

Vinny decided to skip the shower, doused himself in aftershave and deodorant, and dressed.

Jeed was still showering when he pushed the bathroom door open.

"Honey, I go for drink with Keith," he said, sticking his head round the shower curtain.

She covered her soap-sudded breasts and turned round, smiling. Vinny pecked her on the lips; the jet of the shower dampened his new Armani shirt.

Outside the hotel he looked round for a taxi. He looked at Payathai Rd in front of him. The traffic was gridlocked.

"Fuck this." He skipped round the corner.

A tuk tuk driver was sat in the seat of his vehicle reading the paper.

Vinny nodded to him. "You go Khao Sarn Load?"

The guy folded his paper and smiled. He nodded with a wide, toothy grin.

Vinny jumped aboard then caught himself. "*Tow rai?*"

"Fibe hunlet baht." The guy smiled over his shoulder at Vinny in the rear.

Vinny choked. "*Mai ow*. Too expensive." He got out. "You think I dickhead? For Khao Sarn sixty baht."

"OK, two hunlet," the guy replied.

Vinny shook his head. This was why he normally stuck with taxis; there was no fucking about with the fair, they just switched the meter on. Tuk tuk drivers tried to inflate the price, then halfway through the journey they would try and guide you towards a massage parlour or tailor's shop where they'd get a commission. The only advantage of using one was that they could nip in and out of traffic, and Vinny was late.

"Sixty baht, man, or nothing." At this rate it would be quicker walking.

The guy spun his wheelbarrow/scooter combination around and pulled up alongside Vinny.

"For you one fipty."

Vinny looked at the floor and carried on walking, shaking his head.

"OK, one hunlet."

Vinny looked at his watch it; was 7.30 already.

"OK." Vinny jumped in.

He sat on the vinyl seat and spread his arms wide on the ornate chrome-plated railing that surrounded his chair. The driver restarted the engine that he'd turned off while they agreed on a price. Vinny smiled as he shut his eyes and let his head fall back; his head jumped forward as the machine hiccupped into motion. The guy hurled the vehicle at the stream of traffic in front of them regardless of the carnage a collision would cause. Vinny shook his head and clenched his teeth. This was going to be a nerve-jangling ride; tuk tuks always were, which was another reason why he preferred taxis. They stopped abruptly six inches from a passing Mercedes as they edged their way into the main road. Vinny looked at the guy in the driver's mirror. He had a hardened face and was smiling his wide, toothless grin at Vinny through the mirror.

They found a gap in the traffic. Bangkok's answer to Barry Sheen revved the throttle on his hand control and they picked up speed. The tarpaulin roof designed to keep passengers safe from the elements ruffled in the wind. Vinny felt dangerously close to the vehicles around him. He rummaged in his pocket for a cigarette and popped it in his mouth. The driver saw his action in the mirror and turned round with a lighter in his hand. Vinny saw a wagon crossing their path ahead.

"There's a fuckin' van," Vinny shouted in exasperation.

The guy smiled, nodded and turned back to the traffic. Vinny cursed and lit his own cigarette. They pulled up at a traffic light and the guy mimicked smoking a cigarette to Vinny. Vinny passed him one.

"You wan' massard? Sexy lady? Thai lady?" The guy was ignoring the tide of traffic again.

He held up a laminated card covered in pictures of immaculately preened ladies.

Vinny held up his hand and shook his head.

"Oh," the driver nodded and lowered his voice. "You wan' sexy boy."

Vinny held his hand across his face. The traffic started to move and they trundled forward until they hit a bottleneck in the traffic and sat for five minutes in the slipstream of an old diesel lorry that was in need of a service. The dense plume of fog made Vinny cough and choke, and when they cleared the nauseating plume he had to stick his head out of the carriage to get a lungful of relatively clean air.

They pulled up outside the police box at the end of Khao Sarn Road. Vinny got out and handed the man a note, and walked off without any pleasantries.

He wove his way through the cluster of tuk tuks, motorcycles and taxis.

"Sir, you wan' tuk tuk?"

"I've just got out o' one," Vinny cursed.

He joined the throng of humanity that individualised Khao Sarn Rd. It wasn't a Thai populous like Siam Square, or full of sex-starved foreigners with Oriental women like Soi Nana. Khao Sarn Rd was the home of the backpacker. People in their early twenties weaved in and out of a chaotic tapestry of stalls that sell souvenirs. Most of them looked like they were on a twelve-month trip following their university graduation; an expedition to 'find themselves' at their parents' expense before entering the world of work. Some of them looked like they'd been finding themselves for a good ten years without the aid of soap. Matted hair and tie-dyed cotton were very much in vogue. The establishments that lined the street were often multifunctional; cafés at floor level, internet cafés on the floor above with the remaining four floors being divided into rooms for travellers to rest in before heading off somewhere with a beach or elephants.

Vinny saw the one he wanted. The peeling sign above the entrance said HELLO RESTAURANT. The entrance area was full of tables older than Vinny covered in plastic tablecloths. He squeezed his way through two stalls; he couldn't help eyeing up the cheap electricals and counterfeit CDs as he passed through. Keith was sat at two tables joined together, sipping at a beer.

"All right, man?" He smiled at his best buddy.

"All right, Vin?"

"Shit hot. How was the weddin'?"

"Bang on."

"Did Harpers and Queen turn up?"

"Aye. Prince Charles and David Beckham were guests of honour."

Vinny laughed and pulled up a chair. The next table was occupied by a guy in his thirties in a vest and baggy purple cotton trousers. His hair was well on its way to turning into dreadlocks and was tied back from his face. He had a silver ring through one of his nostrils and a knapsack kept him company in the next chair.

"Y' eaten?" Vinny picked up a laminated menu.

"Not yet."

"Grab summat 'ere and have a few bevvies?" Vinny suggested.

"Might as well." Keith picked at his cigarette. "Got a light, mate?"

The question was aimed at the occupant of the next table.

"Sure." He had an American accent. He flicked the light at Keith, who ignited his cigarette. "Just flown in from Delhi. It sure is great to get the feel of a country." The guy was obviously alone and in need of a friend.

Vinny looked up from the menu. "Can you recommend any of the food here?"

"The cheeseburgers are great."

Vinny tried to conceal his sniggers.

A waitress arrived with a pad in her hand.

"What y' avin', Keith?"

"I've got used to that *Tom Yam Kai* upcountry."

Vinny looked back at the menu. "*Nueng Tom Yam Kai*, *nueng Tom Kha Kai* and *sawng* Carlsseberg." He sounded like a native speaker.

The American cowered in embarrassment. The waitress scribbled on her pad and disappeared.

Vinny and Keith ate, drank and chatted. They paid the bill and headed down the road, trying to keep their tempers as people knocked them with rucksacks or just stood in the way.

Vinny guided Keith into an open bar called Sidewalk Café. Its freshly painted walls and newer furniture earmarked it as the classy bar of the street. They took a seat and waited to be served.

"So will you miss Bolton?"

Vinny sniggered. "What the fuck do you think?"

Keith smiled jealously. "I'm not lookin' forward to the cold and pissin' rain."

"So what's this bird like then?"

"All right, like."

"Did you nob her?"

"Aye."

"I was expectin' you'd just get wed and they'd fuck her off on a plane."

"Nah. They need photos an' shit so they can prove it's a kosher relationship. Spent the whole week with her."

Vinny was starting to get curious of his mate's nefarious nuptials. "What's her name?"

"Mem." Keith smiled a proud smile. "I feel a bit of a cunt fuckin' 'er off to a knockin' shop the other side of Manchester. She thinks she's goin' workin' in a Thai restaurant."

Vinny winced and screwed up his face. "Ten punters a day till she's paid off a twelve-grand indenture."

Keith shrugged and looked uncaring. "It's my debts paid off an' I've had a free holiday. Decent shag as well."

"You're a callous cunt, you are."

"Are we off down Nana?"

"I need to sort out a few things down this end first." Vinny looked round at the rest of the punters in the bar.

Vinny squared off the details of what Keith had to tell the police when he was pulled in for the inevitable round of questions.

At the next bar Vinny steered Keith towards a table where a guy was sat alone.

"All right, man. OK if we join you?" The stranger looked up from his book.

"If you like." He was Australian by the sound of it and a little better dressed than their earlier companion.

The waiter spotted Vinny and Keith without drinks and approached them.

"You wanna beer, man?"

"Sure," the guy gulped.

It wasn't an offer that got turned down often.

"So where you been?" Vinny continued with his line.

"Been down near Penang for a while." The guy closed his book.

"Yeah?"

"Yeah, just kicked back with a few mates for a while." The guy, like a lot of travellers, seemed at ease with strangers.

"Where you off to next?"

"I'm off up to Laos in a few days." He looked exited.

Vinny nodded and ceased his questioning.

When the beers arrived Vinny took a few swigs but left most of his beer before heading to the next nondescript bar/restaurant, where he again approached a guy sat alone. Keith tagged along, wandering what he was up to.

The guy was sat smoking and drinking.

"All right, man," Vinny started off the conversation.

Dan was an Aussie like the previous guy. He seemed glad of the free beer and conversation, and had been bumming around the islands close to Phuket for a couple of months.

"Where you off next?" Vinny enquired.

"I fly off to Mexico tomorrow."

"Shit hot." Vinny meant it. "Wanna do us a favour when you're there?"

"Depends." Dan looked cautious. "Will it cost me anything?"

"Quiet the opposite." Vinny smiled mysteriously.

"What is it?" Dan's curiosity had been aroused.

"Can't say round 'ere. Too many people."

Dan started to look a bit paranoid. "So what?"

"Go somewhere else, we'll 'ave a chat." Vinny swigged at his beer.

Dan appeared nervous as Vinny settled the bill.

He followed as Vinny crossed the road with Keith at his side. They nipped down an alley about three feet wide, lined with painted corrugated sheets. Vinny dodged the stagnant puddles in the patchy worn concrete floor and looked over his shoulder. Dan didn't look the least bit happy; getting dragged down a dark alley by two guys he'd met less than half an hour previously fuelled his paranoia and it showed on his face. They got to the end of the alleyway and arrived at a slightly wider alley, with a tiled floor and a covered roof. There were a few shuttered shop fronts and a small one to their right still open. It had a few roughly made low tables with cushions for seating and pictures of classic motorbikes on the wall. There was a fridge with beers in it and a Thai guy with his hair in dreadlocks and a Bob Marley hat sat in a corner.

He looked over to the three guys and placed three beers on the table.

"So what is it then?" Dan took the bull by the horns.

Vinny reached for his wallet and pulled out a cash card. He checked it was the right one and tossed it onto the table in front of Dan.

"Happy Christmas."

Dan picked it up and looked at it then put it down on the table as if it was contaminated. "What is it?"

Vinny laughed. "What does it look like?"

"A cash card." Dan was confused.

"And if I give you the PIN you can draw a hundred quid a day on it till it cancels." Vinny sat back.

Dan picked it up again and eyed it. "So what's the catch?"

"There isn't one."

Dan looked back at Vinny. "So I just use it and there's no comeback."

"Yeah."

"Why would you do that?" Dan looked Vinny in the eye.

"I need to create a diversion. If you use it for a week and throw it away you've got seven hundred beer vouchers." Vinny gave him his best trustworthy face. "Just think of it as your good deed for the day."

"Why do you want to create a diversion?" Dan seemed in two minds.

Vinny sucked his lips. "Can't really say." He scratched his head. "If you don't want it…"

"No, no, I'll do it." Dan pulled the card closer to himself. "What's the PIN?"

Vinny smiled and scribbled it down on a scrap of paper. "You can use it till about the eleventh, then throw it away."

Dan half smiled, half frowned and put it in his shirt pocket. "Whose Vincent Croston?"

"Me."

"We off down Nana?" Keith stood up.

"Can I buy you guys a beer?" Dan looked expectantly.

"Nah, be all right, man. Enjoy it."

At 3.30am a taxi pulled up outside the Asia Hotel. The driver looked in his mirror as the drunken farang tried to see the denomination of the notes in his hand. He didn't bother telling the guy that he'd paid a hundred baht over the odds. He just sat and waited patiently as the drunken guy who'd paid hugged the other guy for three minutes, and tried not to laugh when they proclaimed their love for each other.

"Why won't you tell me what it's like shaggin' a lady boy?" the taller guy asked.

"You have to find out for yourself."

The guy that got out looked sad, and when he shut the door he shouted, "Fuck England!" at the top of his voice.

It took a lot of sleep, a good meal and a few hours staring at MTV in his room before Vinny was fit for conversation. Jeed could sense him coming to and sat on his knee. She'd spent most of the afternoon trying on her new Armani threads in different combinations and posing in front of the bedroom mirror.

"Honey, you can phone airport for plane to Ko Samui?"

Jeed got off Vinny's lap and went over to the phone. She rang reception and nattered in Thai for a moment then wrote down a number on the pad. The number she dialled took a while to pick up. Jeed spoke for a while then went silent as a faint voice replied at the other end. Vinny's sweetheart nodded as he looked over proudly. He had a brainstorm and ran over to her. He took the phone and covered the receiver. Jeed looked shocked.

"My name Jim Bradley," he whispered. "No Vinny."

Jeed smiled. "OK."

He gave her back the phone and she carried on talking.

When she put the phone down she looked up and smiled. "Toomollow we go Ko Samui, thlee o'clock."

Vinny hugged her. "OK, in the morning I go see friend. Need to finish some business."

With the help of a pill from the chemist and four whiskies on the plane, Keith had managed to sleep most of the way back from Bangkok. When the connecting flight from Amsterdam landed in Manchester Mem gathered her belongings, keen to take up her new post as head waitress.

They passed through Customs and Passport Control without difficulty and Keith walked by her side as they entered the arrivals lounge. Vicky was waiting for them with a sullen-looking guy in his forties. They walked through the sliding doors into the cold, grey January Manchester morning. Vicky guided a wide-eyed, expectant Mem off to the car park. Keith joined the queue for the taxis. He felt sorry for Mem, but not as much as he felt the cold.

They arrived at the airport at 2 o'clock and paid for the tickets. Vinny had had a phone call at the Hotel from Jensen felt a wave of relief knowing that he had been weighed in the 5k for his part in the plan. Now at least he could relax without fear of reprise, from Jensen at least.

In the departure area they watched people taking seats and waiting for the flight. Propellers powered the Bangkok Airways plane they boarded and the flight across the gulf of Thailand was bumpy to say the least. Occasionally the engine noise would dim audibly and the plane would drop agonisingly by a few feet before the engines powered up again. Vinny held the armrests tightly and when they approached the lush green island of Ko Samui he said his final prayers. The plane adjusted its path as it started to descend, which made Vinny close his eyes and prepare to meet his maker.

When the plane bounced on the runway he started to shake. From the bump of the tyres on tarmac and the give before they bounced, he could tell they weren't fully inflated. The engines whirred louder in reverse and the plane came to a halt. Vinny unbuckled his seatbelt and bolted for the rear door. He stood in the doorway sweating, and when the hatch opened he dashed onto the staircase. Intense heat greeted him. He stopped at the top of the metal stairway and looked around him. For the last hour he'd been consumed with fear of death and he wanted to get out of the plane as quickly as possible but the view of his surroundings slowed him. Beyond the stretch of tarmac they'd landed on were deep green palm trees covering the steep-sided hills around him. Vinny could smell warm sea air. The terminal building was 300 yards away, surrounded by lush green grass. It had a sort of woven thatched roof and was supported by wooden props. At the bottom of the stairs was a long white vehicle with rounded ends, bench seating and a canopy roof. The wheels were obscured by white bodywork that almost reached the floor. Vinny inhaled a deep lungful of air and smiled. Ko Samui had a calming aura that wafted out of the palm trees.

'Take it easy. Smile,' the place said, and Vinny did.

He sauntered down the steps and waited at the bottom for Jeed. She trotted down the stairs looking glamorous in her new Armani trousers and jumper. Vinny held her hand as they walked to the bus. They took a seat and smiled. As the rest of the passengers joined them they smiled as well. The bus glided across the tarmac to the terminal. Ever the gentleman, Vinny hopped off first and held out his hand to help Jeed off. They walked up the steps to the terminal and waited in the cool of the shade. Vinny looked round at the complex of bamboo buildings. The concrete floor was clean and the seating was simple and neatly arranged.

He took Jeed's hand. "Is nice airport."

"Yes." she smiled. "Beefor Jeed no come."

A small van pulled a trailer from the plane stacked high with baggage. Guys in Bangkok Airways uniforms unloaded them and dumped them in a chained-off section of concrete. Vinny spotted his and pulled it to one side. When Jeed's arrived he pulled hers out and they headed out of the airport. A group of minibuses and pick-up trucks were congregated round the wire gate at the entrance to the airport. Scruffy Thai men stood around in groups, chatting and laughing.

"Wait here." Jeed dropped her bag and walked off to speak to a group of taxi drivers.

She returned after a minute or two frowning.

"What's up?"

"No goot. Today boat finit. Lass boat four pm." Jeed pointed at her watch; it was 4.15.

"We can get bungaro Chaweng, get boat toomollow."

Jeed nodded and picked up her bag. They walked arm in arm to the group of drivers and the one Jeed had been talking to smiled and guided them to a pick-up truck. He helped them dump their bags in the back. They climbed on board and sat on the bench seating. The driver walked off and went to talk to his mates. Tourists formed the majority of the exodus from the terminal building. Among the throng was a fresh-faced guy in khaki cargo shorts and a counterfeit Diesel T-shirt. He seamed a little weary under the weight of his rucksack. He approached the group of taxi drivers and leaned forward under the weight on his back as he spoke to them. The driver of Vinny and Jeed's conveyance pointed at his truck and the guy trudged over.

When he got closer he smiled. "All right?"

Vinny looked up as the guy hauled his pack into the van, and nodded.

The guy climbed in. "You off to Chaweng?"

"Yes," Jeed answered.

"Wanna fag?" The guy held out a packet for Vinny.

"Cheers, man." He took one and lit it himself.

Jeed declined.

"What's your name?" asked the stranger, brushing back his light brown hair.

"Errr, Jim." Vinny smiled. "Jim Bradley."

It was the first time Vinny had used his new name in front of a farang. Up to now he'd given it in at the hotel where they weren't to know, but with this guy it was like a game. The guy could have been from Bolton for all he knew, although he had a hint of a Midlands accent.

"You?"

"Danny." The guy sat back.

Vinny laughed, thinking back to the guy he'd given his cash card to the other day.

"What's funny?" The guy looked indignant.

"Nowt, mate. Private joke." Vinny held out his hand for Danny to shake. "This is Jeed."

"Nice to meet you, Jeed."

A couple more people locked in their own conversation joined them and the truck drove out of the airport car park and onto a narrow concrete road. The road wound its way into the palm trees. Vinny felt the breeze on his face. Occasionally they'd pass a turn-off cut into the jungle with a small wooden signpost. The van passed through the depths of the palm forest and headed down a hill. The outline of a town started to appear in the distance and the traffic got heavier. The road they were travelling along became lined with bars and the occasional posh-looking hotel set back from the road. The pick-up turned down a small cutting between a group of flat-roofed shops and came to a halt.

The guy beckoned for Vinny, Jeed and Danny to get out and helped them with their bags. He pointed at a gate and drove off.

"Looks like we're here." Danny smiled at the simplicity of their arrival.

"OK, we go bungaro." Jeed forged on through the gate.

Vinny and Danny followed. A footpath led into the palm trees. On one side were small wooden huts with pointed roofs and balconies, on the other a long whitewashed building with doors spaced evenly along it and a walkway.

At the end of the path was a thatched open-sided building with bamboo tables and chairs near a bamboo bar. A girl in her late teens was looking through a book on the counter.

"*Sawasdee ka.*" Jeed started the exchange.

"*Sawasdee ka*," the girl replied.

Vinny ignored the conversation and walked through the restaurant. They were right on the sea shore, in the middle of a mile-long cove with ten yards of beach leading down to a shallow, clear blue sea.

Vinny put his hands on his hips.

After a few bursts of rapid fire Thai Jeed beckoned to Vinny. "Can pay thlee hundlet baht?"

Vinny obliged.

Danny tried to make himself understood and with a bit of slowly spoken English parted with some cash. The girl picked up two keys tied to small pieces of bamboo and took them to their new homes in the long building.

She showed Danny his first, then Vinny and Jeed. It was basic but cosy, with a light bulb and fan suspended from the ceiling, a double bed and a separate tiled room at the back with a toilet, a sink and a shower attached to the wall.

Vinny dumped his bag on the bed and went to sit on the chair on the porch. Jeed went to use the toilet.

"Honey, we go get food?" Vinny suggested when she reappeared.

He could hear movement being in Danny's hut.

"We ask Danny come with us?" he added when she nodded in reply.

Vinny jumped down the small set of steps. He felt the sand of the footpath give a little beneath his weight.

"Danny." He leaned on the railing outside Danny's home.

Danny appeared in the door with his top off. "All right, man."

"We're off for summat t'eat if you wanna tag along."

"Yeah, just give us minute."

Thirty minutes later they were sat at a table in an open-air restaurant on the main road, weighing up the menus. Vinny had elicited that Danny was from Coventry, he was 24 and had inherited some money so had quit his job and was out to enjoy himself for 12 months.

Jeed got up and went to the bathroom.

"So how much you payin' her then?" Danny asked innocently.

Vinny laughed. "In any other country in the world that would have got you knocked out."

"Sorry, man." Danny blushed.

"No problem. How long you stayin' in Ko Samui for?"

"About three weeks. I've got some mates turnin' up in Bangkok so we'll take it from there. You?"

"Off to Pha Ngan tomorrow if you fancy it."

"Nah, I'll stay here for a while first."

They ordered and ate. Danny headed off up the main road to trawl the bars and find a woman. Vinny and Jeed went back to the bungalow to sit on the porch and act like teenagers.

Jeed smoked a few joints and swigged on the beers that Vinny had brought back from the fridge in the shop. As it grew dark they watched lizards appear and scurry across their porch and the wooden balustrades while they made soppy romantic small talk in a pigeon mix of Thai and English.

At about 1am Vinny stood on the balcony in his shorts enjoying a post-coital cigarette. Through the dark he saw the outline of two figures strolling down the path. As they reached the halo of light from the balcony light bulb he could tell it was Danny with a slender Thai lady in a short dress.

Vinny got back in bed.

"Jeed, I see Dan with lady." he rubbed her leg playfully.

She stubbed the joint she'd been smoking out and cuddled up to him.

Danny sat the girl he'd met down on the edge of the bed and kissed her.

"Beefor seckt you hab showa." She recoiled from his kiss.

Danny undressed, spent ten seconds under the cold drip in the bathroom and paraded back into the chamber with his stomach held in and a towel wrapped round his waist. She was where he'd left her filing her nails. He sat next to her and kissed her cheek. She picked up her handbag and clopped off in her high heels to the bathroom and locked the door.

Danny lay back and smiled at his prowess. The mental clock started ticking; the shower carried on dripping. He smoked a cigarette. There was no sign of the shower stopping so he discarded the towel and got under the sheets.

"That'll be a nice treat for her." He rubbed his crotch and shut his eyes with his hands behind his head.

When his lady appeared from the bathroom she had a towel wrapped round her. She paused in the doorway and Danny smiled at her feminine outline.

She walked round to the light switch by the front door and flicked off the main light. The room was dimly lit by the glow from the bathroom.

She climbed into bed without removing the towel. Danny kissed her and tugged at the loose knot of cloth that kept it in place. She slapped his hand and tightened the towel. He sat up a little shocked then laid back, thinking it must have been a tease.

She pushed his chest back down and bent to service him with her mouth. He felt her lips on his member then a terrifying thought crossed his mind.

Danny yanked at the towel again. "Shit."

His fears had been confirmed. The lady had a penis. Danny turned as white as a ghost. He pulled the sheet to his chest and recoiled off the bed, shaking in terror.

"Fuckin' hell, get out!" he screamed.

The transvestite put on her best menacing look.

"I want money."

"Fuck off, just get out." Danny's voice was filled with terror.

"You choose me, you must pay."
"I don't pay blokes." Danny backed into the corner.
In the next room Vinny stirred from the embrace. He could hear voices.
The lady boy stood up, unashamed by his appearance, and strode towards the cowering Dan; he raised his right hand and threw a fist at his face.
Danny stood upright and, in fright, threw a fist back with his face screwed and his eyes closed.
He felt another punch returned and it landed on his cheek. In fury he pushed forward and the person in front of him doubled up. Danny threw his arm over her neck and pulled her tight into a headlock. With his spare hand he threw punches in the katoey's face. She struggled and pushed then bent to her knees. Danny was about to let go, but with a Herculean surge of strength she straightened and pushed back the two yards to the adjoining wall.
Danny felt the wall give.
Vinny sat up in bed as he felt the wall shake.
Danny pushed back but his sparring partner pushed again with a surge of enraged inner strength.
This time the wall didn't hold. It only helped lower the velocity as Danny and his new friend went crashing into Vinny's chalet in a hail of plasterboard and dust.
"Fuck me!" Vinny sat up to welcome his uninvited guests.
Danny was sodden with sweat. His eyes were bulbous with shock and he looked a lot younger naked. His assailant, an-odd looking creature, had long hair tied up above his head, make-up, a penis and the outline of breasts born from hormone pills.
Vinny stirred from his drowsiness.
"You fuckin' freak." Danny weighed in with punches.
"You choose me, you pay."
Vinny looked at the half joint lying in the ashtray, shook his head in disbelief and shut his eyes but the dream didn't go away.
They were still there. Fighting in his bedroom.
"Oh my giddy aunt."
Vinny sat up in bed; Jeed was hiding under the sheet. He crawled out, covering his modesty with his hands, and pulled on his shorts.
The lady boy had manoeuvred Danny against the breezeblock front wall and was pummelling him with girl punches.
Vinny spun him round by pulling at his shoulder and smacked him flush on the jaw.
"Get the fuck out o' my room."
The boy cowered and ran off through the recently made manhole, and started setting about everything in the place.
"I go when get money," he started yelling.
By now the other inhabitants of the complex had become aware of the commotion.

Vinny rummaged in his bag and threw Danny a pair of shorts; he went outside and the occupants of the bungalows opposite were stood on their balconies giggling at the spectacle.

The lady who ran the bungalows appeared, rubbing sleep out of her eyes, and walked into Danny's room. Danny walked back in looking apologetic.

Soon the police arrived and carted off the two destructive pugilists.

The lady apologised to Vinny and gave him and Jeed a couple of free beers in the restaurant, while her husband patched in a new piece of plasterboard with masking tape.

island life

Vinny woke at 11am. He felt like death. His mouth was dry enough to keep matches in. The sheet crumpled on his leg was damp as was the patch of the mattress he'd slept on; he wiped his sweat sodden brow with his hand. He sat up carefully so as not to disturb Jeed, then climbed over her and gingerly put his bare feet on the worn wooden floor. There was a plastic bottle of water on the table where the fan was and he tried to open it. The seal was unbroken and he had to rip into it with his teeth before taking a glug of lukewarm water. He opened the door and spat it onto the porch before taking another mouthful and stepping outside.

"Shite." His foot hit a patch of wood that had been exposed to the sun and it hurt. Hopping back inside, he put on the shorts he'd worn last night and his trainers before heading out into the sun again. He rested his hands on the porch barrier. The sun made him smile. The plush green foliage between the bungalows radiated life and the hint of blue from the sea to his right capped it.

The previous night's events were still making him chuckle.

Two Thai girls walked past towards the restaurant/reception and giggled when they saw Vinny bare bellied. He smiled at their angelic faces then looked down at his beer gut. He shook his hips and his belly wobbled in time. Sweat was forming on his brow again so he took a swig of water.

"Winnee." Jeed was stirring.

He turned and pushed the rickety wooden door open.

"Winnee, you hab *nam*?" she croaked.

"No Vinny. I Jim." Vinny lowered his voice.

Jeed's body was mummified in the sheet. A slender brown arm extended from the swaddling and he handed her the bottle. Her hair appeared from her cocoon and the bottle was tipped into her mouth. She held it up and Vinny placed it back on the table. Her head disappeared under the sheet again. Vinny pushed the door to. He climbed on top of her legs and started to massage her lower back.

Fuck it. Dawn strike, he thought and undid his shorts.

The aged wooden beams and planks of the chalet creaked and groaned in time with their lovemaking. The quarter-inch thickness of door did little to spare the world from Jeed's panting and gasping as Vinny asserted his land rights.

Afterwards they hugged and shared a cigarette. Vinny went and stood under the cold water that trickled out of the showerhead in the bathroom before dressing and traipsing down to the restaurant/reception by the beach. He sat in the bamboo chair at the bamboo table and eyed the menu.

Jeed sauntered down the footpath full of smiles. Her hair was damp and she took a cigarette from Vinny's shirt pocket before sitting opposite him. She nattered in Thai to the girl behind the counter. Vinny ordered the full breakfast.

He looked out onto to the beach. It was beginning to fill with Westerners rolling out mats, stripping down to their bathing costumes and oiling themselves up for a day's sun worship.

Vinny smiled at Jeed; he was really starting to relax now. "Jeed, we can stay here a few days before Ko Pha Ngan?"

"Up to you."

The breakfast arrived and Vinny tucked in. A Western couple strolled past the front of the restaurant; the guy was wearing a Bolton Wanderers shirt. Vinny gulped, froze then held the menu in front of his face. When the couple had strolled out of sight Vinny lowered the menu. He was sweating a lot more than before and his hand was trembling. He pushed his breakfast away then dashed back to the bungalow.

Jeed trotted up to find Vinny pacing up and down the gap between the bed and the bathroom, tugging heavily on a cigarette. He'd already packed their bags.

"OK, quick, we go get boat. Vinny threw his cigarette into the bathroom and took Jeed by the hand.

"Why you aflai?" Jeed put on a look of concern and stroked his face.

"I see man from Bolton."

"Iss no ploblem. He no see you," Jeed pouted to calm him.

Vinny sat on the edge of the bed with his head in his hands. Jeed joined him and stroked his back. She kissed his neck and he sat back, stroking her leg.

"C'mon, we're goin'." Vinny picked up the bags and stormed out of the shack. He started to forge up the sandy footpath.

"Winnee."

Jeed was chasing after him, barefoot. Her feet gave way as she tired to speed march through the sand and he couldn't help laughing. She looked like Bambi taking her first steps.

"Winnee." She grabbed his hand.

"No Vinny. Jim."

"OK, Tchim," she scowled. "Must see lady for loom."

Jeed stamped her foot in the sand and dragged him back towards the chalet. She pushed him up the steps to their door and followed him. She pulled the door to, closed the padlock and pulled the key. She pushed Vinny onto the chair and pointed at him. "Waiting."

Vinny stood up.

She pointed again. "Waiting you!"

Vinny obeyed with a smirk on his face while Jeed Bambied through the sand to reception. He rummaged in his bag and pulled out the Yankees sun hat and his sunglasses.

Jeed trotted back smiling and Vinny picked up the bags. They walked onto the main road and sat on the pavement to wait for a taxi. Eventually they managed to flag one down. The taxi drove out of town along a dusty concrete road that almost hugged the coastline. The lack of traffic was a tonic after Bangkok. Vinny enjoyed taking in the scenery and odd glimpses of the sea. After ten minutes or so he noticed a monolith that seamed to be on a spit in the sea; the peak was gleaming in the sun. He pointed it out to Jeed.

She looked up from the text message she was sending. "Iss Buddha."

They passed the Buddha, which up close was massive. Probably twenty feet high on a pedestal out in the sea; it held Vinny's attention all the time it was in view.

The taxi turned off the road and ground to a halt. Like at the airport there were taxis and pick-up trucks parked haphazardly while scruffy Thai men stood around chatting.

A flimsy-looking jetty made of hastily cut planks jutted out into the sea. There was a bamboo and wood building inland and to the left of it people were sat around chatting or reading at tables.

Vinny paid the driver and hauled the bags over to the building. He picked a table. There was still a tray with the remains of someone's lunch on it but it was the only one free so he took a seat. Jeed was talking to a Thai bloke behind a counter while Vinny gazed out to sea.

"Tchim."

Vinny lit a cigarette.

"Tttcchhiiiimmm." Vinny hadn't got used to answering to his new name and the Thai pronunciation made it harder for him to pick up on. He recognised Jeed's voice though.

"Tchim. Hab money for tiikette?" She gave him a commanding look.

Vinny looked up from under the brim of his hat and sauntered over.

"*Tow rai*?"

"One hunlet sickty baht."

Vinny paid the man and let Jeed keep the tickets.

They took a seat and ordered soft drinks. Vinny sat back and weighed up the rest of travellers waiting for the boat. There were none of the sex-tourist types he'd felt so at home with in Pattaya. Most of them were foreign to Thailand, mainly European and mixed gender, sat around chatting. Shorts and bright T-shirts were the order of the day. There seemed to be an abundance of henna tattoos around female ankles or male biceps. Most of them seemed happy, relaxed and healthy. The folk sat around in groups of four or five minding rucksacks, while plastic bottles of water and packets of tobacco and cigarettes adorned the tables.

Vin noticed a group of guys near the railings at the far end of the building. They looked Italian; darker skin and jet-black hair. Some of them were perched on the fence and others were strutting and posing in front of their buddies with much more coquettish mannerisms and hand gestures than the rest of the travellers. Vinny took a dislike to them. There were no fans in this particular restaurant/departure lounge and the heat had an effect on the pace at which people went about the business, just sitting down made Vinny sweat. He quickly drained the bottle of orange Jeed had bought for him and bought himself another.

He looked out to sea at the green lump in the distance. It was going to be Vinny's bolthole for a while.

A blob in the ocean seemed to be moving towards the jetty. Vinny looked up at the sky. It wasn't as clear as it had been earlier.

At the table he spent his time watching the blob slowly get bigger and eventually turn into a boat. As it drew closer he could hear the low throaty growl of the engine. When it came to within a hundred yards of the jetty the pilot cut the engine and let it drift. He started the engine to dock it as a group of well-tanned Thai guys went through the well-rehearsed routine of throwing ropes and tying the boat to the jetty. The people waiting stirred into life, hauling rucksacks onto their backs and tramping down to the jetty.

One of the guys pushed a walkway onto the boat and a row of weary-looking figures made their way down the plank.

The outbound travellers, including Vinny and Jeed, gathered at the start of the jetty. As the departees approached Vinny started to notice that most of them wore washed-out and haggard expressions on their faces. Some had a leg or hand wrapped in bandage and used the hobble as their preferred mode of transport rather than the walk.

As they left the jetty, cries went up behind them. "Taxi, taxi, taxi. Airport, Chaweng, Lamai."

Jeed showed their tickets to a man and they walked down the jetty. At the gangplank Vinny paused. He had to traverse six feet of sea and the drop was a good ten feet. He held his breath, closed his eyes and strode.

He looked to the heavens in thanks for being delivered on deck without making friends with the ocean. The hand he held out for Jeed was still trembling from the ordeal when she grabbed it and jumped aboard.

Vinny let go of his bag and pushed it up against the cabin. He sat down and patted the space next to him for Jeed to join him. She lowered herself daintily and sat forward. Vinny stretched out and rested his feet on the layers of blue paint that protected the wooden deck from the sun and the rain. People sat around in huddles, chatting and laughing. Some went below deck to make use of the bench seating.

A low throaty growl sung out from the innards of the boat and a black cloud of smoke belched out of the back.

Vinny heard some cogs clang and grind and felt the deck shudder, then he felt the circular motion of a driveshaft somewhere in the depths start to whir. The boat reversed out into the shallow sea for twenty yards, then the engine cut. The boat carried on drifting under the momentum and started to turn in an arc. Someone fired up the engine again. The boat turned in a circle and started to lurch off into open sea.

From its seat on the headland to their right the big Buddha emanated good luck and safe passage on the seafarers.

Dressed in brand-new Armani shorts and T-shirts, the happy couple felt superior to their maritime mates.

The Buddha started to slip out of view and the boat gathered pace.

In open sea the swell of the water became noticeable and the boat rode up and down at ten-second intervals. When it crashed into the crystal-blue breakers, almost vaporised saline splashed on deck.

Vinny felt his face getting damper and wiped it dry with his hand. He looked to the sky and noticed the blue of the sky was being replaced by grey. The water on his face was more rain than sea spray.

He nudged Jeed. “We go downstair?”

She nodded and they stood up, dragging their bags down the wooden steps to the lower deck; they started an exodus of open-air travellers avoiding the rain.

Vinny managed to squeeze himself and Jeed in next to a couple of youngish-looking European girls who were leafing through a Lonely Planet Guide. The lower deck afforded them shelter from the rain, but the swell was more noticeable, and Vinny started to regret the few beers he’d had last night. His stomach was starting to churn. Closer to the prow on the other side of the boat there was a commotion; a guy in his early twenties was making a dash for the slat window in the gunwale. He thrust his head out of the window and let out a wretch that was audible throughout the boat. His vomit plumed along the outside of the boat and splashes of bile and half-digested vegetable blew back into the lower deck to the disgust of the people sat behind the guy.

The wretches continued and the unmistakeable odour of vomit filled the cabin. Vinny’s stomach started to churn and he felt light headed. He clutched his stomach and thrust his head between his knees. Prior to the vomiting he’d been a bit queasy, but the noise and smell sent him into meditative state.

He repeated his mantra. “I ain’t pukin’ up. I ain’t pukin’ up. I ain’t…”

The vomiting stopped. Vinny waited 30 seconds before sitting upright. As he opened his eyes he saw the guy dash for the window again and hurl his innards through the gap.

“Oh man.” He didn’t suppress his whisper, and returned to his yogic position. “No pukin’. No pukin’, Vin, no fuckin’ hurlin’.”

He chanced a glance outside and saw that the rain had abated, grabbed his bag and dashed back outside.

The sea breeze was thankfully free from pungency and Vinny breathed a sigh of relief having rid himself of the gastric stench that had invaded his nostrils.

He heard another wretch and the splatter of carrots on wood, and he laughed at the poor guy's misfortune. Jeed emerged from the cabin with her cute little nose turned up as she wafted the pong away with her hand.

They rested on the aqua-blue railing and viewed their new island home as its features became more distinguishable.

The shoreline could now be identified clearly. It was a series of white-sanded coves fringed by palm-treed thickets. The steep slopes that rose from the shores were all forested and littered with pointy-roofed bungalows on stilts.

The engine cut for a minute while they drifted towards the jetty, and cut in again while the boat was piloted in and docked on a sturdy post in the sand.

The jump across onto the plank was a heart stopper but Vinny and Jeed made it onto dry land in one piece.

Once ashore there was another gaggle of haggard-looking departees who looked in need of sleep, a wash and a haircut.

Under his sunhat and behind his sunglasses Vinny felt assured of his anonymity.

A few people were sat around looking at their watches, chatting with leavers or waiting to see if an arrival had made it onto the boat.

A group of youngish Thai guys stood around and as people made their way ashore, wide eyed with trepidation, they started to buttonhole people.

"Bangarow, Bangarow, Bangarow." They'd wave and smile wide grins at anyone with a rucksack.

Groups gathered away from the touts and sent spokespeople forward to negotiate.

Vinny set down his bag and wiped the sweat off his brow. The sea spray had left a layer of salt on his skin. It was new sensation for Vinny and he couldn't work out if it was novel or nasty.

"You can talk to man?"

"Yes," Jeed nodded.

"I want somewhere quiet," Vinny added. "Peaceful." He put his hands together at the side of his head to mimic sleep.

She tottered off to speak to one of the guys, whose eyes lit up when he saw her approach. They exchanged a few words and she returned holding an address card.

"You get?"

"Yes." She eyed the card.

"How much?"

"Two hunlet baht."

Vinny gulped, pleasantly surprised at the cost. It was about a tenth of the price of the Asia where he'd holed up in Bangkok two nights before.

She passed Vinny the card and he read the information. "Coconut Home Village, Ban Kai, Ko Pha Ngan. A nice place under coconut palms. Recreation in quiet atmosphere. Refreshing with sun, sea and flower bloom. Enjoy with Thai and international foods."

The guy Jeed had been bargaining with sauntered over and brushed his shiny black hair back from his face. He picked up Jeed's bag and walked over to a pick-up truck and humped it into the back. Jeed waited for Vinny to set off before following him. Vinny hauled his bag in the back without the guy's acknowledgement. The pair stood by the truck as the bloke went back to his mates.

"Honey, Jeed want dlink." she looked at him expectantly.

"OK." He reached for his wallet. "For Vinny also. Shit." He bit his lip. "For Jim."

She tottered off with two hundred-baht notes. Vinny looked round. They were on a wide patch of compacted sand, which had ruts where tyres had cut tracks in wetter times. There was a row of whitewashed buildings with aluminium doors opposite him. One was a shop, one was a café of sorts and the other a travel agent. Behind him was another concrete building painted a sort of beige/yellow colour. The windows and door were brown smoked glass and either side of the door were large brown glazed ceramic pots. Above the door was a piece of wood with JUNGLE GYM painted on it.

Vinny decided to give it a closer look. He pressed his face up against the window and made a tunnel with his hands to fend off the reflection. He could make out the outline of gym equipment, and in the centre of the room was a boxing ring. A photocopied sheet of paper selotaped to the door listed activities, including Thai boxing, yoga, weight training and aerobics. Vinny looked around him and tucked next to a bush was a red punch bag fitted by a chain to a wooden scaffold.

Memories of his Thai-boxing training came back and he walked over to it grinning; he stood on the balls of his feet, ducked imaginary punches and launched a graceful arching roundhouse kick with his right leg.

Thwack! His shin hit the bag and he yelped.

"Fuckin' cunt." His shin was yelling with pain and his knee nearly gave way. He felt the bag, and the give in the fabric suggested it was filled with half-solidified concrete. He hobbled back to the van and rested on the footplate below the tailgate without putting any weight on his right foot.

When Jeed tottered back from the shop with a bottle of water and two cans of Fanta, he smiled and gritted his teeth, not wanting to let her know he'd dropped a clanger.

The guy who'd been attentive to Jeed headed over with a group of four pasty-faced girls wearing hiking boots and carrying rucksacks. They looked at Vinny and Jeed with a hint of disapproval. Vinny couldn't work out whether it was because he wasn't a backpacker spending a week in every capital city in Asia and eating out of a wooden bowl, or if it was because he was with a girl who looked like a whore. It was probably both.

The girls hauled themselves on board and Vinny and Jeed followed suit.

The four fair-skinned ones started nattering away in faint Irish accents about when Fay was getting in from Laos, what a laugh they'd had with the taxi driver in Delhi and how they'd all miss Penny so much even though she did get a bit bitchy in Chiang Mai.

The tout got in the cab and started the engine. They headed of up a dusty track, bumping and rolling through ruts in the dirt road, and within five minutes they'd left the cluster of concrete and wooden buildings behind.

The dirt road climbed an embankment and the pick-up had a job doing the same. The gradient was one in four and the driver had to crunch into a low gear to embark on the attempt. At first the truck did OK, then Vinny felt it falter. He shot Jeed a worried glance. He felt the clutch go in and the momentum drop. The gears crunched again and a thick cloud of pungent black diesel smoke belched out of the exhaust as the momentum picked up. Vinny had to hold on tight as they rocked and jostled up the uneven track. They reached the crest of the hill to see a 50-foot drop; a similar pick-up was making its way up so they paused to let it pass, then descended. In the dip at the bottom they had to pause again to let another pick-up pass. A girl on a scooter pulled up behind them and shot off ahead with her hair billowing in the wind when the road was clear. After a few more undulations that made Vinny clutch hard onto his seat, the road levelled off and they sped past a couple of whitewashed family houses.

Eventually the driver pulled over next to a footpath. A woman was waiting and greeted the driver. Vinny went to get off but Jeed stopped him.

"Next one." She pointed down the road.

The girls hauled themselves out with their bags and Vinny had to bite his lip while they argued for what seemed like half an hour over the paltry amount they owed the driver.

About half a mile down the road they pulled up next to a wooden sign saying COCONUT PALM VILLAGE. A smiling lady was waiting by the sign with a toddler at her side. They disembarked and gave the driver some money.

"*Sawasdee ka*." The lady smiled politely.

"*Sawasdee kra*p."

They followed her down a narrow sandy footpath worn into the dry grassland. After a bit of weaving and avoiding falling onto a barbed-wire fence, they came into a clearing where there was a large wooden shack with a porch covering the same amount of floor space in front. The porch contained a few tables and chairs, and a guy with long blond hair sat eating at one of them.

The lady called out as they arrived and a girl in an apron approached from behind a counter with a key on a piece of string, which she handed to their guide. A couple of light brown dogs of indeterminate breed lay asleep under one of the tables on the porch. They walked through a gap in the thicket and saw the sea and Ko Samui in the distance. There were ten wooden bungalows on stilts facing in a semi-circle round a clearing. The lady guided them to one at the right and undid the padlock, letting the door squeak open on their new home.

Vinny threw in his bag and smiled.

The lady spoke to Jeed.

"Tchim, lady want money. Can gib?" Jeed explained.

"How much?"

"You stay one week. Twelb hundlet."

Vinny sorted it out and dragged Jeed inside for a roll on the bed.

They showered together under the cold drip from the showerhead in the tiled white room at the back, and dried off quickly.

Vinny dressed and lit a cigarette then stood on the balcony. The place was rustic but it had a sort of tranquil air about it and, as he rested his hands on the rail at the front of the balcony, he smiled but wondered what there was to do. Next door's occupants had a hammock strung up on the rafters above their balcony. He stood back and noticed that Croston Villas had the same luxury wrapped round a beam to save it flapping in the wind. He stood on the plank at the end that served as a seat and, with his cigarette in his mouth, unfurled it. It dropped down with a satisfying flutter and swung for a minute under its own steam before drawing to a calm halt.

He put his hands in the sag in the middle and felt how strong it was, then looked up at the nylon rope holding it in place. As he applied more pressure to the centre it wobbled. His first attempt to enter involved placing a knee in the middle of the cloth and grabbing the narrow part near the rope with one hand. It felt steady so he raised the next knee. The section under his hand lowered and catapulted the resting knee up into his chest, and sent him recoiling onto the floor. His cigarette fell from his mouth and rolled through one of the gaps between the floorboards.

"Shit."

Jeed's soft singing voice hummed gently out of the bathroom, muffled by running water.

On the second attempt he managed to manoeuvre himself into the kneeling position in the centre of the cloth whilst holding onto the chord with his left hand. He heard a creak and a blonde girl in a sarong with a towel wrapped round her head stepped out of the door of the bungalow to his right. He turned and raised his left hand to wave and went reeling backwards onto the floor. She didn't notice him and lit a cigarette.

From his crouched position he noticed her perch her behind daintily in the middle and gracefully swing her legs inside and lie back.

Vinny had it sussed. He sat down in the centre, shut his eyes and counted to three.

"One, two, three…" With an Olympian surge of strength he swivelled his behind and lifted his feet.

The effort used was a little excessive, but sort of got him where he wanted to be. His left leg was hanging out of the far side but his right was in place. The part of his body Vinny normally used for sitting on was acting as a hinge between his legs and torso and, although he was sure it didn't feel as comfortable as he'd expected, he decided to stay put with it lying four inches higher than his face. Having his chin pushed into his chest by the torque from the fabric didn't feel right either, but beginners were grateful for small victories.

He heard the shower stop dripping and the bathroom door being pulled open. Jeed's gentle footsteps creaked towards him. She rocked the hammock and his heart stopped as he felt himself heading for the floorboards for a third time, but he heaved a sigh of relief as he sort of stayed in place.

"Honey, Jeed hungly." She leaned into his cocoon and kissed his lips.

"OK. Vi… Jim hungry also. Where we can go?"

Vinny bravely sat up in the bungalow and looked round. One of the dogs was stood on his hind legs licking the worktop in the open kitchen area.

"Can eat at house."

Vinny felt his stomach move at the thought of the dog licking his plate free of germs before his food was served. "You know restaurant?"

Jeed tottered off to the family house and spoke to one of the girls. When she came back she explained that there was a village not far away where they could eat.

"OK, we go." Vinny jumped up and fell on top of Jeed.

She laughed at his clumsiness, while he dug his sandals out from their new home.

They strolled hand in hand to the road and started to walk in the opposite direction from the way they'd come.

After five minutes or so they heard the sound of an engine behind them and looked round. Through the rapidly approaching dusk they saw a pair of headlights; the vehicle slowed and, as it drew level with them, stopped. It was a baht bus similar to the ones in Pattaya, only dirtier. They hopped aboard and spent ten minutes travelling down a straight but bumpy stretch of dirt track until they reached a village. To the relief of Vinny's behind the road was concreted and the shops and restaurants that lined the wide empty streets seemed quiet but civilised.

They found a reasonable looking restaurant with a bar and pool table under the same roof. A foreign guy was sat at the bar and seemed known to the staff as he made constant conversation with them.

They ordered and ate over a couple of beers.

With the meal done they went and sat at the bar.

They spent the evening there and chatted with the guy, who told them that the place they were in was called Thong Sala. It wasn't really the main place;

Haad Rin, where they'd landed, held that title. It was quiet at the moment because the beach party on the full moon had been preceded by Christmas and followed by New Year's Eve, which had led to five fatalities for one reason or another. Most of the hoards had moved on, either home, next stop on the world tour, or a small minority to the mental hospital on the mainland.

When they got back to Chez Croston at around 1am they smoked a few joints on the balcony and went to bed.

They were woken abruptly at six the next morning by the roar of a couple of engines being fired up. They sounded like thunderous old tractors on a farmyard. Vinny rubbed his head and walked onto the porch to see what was causing the racket.

In the shallow sea on their almost private beach there were two ornately painted longtail boats with heavily tanned guys tending outsized engines strapped to the back. Vinny looked in dismay at the peace breakers and shook his head. He went back to bed and after half an hour of disturbed peace the boats chugged away and he went to sleep.

At around midday they rose, ate and lay in the hammock till teatime, then ate at the same restaurant in the evening.

Keith took a day to get himself straight before heading back to the stall. Ricky had taken care of things while he'd been away; the cold and damp were painful as he sat huddled behind his stall scowling at shoppers and nursing a coffee to keep his hands warm.

On Saturday Ricky helped out as well. Come lunchtime Keith needed a slash and nipped to the public toilets that served Bolton Market.

The cold wasn't doing him any favours and he had to struggle through the thermals to find his best friend. He looked down at the steel trough and the cloudy river of piss with its islands of pubic hair and banks of smeg. He looked up at the ceiling and prayed for inspiration but the flow wasn't forthcoming so he looked down and tensed and pushed with his stomach muscles to try and create a flow.

A green blob of mucus oozed out of his japseye and landed in the trough with a plop before the flow of reconstituted coffee made its way towards the sewers.

"Shit." He pulled back his foreskin to look for traces and pissed on his hand.

The urine washed away the little blob before he had time to inspect it but it had definitely been there. He looked back at the wall. Maybe he'd been mistaken.

Walking to the burger van before the stall, his mind started to work overtime about AIDS, herpes, syphilis.

When he got home at night and used his own toilet the same thing happened and some green slime had appeared under his helmet when he'd inspected it.

"Bollocks, bollocks, bollocks." He opened a can of lager in front of the TV and cursed his bareback adventures on Soi 6.

On Monday morning he rung the VD clinic at Bolton Hospital. The discharge had become more noticeable over the weekend, but they couldn't fit him in until Wednesday so he had to wait. In the meantime pissing became unbearable. Every last drop felt like he was passing razor wire down his urinary tract.

When Wednesday came he dressed and drove to the hospital, and was worried that he'd not been able to avoid passing water for the full four hours prior to the appointment. The STD clinic was in a brick building tucked away in a huddle of outbuildings to afford patients a little anonymity when baring their parts for prognosis.

Keith followed the signs to the Centre for Sexual Health with his head bowed and a feeling of deep trepidation. A humourless grey door at the top of a disabled ramp stood between him and a doctor, who was looking him sternly in the face and, in Keith's mind, saying, "Were sorry, Mr Rossi, but you've contracted a rare tropical strain of *Lasciviovengosis*. Have you made a will?"

"Err, no."

"If you make it back to the car park it'll be a miracle."

He controlled his schoolboy urge to run away, and pressed the buzzer. The lock was released and he pushed the door.

Reception was a sterile-looking area. The girl behind the desk in her blue-check nurses uniform looked up.

"Have you got an appointment?"

He nodded.

"What name is it?"

"Ryan Giggs."

She looked up, smiling; it was the first name that had come into his head.

The nurse passed him a form to fill in and he fabricated all the details except his mobile number.

Waiting rooms were never the most exciting places and this was no exception. There were one or two people sat around and he tactically picked a seat where he could avoid eye contact. After ten minutes of staring at the floor he heard a female Asian doctor in her forties calling out his new name. The other incumbents looked up as he walked towards the door.

She led him to a consulting room where he explained that he had a green discharge; after he'd used the lavatory to provide a urine sample she made him remove his lower garments and lie on a treatment bed.

The lady left the room with his sample in her hand. She didn't bother shutting the door. Keith closed his eyes. He heard staff walking the corridor as he lay helpless with his tackle on display.

The doctor returned with her hands in medical marigolds and inspected Keith's malignant manhood.

"OK," she said sternly. "It looks like gonorrhoea. I need to take a couple of swabs for testing."

Keith found the ceiling a good distraction from his shameful scrutiny.

The doctor walked away and came back with a bowl in her hand. When he looked up Keith saw her holding a wafer-thin, shiny steel probe with a blob of cotton wool on the end. It must have been eight inches long. He closed his eyes and gritted his teeth.

The probe went down his contaminated conduit. As the doctor pushed he held his breath in anticipation and closed his eyes. When she stopped pushing he opened his eyes. She saw the reaction in his face and jammed it another quarter inch down his shrunken violet; he let out a strained growl and clenched his buttocks. On it's return journey the probe seemed to scrape and jar at every point of his soft tissue and it left him sore.

"Just one more." She smiled like a sadist.

Probe number two was cripplingly painful on its way down and she pushed it as far into him as was possible. It felt like it was almost passing through his pelvic bone.

With the part of her job the doctor seemed to enjoy most complete, Keith sat upright. He grabbed his groin and whimpered.

"I promise I'll never go bareback again, honest."

The doctor seemed proud of the punishment she'd administered. She took a blood sample and explained that, although it appeared as if he had gonorrhoea, the tests were in case he'd picked up anything else.

Keith left looking sheepish and feeling violated with a prescription for Cefixine to be taken three times a day for a week.

Wednesday was early closing at the market so he packed up early. He felt paranoid speaking to customers; he could smell the infection wafting up from his groin and seeping into his underwear as he stood trying to flog tracksuits.

In the car on the way home he dialled a number on his mobile phone.

"Royston. Hiya, it's Keith."

"How are you, man?"

"Not bad."

"How was Thailand?"

"Oh, you know, up and down."

"What do you want?"

"Do you still go in the Arrers?"

"Aye."

"Does Sheila still put out after hours?"

a sunny afternoon

Doing fuck all suited Vinny, especially with half a million quid in the bank. The only inconvenience he had to suffer was the boats firing their engines at six in the morning and the crap quality of the speakers he'd wired up to his Walkman. Brunch at Coconut Palm Village, followed by a couple of joints and the afternoon spent lazing on the beach or in the hammock, became a routine he stuck to with uncharacteristic discipline. Within three days he'd become an international-standard hammock jumper, capable of getting in without slip, fall, loss of cigarette or dignity. Attaining perpetual motion was a feat that seamed within reach, although he still had to dip his feet an inch to keep it swinging on the day the unthinkable happened – Jeed ran out of weed.

Anxious to keep a low profile, they'd stuck with the same restaurant each evening; it was quiet and Vinny had got friendly with TJ, the guy who'd been at the bar on their first night on the island.

Vinny gave away little information about himself other than his assumed name. His accent gave away most of the other data TJ had on him.

TJ was a cool guy. He was in his early thirties, Canadian and worked as a guitar technician for touring rock bands, and had spent the last ten years on the road so could spot most accents without too much effort. When he wasn't touring he'd put his feet up anywhere with a beach and available drugs. Thailand was his favourite.

Conversation was restricted primarily to musical tastes, games of pool and whose round it was, while Jeed nattered with the lady who ran the show. TJ was happy to recount tales of rock-star excess and well-hidden cock-ups while Vinny listened.

That night, out of earshot of the restaurateur, Vinny explained that they needed some grass. It was more at Jeed's behest; Vinny was a take it or leave it guy.

"Yeah, sure. But we'll have to go to Haad Rin."

He knew where 'Chez Croston' was and promised to call round next evening.

When his shaven head appeared through the woods Vinny was leaning on the balcony rail picking his nose.

"All right, man." He wiped his bogey on the hammock.

"Hey." TJ raised his hand.

"Jeed, we go Haad Rin."

Vinny enjoyed the ride in the bus. The darkness and the creak of the crickets gave the island an adventurous eeriness.

The bus picked up one or two more other people on the way and drew to a halt at a clearing where three more buses sat unattended. The floor was churned and muddy. They hopped out.

"Haad Rin Central." TJ laughed.

"You what?"

"That's what this place is, Haad Rin Central. The bus terminal."

They walked into the dark and down an alley between two buildings, emerging onto a concrete pathway inhabited on either side by shops, travel agents, open restaurants and pharmacies.

The people walking to and fro were a mix of European-looking folk mainly, all young, tanned, healthy and smiling. Some scooted to and fro on scooters while others ambled slowly, avoiding ankle bites from stray dogs and swatting airborne insects. Vinny got a few disdainful looks for being an exploitative misogynist. The righteous ones got a contemptuous snarl back.

They came to a junction, which seemed to be a sort of focal point. There were a couple of stalls selling fruit shakes, sandwiches, pancakes and satays.

Like Khao Sarn Road, the inhabitants of Haad Rin seemed to have a penchant for brightly dyed cotton, facial piercing and braided hair.

They turned left down a quieter, narrower pathway. The smell of barbecuing meat wafted into Vinny's nostrils and, as he looked for the source, he felt Jeed tug his hand. A woman stood behind a blackened half oil drum with a grill on top. She was old and toothless but was smiling happily and tending a few satays.

Jeed ordered and they stood and watched the freaky people walk by.

With a bagful of food they carried on down the path. The beach was in sight and at the entrance a dark-skinned European with long hair and a beard stood twirling tennis balls on lengths of string. There was a big bar at the bottom of the path pumping out dance music and the guy was twirling the balls in some sort of rhythm to it.

Vinny had a satay in his hand. TJ edged past him. As Vinny stepped sideways one of the balls knocked his food from his hand as he was putting it to his mouth.

"You fucking tithead."

The guy carried on unawares. As Vinny passed him he could see that his eyes were shut.

"There's folk trynna get past, you prick."

He carried on being expressive regardless of the inconvenience he caused. Vinny shook his head and caught up with TJ, who was waiting by another grill where toasted sandwiches were being cooked by an old lady and her daughter. A pack of stray dogs were gathering and yapping, hoping for scraps. A young guy, probably the restaurateur's son, was sat against a wall keeping them away with pebbles and a catapult.

The beach looked impressive. White breakers rushed out of the darkness that shrouded the sea. The sand was soft and white, and Vinny looked all around. Either side of him for about a mile were large open bars sporting coloured flags and lighting rigs in mixed states of occupancy. Some of the bars had chosen to lay out low tables on mats with little oil lamps on the 30-yard stretch of sand between them and the sea.

"'S all right, this gaff," he nodded at TJ. "'Part from all the nobheads."

"It gets kinda freaky towards the full moon."

They walked down the beach and Vinny held Jeed's hand, feeling all soft hearted.

TJ forged a few yards ahead and mounted the concrete steps to a bar. As Vinny approached he whistled.

Vinny looked up.

"Watch your head on the netting."

"What?"

He walked into a volleyball net hung from the edge of the bar.

TJ shook his head.

They took a seat at the bar; like the rest of the bars on the beach it was basically a concrete floor with a roof held by wooden posts, a few tables and chairs, and lighting to give it a disco feel.

"What's this place called?"

"Big Boom."

Big Boom's fingerprint decorations were coloured strings, which were stretched in the roof space and sidings, illuminated with fluorescent light to give it a gaudy but psychedelic feel.

As with all the other bars the staff were Thai and the customers young foreigners.

Vinny felt a chill from the sea breeze as TJ ordered drinks.

"Guys, I just godda go chat with someone." TJ spun off his stool and headed off down the beach.

He returned ten minutes later and carried on drinking and chatting. The barman was friendly and offered them cigarettes when he took one from his packet, and offered them CDs to choose from.

TJ suggested another bar and they headed up the beach.

"Wanna try that one?" He pointed at a building outlined by coloured lights on the hillside. They strolled towards it through the white sand. "Here." He passed Vinny a plastic packet of grass. "It's five hundred."

"Give it you in there?"

"Sure. You gotta be kinda careful with the police round here."

Vinny laughed at the thought of getting caught with a few quids' worth of weed when he had half a million in misappropriated cash in the bank.

"I'll bear that in mind." He passed it to Jeed to put in her bag.

They reached the end of the beach and had to jump up a concrete step to get up the stone stairway that led to the bar. In the dark they had to tread carefully to keep their footing. At the top of the staircase, they reached a small doorway that opened up into the bar. The first thing Vinny noticed was a pile of shoes and sandals by the door. They walked in and felt the varnished floorboards creak beneath them. In a corner a few people were sat on cushions with their legs crossed, chatting and looking stoned. An empty hammock swung above them in the breeze.

They sat round a table on a lower deck with a Ludo set on it and looked down on the beach and bars and lights. The bar had about four floors at different levels, all linked by little wooden staircases, and was spared from crashing onto the rocks below by wooden stilts.

In a corner on their level a girl in a tie-dyed headband was giving a guy who needed a shave a head massage as he rested in her lap.

"Wanna play Ludo?"

They set out the pieces and TJ explained the rules in case they didn't understand. He threw down a packet of king-sized cigarette papers. A minute ago he'd been warning them to be careful. He rolled a joint and started toking away while Vinny looked around uncomfortably.

"We're OK in here. Want some?" He passed it to Vin.

Vinny took a couple of tugs and only half inhaled. Jeed nipped to the toilet so he had to hold onto it for a little longer than he wanted to, and was glad to let go when she returned.

He felt the weight of his eyelids increase. The lady giving the head massage was talking about him in code to her friend. TJ worked for Interpol and was trying to get him to implicate himself in the assassination of JFK.

He leaned back and looked at Jeed happily sipping her drink and tossing the dice with the joint in her hand.

"So, what is it you do Jim?"

Vinny started to panic. "Nowt really."

TJ was definitely onto him.

"Yeah. Sounds fun."

Vinny stared at him as he took his turn to throw the dice.

"It pays well." The paranoia flew out of him and he started to laugh at himself.

TJ picked up another cigarette paper.

"Oh man. 'S makin' me paranoid that."

TJ smiled. "Sure, OK." He rolled a smaller joint as they took it in turns to occupy their hands in the pretence of trying to win at Ludo. He passed the joint to Jeed, saving Vinny the embarrassment of refusal. She refused in sympathy with her boyfriend.

"It's OK, Jeed, smoke," Vinny insisted.

She accepted.

"Maybe you wanna try the mushrooms?" TJ sat back.

"They're worse, aren't they?"

"They're kinda cool. I'm havin' a cup." TJ dusted some light hemp ash off his legs and went to the bar.

Vinny moved his cushion next to Jeed and lay with his head on her thigh. He looked into her face and smiled. She tapped his nose with her finger. TJ returned with a small plastic cup and a straw, and took his throw.

"Ahh, fuck it, I'll get some," said Vinny, and he made an effort to stand.

"Share mine if you're not sure." He passed the cup over to Vinny, who took a few sips at the thick, sweetened shake.

"They don't taste too bad, them." The glutton in him sipped the cup until it was only a third full before he realised his greed.

He passed the cup to Jeed.

The game sort of ground to a halt as TJ started telling jokes, and within half an hour the one about the chicken crossing the road was hilarious.

Vinny started to like the light-hearted feelings he was getting and got two more shakes in apology for devouring the first.

They decided to head back down to Big Boom, the descent of the staircase made easier with fits of laughter.

At the table on the beach TJ told them about a notorious local lady boy who made a habit of attaching himself to the inebriated and buggering them on full moon night.

"That's nothin' that, man." Vinny shook his head.

"Why, you know somethin'?"

"Jeed, you tell TJ about *katoey* Ko Samui."

"OK. In loom Ko Samui, me, Winny sleeping and man come loom wis *katoey* boxing." She nodded at TJ, proud and satisfied that she'd told the story in full. She hugged Vin and looked at him lovingly. "Zen poliit come. Man *katoey* going."

TJ tried his best to laugh.

Jeed went to the toilet again and, when she was out of earshot, TJ said politely, "What was that thing about the *katoey*?"

Vinny sniggered to himself. "Oh man, you had to be there."

He recounted the full story about Danny and the ladyboy smashing through the wall and carrying on with their naked boxing match until they were carted away by the police. It had TJ doubled up in a paroxysm of laughter.

Jeed made her way back through the sand. "Winny, I'm see Danny. Him coming."

Vinny turned and saw their mate from Ko Samui heading down with a beer in his hand.

"Friend o' yours, Vinny?"

"Why did you call me Vinny?" He shot TJ a hard stare.

"Jeed just called you that." He was apologetic.

"Fuck." He held his head in his hands. "Never call me by that name, OK. Jeed, no Vinny, Jim."

He looked at the stars, which each had there own individual tint and had started to sway restlessly.

"Alroight, mate?" Danny was smirking.

"Let you out, did they?"

"Arr. 'Ad to pay the bloke lady thing five 'undred and the bungalow five thousand for the wall. Let me go the next day."

"Did they put you up in a nice room?"

"Oh arr. Robbed the dressin' gown out o' the 'ealth spa."

"Danny, this is TJ."

The four laughed, drank and smoked until the early hours. Vinny forgot Jeed's slip-up on the pseudonym and they fucked in a room full of psychedelic swirls when they got home.

When the bell rang for last orders in the Three Arrows, Royston went to the bar to get himself, Gorey and Pemmy a final pint.

"Three lagers when you're ready, Sheila." He flashed his teeth at her as he put a ten-pound note on the bar.

"Take you're time with them, Roy. You can stay back when I've cleaned up." She thrust her wrinkled cleavage towards him.

Graham, her husband, always went to bed around midnight on Saturday. He coached a Sunday League soccer team so did his drinking on a Friday.

Their Saturday-night soirées were quite regular. Royston and the boys were too lazy to go into town and Graham was past his peak on the matrimonial front so it gave Sheila a chance to satisfy her urges. They didn't do it every week in case Graham got suspicious but once or twice a month she'd let a few stay behind along with one of the barmaids, and more often than not it turned sordid.

The pub emptied and Graham and Sheila did the rounds cleaning tables and collecting glasses with a Berkeley hanging out of their mouths.

Graham had a pint with them and went to bed.

After a few double gins Sheila was getting loud, smutty and tactile.

"So who's the lucky boy tonight then, Sheila?" Royston smirked as he sat slumped in the chair.

"I'll have a few more gins then decide." She was floating on air.

Royston nipped to the toilet. He removed the light bulbs from both ladies and gents then sent a text on his mobile.

Half an hour later it had been decided that it'd be Gorey first, Royston second and Pemmy last. They made her down a quadruple gin then a double Scotch.

Gorey headed off to the toilet and Sheila followed a minute later.

She made a fuss about the lights being off but was quick to lie down in the cubicle.

Gorey always enjoyed the depravity of sleeping with a woman older than his mother and laughed into her chasm as he undertook the arduous task of turning her on.

Eventually he tasted piscatorial dampness and told her to turn round. He embedded himself in the first door Sarah had passed through and worked away, bouncing back and forth on the blubber of her behind.

Royston unlocked the front door and let Keith in. He had his collars turned up against the cold and rain. He pulled at the crotch of his jeans to stop them sticking to the bacterial adhesive in his underwear.

"All right, Roy?"

"Wicked."

Roy's cheeky, mischievous grin pleased Keith. They shook hands and Royston placed the baseball cap he was wearing on Keith's head.

"What's the state o' play?"

"Middle of act one. I put a trip in 'er drink half an hour ago so give it ten minutes she won't 'ave a tube o' glue." Roy pushed the door to quietly.

Keith trod gently across the worn brown linoleum floor and took up the seat where he'd had his collar felt. Roy went over to the bar and held a glass under the lager tap for him.

"So what's new?" asked Keith.

"Ah, fuck all. You've missed nowt in Bolton."

Gorey re-emerged from his congress wiping his mouth. "It was 'ard work, that. Where's my pint?"

"Good luck, man." Gorey punched Keith's knuckles. "Trap one in the gents."

He walked to the loo with his hand down his trousers, thinking of Nan from Tilac. It didn't have the desired effect straightaway and he had to hover outside the door for a while, teasing himself by hand until he was aroused.

"Bloody 'urry up, will you, Roy," he heard Sheila squawking from within.

"Just comin'." He covered his mouth with his hand. When he pushed the door open he saw an oversized grey/white posterior pointing at him from the door of a cubicle. Letting his trousers fall he waddled over and dropped to his knees behind her. He had to hold his member steady in his hand and concentrate hard on Nan's tanned body and angelic face to keep himself erect.

"Fuckin' 'ave that." Keith smiled the sweet smile of revenge as he pushed himself in.

"You must be feeling the cold, Roy, love," Sheila quipped with drunken sarcasm.

"You'll feel summat soon," he cursed through his breathlessness.

Keith pumped strong and hard while he sunk his fingertips into the saggy white flesh of her behind. Might as well leave a few finger marks for Graham to inspect.

After five minutes the vengeful act became surprisingly satisfying for Keith and he pulled out with a grin. He buttoned up and stood back. Sheila was still on all fours waiting for the third musketeer.

"Fuckin' slag." He hurled his foot at the offensive mountain of flesh in front of him and recoiled as his toe buried itself somewhere he'd rather not think about.

After his night on the mushrooms Vinny started to warm to Ko Pha Ngan. Even some of the people seemed decent enough and he became friendly with a few who didn't give Jeed dirty looks. He didn't like the Israeli's though.

Mushrooms and beer on Haad Rin beach became a regular event for a week until he started getting weird spates of deja vous and paranoia while lying on the beach in the afternoon. Beer became his escape after that.

On the second Monday in January John Moston walked into his office at midday. His head was still cloudy from almost non-stop drinking since Friday lunchtime, and the seasonal drop in sales left him in a less than exuberant mood.

At 12.30 he bollocked the team leaders from the sales division and at 1.15 he went to the pub for lunch.

He was practising his putting with a tumbler of whisky on his desk when the phone rang.

"Moston."

"Hi, Mr Moston, it's Richard from Accounts."

"Fuckin' 'ell, what's up?"

"Errr… well, err… there seems to be a bit of a problem."

"Spit it out, lad."

"Personable Computers have sent us another invoice for that Unix thing we bought and claim not to have received payment."

"Tell 'em to fuck off."

"Well, I've spoken to them and it seems like there's sort of… I don't know how to say this."

"I'm listening." Fatty Moston put his golf club down and grabbed at the glass.

"The account we paid the money into isn't actually their account."

"You fuckin' halfwit. I pay you to take care of my money, not send it all over the place. Check you've put the right account number on the payment then tell the bank, and don't bother me till you've got some good news." He slammed the phone down and rattled a ball into the wastepaper basket, emptied his glass and went home.

"It really suits you, that, Sue." Toni sipped at her coffee.

Sue put down the blouse she'd been holding up against her body and rummaged in her Kendal's bag for the next item she wanted to show off.

The phone rang. "Sue Robbins."

A voice started chatting.

"Are you sure?"

Toni recognised a frantic tone even on someone else's phone.

Sue went white. "Have you called the police?"

Vinny was lying in the hammock with his hands behind his head. Jeed sat on the railing at the front of the balcony with his penis in her mouth. They were going to head down to Haad Rin in half an hour for another night on the piss.

When Keith got home on Tuesday night DC Davenport's Ford Sierra was waiting outside his flat.

"Keith."

Keith looked round as he was pushing the yard gate open.

"Oh, how nice to see you, Mr Davenport." He stubbed his cigarette out on the damp cobble.

"Can you spare us a few minutes?"

"Not really, I'm washing my hair tonight."

"We'd like to ask you a few questions about Vincent Croston."

"Fire away."

"We'd prefer to do it at the station…"

"And if I don't agree you can arrest me." He shook his head and jumped in the back seat.

"Lovely shade of magnolia you've chosen, Mr Davenport." Keith rocked back in the interview-room chair with his hands in his pockets.

"Mr Rossi, this is Detective Inspector Fawcett of the Greater Manchester fraud squad."

"Any relation to Farrah?"

"He'd like to speak to you about Vincent Croston."

DI Fawcett wore a well-fitted dark blue suit, unlike Davenport who wore black polyester trousers and a grubby checked sports jacket.

"Your friend Vincent's been a very naughty boy."

"I know. He didn't send his mum a Christmas card," Keith sighed.

"He's misappropriated half a million pounds."

"You what?" Keith let the chair fall forwards and his jaw drop.

"He's misappropriated half a million pounds that should belong to Personable Computers. We wondered if you knew anything about it."

Keith shook his head, wide eyed.

"Let me try and jog your memory. Globe Hop Travel. John Moston. Duxbury Gardens Golf Club." Fawcett raised his eyebrows.

"You're kiddin' me on."

"We believe you were with Vincent when he—"

"Yeah, yeah. Vinny got a tip that this guy wanted to buy a computer and that he'd be there one Friday so I went with him. Moral support while he buttered him up, like."

"And what's he done with the money?" Fawcett fixed him with a stern glare.

"How do you mean?"

"Cut you in, did he?"

"I'm sayin' nowt without a solicitor."

Under the scrutiny of the duty solicitor Keith didn't put a foot wrong. The only information that Fawcett got was that the last Keith saw of Vinny was when he'd said goodbye before heading off on a trip upcountry. He mentioned that Vinny had been buying drinks on the 23rd, and he mentioned being shocked when Vinny wasn't on the plane home although he had hinted on cashing his chips and going on a world tour.

Vinny deliberately chose a terminal in the corner of the internet café where he was out of view when he checked his email. He'd given Keith an address so he could keep in touch.

Do you remember this guy?

All right, Jim. Remember that bloke who was in Pattaya with me? He's been a real bad lad. It was a fucking surprise to me when the coppers pulled me in about it. I've scanned in the front pages of Friday's Manchester Evening News and Saturday's Bolton.

Let us know if you see him round.

Keith

Vinny opened the attachment. MAN HUNT IN HALF MILLION FRAUD was the headline. There was a quarter-page picture of him in a shirt and tie. He remembered it. It had been taken at one of the Christmas parties when he'd been at Intra Tech. At least they'd been decent and shown one of him holding a pint. He looked a lot younger.

The rest of the page was filled with indirect links to him and the half million that Globe Hop had sent to the bank in Switzerland. Whoever had written the article was careful not to say that Vinny had pulled off a fraud, only that police were looking for him in connection with it. They said the last time he'd been seen was in Bangkok and that the police were in contact with the authorities in Thailand and Mexico, where his cash card had last been used.

The *Bolton Evening News* led on a different tack. MOTHER'S PLEA TO MISSING MAN. Vinny's jaw dropped. They had the same Christmas-do picture, but also a professionally taken one of his mum in her specs, looking solemn.

It started with details of why the police were looking for him, then followed on with an interview with the greying Mrs Croston. She said she was missing him, protested his innocence and pleaded with him to come home.

Vinny hit 'delete' before he'd read it fully and walked slowly out of the internet café stroking the back of his head. He was twenty yards up the road when a girl tugged at his hand. There was a tear in the corner of his eye and he rubbed it away.

"You no pay for email."

He gave her a hundred baht and carried on walking.

He sat on the steps of an empty bar with his head in his hands. Jeed spotted him. She trotted over with the bag of cosmetics she'd been to get. It didn't take much to work out he was upset. Quietly she sat next to him. After a minute or two she stroked his back and kissed his temple.

"Tchim OK?"

Vinny wiped his face with his hands and sighed. "We get drink."

Since being on the island he'd left drinking to the evenings but he put that to one side on this occasion.

The tall guy in his late thirties with shoulder-length hair that served him eyed him cautiously.

The centre of the roomy watering hole had a table surrounded by big, low circular chairs where you could curl up and assume the foetal position. That suited Vinny fine. There was a canvass displaying a picture of a smiling sun hanging from the ceiling and when Vinny looked up the warmth of it washed away the sorrow he felt for his mum.

Vinny got pissed that day, quietly and mournfully.

Jeed propped him up on the way to Haad Rin Central and pulled his shoes off when he fell on the bed.

Vinny noticed the island get busier as the full moon approached. The empty bungalows at Coconut Palm Village filled and he made sure he wore his sun hat when he wondered away from the balcony.

He had a friend in TJ and when the bars in Haad Rin started to get crowded they drunk in Thong Sala instead.

On the night of the full moon Vinny looked at himself in the mirror after shaving.

"Fuck me, I'm black." He didn't recognise the dark brown guy staring back at him. He'd had his hair cropped for 60 baht at a barber's and what was there had turned a mid-brown colour in the sun. When he'd left England his hair had been black.

Sweating had become second nature in the air-con free bungalow and bars, and he'd lost weight. You could almost see stomach muscles and ribs.

TJ turned up at 8 o'clock and they got on a baht bus and headed for Haad Rin. The bus was full of wide-eyed foreigners enthusing about their first full moon.

Halfway to town the baht bus pulled up at the side of the road. The driver got out with his cell phone glued to his ear. He walked to the back of the bus and banged the sides.

"What the fuck's goin' on?"

He appeared at the tailgate and unlocked it.

"Lodebrok. Lodebrok."

"What's he sayin'?"

"Polliit. Polliit."

"Shit." The rest of the partygoers wore the same feared expressions as Vinny as they got out of the van and retrieved contraband from shoes and pockets.

"What am I gonna do wi' these?" Vinny produced the bag of six Es that Jeed had managed to weed out from a Thai girl she'd got pally with.

"Same as I'm gonna do with mine." TJ smiled wryly as he showed Vinny the three he'd acquired. He poured them down his neck and washed them down with some water.

Vinny bravely necked three while Jeed had one and a half, and he donated the remainder to a Swedish guy who'd planned to get some in town.

After ten minutes of frantic ingestion they carried on towards town.

They hit a collection of parked-up vans and waited. After twenty minutes they reached the collection of police with torches and batons.

Vinny was in the midst of the most orgasmic narcotic flourish he'd felt since his first E in the Hacienda in 1989.

He clenched his teeth and grinned with dementure as the policeman frisked him and ran through his pockets.

Haad Rin was awash with humanity. The crossroads where the woman made sandwiches was almost impossible to negotiate.

Vinny had to push unshaven Israelis in baggy trousers out of the way.

The beach was rammed full of lunatics dancing in crowds to the music from the sound rigs that had been erected outside all the bars on the beach.

They made their way to Big Boom. The volley-ball net had been taken down and their normally quiet resting place was awash with Europeans in their twenties dancing to sounds the DJ played. Vinny had all the inspiration he needed and spent hours dancing behind Jeed's peachlike behind.

As midnight approached the tide got higher and for a while the party stopped along the beach as the sea invaded the dancers' territory and lapped at the concrete lips of the bars. The tide disappeared as quickly as it had encroached. Vinny was ready to a take up his position behind Jeed and wave his arms and stomp his feet when a drunken guy tapped him.

"All right, mate. Got any pills?" He knew the accent; it was from within five miles of Bolton.

Vinny's heart stopped. He grabbed Jeed's hand and dragged her away, and lowered the brim on his sunhat to shield his face from the world, leaving the guy left wondering what he'd said that had caused offence.

Jeed knew something had set him off but didn't bother asking what. TJ was nowhere to be seen so they went up to the bar on the hill where they'd first tried mushrooms. It was packed to the rafters and Vinny wondered if the stilts would hold. The sight from the ledge as they looked out over the curved beach packed with 10,000 revellers dancing like maniacs to the variety of music was something to be savoured.

After a while they headed back down to the beach. Vinny decided to avoid Big Boom. There were too many English and with his profile in the press he wanted to avoid recognition.

They found a bar further down playing hard techno. The crowd seemed to be predominantly Israeli. The DJ was set up in front of a canvass with the words VINYL CLUB sprayed on top of a psychedelic montage. They got a drink and started dancing but got jostled by young guys with aggressive facial expressions.

They walked back onto the beach and saw guys planting fireworks the size of baseball bats in the sand. When they went off the crowd had to scurry for cover in case they didn't take the planned trajectory.

Vinny and Jeed strolled through the crowds and decided on a quiet bar in one of the sandy lanes leading off the beach. They sat and watched drunks walk into walls and weirdo guys in sarongs walk past waving their hands in the air while their eyes were fixed on the celestial kaleidoscope.

The three pills were subsiding now to Vinny's relief. The earlier part of the evening had involved some pretty intense sensations in 'Vinny's World' and being able to focus on things was welcome respite from wobbling in the sand and wondering why the it had a peculiar circling motion to it.

Jeed was still moving and rubbed her behind into his crotch as he held his hands round her front.

He was considering getting the next baht bus back to Chez Croston when he saw TJ swaying through the crowd and having his attention caught by a group of blonde girls and bikini tops.

"TJ."

TJ turned around but couldn't hear who was calling.

"TJ." Jeed joined the call.

He spotted them and swaggered over. His shirt was plastered to him by perspiration.

"Hey, guys."

"Y'all right?" Vinny slopped a wet kiss on the back of Jeed's neck.

"You comin' up the Backyard?"

"What's the Backyard?"

"They have a party till about midday."

"Nah, me and Jeed are goin' home in a bit. I'm flaggin'."

Jeed stomped her foot in the sand and TJ smirked.

"You want go party?" She nodded and made her eyes grow in expectation.

"I want go home for boom boom." Vinny did his best to look washed out.

"Honey, we boom boom too muts. Jeed want dancing." She frowned at him.

"I tired."

TJ got himself a drink.

"Man, I'm gonna get grief if we don't go this Backyard gaff, but I'm startin' to nod off."

"Try a diet pill."

"Eh?"

"Go the chemist. They'll keep you going for a few hours."

Vinny left Jeed to chat with TJ and headed through the slightly thinner crowds to one of the islands pharmacies. There was queue of people in bandanas holding drinks and looking strung out.

"You got any Es?" the girl behind him whispered.

He chose to ignore her.

When he reached the front the counter he hesitated. "Err… I want, err… amphetamine," he spat it out.

"How many?"

"Two." He held his fingers up.

The guy looked like he needed a dose of his own medicine. He rummaged in a jar and put two transparent capsules filled with odd-looking crystals into a tiny brown paper envelope for Vinny.

When the sun came up they walked down to the beach to watch the depleted revellers dancing barefoot in the breakers. One or two people were lying in the sand motionless.

TJ took them on a walk up a steep, narrow footpath. Thickets of bushes and trees surrounded them as they climbed the headland at the low end of the beach.

When Vinny was bathed in sweat and ready to give up, they found the Backyard. It was a big bar, ramshackle and constructed of lightweight material, but jam packed with die-hard hedonists eager to wear out their shoes.

Vinny propped himself against the bar. Jeed joined the throng but didn't stray too far from her benefactor.

The diet pills did their job.

TJ was dancing with group of blondes that had caught his eyes earlier.

Vinny gulped at his beer. When he looked up, one of the blondes was next to him. She wasn't trying too hard to grab the bartender's attention.

"Hi." She smiled seductively.

"All right."

"Wanna share some whisky?" She had an Aussie accent and an expanse of golden tanned midriff that made Vinny's hands sweaty.

He could hardly refuse.

She ordered whisky and Sprite. It arrived in a sort of bucket full of ice with straws hanging out of it.

Vinny sunk his mouth in. It had a sickly sweet tang.

She sipped daintily. Vinny sucked hard on the straw. Before long it was gone.

"Looks like my round." Vinny watched the bartender pour a quart bottle of whisky into the bucket along with a small bottle of energy drink.

Vinny polished it off again. The girl went to dance and smiled every time she caught his eye.

Pissed and full of drugs, Vinny forgot about Jeed. He smooched over the dance floor and did his best to impress her with his moves. She egged him on. Before long he was dancing a little closer than he would have done if he had known Jeed was watching.

Hardly anyone noticed the pretty Thai girl storming off with tears running down her cheeks.

When a tall athletic guy approached the girl she switched her attention to him.

Vinny went back to the bar and scanned the room for Jeed. He sat and waited for her to return from the toilet.

It was 10 o'clock in the morning when he realised she must have gone home.

Vinny stumbled back down to town. He walked along the beach, which was strewn with dead bodies and empty bottles. He took a baht bus home with a few casualties who looked ready for a good sleep or some form of lobotomy.

The sun in Coconut Palm Village made him smile. The family who owned it went quiet when he walked past.

In readiness for a passionate embrace he smiled as he pushed open the door of Chez Croston.

An airborne shoe brushed past his face and he felt Jeed pushing the door away from him.

"Let us in, blossom," he croaked after 60 cigarettes and 40 beers.

"I'm hate yooooo!"

"Time o' the month?" he muttered and scrambled into the hammock.

He wasn't sure how long he'd been asleep, but the ashtray hurt when it hit his face. It hurt a lot more the second time.

Jeed was possessed.

"Why you butterfly me? I know you fucking lady."

The ashtray crashed onto the bridge of his nose and he felt his skin break.

Jeed's eyes were blackened from crying.

"I no butterfly." He wrestled the ashtray out of her hands and wiped the blood off his face.

Jeed ran back inside and jammed herself behind the door. Vinny kicked at it but it didn't move. He could hear sobbing. He sat back at the railing and heard scrabbling from inside. When the door opened he smiled his best apologetic smile but Jeed ran at him with her fists flying.

Vinny laughed at the ludicrosy of the situation and grabbed her by the wrists.

"You no lub me. Why I no goot. You boom boom lady falang. I watching."

Vinny threw her into bed.

yet I know

Jeed eventually stopped crying at about midnight that night. Vinny slept in the hammock.

It took three days before she spoke to him, and that was only because she wanted money for food.

After a week of sleeping on the hammock she actually started to speak to him more, without smiling though.

He'd spent a fair amount of time explaining that swindling half a million quid wasn't something he'd do for any old woman.

When he got badly bitten by mosquitoes sleeping on the balcony she let him back into the bed, and surprisingly obliged in the coital department. He was expecting to have to wait another week or so for that.

Since they'd escaped from Bangkok she'd spent about an hour a day on her mobile phone, usually in the afternoon to some friend or other. Occasionally she'd recount some information about Ohn finding a new boyfriend who'd ended up dumping her, resulting in a session of drunken self-pity; sometimes she'd tell of her younger brother who'd got in trouble at school.

It was about a fortnight after the full moon when she got the call. Vinny was playing frisbee on the beach with the German guy who'd moved in next door.

"Tchiim," he heard her calling out and made his excuse to leave. "Tchiim." He mounted the steps, sweating. "I'm talking telephone Ohn." She looked worried. "She say man polliit looking. Want look for Winnee."

"Eh?"

"Polliit come to bar Pattaya. They'm look for Winneee."

"Shit." Vinny stopped in his tracks and held his head. He paced up and down wiping sweat off his face as he searched for ideas. "Ohn say I in Ko Pha Ngan?"

"No. Ohn no speaking. She say not know yooo."

"OK."

Vinny got his wallet from the depths of the bungalow and dug out Pete Jensen's card. It felt funny holding Jeed's mobile. "Hiya, Pete."

"'Ello." He sounded near death.

"Pete, it's Vinny."

"'Ow can I 'elp?"

“Errrrr… I’ve ’ad a whisper. Some copper’s been asking round Pattaya for my whereabouts.”

“Give us a day or two, I’ll sort summink out. This your number, is it?”

“Yeah. Make it quick, will you?”

Pete cut the call. Vinny was still restless. He started to dial England but hung up.

The next two days were spent anxiously drinking too much while Jeed massaged his temples and his ego. She actually shared a little of his anxiety.

Vinny was having a piss when Jeed’s mobile rung.

“Tchim.”

He splashed his shorts.

“Tchim. Man want speak wis Winnee.”

“Hello.” Vinny fiddled with his flies as he held the phone.

“Vincent, it’s Pete,” a faint voice croaked.

“Yeah.” His heart was fluttering.

“Vincent, I’ve spoken to a friend of mine at the police station in Pattaya.”

“What’s he said?”

“Well, the officer in charge of your investigation, a Mr Purachai, says that he can send a letter back to the police in Manchester saying you aint in Thailand.”

“Shit hot. When can he do it?”

“Well, the problem is he’s got a credit card bill that he can’t pay off. I’m sure a man of your warmth can understand how distressin’ this is for ’im, and he needs a donation…”

“How much?”

“He’s asking for ten thousand.”

“Ten thousand baht. No problem.”

“No, no, Vincent. He wants ten thousand pounds.”

“Fuckin’ ’ell.” Vinny’s hand started to shake and he felt short of breath.

“Cunt. Won’t he bargain?”

“I’ve already bargained him down for you.”

Vinny looked at Jeed smiling up at him, and thought of England.

“OK. How do I get it to him?”

“Well, we’re forgettin’ my friend in the police department who needs taking care of and, of course, there is my arrangement fee.”

“Bottom line.”

“Twenty.”

“Fifteen.”

“Because I like you, Vince, I’ll cut mine down and call it eighteen.”

“Done.”

They sorted out the bank account it needed transferring to and Vinny threw the phone at the back wall of the bungalow.

Vinny got the baht bus to Thong Sala and arranged the cash transfer at the local Thai Farmers Bank.

He was seething at the cost when he got back. Jeed dragged him onto the bed in the bungalow and gave him the time of his life.

Vinny relaxed a little knowing that the police had been paid. By the time the full moon came around again TJ had gone on the road with some German heavy metal outfit and Danny had met up with his mates from back home.

After the previous full-moon incident Vinny was extra careful not to give Jeed any cause for drama and kept his eyes to himself. This time they took it easy and went to bed when the sun came up.

Bliss became boring and Vinny spent a lot of time pacing around and looking for things to do. He started to train regularly at Jungle Gym, where he'd banged his foot on the day he'd arrived on the island.

The female instructor gave him a hard time, but soon the cobwebs on his Thai-boxing skills and the flab round his abdominals started to disappear. Jeed watched on proudly as he went through his paces, whirring the pedals on the exercise bike in the corner.

A couple of times Vinny woke with a start in the middle of the night thinking he was back in England. He had the horrid vision of himself lying alone on his futon in the cold.

Occasionally he lay in the hammock, smoking and wondering if he could pull off the same scam again.

He hatched a plot to enter Australia as Jim Bradley with a fictitious CV and references, and to try and pull the same trick again.

Jeed started to get bored as well. Occasionally she'd sulk for a day or two then spend ages talking on her phone.

The third full moon passed and Vinny and Jeed actually avoided Haad Rin altogether.

Vinny got sick of all the wide-eyed youngsters and his conversations and congress with Jeed became a little flat.

A couple of weeks later they were sat in the restaurant in Thong Sala having dinner when Vinny took the bull by the horns.

"Jeed, you want go back Pattaya? We can buy bar?"

She put her knife and spoon down, leaned across the table and kissed his forehead.

When they got back to the bungalow that night she phoned Ohn and jabbered on in Thai using the joyful tones Vinny hadn't heard for a while.

He smiled to himself as he sat on the balcony smoking a joint.

"Honey," came Jeed's voice.

Vinny stubbed out the joint and headed indoors.

"Honey. Ohn say man selling bar Soi 7."

"Yes? How much?"

"Ohn not saying."

The next day they packed up and got on a plane to Bangkok. Thankfully it was a jet and they glided through the sky rather than hiccupping the way they had in the twin prop.

April was the hottest month of the year. In the taxi to Pattaya Vinny was sweating profusely despite the air conditioning being on full blast.

The smiling couple checked into the Nova Lodge on Soi 7 as dusk drew in.

They showered and dressed and when they got to Tommy Bar Jeed was greeted with hugs, kisses and whoops of delight from Ohn and the rest of the girls.

Paul was sat at the bar drinking by himself.

"Fuck me, Lord Lucan."

"All right, Paul. How's Stez?"

"Oh, he's fucked off up Udon Thani wi' the tequila girl."

"Yeah?"

"Oh aye, wedding's planned an' all sorts."

"What've you bin doin'?"

"Shortenin' my life expectancy."

Vinny laughed.

"There's a sweep on what'll finish me. Favourite's liver failure, but you can get good odds on HIV or lung cancer."

The pair looked over the bar at the girls laughing and giggling and feeling at Jeed's slightly worn Armani clothes.

"We off down town?" Paul stubbed out his cigarette.

"Fuck me, I thought you'd never ask."

Vinny OK'd it with Jeed and they headed for South Pattaya. Jeed didn't mind; she was well on her way through a bottle of Mekong with the rest of the girls.

They took a seat in Happy a Go-Go.

"Fuck me, it's good to be back. No nobheads with dreadlocks and rings through their noses."

An ashtray hit Vinny in the face.

Paul got up and started to walked out.

"What the fuck's up?"

"Sorry, Vin, been a bit of a butterfly. Not that popular in a few places."

"How about Dollhouse?"

"Done seven of 'em in there. Might be a bad idea."

Vinny laughed. "Dirty bastard. Any road, can you call us Jim from now on?"

They spent the night drinking in the few bars left in Pattaya where Paul's licentiousness didn't put his life at risk.

When they turned up back at Tommy Bar at around 1.30am Vinny was greeted by a drunken Jeed and jealous smiles from the rest of the tanked-up bar girls.

Paul got a few whispered frowns for turning up with yet another lady.

They ignored the 2am curfew and drunk until it turned light.

At 7am they stumbled the few yards back to the Nova Lodge and fell asleep on the strangely comfortable bed.

The fully functional shower had Vinny smitten and he spent almost an hour under its powerful warm blast when he finally woke in the late afternoon.

"Honey." He stroked Jeed in bed.

There was little sign of life so he went and had a cigarette on the balcony. When he returned she was cocooned in the sheet so he went to eat in Rosie O'Grady's.

When he got back to the room she was singing in the shower. He couldn't tell if it was a badly interpreted English song or one of the soppy Thai love songs the girls were playing in the bar last night. She had a sweet voice anyway.

When she dried and dressed she took his hand and kissed him.

"We go look bar?" She smiled and dragged him out of the door.

They wove through the complex of beer bars that cluttered the lower end of Soi 7. Jeed dragged him up to one on the concrete plinth that was closed and had upturned stools in the middle of the rectangular serving area. It lacked a pulse. The counter's entrance hatch was at the far end of one of the longer edges that ran parallel the next open but empty bar.

Jeed trotted over and ducked behind the bar.

"Hey, sexy man, you wan drinking Tchim Jeed bar?" She leaned her elbows on the counter and gave him a smile that would have lit the Albert Hall.

Vinny fell in love again. She held her hand out and guided him round from the inside. He felt a homely glow as he ducked under the counter and walked across the dusty floor of the bar and joined Jeed at the edge with his elbows on the bar.

They watched the world go by. It was noticeably quieter than last time he'd been on Soi 7 in January, but there were still bar girls calling out and punters walking past with their newfound loves.

Vinny shut his eyes and saw himself, surrounded by his harem, with Jeed sorting out the squabbles and Vinny keeping the punters happy with witty conversation. When he opened them Jeed was smiling at him.

"OK, yes, we buy."

Jeed jumped for joy.

"Only if price OK."

When they went back to Tommy Bar Jeed sat close to him and stroked his chest. Paul looked dismayed when he arrived and saw them pawing each other.

Jeed nattered to Ohn. She went and made a phone call at the back of the bar then returned and nattered with Jeed.

“Honey, Ohn say man from bar come toomollow.”

The next day a fat guy wheezed his way down Soi 7 in a vest and shorts. When he took his seat at the bar he brushed back his sweat-sodden hair from his wrinkled forehead and ordered a glass of soda. Vinny looked at the course bulbous veins characterising his lower legs.

“Do you know if Jim’s about?” he asked in a thick Australian accent.

“You’re talking to ’im.”

“I’m Bruce. You’re interested in the bar?”

“Fuck me, an Aussie called Bruce.”

“I can’t apologise for the predictability of it. How’s life?”

“Shit hot.”

Vinny liked him. They shot the breeze for a while. When it came to brass tacks Bruce stuck his neck on the line and asked for half a million baht.

Vinny coughed to show his shock. He’d done his homework by looking at the classified section of the *Pattaya Mail* and talking to Jeed.

With a bit of toing an froing, he settled at 300,000 baht. They shook hands and had a beer, and Bruce agreed to come back the next day with a contract.

They took the contract, written in Thai, to a local lawyer’s office. In return for a fee he looked it over and gave it the thumbs up.

Jeed signed as the new owner. Foreigners weren’t allowed to own property in Thailand and, after exchanging paper and a wad of thousand-baht notes, they proudly took the keys for the locked fridges to their new venture.

They bought some beers and sat proudly at the bar drinking. Paul and Ohn were invited over to join them and they sat and got drunk in celebration.

The name they were going to call it was high on the list of conversations.

Burnden Park was Vinny’s first suggestion, but he backed down when he realised it might draw attention from Boltoners.

Me Happy was Jeed’s first suggestion.

Paul chipped in with Scabby Old Boot, which was dismissed immediately.

“How about Jim and Jeed?”

It was met with a frown. “Cannot iss Jeed and Tchim?”

“Errr… Very Happy?” Vinny offered by way of an apology.

By the end of the night they settled on Me Happy.

The next day they rented an apartment on Soi Nakula. It was half a mile away from Soi 7 and overlooked a boatyard. The view from the balcony was of ramshackle old fishing boats in a compound waiting to disintegrate, making the sand more habitable for plants. A month’s rent was the same as four nights in a hotel. It didn’t have a reception or restaurant, but they had a kitchen, a living room, a bedroom and maid service once a week. The complex had a pool as well.

They worked hard for a week cleaning and painting the bar, and stayed in on the evenings. It had been years since Vinny had done any physical work and it told on him. Jeed massaged him back to life at night.

One night after a couple of beers, once he'd come round from his one-hour post-toil snooze, he felt cheeky and squeezed through the chicken-wire gate of the boatyard and pinched a reasonably fresh piece of plank, and dashed back to the apartment with it.

"Honey, can make sign." He held it proudly above his head as he walked through the door.

She hugged him proudly with a knife in her hand from chopping vegetables.

"OK, when made sign we can open bar." Vinny nodded and kissed her forehead.

"Cannot."

"Why cannot?"

"Need ladee."

"No problem. We ask lady from Tommy Bar, your friend."

"Iss ploblem," Jeed sulked. "Must pay bar for lady working."

Vinny pulled back.

Jeed had to settle him and explain that if a girl was already working in a bar he'd have to pay the owner.

"OK, how we can do?"

"Jeed speaking friends and asking."

Vinny sucked his lips. "Well, it's gonna be a tough job choosing."

He felt an elbow in his ribs.

"Jeed, can find. I no want Winnee working too hard."

The next day Vinny sat at Tommy Bar while Jeed spread the word that they needed girls to work at the new bar.

Vinny was little despondent on the opening day. He'd been looking forward to having it open by the end of March.

Paul turned up at tea time.

"All right, Vin. I mean Jim."

"Y'all right, Paul? What've yer done today?"

"Three shag's, nine shits and a wank."

The extravagancies of Pattaya's lifestyle never ceased to amuse him.

"Lookin' forward to getting' Me Happy off the ground?"

"Aye, can't wait." The pair turned to look at Vinny's new investment.

A couple were walking round the newly decorated but as yet unopened watering hole. He was European looking; she was Thai.

Vinny thought nothing of it until the guy lifted the bar top and walked inside and spread his arms triumphantly.

Vinny walked over a little exasperated.

"Wassup, mate?" Vinny stood in the gap in front of the guy.

"Ah, you know, just savouring my empire." He gleamed and spoke with an Australian accent.

Vinny cracked him on the chin. The training on Ko Pha Ngan was still fresh and the guy fell to the floor.

The girl launched a verbal tirade on Vinny at his actions. The guy slowly got to his feet, dazed.

"You've made a mistake, mate. Fuck off." Vinny made the hitch-hiking motion with his thumb.

Jeed noticed the commotion and steamed over, berating the girl in a flurry of Thai.

"Nah, mate. Just bought it today." The guy seemed calm under pressure and produced what looked like a contract from his pocket. "Off a fellow countryman called Bruce."

The guy placed the contract on the counter. Jeed craned her neck to look at it. As she read, her face started to darken.

"Jeed, is it mistake?" Vinny was sure it was a mix-up.

"They buy also."

"Eh?"

"Paper say man Kevin Harding buy also."

The Aussie nodded his head in satisfaction. "That's me."

Vinny held his head in his hands. "Sorry, mate, I've got a contract same as that. With Jeed's name on it."

A horrible thought dawned on them both at the same time.

"I'll call Bruce." The Aussie reached for his mobile phone and dialled.

Vinny heard a dialling tone. "Bruce, it's Kev."

The line went dead. Kev hit redial and started pacing up and down.

Vinny sighed. "It's no use, man. It aint 'appenin'."

"Well, I want my fackin' money back!" The guy's eyes were popping out of his head.

Vinny opted for time out. "Kev, mate. We ain't gonna sort this out now. How about we both go home and speak to the lawyers and come back tomorrow. Say three o'clock?"

"I knew I shouldn't trust a guy from Perth." Kev stormed off with his girlfriend.

Vinny walked back to Tommy Bar shaking his head and drank a beer. Then he nipped off to an internet café and emailed Keith.

Keith

Hope you're well. No sign of your mate Vinny. Can you do us a favour and get that Eddie's phone number off Vicky?

Cheers

Jim

Vinny and Jeed waited at the bar for Kev the Aussie to turn up. At around 3.30 he arrived with his girlfriend and a concerned-looking Thai bloke.

"Mate, I'm sorry I chinned you last night. I reckon the best thing we can do is sort this out legally." He was putting on his best mediator's voice.

"Fair dinkum," he nodded. The Thai bloke who'd been watching backed into the safety of the bar.

"Just to play fair…" Vinny knew the name on the contract was Kev's and they'd just get laughed at. "Do you wanna find a neutral lawyer? 'Cos the ones we've both used already are gonna give biased views."

"Sure. I'll ask the Mrs." He turned to his girlfriend. "Lek…" He started nattering in Thai to her.

As Kev was chatting to Lek to find a suitable solicitor a fat guy pulled up on a motorbike. He was in his forties, had his hair tied back in a ponytail, was in need of a shave and his hairy chest, legs and arms were exposed to the sun by him being clothed in shorts and a vest. A girl no older than eighteen sat on the back of the moped with a plank on her lap. There was a cardboard box displaying the CARLSBERG logo strapped to the back of the bike.

The guy got off, unclipped the box of beer and hauled it onto the bar top.

Kev didn't notice but Vinny's eyes got wider. The guy's girlfriend pranced up to the bar with the plank, and the guy produced a hammer from his pocket and hammered the sign into one of the posts, renaming the disputed territory as Braveheart.

"Y' all right, guys?" he wheezed in a broad Glaswegian accent. "Be open tonight roond seven bells. Brang yer cash."

Vinny started laughing. "Just bought the bar off Bruce have yer?"

"Aye, that's right." He started unloading bottles onto the bar.

"Might 'ave a problem there, our kid. Me an' Aussie Kev just done the same thing."

The guy stopped in his tracks. His young assistant looked Vinny in the eye mournfully.

"I got a receipt and a contract sayin' me 'n' Nok are rightful owners." He looked like he was about to have an aneurysm.

"So have we."

"I got a hammer an' three brothers," the Scot replied and raised his hammer in an upright position.

"Where's your brothers, mate?" Kev had taken a moment to cotton on.

"Glasgow."

Vinny and Kev started to laugh.

When the solicitor went home to his family for tea that night it must have made interesting listening as he recounted how he'd had to act as referee as three enraged farangs and their girlfriends tried to scream each other into submission over the ownership of some worthless slab of concrete, four beams, a roof and a few stools thrown in.

The solicitor made an appointment for them all to return next week, while the beguiled agreed to try and track down Bruce. For some reason the Scottish guy was as keen to avoid police involvement as Vinny. Kev was just relieved that the lawyer might be able to track Bruce down when he heard he had no rights of ownership as a foreigner.

When they met at the bar half an hour before going to the solicitor's, Vinny introduced them to Barry from Birmingham, who'd fallen for Bruce's ruse as well and had arrived looking proud a couple of days later.

They all shared their dismay, cursed Bruce, and nobody was surprised when they all admitted they'd had no luck in tracing the antipodean conman.

Vinny looked at his watch, then looked down the street. He saw a tubby policeman motoring up the street on a motorbike, and he wondered where Eddie was.

The policeman pulled up near the bar and Vinny smiled as he saw Eddie, with his villainous glare and black designer clothes, dismount from the back of the *gendarme*'s motorbike.

Vinny cleared his throat.

"Sorry to do this to you guys." He put on his best orator's tone. "But I'm gonna have to claim the bar as my own."

Eddie swaggered towards them confidently. He pulled out a meat cleaver that was tucked in the back of his trousers and a pistol from his pocket.

"Ebelywon. You gib paper for baar to my flend Tchim. You no do. I kiil you." He let his pistol off into the roasting afternoon air.

The policeman looked on and nodded. Three more motorbikes converged on the bar. Each had a passenger, one in police uniform, the other two looking villainous, all three of them carrying assault rifles, and they all trained their guns on the crowd.

Vinny passed round slips of paper for the guys or their partners to sign, all of whom complied whilst shaking their heads. Surprisingly none of them wanted to hang around for a drink.

turn like a wheel

Songkran wasn't quite how Vinny and Jeed had planned it. Traditionally it was a festival celebrated in the middle of April when the Thai's celebrate the end of the dry season by pouring a small amount of lightly scented water over the hands of their elders. In modern times it had been bastardised and had become a ten-day orgy of drink and drug-fuelled excess.

A national water fight lasting from dawn to dusk, where hoards of normally reserved Thais drew upon their reserves to drench as many people as possible during the festival, had replaced the reverent anointment of grandparents.

In the year 2000 over 400 people died during the period; the majority of deaths were the result of drunken accidents.

Vinny spent the festival stood behind the bar of Me Happy with Jeed and the four girls she and Ohn had commandeered to work for them. Vinny didn't get involved in the acquisition of hostesses; he just handed over a chunk of cash.

Since Eddie and his friends had been so generous in their capacity as arbiters Vinny felt obliged to let them drink at the bar. The fat policeman didn't really abuse the privilege; he just turned up every day for his free bottle of Johnny Walker. The thin policeman who'd waved his Kalashnikov seemed to have an insatiable appetite for the Thai brand of whisky, Mekong. Eddie and the rest of his non-uniformed cronies joined the thin policeman at the bar on a daily basis and made Vinny and Jeed very popular at the wholesalers. After three weeks of hospitality Vinny worked out that it would have been cheaper just to turn his back on the bar and cut his losses. He even considered contacting Kev, Barry or the Scottish bloke and donating it to them.

Vinny heaved a sigh of relief when thin policeman stopped drinking at the bar and he wasn't the least bit surprised when he read in the *Pattaya Mail* that he'd been arrested by undercover police officers from another force for his involvement in the supply of yabba, Thailand's own brand of methamphatamine. At least it explained his capacity for drink.

The girls did their best to tempt in customers at first, then gave up when they realised Eddie and his mates scared them off by leaving their pistols on the bar.

Vinny heaved another sigh of relief when one night Eddie said he was off up to the Burmese border to help his friends in the Wa (whatever that was), and politely turned down his offer to come along for the ride. That night the guys shot a few holes in the roof before rolling home at 6am.

On 7 May, Keith stood at the stall. He'd given up charming housewives and young mothers into buying a new football strip for young Johnny, and spent his day warming his hands on a plastic cup of coffee and staring at the sky, dreaming of his return to Bangkok and of splashing out on three girls from Long Gun on his first night.

When women did come and look at the stall, he'd look at them, baulk at the size of their hips and grunt, returning his eyes to the go-go bar in the sky.

He didn't notice DC Davenport with his anorak over his sports jacket.

"Keith Rossi." Keith looked him in the face and gave a slight resigned shake of his head.

"Need a new rugby shirt for the Mrs?"

"Keith Rossi, I am placing you under arrest. You do not have to say anything…"

He walked with them to Davenport's Sierra and took a seat in the back. He recognised Fawcett from when he'd been interviewed about Vinny.

"What is it this time?" He did his best to rub the muck from his shoes on the carpet.

"You've been smuggling aliens into the country." Davenport looked at him smugly in the mirror.

"Oh aye, yeah. Did I not tell you I popped Mork from Ork in my suitcase last time I were on Mars? Felt sorry for him 'cos he said he were missin' Mindy."

Keith had been half expecting this and had prepared a little routine.

They sat him down in the interview room and waited for the duty solicitor.

"Keith, we know you're involved in the supply of cocaine, organised football violence, global fraud and the trafficking of prostitutes. What next? overthrow the fucking council and form a banana republic?"

The solicitor arrived.

A stern-looking guy in a brown suit entered and sat next to Davenport.

"Mr Rossi, I'm Detective Inspector Brian Rubens." He was greying, with heavy lines round his face and a conspicuously manifest nose.

"Afternoon."

"Mr Rossi, we believe that whilst in Thailand on the twenty-fourth of December you were married to Rungnapa Chatunchak." He looked up from his notes.

"Yep."

"Mr Rossi, when was the last time you saw Rungnapa?"

“Err, not sure. It were about the eighth, ninth o’ Jan. Got ’ome from work that day and she’d left a note sayin’ she’d fucked off back to Thailand ’cos England were too cold.”

Rubens raised his eyebrows. “Did that not surprise you, Mr Rossi?”

“Well, all she did were stay in bed and moan. It didn’t really surprise me. To be honest she was getting’ on mi tits anyway.” Keith kept his poker face on.

“Mr Rossi, would it surprise you to find that, in a raid earlier today, of the Siamese Paradise Health Club in Stockport, officers from the Greater Manchester vice squad found Rungnapa Chatunchak being held against her will and forced to have sex with customers?” Rubens sat back with self-satisfaction daubed across his face.

“Funny old world innit.” Keith looked him in the eye.

“Mr Rossi,” Rubens fixed him. “What is your relationship to Victor Romerez?”

“Who?”

“Victor Romerez.” Rubens sat back again.

“Eh…” Keith’s brow was starting to furrow.

“Mr Romerez is a transsexual, originally from Spain. He is known locally as ‘Vicky’.” Rubens held up a police ID photo of Vicky with a hint of stubble.

“Fuck me. Jesus fuckin’ ’ell… Christ.” Keith held his head in his hands.

The duty solicitor cleared his throat. “Err… I think my client would like to suspend the interview for a while.”

Vinny slipped into a blithe routine of sitting with customers in the late afternoon at Me Happy, drinking and drinking until late with whoever was around. Paul disappeared to Phuket after two bar girls appeared one afternoon and set about him with the heavy halves of pool cues for lying to them.

Vinny’s daily waking time was around 1.30pm. Jeed would invariably have got up and gone to open the bar or run some errand, and had a habit of returning while he was showering and made sure he was satiated before he went to play host for a few hours.

On 22 May, he had an afternoon drink in Me Happy. He decided to sleep for a couple of hours before the evening drink so walked home.

The welcome girls in the bars nearby didn’t falter in their attempts to get him to pay for their services despite the fact that half of them knew he was spoken for.

A girl in platform soles stood in his path and smiled.

“*Mai ow crap*.” Vinny politely tried to dismiss her.

She grabbed his hand. “Today, sir, I hab speciar offa.”

“Wow,” Vinny played along.

“Yes.” She gave him a seductive wiggle. “Today you buy pussy, get ass for flee.”

Vinny broke into a giggle, wrenched his hand free and carried on walking.

He got home and slipped his shoes off and got a carton of orange from the fridge.

He was sitting on the balcony in the sun reading the *Bangkok Post* when he heard a knock on the door. He padded over to the door and opened it.

The sight that greeted him made his heart stop.

Four policemen.

"Wincent Croston?" The senior one with thin lips smiled at him.

Vinny felt short of oxygen,

"Errrr, no. I James Bradley. I show passport."

The police officers walked into the flat. Two of them were carrying batons.

Vinny was about to shut the door when two English guys who were further down the corridor entered.

"All right, Vince?" A small guy he vaguely recognised in a sun hat shook his hand. "Lovely place you've got here."

He was grinning like a Cheshire cat. Vinny didn't recognise the taller one.

"I'm DC Davenport." He shook Vinny's hand. "We met in the Arrows that time I felt Keith's collar."

Vinny felt an overwhelming desire to empty his bowels.

It didn't take the police long to find Jim Bradley's passport with Vinny's photo in it. They gave the rest of the apartment a quick rifle, but didn't find anything of interest.

The police station wasn't the most inspiring building in the world. They took him into a room where he was photographed and fingerprinted, then into a large interview room where a serious-looking inspector sat behind an officiously large desk. The thin-lipped policeman and the two English guys joined him and the inspector eyed his passport.

"Wincent Clot ton. We belleep you entar owa countlee irreagary on thirty-first Decempa. Using the pattpor of James Bladley. Your photogra ant fingaplinn confim your ID."

Vinny cursed the day he'd been caught shoplifting in 1987.

"You will appear bepor Pattaya Magistlay in fibe days to ansa charge." The inspector picked up the papers on his desk and straightened them.

"Can I see a lawyer?"

"Man will come toomollow flom Blitit Empassy to organy your deffent."

The inspector got up and walked out.

Davenport smiled. "I'd save you're breath mate. We've got an agreement. They want you out of the country as much as we want you back in England. Where's the money?"

"Up my arse, second shelf on the left."

They took him to the detention area. 'Cell' was the wrong word for the place they put him. It was a cage crammed full of people. Some were lying on the concrete floor, others were standing. The lucky ones got to hang onto the inch-thick steel bars for support. There was a hole in the floor in the corner and the smell of putrid human waste wafted up from it.

Vinny started to sweat. After two hours standing shoulder to jowl with the other twenty upright inmates the forty detainees performed a silent heaving manoeuvre and the ones standing took the place of the ones lying on the floor.

The cage itself was in a room containing four other cages, all containing the same number of people.

On Vinny's second shift in the upright position the police dragged a guy who was protesting in what sounded like Italian to one of the other cells. He was clad head to toe in designer clothes and had sunglasses resting on his forehead.

After eight stints in the upright position and an equal number lying on the floor vainly attempting sleep, two policeman came to the cage and shouted Vinny's name. He pushed his way through the prisoners carefully. By now he was so dehydrated he'd stopped sweating and his skin was covered in a film of grime.

They took him to an interview room were an English guy sat behind a desk. He was dressed smartly in a shirt and tie, and was in his mid-forties.

"Mr Croston. I'm Duncan Fairbank. I work for the British Embassy in Bangkok. My job is to help people who have got in trouble with the law and ensure they're being treated fairly. Are you OK?" He had a kind face and gave him a considerate smile.

"Bit cramped, like." Vinny laughed to hide his shame.

"I've brought some food for you. Is there anything else I can do? Anyone you want to contact?"

"Yeah, can you get us a lawyer and get in touch with Jeed?"

Vinny gave Duncan details of where to find Jeed, and Duncan conveyed his lack of optimism that Vinny might be allowed to stay in Thailand.

When he got back to the cage, Vinny shared out the food and cigarettes from the bag Duncan had given him. It seemed to be the protocol.

On the second day he was taken out of the cell again. He was hoping Jeed had come to visit him.

It was Duncan Fairbank again, this time with a fresh-faced lawyer.

Duncan explained that he'd been unable to find Jeed at the bar, the apartment or on the phone number he'd been given.

Vinny spoke to the lawyer. He explained that he had money in a bank in Switzerland, and was willing to pay the police and the judge whatever sum of money was required to allow him to stay in the country.

The lawyer nodded. That was how things were done in Thailand. He asked Vinny to give him Jim Bradley's bank details and sign a letter as Jim allowing him access to the account.

Vinny went back to the cell with another bag of food from Duncan, satisfied that in a few days he'd be a free man again, only a few thousand pounds worse off.

As he waited for the cage to be unlocked the Italian was escorted out of his cage to an interview room, having been stripped by his peers of all his designerwear except his underpants.

Vinny started to get anxious as the day of his court appearance drew close, having had no word from the lawyer.

When judgement day finally arrived Vinny felt noticeably thinner and a faint croak had replaced his voice.

The lawyer waited for him at a briefing room in the courthouse.

Vinny nodded to him expectantly as he took a seat in his handcuffs.

"Have you sorted all the money out for the police and that?"

The lawyer gave him a painful look. "Mr Clot ton, there iss no money in the bank accou' you tell me."

"Yer what?"

The judge was swift to declare Vinny a *persona non grata.*

They took him back to the station where he spent another day in the cells, then at midday he was hauled out and escorted to a police van. DC Davenport and the other policeman were there with him.

"Don't mind us hitching a lift, do you, Vinny?" Davenport smirked.

Vinny fell asleep. It was the first time in a week his behind had felt cushioning and he'd had room to stretch his legs.

He woke as they were approaching the airport. Vinny looked at the outskirts of Bangkok and his tear ducts became moist.

They drove through a side gate manned by guards at Don Muang and he was taken in handcuffs to an office where an immigration official stamped some papers the policemen had brought and gave them to Davenport.

After waiting in a room patrolled by vicious-looking guards with batons, Vinny was escorted to a departure gate. He was the object of the waiting passengers curiosity.

His uniformed chaperones took him on board the plane and guided him to a seat next to Davenport. Vinny smelt alcohol on his breath. The guard gave Davenport the keys for Vinny's handcuffs.

When they landed at Heathrow, the other guy with Davenport officially arrested Vinny for fraud.

Dressed in knee-length shorts and a T-shirt, Vinny shivered in the prison van on the way to Manchester. The van was divided into mini-cells and he couldn't see the outside world.

They arrived at Bootle Street police station where he was charged and taken to a cell. When the door slammed shut Vinny fell to his knees and cried on the floor for an hour.

When he stopped crying he sat on the bed and stared at the floor. He didn't eat the meal that was shoved through the observation hatch.

Vinny was given access to a lawyer, who explained he could face up to fourteen years in prison for his crime, and advised him to plead guilty in court and also make efforts to return the money.

Vinny gave the guy details of Jim Bradley's bank account and signed a letter allowing him to obtain a statement.

The next time they met, his brief produced faxed copies of statements from the Swiss Bank showing that, since the beginning of April, there had been 45 transfers from Jim Bradley's account of approximately £10,000 to an unknown account in Thailand.

Vinny's head hit the interview-room desk. He remained silent for ten minutes.

"I don't know who the fuck's got to the money."

Pete Jensen lay on his front on his sun lounger by his pool. There was a bottle of white wine in a cooler and Jeed was sat on top of him in a bikini, massaging his sun-freckled back.

"All right, Pete?"

Jeed eased off and Pete turned her head.

The maid had let Fatty Jarvo in and he was red faced and eager as he walked across the garden towards Jensen.

"Ah, Mr Jarvis." Pete put on his dressing gown and took a seat at the table.

"There's another one just landed. Perfect. Met 'im last night in the Freelancer Bar," Fatty Jarvo wheezed and showed a self-satisfied smile.

"Yeah? What does he sell?"

Jeed joined them at the table.

"Some sort of industrial filters. Clean the smoke factories let out or summat."

"How much do they sell for?" Pete held a cigar, which Jeed lit for him.

"Three hundred thousand Aussie dollars a piece, he reckons. I'm meeting him tonight down Soi Yamoto 'bout seven."

"Jeed, nip inside and get another bottle of wine, love." Pete exhaled a plume of blue cigar smoke.

She obeyed.

"What happened to that last dickhead from Bolton?" Jarvo was sweating.

"He got deported about two weeks back."

"Yeah?"

"Funny thing is, his mate got collared for acting as a mule with some bird for a massage parlour in Manchester." Pete smirked. "So 'e probably thinks it's 'im that grassed."

Jarvo and Pete doubled up in laughter.

"Why didn't you just bump 'im off like that daft Scouser?"

"It'd start looking a bit suspicious if blokes wanted for switchin' invoices disappeared with a bird called Jeed and then got shot, wouldn't it. Anyway, it was good having Jeed out of my hair for a few months."

Jeed trotted back from the house with a fresh bottle of wine.

Pete stroked her behind as she bent over to pull the cork out. "I feel so lucky havin' a wife who helps so much with the household budget."

Pete smiled a murky grin as she poured out three glasses of white wine.

"Jeed, darlin', Jarvo's got another guy we're gonna set up. Can you go work your magic on 'im down Soi Yamoto tonight?"

"OK." Jeed's mobile rang.

She walked into the house to take the call.

Jarvo tried to hide his lascivious grin as her bikini-clad crotch passed his face.

Pete reached into a carrier bag under the table. "It's all there. We managed to get twenty-seven million baht out of his account in the end."

"Usual ten per cent?" Jarvo wafted his face with a four-inch pile of thousand-baht notes.

"Of course." Pete said begrudgingly. "You know, I've been getting worried about her. With the first three she was so detached, you know, phlegmatic. But I started to get the feelin' she actually liked that Vince fella." Pete looked at Jarvo, waiting for his opinion.

"Nah," Jarvo shrugged it off. "She knows where 'er bread's buttered."

After appearing before the magistrate, where Vinny had pleaded guilty and been refused bail, he was transferred to the remand wing of Her Majesty's Prison, Manchester, or Strangeways as it was known before the riot.

On the first visiting day his mum and dad arrived. He couldn't look them in the eye. His mum tired to hug him but personal contact wasn't allowed.

They were in a room full of uniformed felons being visited by relatives and friends.

"Well, we're glad your home." His mum tried to put a brave face on.

"Thanks."

"And we're sure you'll be found not guilty. You can come and live with us. Dad's cleared out your old room."

Vinny's patience snapped. "Mam. I'm fuckin' guilty and I aint coming home."

He got out of his chair and stormed over to the guard, asking to be taken back to his cell. They wouldn't allow it and he had to sit and scowl at his parents for another 25 minutes.

When he got back to his cell he sat on the edge of the bed and cried like an infant. He pulled the sheet off his bed, ripped it in half, tied a noose in it, then ran the length of sheet behind the bars in the window.

As the knot tightened round his neck he felt short of breath. When the world became dark he saw Jeed lying naked on top of him, giggling playfully.

Jensen lay asleep in bed. Jeed was dressed. Her hands shook as she held the pistol to his head. When she pulled the trigger the gun jumped in her hand. She wiped the blood and shards of shattered skull off the overall she'd worn especially for the occasion.

The doctor checked for a pulse on the corpse the prison officers had cut from the improvised gallows.

Jeed sat in the internet café. She checked what she'd written on the screen.

Vinny Darling,

I hope you are OK. I know monkey house no good, but I think monkey house England better monkey house Thailand.

I tell you now that I have money that you take.

Please not for angry me Vincent because I'm love you. You wait and when you finish can come Thailand. Jeed have all money for you.

I go to praying at Buddha and ask for you to be safe.

You my love forever

Jeed.

She hit send.

Big Changs alround

Thanks are due in no particular order to the following people for their help, encouragement, friendship and inspiration (both close up and from afar) or for putting up with me when I'm drunk

Mam, Dad, Helga, Helena and family all round, Pommy Keith & Touctic, John, Sarah and all the Fish, Ckrisg, Mike, Dave and all the Gores, Tussanee, Wez & Danny, Rusty, Bri Cannon, Dr Paul/Fiery Jack, Lee Gritty, Steve O'Connor, Steve K & Francis, Chum, Glen Hornby, Pat Kane and Lal, Easy Kev, Easy Andy, Jeed, Lin, Liam Hitman Harrison, Drew Slater, Scott Millwall, Johnny, Kenny & Roger, Baz Eden, Chubby Chris, Geoff Dogs Bar, Gerry Potter Chloe Poems, Pricey (808), All at Jitty's, Dom Berry, KSR John, Geordie Claire, Dave Ball, Bob Hippie, John Canny & Poon, The Saddlers Ben & Steve, Jitty & Sarah, Gareth Parry H & Deacon (both Cardiff), Brummy Jay, Steve & Mad Jim, Ian Ince, Erika, Aussie Keith, Sandy Holt, Danny Blue Cat, All at Nana Coffee shop, Gwen & Mike, Sean Kelly, Connor A, Gordon Zola, Tilac Bar, Chris Dawson & family, Steve Reilly, Lee Penders & Joanna, Pete Slater & Mike, Nong/Nigel (we love you forever), Jason and Peow, Mike Vegas, Bangkok Mouth Phil Williams, H Mr Paul, Moggy doorman, Si Shep, Marcel, Ben Yai, Paul Henderson, All at Metro Stockport, Roy, Oliver, Eddie & Joe, Bernard Trink, Barry Crowther, Girl from Chaiyapoom, Sean Bangkok Butcher, Gavin Scouse, Stickman, Kev Mac, Frank & Julia Lake, Monkey, Tommy Dodds, Khun Kong, Darren Philips, Hughie Quirk Halifax, There's only one Stevie Dicko, Munchshak Chris, Nick French, New Order, Nervous Dog, Marlboro & Marlboro Lights, Steve Byrne, Geordie Alan, Dani Bruppacher, Steve Miles, Khun Sanuk, Mango Sauce, Mick Rutter, Tanonsak, Bazzer (sorry man), An, Ender, Pat & Mrs McGowan, Camille Limbo, Pe7e (get well soon), Needles, Linton, Ian Blacks, Rick, ACR, Andy Southampton, Arthur Guiness, Kennie Burt, Jess, Simon Wigan, Kung Fu Kev, Rob Sankey, Shelly Grimshaw, Kent Martin, Jane Deacon, Add, Lao Hu Li/Frank Truman, Marrisa & Wendy Jungle Gym, Jemma, Jacko, Nok, Clarkey Stuart & Alison, Scott & Jamie Halifax, Marty Artwork and anyone else who's door I've darkened.

Cheers

Printed in Great Britain
by Amazon.co.uk, Ltd.,
Marston Gate.